WINTER WAR AWAKENING

ALSO BY ROSALYN EVES

Blood Rose Rebellion

Lost Crow Conspiracy

ROSALYN EVES

WINTER WAR AWAKENING

BLOOD ROSE REBELLION

VOLUME III

ALFRED A. KNOPF  New York

THIS IS A BORZOI BOOK PUBLISHED BY ALFRED A. KNOPF

All rights reserved. Published in the United States by Alfred A. Knopf, an imprint of Random House Children's Books, a division of Penguin Random House LLC, New York.

Knopf, Borzoi Books, and the colophon are registered trademarks of Penguin Random House LLC.

Visit us on the Web! GetUnderlined.com

Educators and librarians, for a variety of teaching tools, visit us at RHTeachersLibrarians.com

Library of Congress Cataloging-in-Publication Data is available upon request.
ISBN 978-1-101-93611-5 (trade) — ISBN 978-1-101-93612-2 (lib. bdg.) — ISBN 978-1-101-93613-9 (ebook)

The text of this book is set in 12.5-point Bembo.

Printed in the United States of America
March 2019
10 9 8 7 6 5 4 3 2 1
First Edition

For Andrew & Oliver, who think there's too much kissing in my books, but let me write them anyway.

I can read the stars: blood and blood
everywhere. Brother kills brother, nationalities
massacre each other implacably and insanely.
They mark the houses they seek to burn down
or destroy with the sign of the cross in blood.
My life has gone up in smoke! Pest is gone.
Roaming troops devastate everything we
had built.

—SZÉCHENYI ISTVÁN'S DIARY, 1848,
FROM STEPHEN SISA'S *THE SPIRIT OF HUNGARY*

Liberty and love
These two I must have.
For my love I'll sacrifice
My life.
For liberty I'll sacrifice
My love.

—PETŐFI SÁNDOR

CHAPTER I

Anna

Austria, late September 1848

These mountains gave nothing back. You might offer your secrets to them, and they would be kept safe in the folded rock and jagged crevices.

You might tally your fears against them, and they would be swallowed by the immensity of stone.

You might throw yourself at them and never return.

We were too few, the five of us against these mountains, against the praetheria who might be holding my cousin Noémi in a cave buried somewhere in that imposing stretch of rock—a handful of dust against the weight of the mountains.

Night fell swiftly as we set up camp, a sweep of ink blotting out the Austrian Alps rising all around us. The walls of a military fortress, clamped on high rocks behind me, disappeared as though someone had dropped a curtain over them. But I could feel the mountains even so: craggy stone sentinels piercing the sky overhead, monoliths that would crush me as soon as shelter me. Though the September evening was mild, I shivered in the too-large secondhand dolman I wore over a boy's shirt and trousers. I wished that Gábor were here, to share his warmth—or that Mátyás would let us start a fire. But my cousin was being uncharacteristically cautious.

I squinted into the night. The mountains facing us were no longer visible, except as a wash of black at the base of a star-strewn sky. Somewhere in that darkness, Noémi waited.

Assuming, of course, that the information we had pieced together in Vienna was correct.

Two months earlier, Noémi had disappeared from Vienna while I was crusading unsuccessfully on behalf of the praetheria, the creatures I'd released from the Binding spell. Before I could do anything to recover her trail, my own life had imploded, and I'd been hunted from Vienna, running until I'd stumbled across Mátyás and Gábor on the *puszta*.

Together, along with some outlaws Mátyás had befriended, we searched for Noémi in Buda-Pest and at Eszterháza before returning under cover to Vienna to comb the city for clues. The few crumbs of information we found there had led us to an unlikely road into these mountains, pressed like teeth against the sky.

Had we made a web of nothing—built a trail out of strands that, when pinched together, would vanish?

A flare tugged my attention back to our small camp. Zhivka held a tiny flame in her hand, and it danced, a sensuous weave of light and heat. Mátyás batted irritably at her. "Put that out. Someone might see it."

She swung her hand out of reach. "Oh, don't be such a wet wood. And who should see us here?"

Any number of people, I thought. Austrian soldiers, come to haul me back to Vienna to suffer a death sentence for the magic that had killed Mátyás and broken the Binding. Or those same soldiers, to collect the bounty on Mátyás's head, as he and Bahadır had spent the summer as bandits on the Hungarian plains, because apparently dying once had not put sufficient fear of death into him. Or to arrest the praetherian women, Zhivka and the lidérc, for flouting the imperial Hapsburg ruling that all praetheria be sequestered. We had been cautious while gathering information in Vienna, but the lidérc stood guard some hundred or so feet from camp even now, in case our caution had not been enough.

"You said yourself that praetheria sheltered in the caves," Bahadır said, his dark eyes fixed on the flame in her hand. His voice was soft, but a tightness about his eyes revealed some of his tension. "If they find us here, they will kill us before we can betray their location."

It was not the nameless praetheria in the caves I feared: it was the praetherian Vasilisa and her wolves. My shoulder still ached where one of her great beasts had gnawed it— she had chased me down and damn near caught me, just before Mátyás found me. Well, it was not *only* the nameless praetheria I feared.

"And if they should see me, they will see only a samodiva on her way to join her sisters." The flame maiden in Zhivka's hands somersaulted, her body forming a neat ring. "You think everything is a trap. I cannot tell if this is caution"—her voice turned sly—"or fear."

Bahadır shot to his feet. "I believe it's my turn to keep watch."

Mátyás looked at Zhivka after the Turkish boy had vanished into the shadows. "That was not kind. Had your father and, later, your best friend been killed before you, you might see traps everywhere too. He is not a coward."

"I did not say he was. If he thinks I did, it is his own conscience that pricks him, not me." Zhivka drew the fire around her, a flaming shawl against the brightness of her hair. I wished I could borrow it from her without burning and press its heat against my throbbing shoulder. Then she sighed and let the fire flicker out. "If you are so worried, I will explore the caves tomorrow and report if I find your sister."

"Thank you," Mátyás said, his voice a trifle stiff.

"I'll go with you," the lidérc said, stepping toward us on her bare goose feet. She'd discarded the boots she wore in more civilized regions. With boots on, she appeared very nearly human, until she met your gaze with her opaque black eyes or grinned to reveal her sharpened teeth. Without boots—well, she had rather the look of a housecat, a predator that only pretends to be domesticated.

Zhivka lifted an eyebrow. "I did not think climbing a mountain was something you enjoyed."

The lidérc returned a long, steely stare. "It's not. Neither is spying on my kin. But I offered to help Mátyás find his sister, and I mean to keep my word."

Zhivka dropped her eyes and did not answer, and I wondered what message had passed unspoken between them.

Shadows curled in around us. I inched toward Mátyás, drawing a blanket over me. Despite the trees surrounding our camp, we were too exposed here.

Mátyás turned to smile at me, and his teeth gleamed faintly in the starlight. "Tired?"

My body was heavy with exhaustion, but I was not tired. There would be no rest here on the hard-packed earth, no rest while finding Noémi was a possibility, halfway up a mountain I could no longer see. "No."

"You should try to sleep," Mátyás said. "We've a long climb tomorrow."

I lay back on the ground, my head pillowed against my arms. Tracing the bright lines of stars with my eyes, I tried to scry them, searching out a future that led us to Noémi and not to capture or death.

But if the stars had an answer, I could not read it.

〤

Bahadır came in from his watch and Zhivka took his place, and still I could not sleep. I inhaled, long and slow, and blew the breath out, my hands steady on my stomach as it rose and fell. And yet this breathing trick, which usually calmed me, did nothing to still the voices chattering in my head.

So I thought of Gábor instead, deliberately turning my

thoughts and spooling out my memories of him, slow and luxurious, until they replaced the stars overhead, until I no longer minded the anxious thrum of my heartbeat in my neck. If those memories hurt, I preferred that pain to the dull ache of fear.

Nearly three months earlier, Gábor had left me in Vienna, telling me that no relationship between us could prosper, that the distance between us was too great. I had filled the silences after his departure with rage: angry that he presumed to decide our future without asking me, angry that we lived in a world where social status should matter so much.

But then the archduchess had learned of my role in the broken Binding and sentenced me to death, and in escaping her I had become a fugitive, and the distances that had once seemed so great began to shrink. What was social standing to a girl who had nothing left to lose?

Awake in the darkened valley, I skimmed over the memory of those days spent hiding and hungry, skipping past the soldier Emilija Dragović tracking me down and Vasilisa cornering us both with her wolves. I remembered instead how Mátyás had found us just in time, how Gábor's fingers had been so gentle on the wound in my shoulder.

I set my own fingers against my shoulder, re-creating that soft weight.

After the rescue, I had begun to hope (cautiously, carefully) that Gábor and I might find our way back to each other. Our first task was to take the unconscious Emilija to the Buda-Pest hospital where Noémi used to work; our second was to find Noémi. For these joint tasks, we shared a horse on the road to Buda-Pest; every day, Gábor wrapped his arms around me, and we talked, and sometimes he pressed featherlight kisses on my hair, brushes delicate enough to be accidental, kisses I pretended I did not feel, though I wanted to turn and catch them with my lips. At night, he watched me, an unguarded expression on his face that brought a blush to my cheeks. While the others shared stories, I told him English fairy tales, and he sang Romani songs from his childhood. We talked of everything and nothing, our quiet voices embroidered around the others' laughter.

For all he said before he left Vienna, he had never said he did not care for me. I had begun to believe that meant something.

But then sixteen days ago, I left him behind in Buda-Pest. For sixteen nights, only the memory of his voice had followed me into my dreams.

We had all been crammed into a dingy hotel room in Pest, disheartened by a week's worth of searching for clues to Noémi's whereabouts with no success. Mátyás suggested that we go back to Vienna, where she had disappeared, and we had agreed.

Then Gábor had spoken. "I'm staying." He was standing near a dirty window, looking out on the street below. A chill had washed over me, and I looked at him, studying his severe profile with a growing lump in my throat.

"You're staying?" I echoed, hearing how foolish the words were as soon as they left my mouth. I thought of the nights we'd spent beside the fire: had I misconstrued everything?

"I mean to enlist with Kossuth's army." He hesitated, his glance flickering around the room. "It is not that I don't

7

care what happens to Noémi. I do, and I understand why you wish to go. But Hungary is my home, my family's home. My first duty is to them."

Bahadır murmured something in response. I said nothing. The room swirled around me, the air strangely dense. Gábor was going to war. I might never see him again.

I had no claim on him. No right to protest his leaving, no say in his decisions, no sense to feel as betrayed as I did.

My head understood the barriers between us—that we belonged to different worlds, that his family did not want us together any more than mine did, that perhaps he did not care for me as I did for him. But my heart could not accept them. These last weeks had taught me I could live without luxury, could even live outside society. But I did not want to live without Gábor in my life.

"Excuse me," I said, standing up suddenly and then stumbling from the room, my gaze unsteady and unfocused. I needed air. I crept along the dark hallway, down the stairs, and through the smoky common area to a door opening onto the cobblestone street.

Dusk was falling, a gentle drift of grey against the sun-warmed rock. I walked past the front of the hotel to the alley flanking it, where I could bury myself in the shadows and indulge in self-pity and tears.

I could not grudge Gábor's choice of home and family over me. For all the things I loved in him—his courage, his kindness, his bright curiosity—what did I have to offer in exchange? Everything I owned had been stripped from me, and any intrinsic gifts I might have were tainted by my chimera self, the dual souls that broke spells and trailed havoc in my wake. What man of sense would knowingly link himself to all that?

I should simply have to steel myself against my heart's fruitless yearning.

"Anna?" Gábor's voice echoed in the deserted street.

I froze. There was nothing dignified in my tear-stained cheeks, in the sniffles I was trying hard to suppress. Gábor couldn't see me like this. My mother's tart voice echoed in my ears: *Serves you right. Self-pity is never pretty.* I swiped the sleeve of my shirt across my face.

"Anna?" His voice came again, closer, and then he was standing before me, his hands reaching for mine. His bare fingers were warm, his palms slightly callused.

I should have pulled away, but I wanted this last touch. I wanted to remember the weight of his hands around mine. I looked down at our entwined fingers, both to hide my reddened eyes and to avoid seeing the pity in his. My tears betrayed too much. His breath huffed against my cheek as he sighed.

"I did not make this choice lightly," he said. "And I do not make it to hurt you."

"I know," I said. And I did, though my lips found it hard to shape the words. I wanted to get through this conversation as quickly as possible, with at least some of my dignity still intact.

"Would you please look at me?"

I raised my eyes, though my heart hurt at his nearness, at the familiar, beloved planes of his face: brown skin stretched across sharp cheekbones, the wide, generous lips that creased at the corners when he smiled. In the dimming light, his dark eyes were pinched, in the way they always were when he was nervous, or guarded. The tightness around my chest began to ease. Perhaps I was not the only one hurting.

"Hungary is my home. I cannot see her overrun and do nothing."

"You might be killed."

A smile tugged at his lips. "Says the woman who is going to Austria, where there is a price on her head." The smile faded. "I might die whether I choose to fight or not—and I would prefer an active death. I would prefer to try."

I knew that. It was one of the things I loved about him. Only . . . "I don't want to lose you again," I said, so softly the words seemed to evaporate in the air.

But he caught them anyway. "Would you want me to go with you, knowing that I contribute little to your search, knowing that my duty and my heart dictate I should be elsewhere?"

I stared at him, fumbling for words. Like a soldier asked to breach a wall with his bare hands, I was cowed by his question, by the immensity of things left unsaid behind it. Much as I wanted him to come with us, I knew I could not ask it of him. His duty was the one barrier I had never—and did not ever hope to—overcome. I might dismiss our social differences and our families' disapproval as flimsy obstacles. But against his duty, his burnished honor, his pride—I might break myself against those shining walls.

Better to bend than break.

"Of course you should follow your conscience." My voice shrank. I was not good at these conversations. I did not know how to make myself vulnerable, to say what was in my heart without being ridiculous. *I love you,* I wanted to say. But I could not bring myself to speak the words without some guarantee they would be returned. "I . . . will miss you."

"And I, you." Gábor dropped his gaze and dug through a satchel hanging at his side. He plucked out a fistful of papers. "I've brought something for you." He handed two of the pages to me. At the top of one was written "To"; at the top of the other, "From."

"It's a gift. A small magic. An Elementalist in Pest helped me make them. Whatever is written on the 'to' sheet will appear on my 'from' sheet." He held up his other hand, showing two identical papers. "And anything I write on my 'to' page will appear on your 'from.'" He tapped the paper I was holding. "The words will remain until you say *'Változz át üres lappá!'* Then they will vanish." He paused, the crooked line of his brows uncertain. "That is, if you want the pages."

His diffidence touched me. Perhaps I was not the only one fumbling for the right words to draw us together. "I do. I do want them." Such magic could not have come cheap. What had Gábor given up for these pages? For me? To have had these made on short notice and at such expense meant he did not want to lose me any more than I wanted to lose him. Paper and ink might make for a frail connection, but the sacrifice behind the pages spoke of something deeper.

He tucked his papers back in the satchel, then cupped my chin in his hand. My pulse pounded beneath his thumb. "I

11

need you to know this: I am not staying because I do not care about you or Noémi. If this were just about me and what I want, I should not hesitate to come with you. But this war is not what I want."

He took a long breath. "I do not know what our future will look like if we survive the war. I only know that I am tired of trying not to be with you."

My heart thrummed unevenly. *Our future.* "We don't have to know the future yet. We just have to want the same thing." Feeling greatly daring, I dipped my chin so that my lips brushed a kiss against his palm.

As though that were an invitation, Gábor slid his hand around my neck to cradle the back of my head, tangling his fingers in my short hair and setting his mouth to mine.

His lips were soft and warm, and in the gathering darkness I melted into him, putting everything I could not say into my kiss. *I love you. Be safe.*

Kissing him felt like a greeting, a farewell, and a benediction all pressed together. And though we lingered in that alley as long as we dared, it was not enough time.

By morning, I was gone.

I let the memory fade from me. It held a peculiarly pleasant pain—I could not remember that moment without being buoyed by Gábor's promise . . . and also weighted down by the distance between us, the uncertainties haunting us. My aching heart merged with the ache in my shoulder, and I sat up to rub at my collarbone.

A light flickered from the trees where Zhivka stood. Probably the samodiva was playing with fire again. At least Mátyás was too deeply asleep to be moved by it. I watched the light, the long-short-long-long of it, as though it were a pattern, a language I could almost grasp. Then the flame winked out.

A moment later, footsteps fell across the grass: Zhivka returning to the camp. Her gaze lit on me, and she stiffened imperceptibly, as though I had surprised her. Then she laughed softly. "Good. You're up. I thought I should have to wake you, and I detest pulling people from pleasant dreams. It feels cruel, like eating the last piece of dessert before one of my sisters has had her share."

I didn't like standing watch and knew that Mátyás sometimes took a longer-than-fair-share to spare me when he could. I didn't like the way the darkness came alive with noises: every cracking branch sounded like a threat to me. I didn't like the way the night made me feel smaller than I already was, or the way even a knife in my hands felt flimsy. But Zhivka was waiting, the smile on her lips deepening into a smirk, as though she guessed at my thoughts. I pulled my boots on, hauled myself to my feet, and walked into the dark alone.

CHAPTER 2

Anna

I passed an uneventful watch, punctuated by a handful of unidentified noises that sent fear spiking through my body, rendering me momentarily extra-alert until the stillness lulled me once more.

Dawn crept into the valley little by little, a broth of warm gold light filling the stone basin. Somehow the mountains looked even more daunting that morning, with steep blue shadows carved out on the bald grey stone. Hardy evergreens clung to the lower slopes.

Zhivka and the lidérc set off just after breakfast. We watched them climb the mountain, their progress slow and careful as they zigzagged their way across the rough terrain. They were not particularly worried about being seen, as any human who spotted them from the valley floor would mistake them for climbing enthusiasts, and any praetheria would assume they were seeking shelter. Only when their shapes had diminished to tiny specks did I turn away.

I helped Bahadır brush the horses until their coats gleamed, then reread Gábor's latest letter. He wrote mostly of outside news and little of what I really cared about— Gábor himself. He glossed over the fact that he had joined Kossuth's army and had been sent to fight invading Serbs along Hungary's southern border, describing instead how martial law had been declared in Hungary following the murder of some count sent to bring order to the resistant government. The glossing frustrated me: did he think I would worry less if I knew less of the dangers he faced? I could invent more than enough worries to fill his gaps; I'd rather he wrote too much than too little.

I pulled out the paper Gábor had given me and a pen to answer him, but found I had nothing to say. Voicing my fears that he might be injured or killed in a skirmish would scarcely help him, and most of my attention was fixed on the mountain, my thoughts trailing the two women who would return to tell us if we had found Noémi or only chased a rumor. I put the pen away, then tapped Gábor's letter and whispered the phrase that would make the words vanish: *"Változz át üres lappá!"*

I had not yet grown familiar with the way the words disappeared from the page, as though they had never existed, as though whatever history they hinted at was only as substantial as a dream. The blank page staring back at me seemed suddenly a terrible omen, and I slid the paper into my bag, where I could not look at it.

Then I waited.

My time in society had not made me any more patient with long hours and little to do, and I paced in frustration. Bahadır slipped away once, then twice, to make his prayers in private. Mátyás fingered a small cross at his neck and tossed a pair of dice on the ground, and then he too disappeared: a crow shaking inky wings against the sky.

The sun scoured along the valley, heat rising from the rocks in waves.

Then Mátyás-as-crow fluttered down before us, and Mátyás-as-human scrambled back into his clothes, exclaiming, "They're coming!" When I looked back at the mountain, I could see them: two spots clambering over the rocks, growing rapidly larger.

Zhivka struggled for breath as they approached; the lidérc seemed unmoved by the climb up and down the mountain, a fact that clearly annoyed Zhivka, as she would not look at the lidérc.

"The praetheria are here," Zhivka said, then drew a deep breath.

"And Noémi?" Mátyás asked.

"Patience, my child," the lidérc said, her pointed teeth showing through her grin. "Can't you see Zhivka is winded?"

"I am not"—Zhivka took another breath—"winded. Your sister is there. In a small opening off the main branch of the cavern. There is a guard by her room, but only one."

"Did anyone mark your searching?" Bahadır asked.

"A few creatures saw us, but no one paid us particular attention." Zhivka waved her hand dismissively, her breath evening out. "There were other praetheria coming and

16

going as we approached the entrance, and it seemed clear they are used to newcomers seeking refuge."

A slight frown creased the lidérc's forehead as she said, "There were glamours across the cave."

"They're nothing," Zhivka said. "Only glamours to hide the cave from climbers. You needn't mind them."

"Did you see anything of Hunger or Vasilisa?" I asked.

"No," the lidérc said.

I let out a slow breath, the worst of my fears alleviated. Now we had only to retrieve Noémi.

"Good." Mátyás squinted up the mountain, thinking. "Can you climb again, or do you need rest?"

The lidérc shrugged, but Zhivka insisted on both food and drink before she was willing to brave the mountain again. I fretted at the delay. Now that I knew for certain where Noémi was, my body itched with inaction. But it was not long before Zhivka finished.

As we began walking toward the mountain, Zhivka turned to Bahadır. "Are you not coming? How convenient— to always stay behind when there might be danger. I thought you said you were not afraid."

"Zhivka . . . ," Mátyás warned.

Bahadır's eyes flashed. "I am not frightened. My faith forbids the practice of magic, and as I will not be shifted or glamoured through magic, I should only endanger your mission. I offered to stay with the horses, to be ready when you return with Noémi."

"I'm sorry," Zhivka said, threading a bit of fire across her knuckles, then collecting the flame in a ball on her palm and holding it toward Bahadır as a peace offering. "I didn't know, or I would not have teased you so. It can be lonely to live a faith not shared by those around you."

Bahadır nodded at her, accepting the apology, and we set off. Mátyás shifted once more into his crow form and launched into the air, swooping lazy circles over our heads while Zhivka cursed him halfheartedly. I stayed close to the lidérc, whose glamour covered both of us with shadows that would turn away unwanted attention. Mátyás offered to shift me as well, but I thought he might need to conserve the extra power, and I had no desire to emerge, naked, in the caverns after he shifted me back. Once in the caves, Zhivka would set a small fire to distract the guard while the lidérc and I freed Noémi, with Mátyás keeping watch overhead. Then we'd flee, Noémi and I beneath the lidérc's glamour and Mátyás on wing.

I had not done much climbing—certainly not anything of this magnitude, at this height. For some time, I focused only on my footing, searching out flat ground and stable rocks. Even as my legs burned with the unaccustomed exercise and the air seared my lungs, I refused to stop and rest, to avoid slowing the others. As it was, I sensed the lidérc restraining her pace, for my sake. The faint prickle of her glamour on my skin set my shoulders twitching, but I tried to ignore it. This was not a spell I wanted to break.

Before long, sweat was running down my face and wetting the back of my shirt and the waistband of my trousers. Thank heavens Gábor could not see me like this—and thank God for boys' clothing. A dress would have made the miserable climb unbearable.

We stopped a couple hours into our climb to finish a loaf of bread, and Zhivka passed around a water jug. I drank deep, the brackish water somehow sweet after my exertion. The landscape spread out in a panorama I had only seen in paintings. The mountains stretched as far as I could see in a bluish haze across the horizon, the nearer peaks crisp and grey-green, the valleys full of shadow and mystery.

It was late afternoon when we reached the rounded mouth of the cave. I could not see the opening at first; it was only when I followed Zhivka and the lidérc through what appeared to be sheer rock that my vision shifted and the dim entrance of the cave materialized. *The glamour.* I could feel the faint spell prickling across my skin, an almost imperceptible weight laid across the lidérc's own glamour. If it made me uncomfortable, well, I had borne worse. I followed the praetherian women into the gloom.

It was much cooler inside the mountain than it had been on the trail outside, and at first I welcomed the bracing air. But as we walked farther into the darkness, the sweat cooled on my skin and I began to wish I had brought something warmer than my light dolman. Zhivka kindled a small flame in her hand—enough light that we would not stumble. I swayed toward her, craving the warmth of the flame, before remembering I needed to stay close to the lidérc for her glamour to work.

The path dipped at a steep angle, and we scrambled downward, sometimes sliding on our backsides. A sharp rock scraped against me, and I winced, both at the unexpected pain and at the suspicion that I might have torn my trousers. Rocks clattered down the chamber before us, heralding our arrival, and I could only pray that the dull roar of voices from the cavern ahead covered the noise. Mátyás was a muted flutter in the darkness above us.

I accidentally dislodged a large rock and sent it tumbling down the path before me, making me jump. The lidérc huffed a laugh.

"You're in no danger, *nyuszikám*."

"I am not your little rabbit."

"But you jump like one." She smiled sweetly at me.

As the long, snaking chamber flattened out, Zhivka let her light fade. This new space had its own light: small glowing globes hung at intervals along the walls. A few figures moved about, their voices echoing across the cavern.

I took a deep breath, inhaling the rock-and-water scent of the caves, bracing for the moment when someone would see us. But no one did: the lidérc's glamour held.

We edged into the larger room, Zhivka and the lidérc walking casually along one wall. There was nothing about them or their movements to raise suspicion. Mátyás flew near the roof overhead, dodging stalactites and hiding in the shadows. I trailed as close as I dared to the lidérc.

This room was colder than the opening, and I rubbed at the gooseflesh on my arms. There was something off about the room, something that set my skin puckering beyond the chill. *It's just nerves,* I told myself.

Zhivka had said Noémi was being kept in a small chamber branching off the left side of this main room, and now she led us toward the branch. I tried to keep alert, to sweep my eyes across the entire room, but as we drew closer, my eyes fixed, magnetlike, on the spot where I should soon see my cousin.

I thought I caught a glimmer of gold—her hair?—when a short, stout creature with knobbled skin and a long, pointed sword broke away from the rock wall. He had not seen us yet, but I drew in my breath. This was Zhivka's cue to light her fire and our cue to dart around the guard and rescue Noémi.

But Zhivka froze, her hands at her side, and I realized—too late—what had bothered me about the room. The pressed-down weight of the lidérc's glamour had grown inside the cavern, and when I focused my chimera sense on it, I felt not just the prickle of her glamour but the bone-deep buzz of a massive spell. This was not a simple glamour to hide the entrance of the cave from uncaring eyes.

"Lidérc," I whispered. "There's a spell here. Can you see it?"

Zhivka must have heard me, because she shook her head, pressing her finger against her lips to signal silence. "It's nothing. Only the spells to power the lights around the room."

But the lidérc was frowning now. "An illusion—too dense for me to see through, but cunningly crafted to deflect attention from its existence, or I'd have marked it before."

Misgiving roiled my stomach. My second chimera soul was agitated now, swirling inside me. It would take only a small gesture to reach out and grasp the spell, to pull it to me and twist it. But we had not been noticed yet: if I broke a massive illusion, we'd surely be spotted.

The guard turned and raised his sword toward Zhivka in challenge. He said something in a language I did not know, and Zhivka answered.

"Anna," the lidérc said, her voice fierce and low, "break the spell."

Alarm bells jangled in my head, and I reacted, plucking a

thread of the illusion and snapping it. I did not see, at first, what had happened, but the lidérc hissed in shock, and I stumbled back, catching myself against the stone wall with my hand.

I snatched my hand away, gasping with pain. My fingers were burning, but not with heat—with ice. The cavern around us had transformed, ice carpeting the floor, great thick swells of it swooping from floor to ceiling, a giant wave turned perpetually still. As the illusion dropped, so did the temperature of the cave, bitter air singing through me.

Why would the praetheria bother to hide the icy nature of the cave?

A spell still buzzed about me—there was more to this illusion. The guard had spotted the lidérc now. He sprang forward, neatly evading the flame Zhivka had finally kindled in her hands. I reached for the spell again, shearing through its heart.

The praetheria milling about the room disappeared as though snuffed, and the guard vanished midstride. Only Zhivka and the lidérc remained, staring wide-eyed across the cave.

CHAPTER 3

Mátyás

A lifetime ago (quite literally, before I died), I found my sister a confounded nuisance. As was the fashion among my friends, I adopted an attitude of affectionate derision toward Noémi, teasing her mercilessly and declaring that few things were as likely to turn my stomach as a mushy declaration of feeling for one's siblings.

Before I died, I'd been something of a prick. (Perhaps I still was, but at least now I was *aware* of my failings.)

When I'd first come back after dying, it had been too dangerous to seek Noémi out, and the itch of her absence had begun to teach me what I'd dismissed in her presence. But when I'd heard she was missing, it was as though someone had pulled a chunk from my heart, as though some critical part of me had gone missing too.

As my crow's wings sliced through the icy updrafts above the mountain where Noémi was trapped, I found myself thinking not of my sister's tirades (which were mostly merited, truth be told) but of the times she had protected me: when she shielded my adolescent drinking from my father by making me devilish-tasting elixirs that cleared up my hangovers, when she steered me away from my first desperate infatuation with a much older woman whose practiced seduction concealed her predatory nature. More than once, Noémi had loaned me money out of her own slim savings and made nothing of it.

We had been good friends, once. I hoped we could be so again.

Damn it, I was becoming maudlin in my afterlife. I needed to be alert, not sentimental.

Ducking into the caverns, I had to fight the crow's natural instinct to resist such confined spaces. The rock felt smothering, a heaviness that was antithetical to everything in my hollow-boned body. I swallowed a *caw* of warning and flew after Anna and the others.

The walls surrounding us were coated in ice, gleaming like gems. Zhivka hadn't said anything about the cold, but perhaps with her samodiva fire-blood she hadn't noticed it. I followed the women into a large chamber, where a massive pillar of ice cleaved through the center of the room. The space was empty, save for the four of us.

I frowned. Where were the praetheria Zhivka and the lidérc reported seeing? I circled the room, trying to spy the side chamber where the praetheria kept my sister. But without flying into the darkened corridors branching off the main room, I could see nothing.

Below me, Anna froze. She and the lidérc had a quick,

furious conversation, and then Anna's eyes slid shut in concentration. Zhivka froze too, her lips pinching together in something like chagrin.

What were they seeing that I could not? A crow's senses did not always register as a human's did. Nor, apparently, as a praetherian's. A stabbing sense of danger raised my feathers, and I fluttered to the ground, shifting as I landed.

A mistake: a million points of gooseflesh lifted on my exposed skin, and the cold of the room sheared through my naked flesh as I crouched down. I let a fine layer of fur grow across my skin. Better—though to judge from the expression on Anna's face, the hirsute look was not one of my best. Or perhaps it was my near nakedness she objected to.

"What's wrong?"

"Illusions," Anna said. "Everything in the cave was an illusion."

"Is Noémi here?" Every muscle in my body tensed. If she wasn't . . .

"We don't know," the lidérc said. "I'm afraid we were set up. We should get out before—"

She cut off as a thousand tiny stars exploded in my vision. Something fine settled over me: an imperceptibly weighted net that tangled about my feet as I tried to turn and run. I stumbled, falling to my knees with a painful thud.

"Run!" I shouted at the others, but they were already moving, Anna and the lidérc scrambling back the way they had come, slipping across the ice.

Zhivka halted beside me.

"Run!" I told her again, shifting into a mouse, something small enough to escape through the net. But as I shrank, the net shrank with me, and my heart turned cold. I shifted again, taking on the shape of a flea, but I could not shrug free of the mesh.

Vasilisa had cast just such a net when she'd tried to trap me and Anna.

I glanced around the cavern, trying to see the praetherian witch-woman, but there were too many obstacles: icicles of stone and rock, light and shadow fracturing around them. If it was not Vasilisa behind the spell, it was someone with power like hers. Either way, we were in danger.

I surged upward, a mountain cat with sharp, scissoring claws. The hunger from so much shifting was starting to gnaw at me, but I ignored it. I could eat when I was free. But my claws and teeth made no difference to the magic mesh, which merely re-formed in the wake of my claws, like sand when you draw a finger through it.

The ravenous feeling tugged at my heart. This was more than the merely physical hunger that shifting brought out in me; this was the deeper yearning that the World Tree called from me. Even here, hundreds of miles from the *puszta,* I could sense the tree, its roots cracking fissures in my soul, pulling every cell in my body toward a powerful, devastating dragon shape. I doubted even Vasilisa's net could hold me in that form.

"Mátyás!" Zhivka cried, and I looked down to find that my cat feet had hardened into dragon claws.

No. I'd given in to the dragon twice before, and the first time, I had nearly killed my friends. The second time,

I *had* killed my friends, my hunger driving me to attack those around me indiscriminately. I shuddered into my own body, the sharpness of bile stinging my throat.

I had been so close to shifting into the dragon shape between one breath and the next, without any conscious decision.

Heart thudding, I glanced around the room. A wall of fire had sprung up before Anna and the lidérc, blocking the exit to the next chamber and the entrance to the cave. As I watched, Anna managed to shatter part of the spell, and the flames vanished. The lidérc made it across the glistening ice, but fire spurted up in Anna's face as she followed, and she fell back.

Zhivka still had not moved.

My subconscious understood her immobility before my conscious mind did, and my stomach tightened with pain, as though someone had punched me. Then three figures emerged from the shadows, and I no longer cared why Zhivka was not running.

A young woman with bone-pale hair: Vasilisa.

A horned creature with the pointed ears and goat tail of a satyr, a pair of loose trousers hitched about his waist.

And a bright-faced woman with fire-gold hair whom I had met once before, when I set her and her samodiva sisters free and Zhivka had stayed behind as a guarantee of good conduct. The samodiva queen.

I looked back at Zhivka. Her lips were tight, but her eyes were steady.

She knew.

She had always known what waited for us here.

"Why?"

She dipped her head, dropping her eyes to the ice floor. "Because my queen asked it of me. And while you are my friend, my sisters have my heart."

Anna was faltering now, sweat running down her face as the wall of fire flared, then sprang up again as her attempt at spell-breaking failed. The praetheria were closing on her, and she could not get out.

But I could get her out.

Maybe.

I had enough energy for one more shifting before I would need food and rest. I could not use it myself—I was trapped by Vasilisa's magic net unless I adopted the dragon form, which I would not do unless I had no other option—but I could shift Anna into something that would let her escape. A bird, maybe. My glance flickered to the samodiva queen, powering the wall of fire. Or something fireproof, like a samodiva.

I shuffled forward, hoping the praetheria would over-look me as they focused on stopping Anna.

I nearly made it. A few more steps, and I'd be able to touch Anna's sleeve.

But Zhivka saw me. "Don't let Mátyás touch her!"

The satyr grabbed me, arms like iron bands tightening across my chest. I tried to throw him off, but he was too powerful. I couldn't shift myself, not if I hoped to have enough strength left to shift Anna. *Iron.* I'd subdued the samodiva queen once by transmuting her hair to iron, a transformation less demanding than a whole-body shape-shift. I changed a few hairs on the satyr's arms to iron, but he didn't even flinch. So much for that idea.

I had only a few seconds before Vasilisa could seize Anna. I'd never shifted anyone from this distance—but then, until a few months ago, I'd never been dead before, either. I still didn't quite know the limits of what I could and could not do since the Lady had resurrected me.

I closed my eyes. There's no real merit to closing one's eyes while spell-casting, but everyone does it. I thought of Anna, the way her dark hair straggled about her face, her long, not-quite-graceful gait.

I thought of Zhivka, the way she held sparks from an open fire in her hands and they did not burn her.

Then I pictured Anna's fragile human skin and hair taking on the samodiva's resistance to fire, and pushed a shape out into the air.

For a moment, I thought nothing had happened.

Then Anna cried out—in surprise, I thought, not pain. At least, I hoped not.

I shouted, "Run!" and Anna-turned-samodiva nodded once and sprinted through the flames. The fire licked at her . . . but did not burn. "Get out! Find Noémi!"

The satyr released me to pelt after Anna, with Vasilisa beside him; the samodiva queen sent spurts of flame ahead of Anna, a conflagration filling the entire chamber before us.

But Anna did not cry out again, so I assumed her shifting held.

My legs trembled; I'd spent too much energy. I slumped to the icy ground, shivering as exhaustion washed over me. I curled my arms around my knees and huffed warm breath against my forearms. I could see the distant reflection of light from the samodiva's fires, but the near fire had burned out and the room was bitter cold, the ice slick beneath me.

Zhivka knelt beside me, kindling a fire in her hands and holding it toward me. An apology? I rolled away from her, though my chilled skin protested fiercely at the loss of her warmth.

I'd figure out what to do next when I'd regained some energy. Food would be my first priority.

But for now, I focused all my attention on a silent prayer.

Run, Anna.

CHAPTER 4

Anna

I raced back through the cavern like a thing possessed, my hands and legs finding purchase in the scree as though they had minds of their own. My lungs burned with the exertion, but I did not stop. The lidérc, her webbed feet providing her with a grip the rest of us lacked, had disappeared ahead of me.

I stumbled out of the cavern, blinking in the brilliant light of the afternoon sun. I paused for just a moment, to reorient myself and grab a gulping breath.

"Zhivka!" the lidérc hissed, emerging from the shadows of a large rock a few feet from the entrance. Her fingers curled, clawlike.

"No," I gasped. "It's Anna. Mátyás shifted me. But they're right behind me!"

Desperation had lent me added speed, pushing me across the slippery, uneven footing of the cavern, but any moment now Vasilisa and the others would be free of the cave.

The lidérc must have believed me, for she grasped my hand in hers and her shadow-glamour prickled my skin. I wasn't sure how much protection such a slight spell would afford us, but I was grateful for it nonetheless.

"We need a distraction," the lidérc said.

I glanced around as we began our descent, my thoughts racing ahead of my feet. Somewhere to hide would be ideal—but the rocky mountainside seemed too exposed, and I was not going back into that cave. In any case, hiding worked only if they did not find us.

It would take us hours to get back to where Bahadır waited, unless we wanted to risk our necks by running down the mountain.

The sky overhead was mostly clear, threaded through with fine white clouds. No storms to offer cover. Maybe a fire? No, the samodiva would walk right through it.

A glint of white at the mountain's summit caught my attention. If fire could not stop them, perhaps snow? I might loosen the new snow from recent storms, but I could not guarantee that a wave of snow would not bury us as surely as our pursuers.

If not snow, then maybe rock. There was a clump of boulders above the cave's entrance. If I could just coax them free . . .

All these thoughts passed more quickly than the time it takes to tell them.

I tugged the lidérc to the side, moving on a horizontal line rather than down the mountain. Focusing on the limestone lip of the cave's entrance, I thought of the tendency of things (even rocks) to crumble over time. I sought out fissures in the scree just above the cave and pressed on them, remembering how I had persuaded the stone foundations at Schönbrunn to shiver apart that terrible night of the archduchess's masquerade ball, when the archduchess sent her guards and magicians to round up the praetheria, when she had sentenced me to death for the magic that killed Mátyás.

A loud crack like thunder rolled across the valley, and a great plume of dust rained around us as the boulders cascaded down. Smaller rock shards exploded through the air, and the lidérc and I threw up our arms to protect our faces. I prayed Mátyás had the sense to stay back in the heart of the cavern, rather than following the others to the mouth of the cave. Noémi would never forgive me if I killed him twice—indeed, I would not be able to forgive myself.

When the dust cleared, I rubbed my stinging arms and looked back at the entrance.

It was gone.

A mound of boulders stood in its place, rocks still rattling over its surface and bounding loose across the slope.

A vast relief settled over me. It was pierced moments later by a sharp pang, as I thought of Mátyás—I'd left him behind, trapped and vulnerable. But he was resourceful, and the praetheria had no reason (yet) to want him dead.

I hoped it would be enough, until we could return to free him.

But now we needed to get away before we were as trapped as he was. My trick would not hold the praetheria indefinitely.

I dusted myself off and caught the lidérc staring at me. "What?"

She shook her head, dark tangled hair falling about her cheeks. "Nothing. Only you look like yourself again. And you're bleeding."

I glanced at my arms. The linen sleeves of the boy's shirt I wore had been torn, and red was seeping through them. I swallowed a curse: gone were the days when a ruined gown was easily replaceable and meant nothing. I had only one spare shirt, and I didn't fancy going shirtless while it was laundered.

Then I did curse: Mátyás had gone into the ice caves with nothing. Even if he did escape, he'd have no money with him, no clothes. And he could freeze to death while the praetheria dug out of the cave.

I looked back at the rockslide. I couldn't leave him like this.

"Come on," the lidérc said.

"But Mátyás . . ."

". . . can take care of himself." She started down the mountain again. "If you don't get away now, you'll be no use to him later."

I hesitated a moment longer, staring at the rocks. A crow called somewhere overhead, startling me into action.

Run, Mátyás had said.

I scrambled down the rocks behind the lidérc.

Ж

We reached the valley just as night began to roll in, long, steep shadows cutting across the gorge. Overhead, the last of the light gleamed against the walls of the hilltop castle.

We explained to Bahadır the dire arithmetic of our rescue attempt, how we had left with four and returned with two.

He started toward the trail we'd just descended, never mind that it would soon be too dark to see his own feet. "We've got to get Mátyás out."

The lidérc hissed in annoyance. "If you climb the mountain now, you'll either get yourself killed or captured, and you'll be of no use to Mátyás. There aren't enough of us to fight the praetheria. We need to find aid."

My eyes strayed to the castle. I nudged the lidérc. "I have an idea."

The lidérc and I gathered a few supplies and started across the valley on horseback toward the castle. Bahadır volunteered to stay with the horses, saying "If Mátyás does manage to escape, someone needs to be here to meet him. The praetheria won't be looking for me."

The moon rose as we rode, full and bright. While I was grateful that its impartial light made our way less treacherous, it also exposed us to anyone who might follow. I listened for Bahadır's warning whistle and jumped at every unexpected sound, from a hare, shooting from the bushes in a burst of noise, to an owl hooting in the distance. A smile, fleeting and amused, flickered across the lidérc's face each time I startled.

A cold wind scoured the valley, and I pulled a cloak out of my bag, wrapping it around my shoulders and thinking of Mátyás, shivering naked in the ice caves. But as we rode and no immediate threat emerged, my body began to shut down, reacting to the intensity of the day's events. I may have dozed once or twice before the lidérc woke me. Curiously, for a woman who might slit my throat as effortlessly as she might pour tea, the lidérc was proving surprisingly restful—and resourceful.

We skirted a small village and reached the base of the hill, where a trail curled up toward the castle. We dismounted, tethered our horses in a grove of trees, and began to climb. My muscles screamed at me, already sore from my scramble up and down the mirroring mountain. "If I never climb another hill in my life," I muttered, "I might die happy."

"You might die anyway," the lidérc pointed out. "Take your happiness where you can."

I glowered at her, thinking the night shadows would hide my expression, but she laughed. We had never spent so much time alone together, but as we paced the trail— the lidérc unflagging as I sweated and gasped—I could not help feeling a sort of kinship with her. When I first came to Hungary, Noémi had told me of the lidérc as a means to scare me, and I had dreamed of her kind as something nightmarish: the *lidércnyomás* that was a Hungarian word for night terror, the weight of a lidérc perched on your chest, pressing the life from you. I had seen her months later, in the streets of Buda-Pest, hunting the soldiers who threatened my friends, and though her mouth had been crimson with blood, she had not seemed so nightmarish then.

Now, in the moonlight, her goose feet dusty and cracking, she seemed so familiar I could not believe I had ever been frightened.

"Why do the others call you 'lidérc'?" I had wondered this for weeks now but had not known how to ask. "Don't you have a name?"

The lidérc turned her black eyes on me, and at once she was no longer familiar or ordinary but a creature who could kill me before I drew another breath. "You should not ask a praetherian her name if it is not freely given. Names have power, and you have not earned the right to mine."

The cool air was bitter on my tongue as I inhaled. "I'm sorry. I didn't mean to offend."

I wanted to ask her more, about her childhood, about her years in the Binding, but her closed expression said she would not welcome such questions from me. In any case, if we were being followed, it was safer to keep silent.

The trail toward the castle was steep, but at least it was maintained, unlike the one we'd forged across the valley. I tried to recall what I'd heard of the castle and its current inmates. At length, we reached the lower walls and a guardhouse. The rest of the castle perched sheer and grim above us, only a few lights still flickering in the darkness.

There were two gates here: a larger arched gate for carriages and carts and a smaller pedestrian entrance set to the left of the main entrance. A square guard tower squatted in the corner, narrow slits forming the only windows.

I knocked on the smaller gate, trying to corral my thoughts into some kind of sense. What could I say that would persuade them to help us free Mátyás? That there had been a rockslide? Or that he had been captured by praetheria?

There was a squealing sound as the hinges shifted and the wooden door swung open. A middle-aged man stood in the doorway, his arms crossed over a heavy belly. *"Ja? Was wollen Sie?"*

"There's been a rockslide. My cousin is trapped in the ice caves across the valley. We need some strong men to free him," I said in German.

"Your cousin is likely dead." The man rubbed his balding scalp. "And this is a prison, not a rescue service."

"Please," I said, adopting my most pious "young lady" expression—and momentarily forgetting that I was dressed as a young man, not a woman. "Surely you can spare a few men. We will pay you." I hoped—I was not altogether certain how much money we had between Bahadır's purse and the one stowed in my bag.

The lidérc whispered in Hungarian, "Tell him Mátyás is táltos and should not be left to die."

The man's eyes swung to the lidérc, flickering from her rather severe features to her dusty feet. He recoiled as though shot, his hand shaping a cross in the air before him.

"Get that *Ungeheuer* away from here!" he said, scurrying behind the wooden door and slamming it shut.

The lidérc stared, unblinking, at the door. "What is *'Ungeheuer'*?"

I took her stiff arm, gently. "Let's go."

"Tell me! Monster, ogre, devil? What is it?"

"Monster," I said reluctantly, wishing I could soften the ugliness of the word. It hung in the dark air between us, the shadows around us rustling with whispers of unspeakable things.

The lidérc blinked once, her eyes still fixed on the door. "He might have helped Mátyás, if not for me."

I sighed. "I don't think he meant to help us, even before he saw you. And his prejudice is not your fault."

She bared her teeth, exposing their sharp edges in the moonlight. "I may not be responsible for his beliefs, but I must live with them anyway."

She turned away from the walled castle and stomped back down the mountainside. I followed, wishing I could undo the world with a spell, as I had the Binding, and re-forge a world where the lidérc and other praetheria would not constantly walk under the weight of another person's hate.

In the next breath I remembered Mátyás, trapped in the ice caves with praetheria who had hunted us. Where did this tangle of hate begin and end? The praetheria hated humans because we had trapped them in the Binding spell and then abused them when they were released; and humans hated the praetheria because we feared them and saw in them our own hate reflected. With a flush of shame, I realized I was not absolved in this: I had brought the praetheria into a world unprepared for them, and I too had feared them, had seen them as something other than what I was. I was learning to overcome that fear, to see the praetheria, like the lidérc, as beings with a center of self as distinct and complex as my own. Still, learning was only a start, a small coin set against the recompense we owed them. Humans had been—were—wrong in our treatment of the praetheria. But I could not believe praetherian vengeance would right that wrong, only multiply it.

Maybe I should not reforge the world, if I had my wish. Maybe I should burn it down.

The lidérc was already mounted when I reached the horses. I swung myself up, grateful for the thousandth time for my trousers. (Really, why were women's clothes so impractical? It's as though designers *wanted* to incapacitate us.)

Ahead of us, the trail disappeared into shadows. The night seemed to be growing darker. I glanced upward to see if the moon had shifted behind a mountain peak or if a cloud had passed across it—and every muscle in my body stilled. Darkness sliced across the edge of the moon.

The lidérc noticed. "What's wrong?" Her tone was softer than it had been earlier.

"The moon—it's not right."

She followed my upward gaze, then grinned. "A lunar eclipse. Have you never seen one?"

I shook my head, feeling foolish. I might have guessed what it was, had not the events of the day predisposed me to spooking at shadows. "I have heard of society parties to watch eclipses, but I have never been to one, and Mama did not think it proper for me to be out of doors at midnight."

"My mother told me the only proper place for a lidérc at midnight was beneath the skies," she replied, still smiling, and I grinned back. She'd never shared anything of her own life with me before. That breath of lightness lifted some of the fury still coursing through me after our encounter at the castle.

We did not slow our pace as we rode back across the valley, but we watched the sky as the shadows crept over the face of the moon, and the white orb slowly turned rusty, then the darker shade of old blood.

Riding beneath the broad dark sky and the carnelian moon, I felt a glimmer of hope. The magnificence in the sky was part of a regular cycle: the moon would change whether it had an audience or not, whether humans reigned, or praetheria, or both, or neither. Somehow that permanence in the face of everything uncertain in my life steadied me. Whatever choices we made, they were not irredeemable. Life would go on, somehow.

That hope sustained me until we reached the clearing where we had left Bahadır.

Mátyás's ugly white horse, Holdas, was missing. So was Bahadır. Bahadır's horse was pulling at her tether, her nostrils flared and wild, her mane matted with sweat.

The lidérc slid off her mount in a sinuous movement and crouched down. She set her fingers against a dark patch on the grass, then lifted them to her nose. "Blood," she said, frowning.

CHAPTER 5

Anna

I was still unraveling the implications of the lidérc's finding (*Whose blood was it?*) when a shadow barreled out of the trees, knocking the lidérc to the ground. She screamed, but it was a scream of rage, not terror.

The shadowy figure raised his arm, and moonlight spun across a metal blade and caught in the horns protruding from a darkly matted head. His chest was bare, and a tail protruded from the back of his trousers.

The satyr from the caves.

He sliced his weapon down, and the lidérc rolled away. She tried to scramble upright but fell back with a cry. She'd been injured in her fall.

I nudged my horse forward, riding at the satyr. He leapt aside and swiped something at my mount's flank. The horse reared up, depositing me on my backside on the ground, my teeth jarring together, and the satyr rushed me.

As I felt frantically around for a weapon, my fingers closed on a rock the size of a small apple. I was useless in this kind of fight. Against a magician, I might break a spell, but against sheer brute force, I had nothing, not even the training a young man would have as part of his schooling.

I lobbed the rock at the satyr. It missed his head, which I'd been aiming for, but struck his shoulder. The blow didn't accomplish anything useful, however, as he continued to advance on me. I clambered to my feet.

"Run, Anna," he said, mimicking Mátyás's cadences with eerie accuracy.

I stumbled backward, and my heel caught on a root. Only the desperate windmilling of my arms saved me from falling. The satyr laughed.

"Is that all the resistance you can muster? I expected some fight, at least."

The satyr caught my shoulders and shoved, and I reeled back, falling to the ground.

Some hero, I thought. *I can't even stand my own ground.*

The satyr fished a length of twine from a pocket and advanced again. I scuttled to one side, away from his reach, and froze.

Some distance from us, a gentle glowing light bobbed uncertainly between the trees. I squinted at it. Was it a lantern? Someone coming belatedly to help us? The light began to grow, expanding like a small sun, a beacon in the darkness. The swelling light pulled a sweet-bitter note of longing from me.

I didn't know what the source of the glowing sphere was, but I had to reach it. The light promised to slake every thirst, fill every half-named desire, meet every ache of need I'd ever felt. I was on my knees, then my feet, scrambling forward before my wits caught up with me.

The satyr pushed past me, running toward the light, and an unreasoning fury burned through me, that he would reach it before me.

"Anna!" someone called, and the light seemed to fade, its pull weakening. I blinked, both fury and need draining from me.

"It's only a projection," said the lidérc. "Part of my glamour. Useful for hunting but not much else." Her breathing was heavy, her words punctuated by panting. "We've only got a few minutes before he sees through the glamour and returns. Help me!"

She was still sitting on the ground, her face pale and set, her lips pinched together. One hand was clamped around an ankle. "I don't know if I've turned it or if it's broken."

I helped her to her feet, and she winced as she limped to her horse. Somehow, with much pulling on her part and much pushing on mine, we got her into the saddle. She rode forward, slashing the leash of Bahadır's horse with a knife so the beast could follow us.

I swung myself into my own saddle, grunting as my mount's trotting gate jostled my bruises. The trot turned to a canter, then a gallop across the valley floor.

It was not long—perhaps five minutes—before we heard hooves pounding behind us. I swung around to see Bahadır's horse. But the horse was not alone; she had been commandeered. A horned shadow crouched across the saddle.

The lidérc hunched over her saddle, urging her horse

faster. "Damnation." She'd picked up a few of Mátyás's speaking habits. "We can't fight, not wounded as I am. We'll have to outrun him."

Night was edging into morning, the faintest grey sweeping the horizon. I blinked hard, willing my body not to slip into exhaustion. "We won't be able to keep up this pace much longer," I said. Already my horse breathed heavy, sweat dampening her neck.

The lidérc sighed. "You're right, though that is a consideration the satyr will not share."

"Can you fight him from horseback?"

"I can—until he stabs the horse from beneath me." She grimaced. "If I weren't injured, we could abandon the horses and try our luck at hiding and hope to lose him."

I tugged on my reins. My horse slowed with a long, whuffing exhale. "Give me your dagger," I said, injecting more sureness into my voice than I felt. "I'll try to hold him off while you run."

The lidérc pulled to a stop. "Can you wield a dagger without stabbing yourself?"

"Yes," I said, somewhat indignantly. I'd handled daggers before, though I ruthlessly suppressed the memory of stabbing Mátyás with a bone knife. I might not be adept, but I could be trusted to know the point from the haft.

The lidérc urged her mount beside mine and handed me a dagger, sliding a second one into her own hand.

We hadn't long to wait. Within moments, the satyr appeared, Bahadır's horse clearly struggling to maintain her pace, her sides heaving. At the sight of us, the satyr slowed and unsheathed a short sword at his side.

He charged the lidérc first. She parried his thrust, her

blade sliding beneath his guard to leave a dark line across his forearm. He hissed, and charged his mount toward her, crushing her injured leg between the two horses. She cried out and dropped her dagger, and the satyr swung his sword. The heavy pommel connected with the side of her head with a sickening crack, and she tumbled forward, to rest across the withers of her horse.

The satyr trotted toward me, his horse trembling beneath him. I held my dagger before me like a talisman, and prayed I did not embarrass myself.

I managed to parry his first attack, though the shock of the impact rattled my bones and buzzed in my head like the aftermath of a spell. As his arm shifted for another thrust, I tightened my sweat-slicked grip on the lidérc's dagger.

I'm sorry, Mátyás. I didn't run far enough or fast enough.

A crack like a heavy branch snapping splintered the dawn, and the satyr toppled from his horse.

When the satyr did not move, I slid down from my saddle and rushed to the lidérc, too grateful for the unexpected reprieve to wonder much at it. She still breathed, though her face was ashen. A trickle of blood ran down her temple. I eased her out of her saddle, huffing as her weight fell against me, which nearly dropped us both. I dragged her away from the horses, laid her down on the ground, and covered her with a blanket scrounged from one of her saddlebags.

Then I straightened, sighing, and turned to deal with the satyr's body.

But someone had already beaten me to the task. Where

the body had lain, a girl now stood; her hand was stroking the neck of Bahadır's mare.

I recognized her at once. It was Emilija, daughter of the Croatian general who had hunted me from Vienna. Following Vasilisa's attack, we'd left her unconscious in a hospital in Buda-Pest. She was conscious now, dressed once more in her Sereshan's uniform: the telltale red mantle, short brown jacket with red braiding, white trousers, blue socks, and sandals. Even in the dim early-morning light, she looked crisp and well rested, whereas I was nearly frayed through with exhaustion.

"Where is my dog?" Emilija asked. Her forthrightness was coupled with an edge that betrayed her fear. That her first concern was for her dog made her seem more human than she had in the two days she'd held me captive. Her dog, a beautiful Dalmatian that had helped her track me down, had been injured when Vasilisa attacked us. But the dog could not stay at the hospital with Emilija.

"I left him with a journalist—Borbála Dobos—in Vienna. She will keep him safe until you can fetch him."

How had Emilija picked up my trail but not that of her Dalmatian? Perhaps she saw me as a duty and her beloved dog as a luxury.

Her relief was palpable, lightening her stern face and lifting her shoulders. "Thank you." She leveled her pistol at me. "But I must still return you to Vienna and the emperor's justice."

At once it was too much: the ice caves, the frantic scramble down the mountainside, the midnight ride to the castle, the harried escape from the satyr, only to come to the same place I'd stood a lifetime ago, when Emilija had first captured me.

I dropped to the ground and began to laugh. I might have cried a bit too.

Emilija flipped one of her neat braids over her shoulder and eyed me askance. "Are you . . . Have you gone mad?"

"No," I said, wiping tears from my eyes. "It is all of a piece with my life right now. Of course you should arrive to save us from certain capture by the praetheria, just to doom me to execution at the emperor's hands. Is this how you thank me for saving your life?"

"I saved *your* life just now. I think we are even. But I am grateful that you brought me to the hospital."

"But not grateful enough to let me go?" My wild laughter ebbed away, leaving me only profoundly tired.

"My gratitude is personal; my duty belongs to my sovereign." Her words called up echoes of Gábor's before we'd parted in Buda-Pest—the words of a person who placed honor before personal interest. I wished I had a fraction of that sureness. Emilija continued, "I *am* sorry. If I could see a way to let you go, I would."

"You might pretend you never found me."

She looked affronted. "I am not so incompetent."

"What of my friend?" I asked, glancing at the lidérc.

Emilija looked at the sleeping woman, noting, surely, the uncanny angles of her cheeks, the goose feet just peeking below the blanket. "I have no quarrel with her. She is free to go."

So Dragović's daughter did not share her father's zealous hatred of the praetheria? Interesting.

Exhaustion crashed over me, and I yawned. "At this moment I do not particularly care what you do with me, so long as you let me sleep." I'd figure something out in the morning, I thought muzzily, crawling toward the lidérc to share her blanket.

"I've already lost so much time." Emilija's words were sharp with impatience.

"I have climbed two mountains and narrowly escaped death today. I have not slept a wink. Unless you mean to tie me to a horse and drive me to Vienna, I will sleep. In any case," I said, "these horses are not fit to be ridden until they've rested."

"Fine. Sleep. But we'll be off by afternoon."

I scarcely heard her. I was already drifting away.

)(

It's astonishing what a few solid hours of rest and some bracing cold water can accomplish. By the time Emilija roused us, and I had splashed water on my face, I felt almost myself again. And I had a few ideas.

The lidérc watched me. The blood at her temple had been washed away, and her ankle was neatly bandaged. "I challenged the soldier to battle to set you free," she said, nodding at Emilija, who stood some distance away currying the horses. "But she refused when she saw that I was injured." Emilija either could not hear us or was doing a very good job of pretending she could not, as she did not once look at us. Her father would not have seen an injured praetherian as grounds for mercy. She had a sense of honor. I could use that.

"You didn't have to do that."

The lidérc shrugged. "I know."

I stood up, swallowing a string of distinctly unladylike phrases as my bruised body registered aches in places I was not aware one *could* ache. On the plus side, Emilija had not bothered to bind me, as she had before. She must have been very sure of her capture.

"I could still run," I said, approaching her, walking slowly so I did not betray how much it hurt to move.

She did not look at me but continued brushing the lidérc's horse. "You did not leave me behind when I was injured, and I am your enemy. You would not leave behind a friend."

"You said my friend was free to go."

A tiny smile danced about Emilija's lips. "So I told her. But she, curiously, has refused to leave you. And so here we are."

I looked back at the lidérc with raised eyebrows. "I thought surely you would stay to help Mátyás. And what of Bahadır?"

"The satyr's attack makes it clear that the praetheria escaped the blocked cave. I would guess from Bahadır's disappearance that they have taken both him and Mátyás somewhere, and I am more likely to find clues to their destination in Vienna than here in these mountains. Besides, Mátyás does not need my help so much as you do—and he would not be pleased to hear that I had let a strange soldier take you back to Vienna to be killed."

I sighed. She was likely right. "A pity that Emilija killed the satyr, or we might have asked him."

"I'm sorry my efforts to save your life inconvenienced

you," Emilija said, brushing more aggressively. The horse skittered away, and she murmured an apology to it.

"Your efforts to see me hanged inconvenience me more," I said. "If I am still to be executed for my cousin's death, you should know that he is not dead." I rather admired how neatly I'd phrased that: no mention that I *had* killed Mátyás, or that he'd been brought back to life. Only that he now lived.

"Why did you not say so before?"

"I didn't know."

"Can this be proved?"

"I've seen him," the lidérc said, limping toward us. She paused, her face taut with pain, and put her arm across one of the horses to support some of her weight.

"You might have seen him too," I said to Emilija, thinking of the first time I saw Mátyás after his death. He had come upon us just in time, after Vasilisa had trapped us with her wolves. "He is táltos. He fought with Vasilisa as a bear just as you passed out."

Emilija's frown deepened. "I . . . might remember that. Certainly, I do not think you should be executed for a crime you did not commit. But I am not the courts—my duty is only to take you back. Someone else must stand in judgment."

"If you take me back as a prisoner, the archduchess will not let me live."

"You do not know that." Emilija cocked her head, a thoughtful expression on her face. "Indeed, the archduchess might welcome you. Her son is dying."

I blinked. "Franz Joseph?" *Impossible.* I had danced with

him only weeks before. He was young and strong and flush with health.

"He fell sick just after that masquerade ball where you were charged. A spell of some sort. The archduchess has offered enough wealth to buy a small kingdom to anyone who can break the spell. So far, no one has succeeded."

Nausea washed over me, making me light-headed. I remembered that night vividly: Vasilisa transforming me into a vision of winter and saying she hoped I'd break a man's heart. And then Franz Joseph had behaved so oddly, acting cold and distant when I first arrived and then drawing me to him in a frenzy, kissing me as though he were possessed. *Or ensorcelled.* Any good student of fairy tales knew that kisses were untrustworthy magic. They could cure one's true love—but they could curse just as easily. Had *I* brought this illness on Franz Joseph?

Emilija continued, watching my face carefully. "You break spells, yes? If you heal him, you might name your own reward—perhaps even a pardon."

"It's a good idea," the lidérc said, surprising both of us. "And not only for the young man. You might use the arch-duchess's gratitude to turn the war. This is not a war any of us can win. Should Hungary somehow manage to stand against Austria and Croatia and Romania, she will fall to the praetheria. And if your armies unite against the prae-theria, they might win. But at what cost to human and praetherian alike?"

The war. In the tumult of the last few weeks—fleeing for my life, being captured first by Emilija and then by Vasi-lisa, and then our frantic search for Noémi—I'd mostly ignored the war, except as it pertained to Gábor. The lidérc's words made me remember, reluctantly, how wide this web of violence stretched. Less than six months after Hungary had been granted independence from Austria, Austria had begun to regret that freedom. The Hapsburgs (most particularly, Archduchess Sophie) had encouraged the minorities in Hungary—Romanians, Croats, Serbs—to petition for their own independence and had covertly sent them money and arms to provoke outright rebellion. Then, when the count who had been sent to bring order to Hungary was murdered by a group of students, pulled from his carriage and hacked to pieces, Austria had declared war outright.

And this was only the beginning. Austria would reach out to her old ally Russia for aid in quashing the unrest that the Austrians had helped manufacture. The Russians, in turn, were led by a tsar who was under the influence of a praetherian, Count Svarog, one of the Four who sought to restore the praetheria to their former glory by inciting a war among humans. If Russia were drawn into the war, the praetheria might destroy Austria and Hungary together before turning on the Russians.

But no one had wanted to listen when I tried to alert them to the praetherian plot. I had not been able to stop the Congress in Vienna from voting to sequester the praetheria. The British embassy in Vienna had ignored my warning. When I had tried to stand against Archduchess Sophie, she had decreed my death, and only intervention by the praetheria had saved me. Even if I wanted to stop the war, there was nothing I could do. Everything I thought I possessed had been stripped from me—family, fortune, a place in society. I had channeled my energy into finding Noémi instead.

And now the lidérc wanted to drag me back into the war. She continued, "The only way to win this war is to stop it before it begins. If the archduchess decrees it, the Austrians will withdraw their army, and others will follow. If the humans will not fight, the praetheria will not attack. Not yet. They are not strong enough to take on hale armies."

I looked at Emilija. "Would your father pull back his armies if the archduchess asked him to?"

"Of course. He's a loyal subject of the Hapsburgs." She frowned a little. "What is this about the praetheria?"

"I'll explain later," I said, thinking. The archduchess did not care for me—but she did care for her son. All her ambitions were centered in him. His life would surely be worth my pardon, which would mean I should not have to live my life in exile or in hiding. I could see my family again—my sister, Catherine, and her new baby; my parents; and my brother, James. Besides, I did not want to see Franz Joseph die from a spell. Not when I could stop it. Not when I might be responsible. But— "I risk my life if I go back to Vienna. If this does not work, I might die."

"If this does not work, we might all die," the lidérc said. "I risk my life every day simply existing in your world."

I took a long breath. She was right. Only luck and a twist of history made my life less precarious than hers. Had there never been a Binding, perhaps today the praetheria would rule, and humans would be hunted.

"All right," I said. "I'll try to break the spell."

)(

Our return to Vienna was not swift, as we had to let our exhausted horses recover and then we ran afoul of autumn rains that turned the roads to mire. But my agreeing to go willingly to Vienna had shifted something between Emilija and me—she did not bind my hands, and she allowed the lidérc to travel with us without comment. I had always seen Emilija as an extension of her father, but it was becoming increasingly clear that she was her own person: she did not hate the praetheria, as he did; she was not ruthless, as he could be; and in the mornings, when the sun shone, she sang Croatian folksongs in a delightfully rusty voice. After a few days, the lidérc began to join in, her voice a low, mournful countertone to Emilija's. I hummed along, my voice scarcely audible. When the lidérc did not know the words, she made them up, and she and Emilija both dissolved into giggles.

I watched them—a fierce soldier and a sharp-toothed creature out of nightmares—laughing together like two ordinary girls, and something curled tight beneath my breastbone began to ease. I could imagine few things more distant from the war Emilija's father waged than the laughter pealing in the autumn light, and those echoing notes sounded like hope.

The second evening of our journey, while Emilija poked at the fire beneath a small pot that held what promised to be our dinner and the lidérc went hunting, I settled on a patch of grass still lit by the fading sun to read the latest of Gábor's letters.

Šukarìja! I hope my letter finds you well.

A group of Romani men have joined my division, though it took some persuading for our colonel to accept them as soldiers rather than musicians: it is a bitter truth that the Romani are often as sought after as musicians as they are scorned elsewhere. In my grandmother's generation, Bihari János played before the emperor of Austria and lived like a nobleman. For this, he was remembered as a Hungarian, his Romani heritage forgotten. I hope someday that when—if— I am remembered, it will be because I am Romani and Hungarian both.

I looked up. Emilija prodded at the fire, oblivious to me. Why did society persist in seeing identity as an *or* rather than an *and,* unless you were a wealthy man? All my life, my mother and society had taught me that because I was a woman—a lady, at that—I must live and behave a certain way. *Or.* Emilija defied such expectations to become a soldier and was held to be a good one, despite being a woman. But to erase one part of her identity was to diminish the other. *Or.*

And Gábor—what must it be like, to everywhere find his talents and gifts undervalued because he belonged to a community without a nation, because he was Romani? Yet he too was many things, many *and*s: Romani and scientist, soldier and friend. He should not have to choose between them.

I picked up the letter again.

The food is terrible—oversalted and undercooked— but somehow eating it while speaking Romani makes it

bearable. My mother tongue is a beautiful one: someday
I shall teach you. We are kept busy during the daylight
hours, but at night, when I cannot sleep, I find myself
wishing you were with me. Then I remember the food
and the indifferent quarters we keep, and I am glad you
do not have to share them. I miss you.

I smiled at his closing: our own food and quarters were
not much better. Though I did not recognize his opening word—it was not Hungarian—I hoped it was some
Romani endearment. His words helped bridge the terrible
distance between us and offered me an anchor, reminding
me there was still much in the world to hope for.

I trimmed my own pen and began to write.

)(

As we drew nearer to Vienna, Emilija grew more talkative.
One afternoon, as we led the horses alongside the nearly
impassable smear of mud that passed for a road, she said,
"Tell me more of this praetherian conspiracy. I thought the
praetheria were all secured in a camp outside Melk."

"I think 'secured' means something different to you than
to me," the lidérc said. "Were the praetheria truly secure,
and safe, we would be protected by laws, not guarded by
soldiers."

"Some of the praetheria are dangerous—we cannot have
them free to threaten peaceful citizens."

"And some humans are dangerous, but most of you remain free," the lidérc said.

"The law is as much for praetherian safety as ours."

"Then perhaps you might have asked us how we wished to feel safe."

Emilija's lips thinned, but she did not argue back. Indeed, the faint pink stealing into her cheeks suggested she might be considering the lidérc's argument.

"You asked about the war." The lidérc changed the subject, returning to Emilija's earlier question. "Some praetheria evaded the sanctuary. Many of those resent this human world—they want to return to the world they knew before the Binding, where they were worshipped by humans. Where they ruled."

Emilija studied the lidérc. "And do you wish for this?"

"Would I be here with two humans if I wished for that world? My kind have only ever been feared—by humans as well as other praetheria." Her black eyes flickered and drooped, and her voice sounded faintly sad. "I should like a world where I do not fear being hunted."

"That sounds very lonely." Emilija combed her fingers through the hair hanging free at the end of her braid in what I was coming to recognize as a nervous gesture. "I know something of that feeling. Because I was not a girl who wished for fancy dresses or the attention of boys, other girls did not know what to make of me. And when I became a soldier, the boys mocked me too. Only my father believed in me. I hope you also have someone like that."

"I had someone once," the lidérc said, her eyes fixed on distant shadows. "Very long ago."

"You have Mátyás," I said, because for all his faults, my cousin's loyalty was adamantine.

"I know," the lidérc said, very low. "That is why I am still here."

58

We told Emilija what we knew of the war, how the praetheria meant to wait until our armies had worn themselves
thin, then attack. I explained that I had tried to leave word
with Kossuth Lajos, with the English embassy, but no one
seemed to listen.

"I am listening," Emilija said. "I was there when Vasilisa attacked us. I believe you. A good soldier fights not
to make wars but to end them. When we get to Vienna,
I will do what I can to persuade the Hapsburg family to
listen to you."

That night, we shared a stew and bits of familiar songs
before dropping to sleep, one by one, beneath the stars.
But in that shared quiet before we slept, a current passed
among us. We were not quite allies but no longer enemies,
either. Words had done that—mine, the lidérc's, Emilija's.
There was a key in that somewhere, but sleep tugged at my
thoughts, and I could not hold it.

CHAPTER 6

Mátyás

A thundering boom shook the ice caves, and then a cloud of ice pellets and debris enveloped me. I coughed on the dust, my lungs burning. With each cough, my shivering intensified, until my whole body trembled with cold.

Here lies Eszterházy Mátyás: He died with fire in his lungs and ice on his arse.

Angry voices reached me, coming nearer. Through watery eyes, I counted the returning figures: one, two, three. I squinted through the lingering dust, but no one appeared to be dragging a captive.

"What happened?" I asked.

"Your thrice-damned cousin tried to drop a mountain on us," Vasilisa said. But though she seemed put out, she did not seem genuinely angry. There was a glint in her eye that might even have been amusement.

Anna escaped. I released a long, burning breath and let the shifting I had cast over her dissolve. She no longer needed the samodiva shape—and I might have need of the power. As soon as I regained enough strength, I planned to shift to something better adapted to the cold. A beaver, maybe, with a nice, thick pelt. Or a wombat, one of those odd, fuzzy Australian badgers. Vasilisa's spell net still hung over me, preventing my escape, but it would not stop me from shifting.

From her crouch beside me, Zhivka said, "His lips are blue. Unless you mean to kill him with cold, you'd best cover him." She'd extinguished the flame she held earlier as a peace offering, and now she would not meet my eyes.

"And spoil the view?" Vasilisa asked, pouting, and then laughed as my cheeks flamed. Would that I could pass that warmth to the rest of my frostbitten body. But she produced a blanket from somewhere—a coarse woolen thing—and flung it over me. I snuggled into the folds gratefully.

"Stop talking about the táltos," the samodiva queen said. "We need to get free of this cave before our quarry escapes."

Vasilisa addressed the satyr who was standing near the mouth of the chamber with his arms crossed. "Silenus, see what you can shift of the rocks. If brute strength will not move them, we shall have to use other means."

Vasilisa frowned, and though she did not look at me, I suspected she was thinking of the spell that bound me. A sophisticated spell like that would take a great deal of power to maintain, meaning she might not have energy to both maintain my spell and cast another one. *St. Cajetan, let it be so.*

While the satyr worked, I slept some. (Noémi always complained about my ability to sleep nearly anywhere, but I suspect she was only jealous.) I woke to an argument. Pretending to sleep still, I listened.

"Are you not finished yet? The night is half gone—the girl will have escaped before we're free."

The satyr growled. "There is only one of me. If you want the rocks moved faster, help me."

"I cannot spell the rocks to move without releasing the spell on the táltos."

I knew it.

"The táltos is asleep. He won't escape."

"But asleep for how long? And a táltos can be nearly as dangerous sleeping as waking—it's just as well this one doesn't seem to know his own gifts." Vasilisa sniffed. "I can promise you, we will make better use of his power than he does."

Did I have other powers beyond the shifting and animal persuasion, beyond the strange dream-walking that I had just begun? Not for the first time, I wished I had let the Lady teach me. Instead, I had refused her, and she had died at Vasilisa's hand. Too late now for recriminations.

"Here, he's twitching," the satyr said. "He's waking up. I'll take care of him."

"No, wait—" Vasilisa began.

Footsteps sounded nearby, then a shadow fell across me, and pain exploded in my head. Darkness dropped like a curtain.

)(

Light filtered red across my closed eyes. The whole world seemed to be bobbing up and down in time with the pulsing in my temples.

I blinked, squinting teary-eyed at the too-bright sun. Was I drunk? Why could I not remember—

Memory returned with the subtlety of a sledgehammer. I was *not* drunk, merely recovering from a head injury. But the light . . . I blinked again, trying to clear my vision. Wind whipped past my cheeks.

I was out of the cave. Clothed—by whom? And moving. What the devil?

Not simply moving—*flying*. Blue-and-green-hued mountains, their tips already kissed with snow, scrolled beneath me. Two feminine arms curled around my torso, and bits of bone-white hair tangled in my vision. *Vasilisa*.

I tore my gaze away from the mountains below and looked around. Zhivka and the samodiva queen had sprouted misty, filigreed things from their backs that must be wings, and Bahadır hung suspended between them in a kind of woven mesh. His eyes were closed, and I could not tell from this distance if he was sleeping, unconscious, praying, or merely sick from the airborne motion.

How had I never known that the samodiva could fly? Then again, in light of what Zhivka had concealed from me, flying seemed a mere trifle. As if she felt my eyes on her, Zhivka glanced over. I turned my gaze sharply forward, but not before registering the hurt in her face. *Good.*

We landed a short time later to eat, relieve ourselves, and allow the women some time to rest. Based on the mountainous country and the changing position of the sun, I deduced we were likely still in Austria and flying eastward.

Bahadır slumped on the ground, his face buried in his arms. I crawled toward him, my head still aching from the blow the satyr had given me. Vasilisa perched on a boulder nearby, watching us closely, her fingers working through snarls in her hair. I did not doubt that if I tried to run, her spell would trip me up.

"Bahadır? Are you all right?" I set one hand on his shoulder.

He flinched, then blinked up at me, releasing a long breath. "Mátyás. You're awake. *Allah'a şükür.*" He ran his hands over his face. "I am all right. Flying does not agree with me, but I am not hurt."

I sat beside him, wrapping my arms around my knees. "How did you get here? And where are the others?"

"I don't know. Anna and the lidérc sought aid from the castle on the mountain. I stayed behind with the horses in case you got free and came looking for us. While they were gone, the praetheria surprised me. They left the satyr behind to wait for Anna."

Damnation. I'd hoped Anna would have more sense than to try to save me.

"But why bring you with them? Why not simply knock you out, or . . ." I trailed off. *Or kill you.*

"He is your insurance," Vasilisa said, though I had not asked her. "Like most of your kind, you are rotten with sentimentality. You let Anna kill you to break the Binding; you let yourself be captured so she could escape us just now. You will not let a friend die for you. So long as you do what we ask, your friend lives."

"I won't be used as hostage," Bahadır said, his eyes stricken.

Vasilisa merely shrugged, indifferent.

"Don't worry," I said, low-voiced. "We won't stay captive long enough for it to matter."

Another thought occurred to me. "Where are the horses?"

"Back by the mountain, if they have not already run off."

Bahadır's horse had been one of many belonging to the *betyárok*, but Holdas—my white horse had been with me for many years. I would miss the brute.

For a full day, I watched the praetheria's travel patterns, trying to gather enough information to plot our escape: our direction, periods of travel and rest, how closely we were guarded. We were clearly traveling eastward— as the day waned, the sun began to sink at our backs, sending light across the shrinking mountains. I thought I caught a glimpse of a faraway city as we descended to a meadow near some trees. Vienna? Hard to tell from this distance.

The women flew for an hour or so before stopping to rest, and they did not fly at night, when darkness made it difficult to see the landmarks that guided their flight. Though they were powerful, they were not invincible.

Our biggest challenge was opportunity: in addition to Vasilisa's spell keeping me tethered, the three women kept us closely guarded. At each stop, one of them remained nearby, keeping watch over us and preventing any open conversation about escape.

When it was Zhivka's turn, I met her tentative smile with a haughty look over her shoulder, as though I could not see her. It was unpardonably rude for a gentleman to cut a lady like that—but then, I had never been a particularly good gentleman, and she deserved it.

It fell to Bahadır to talk to her, to comment on the mild weather and the flight. It was Bahadır who made her smile, then laugh, and when he asked if she knew what our destination was, she did not stiffen as she might have if I had asked.

"I wish I could tell you, but I can't. I can assure you that you will not be hurt; I would not have agreed to this else." From the corner of my eye, I could see her watching me, and I caught the way she leaned toward me, her voice fierce and intent. "When we stopped in Vienna, my queen asked me to bring you to her. Please understand I never meant any harm."

I understood that she had sold us out, that any friendship between us meant less to her than her loyalty to her mistress. But then I remembered the way Zhivka had brought me back to myself with a touch when my dragon shape overwhelmed me, the way she looked at me as though she saw *Mátyás,* and not simply *táltos.* She had flirted with me and mocked me and championed me, and in another world, one where we were not at war, and I had not seen her sisters kill grown men with their seductive glamour, I would have flirted back. I would have kissed her and brought her flowers, orange as her flaming hair.

But in this world, all I could feel was the bitter ache of loss—of our friendship, of anything else we might have been to each other.

"'Understand'?" I said, meeting her eyes for the first time since she'd betrayed us. "Yes, I understand. But that does not mean I shall forget—or forgive." I stood and walked away, as far as my invisible tether would stretch. (Which was only a matter of five paces, but it was the symbolism of the act that counted.)

Zhivka did not try to talk to me again after that.

The first night, Vasilisa put something in the tea they gave us at supper. I fell asleep watching Zhivka and her queen dancing around the small fire they'd kindled.

The next day brought us into Hungary: I knew at once that the glinting lake we skirted was Lake Fertő—I had flown across these fields and hamlets near daily when I had lived with János at Eszterháza. Vasilisa must have been certain of the spell trapping me, since she made no attempt to hide our direction.

When we stopped for lunch, I asked Bahadır, "What are the odds that Noémi is being held in the same place they are taking us?"

He swallowed a bite of bread and said, "If I were a betting man, I would say your odds are probably not good. Why should they make things so easy for you?"

"But someone there might know something." I leaned close, lowering my voice so the samodiva queen, our current guard, could not easily overhear. "Perhaps we should not try to escape until we've seen the praetherian camp."

"It will undoubtedly be harder to escape once we've reached the camp, or the praetheria would not be so eager to reach it."

A bee buzzed nearby, brushing across the grasses in search of some late-blooming flower. I ripped a chunk of bread with my teeth, chewed grimly for a moment, and then said, "You're insufferable when you're right—you know that?"

Bahadır grinned at me, the scar on his cheek pulling tight. "But I am nearly always right."

"Precisely."

We flew into headwinds over some green farmland. The first gale nearly knocked us from the sky. Vasilisa dropped several feet at once, and I clamped my lips on a shout. In crow form, I'd be delighted by such winds, riding the currents with easy joy. But not like this, at the mercy of someone else's dubious powers of flight.

A second powerful wind slammed into us, and Vasilisa's grip loosened. I slipped only a foot or so before she secured her grip, but that instant was enough to convince me.

I would not let someone else determine my fate. We would escape, and then see about finding Noémi. We could track the praetheria, if we had to—but I'd be damned before I let myself be carried through the air longer than absolutely necessary.

As we flew, I considered and abandoned various options for escape. I could not shift my way out of the spell: even if

I could shift myself to the smallest of molecules—smaller even than the threads of the spell—there was no guarantee I could find my way back to myself. The two of us were not physically strong enough to overpower the women, particularly when I was hampered by Vasilisa's invisible net. And Vasilisa would not release the net—except if she were to use her magic against a greater threat.

I needed a diversion.

When I first became a bandit, I fought a powerful *guta* by calling a cloud of birds that drew the creature away and put out its eyes. And yet many of the birds had sacrificed themselves to my persuasion, and each death had pricked me.

Would I ask for that kind of sacrifice again, if needed? Simply because I *could* do something did not mean I *should*.

I was still puzzling over such thoughts when I fell asleep that night, and when I woke again, in the grey light that presaged dawn, an idea had crystallized in my head. I glanced around. The others still slept—all but Zhivka, who watched me with clouded eyes. When she saw me looking at her, she turned away.

Birds were just beginning to stir, a few high sweet calls in the darkness. I cast my inner sense out: a slight brush sent them soaring upward and away. I wanted the other praetheria to sleep as long as possible.

Sweat was beginning to bead on my forehead before I found what I was looking for: not because of warmth, as the day was cool, but because searching had taken longer than I anticipated.

I nudged Bahadır with my foot. When he did not stir,

I nudged again, harder. His eyes flew open, and I set a finger to my lips, glancing quickly at Zhivka to ensure she was still looking away. She was.

Be ready, I mouthed, and Bahadır sat up.

With my táltos sense, I could feel the mass of creatures growing, responding to my call. It was a question only— a request, not a compulsion. Still, there were many that answered, swarming toward us in a mass.

The sound reached us first: a low humming. Within moments, it had escalated to a roar, a steady buzz that reverberated in my head, and then we were surrounded by a cloud of flying insects: wasps, bees, biting flies.

Zhivka heard them at last, too late. She sprang to her feet and shouted, but her words were swallowed in noise, as the insects descended on the praetheria.

With a shriek, the two sleeping praetheria woke and leapt up, swatting at the insects crawling over them.

The samodiva queen ignited, fire flaring around her. I flinched, feeling the hundreds of tiny sparks extinguished in her heat. Insects still buzzed around her, waiting for the fire to subside. Behind her, Zhivka tumbled to the ground, writhing under the biting onslaught. She did not ignite, as the samodiva queen had, but screamed once, a cry so full of anguish that I nearly sent the insects away. But Vasilisa had not released her spell yet, and so I steeled my heart, and we waited.

It was hard to see what Vasilisa was doing through the buzzing black cloud, but I could hear her swearing, a choice mixture of German and Russian. I tensed, preparing to shift. She would need a spell to drive the insects away—and as soon as she dropped the spell holding me, I meant to be ready.

A thunderclap shook the clearing, and Bahadır and I rocketed backward. Pain shocked through my body, sending white and black streaks across my vision. I clutched my head, and the buzzing stopped, thousands of tiny lives wiped out in an instant. And not just the insects: a few unwary birds passing overhead tumbled from the sky; a handful of squirrels caught in the radius of a spell dropped from their nests. The ground around us turned black, carpeted with insect shells.

Vasilisa's spell net still held.

No.

She stalked toward us, her eyes blazing. The right side of her face was angry and red from a handful of bites and stings.

"Did you think you could escape so easily? That a little pain would distract me from the spell holding you? I am not so weak." She surveyed us contemptuously, lips twisting. "I think you do not respect me enough."

She flicked her fingers at us. Beside me, Bahadır groaned and wrapped his arms around his torso. A moment later, I was writhing beside him, fire burning along my skin, as dozens of tiny bites and stings—an echo of those I'd inflicted on Vasilisa—stitched themselves in our own flesh.

When I could breathe again, the samodiva queen stood beside Vasilisa. If Vasilisa had been angry, the queen was incandescent with rage, fire shimmering along her skin and hair. Her eyes were terrible: the dark iris swallowing up the white.

"They do not suffer enough," she said, lifting her hand. Vasilisa put forth her own hand. "It is enough—for now."

"My sister is dead," the queen snarled. "They must answer for that."

Zhivka? I pushed myself to my feet, though my arms still burned and my head still rattled with the animals' death throes. At the far side of the clearing, Zhivka lay still. A breath of wind lifted a fiery lock from her cheek.

Her face was swollen grotesquely, pink and almost unrecognizable.

"But they were only bites," I said. "Stings. Painful but not deadly. She can't be dead." My arm and the side of my face throbbed. I stumbled toward Zhivka, trying to ignore the crunching beneath my feet, and dropped to my knees beside her. Memories flooded through me: of her leading us to a trap in the ice caves, yes, but so much more. Of sitting beside her on the *puszta* and watching the sun set. Of her banter with the other *betyárok*. Her fearlessness and laughter as we rode to challenge some new carriage.

All that brightness, gone. Snuffed out.

My fault.

Bahadır's voice was soft behind me. "Bee stings take some people so. I've seen it before."

"But she was samodiva—" Shock sent my thoughts spinning helplessly. My stomach knotted. Zhivka could not be dead.

"All samodiva bear human blood," the samodiva queen said, her voice ragged. "Our daughters are sired by human fathers."

I wiped my hand across my face. My cheeks were wet, though I did not remember the tears starting.

"I say we kill them now. Life for life," the queen said.

"We need the táltos," Vasilisa said.

"Then let me kill the other."

I turned from Zhivka's body to face them. The samodiva queen was rigid in her anger, fire still curling about her in an unearthly halo. Vasilisa's pale eyes were shadowed. "It was not Bahadır's fault. It was mine."

"Life for life, death for death," the queen insisted.

"Then take my life," I said, holding my hands toward her. Exhaustion washed over me. I was so tired—tired of trying to do the right thing and hurting people instead. Tired of carrying the weight of being táltos everywhere like invisible shackles. Tired of expectations I could not meet.

My life was only borrowed anyway. The Lady should never have brought me back.

There was a long, tense moment as the samodiva queen glowered at us both, her hands lifted as though ready to strike. I braced myself. Fire was not high on my list of ways to die.

Here lies Eszterházy Mátyás: Like the damned, he burned.

"We don't have time for this," Vasilisa said. "Your sister's death will be answered, but not now, not in this fashion. Do what you must for her funeral rites, but then we should be on our way."

The samodiva queen disappeared, carrying Zhivka's body into the trees beyond us. I did not hear what rites she spoke, but we all saw the pillar of smoke rising into the sky, marking the spot where Zhivka's body burned.

I am not sure what Vasilisa read in the samodiva queen's face when she returned, but Vasilisa refused to let her carry

Bahadır or me. Instead, Vasilisa wrapped one arm around each of us and had the samodiva queen tie a length of rope around us to secure us to her.

"Are you certain you can carry us both?" I asked, envisioning the three of us crashing to our deaths. If she meant to kill us, there were less costly ways to do so.

She cast me a disgusted look. "I have carried more."

We launched upward, the samodiva queen trailing behind us. Vasilisa did not fly as fast with two extra weights, and I told her as much. As a reward for my pains, she pinched my arm, hard enough to bruise.

I occupied myself with tracing the roads below us and trying to guess where we were. Heading east, that was certain. This was not a part of the country I had frequented, and I was not sure I could name the cities that spun out below us. Kápolna? Eger?

Vasilisa must have found our added weights more tiring than she admitted, because sooner than I had expected, she began lowering toward a stretch of flat land.

I squinted. Something was hurtling toward us—a quick reach with my inner sense confirmed it was not living. But what—?

Before I could do more than begin to frame the question, a heavy net fell over us. At once we dropped, and my stomach launched upward. Vasilisa cursed furiously as we fell. There was iron woven through the rope's core.

The ground raced toward us, the trees and grasses below us growing larger and taking on clarity with alarming rapidity.

This was going to hurt like the devil.

CHAPTER 7

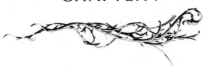

Anna

Vienna unsettled me in the way I imagined an ex-lover might: a place once familiar but where I was no longer welcome. A city with secrets I no longer had a right to know.

I tensed as we neared the southwest city gate, worried that someone might recognize the lidérc as praetherian, or see in me the fugitive Miss Anna Arden. But the guards saw Emilija's Red Mantle uniform and waved us through with scarcely a glance at me or the lidérc. As it was late afternoon, Emilija took us to the flat she shared with her father near the center of the city instead of proceeding directly to the Hofburg.

Though not large, the apartment was well furnished and clean. Emilija showed us to rooms where we could wash away the worst of the travel grime, and then a uniformed maid with frizzled grey hair served us tea in a small parlor.

Before I had even taken my first sip, Emilija began to fidget, twisting her fingers together and chewing on her lower lip. This was wholly unlike her—she tended to go quiet and watchful when anxious, not restless.

I set my teacup on the saucer. "Are you well?"

"No. That is, yes. Only . . . I miss my dog."

"Of course. I can take you as soon as I've finished my tea."

We left the lidérc behind, as she claimed she would rather sleep than go one step farther. Dusk settled over the city as we walked, casting a golden light over the old buildings and cobblestones. Vienna had overawed me once with her opulence and her relentlessly fashionable elite. Now, the city felt merely indifferent. The city had not changed; I had. The girl who had been impressed by wealth and fine manners was gone.

We were still a few blocks from Borbála's apartment when I caught a glimpse of a familiar woman in a black dress, her copper hair braided neatly about her head. Ginny had been my maid—and, in truth, my closest confidante—until she had betrayed me at the archduchess's ball earlier that summer, appearing with other newly trained magicians to capture the praetheria. I pulled back into an alcove before she could see me.

Emilija halted and looked at me as though I had suddenly taken leave of my senses.

Ginny crossed the street toward us. "Miss Anna? Is that you?"

I had not hidden myself quickly enough, it seemed.

Emilija stepped in front of Ginny, barring her access to me. "Who are you?"

"I used to be Miss Arden's maid. You needn't fear me: I'm no snitch."

I slipped out around Emilija. "But you are a traitor."

Ginny flinched. It should not have pleased me to know I could still wound her, but it did. "I did not betray you. Every spell I cast in that ballroom, I did at the request of Her Majesty's government." Her eyes flickered over me, taking in the ill-fitting boys' clothes I wore. The crease in her brow deepened, but she said nothing of my sartorial failures.

"You thought it right that the praetheria should be forced from their homes? That I should be sentenced without trial?"

Ginny pinched her lips together and crossed her arms. "I did not know what they intended. We were told only to exercise our magic on behalf of Queen Victoria. I never meant for you to be hurt—I was glad when you escaped."

The conversation grated on me. I both wanted Ginny to apologize and wanted to throw the apology in her face, so I could hold on to the betrayal I'd felt when she showed up at the ball, allied with the same magicians and soldiers who trapped me. Yet deep down I knew I was being unfair: I was blaming Ginny for becoming a magician instead of a lady's maid—a role *I* had encouraged her to take, a role that opened up many more opportunities than I could have given her.

Ginny continued, "I'm sorry about your friend, though."

The shift away from the ball confused me. Who was she talking about?

"Mr. Skala?" Ginny said.

"William? What happened to him?" My stomach tightened.

"He died in the hospital, after the ball."

It came back in a rush: William, running to tear me away from the soldiers, the spread of blood across his white shirt where a soldier's sword slid through him. He'd fallen, and the soldiers had dragged me away, and then Hunger had pulled me out a broken window and into the night. I hadn't seen William again, hadn't found anyone who knew if he lived or died.

Dead.

William, who was the first rebel I had ever known, and one of the truest. How terrible that his lofty ambitions had come down to this: a moment's decision to try and save me, fueled by personal rather than national interest. A promising story cut off midparagraph, midsentence. I blinked back tears, aware of Emilija shifting beside me.

"Thank you for telling me," I said. "But we must be going."

Ginny didn't move. "There's good news too. You have a nephew: Christopher. A bright, bonny child."

I grasped her arm. "You've seen him? And Catherine? Are they well?"

"They're well. I was just visiting with—"

I interrupted her. "They're in the city? I thought she was returning to England."

"Travel did not agree with her or the baby. She had to turn back. But both are well now."

I shook my head, dazed. *Christopher*. It was a good name. In another world, I might have given him a nickname and carried him on my shoulders and taught him to fish, just as I had taught James. Perhaps I still could, if I succeeded in persuading the archduchess to pardon me. But Catherine was in the city. Whatever violence was about to engulf us would wash over her as well. And the baby.

I did not want this war to become my war; I wanted to stay clear of it. But for Catherine, for my infant nephew, I should have to pray that the archduchess could stop the war before it was too late.

We said goodbye to Ginny and moved on.

Borbála Dobos lived in an unremarkable flat just within the walls of the city. When I rapped at the wooden door, it was opened by a pretty, neatly dressed woman in her thirties, her dark hair just threaded with grey at the temples. She ushered us into the flat, casting curious looks at Emilija.

"Hallo, Marina," I said. "This is Emilija Dragović, here to recover her dog."

A cloud passed across Marina's pretty face—only a hint of shadow and then it was gone. "Of course. Borbála is taking her supper in the dining room. Will you join her? It's rare enough I can get her to sit down to eat two bites together. She's always chasing a story."

The dining room turned out to be no more than an airy nook with a small table crammed into the space, a bright bouquet of chrysanthemums at its center. Borbála sprang up as we approached, pulling a napkin from her trousered lap, but a blur of white and black fur reached us before she did.

The dog jumped up, putting his forelegs on Emilija's

shoulders and barking jubilantly. Emilija laughed and let the dog lick her face before kneeling to tuck her arms around its neck. "I have missed you, Sretno."

Marina turned away, and Borbála altered her course, patting me gently on the shoulder as she passed. She drew Marina to her in a hug. "It's all right. We'll find another dog, if you want one."

Emilija looked up, taking in the two women with a slight frown. "It's true that Sretno is very lovable. I am sorry if caring for him has brought you pain—I am very grateful that he has been so well tended."

Marina smiled, though her eyes shone suspiciously. "He is your dog—he should be with you."

Emilija stood, her frown deepening. Sretno sniffed at her fingers, then padded across the room to do the same to Marina, who rubbed his ears. "My father has gone to war, and after I take Anna to see the archduchess—"

"You're taking Anna to the archduchess?" Borbála echoed, cutting her off. "Why? The woman will slaughter her! Best leave her here with us." She stepped forward, arms crossed, as though she might intimidate Emilija.

"I mean to try and break the spell on the archduke," I said, feeling absurdly touched by Borbála's defense.

Borbála narrowed her eyes at me. "You think she will pardon you? I'd not be so trusting."

"She loves her son." The archduchess might hate me with the passion reserved for demon-spawn, but she would not harm me if there was a chance I could save her son.

Emilija cleared her throat, and we turned back to her. "As I said, my father is at war, and I will likely join him when my business here is done. Sretno is an excellent hunter, but he is not a warrior, and I would not wish to see him hurt. There is no one at our flat to care for him but an old maid. Perhaps . . . ?" Her voice trailed off delicately.

"Of course he can stay here," Marina said, her face already brightening. "For as long as you'd like."

Borbála pressed her lips together in mock displeasure. "And have I no say in this? This is my house, after all."

"You always have a choice," Marina said, stooping to plant a kiss on Sretno's head. Emilija joined her, dropping to her knees and murmuring to the Dalmatian.

Borbála's eyes softened. "Yes," she said. "I know. And that choice will always be you."

I watched the two women, secure in their friendship and love, and wished I had anything approaching their certainty. If I were to choose one person, one place, one thing over and over again, what would I choose? Gábor? My family? Hungary? Would I even get to choose, with war sweeping over everything? Or was my choice already cast—some seemingly insignificant decision that would shape everything else? William had chosen to help me, and he had lost everything—every other choice had been subsumed in that one moment. What would my choice to help the archduke cost me?

)(

A deep green silk dress with copper leaves embroidered along the hem and sleeves spilled over Emilija's arms.

I'd spent the night in a real bed and felt nearly ready for anything. But— "I can't wear that."

The girl who had worn such dresses and had taken tea

with the archduchess no longer existed. And I did not want to be beholden to Emilija.

"A good soldier goes into battle armed and prepared; think of this dress as your armor. The archduchess will not like you better for wearing humble clothes—or boys' clothes."

I sighed. She was right. "Thank you."

Emilija left the room while I washed. It was a relief to unwind the strips of fabric binding my chest, but strange also, as if I'd forgotten the feel and shape of my own body. I did not have to exchange my drawers or the chemise I'd worn under my binding, but I had to call Emilija to help me cinch the corset tight and fasten the gown. The multiple petticoats that belled out the dress hung heavy from my waist. This I had not forgotten: the way a dress made me feel both feminine and weighted down, my breath constricted and my steps precise. I had not realized, until I wore men's garments, how differently we inhabited the world in our clothes.

Emilija and I stared into the small mirror atop her dressing table. My short hair curled unevenly, and my attempts to brush through it with my fingers only made it stand up higher.

"I'm a tolerable hand with a braid," she said, "but your hair is too short for that."

I dipped my fingers into the water in the basin and ran them through my hair again. The wetness made the curl lie down a little. I sighed. "I don't suppose you have a bonnet?" I had never seen Emilija wear a hat—only her hooded mantle.

"Somewhere." She frowned and dug through her wardrobe, eventually producing a faded brown bonnet with a pink ruffle. She looked dubiously from it to my green dress. "It does not exactly match."

"It will have to do," I said, taking it from her and tying the ribbons beneath my chin. I could scarcely march bareheaded into the archduchess's salon. And it *was* an improvement over my curls. "Do you need to bind my hands?"

"Do you plan to run?" She smiled, a delicate curling of her lips. "I do not think a rope is the right ornament for that dress."

We walked the short distance to the palace. Most people paid us little heed, only eyeing Emilija's red mantle warily. Emilija led me past the guards at the palace gate, up a flight of stairs, and through several hallways with an ease born of long familiarity. When she reached a liveried footman standing in one of the hallways, she asked if the archduchess was receiving.

"She has gone out for the morning, I'm afraid. Is the matter urgent?"

"Fairly urgent," Emilija replied. "I've someone here who might help the archduke."

The footman's eyes flicked to me with interest, quickly wiped away as he recalled his place. He escorted us to a small salon and bade us wait.

It was perhaps half an hour before we heard voices and light footsteps in the hall. The door opened and Archduchess Sophie stepped in, immaculate in a pale blue gown, carrying a familiar scent of lemon and bergamot with her. As I studied her, I revised my first impression. Her dress was as neat as ever, but there were furrows around her eyes that suggested a deep strain. My heart lifted. If the archduchess was indeed desperate, she might listen to us.

"My dear Miss Dragović," the archduchess began, hands outstretched to Emilija. Beside me, Emilija dropped a curtsy, and I echoed her. Then Archduchess Sophie stopped, her fingers curling into fists. "Miss Arden."

She was already turning to the footman—with an order for more guards, no doubt—when Emilija said, "Please, Your Royal Highness, hear her out. Arrest her once she's spoken, if you must, but please listen."

Arrest her? Perhaps Emilija and I should have discussed our plans in more detail. That was not how I intended this discussion to end.

The archduchess turned back and nodded once, stiffly. "Very well. Speak."

I explained that I had heard of Franz Joseph's mysterious illness and thought I might try to break the spell.

"I suppose you are here for the reward," she said when I had finished. "Your *ungeschickt* appearance suggests as much. I hope you are not here for my son—he would never marry you now that you have broken our laws."

I flushed and ignored Emilija's curious look. "I don't want your money—or to marry your son. I should like a pardon, and your word that Austria will pull back from war. I want you to command Croatia to do the same."

"You do not ask for much," she said, her voice excessively dry. "Pray, tell me why I should give you these things."

My heartbeat stuttered. If I overreached, I might lose everything. "You charged me with killing my cousin, but my cousin is alive. I have witnesses who will swear to it."

"Do you?" She was beginning to sound bored.

"I've seen him, Your Royal Highness," Emilija said. "He saved my life."

I shot a glance at Emilija. Her chin was high, her voice even, betraying no fear. But it occurred to me then that she was risking much on her faith in me.

"There is, besides, the matter of the praetheria." Briefly, Emilija related what we had told her. "My father is one of your most loyal subjects, and I am loyal to him. I would not lightly speak against his wishes or his plans unless I believed it to be in the best interest of the empire. This is a war we cannot win. We must stop before we are too weak to protect ourselves."

The archduchess tapped her lips for a moment. "I will make no promises until my son is healed. If you succeed— and I am not at all certain you shall—then I shall see you pardoned, and I will do my best to see this war ended quickly."

"Thank you, Your Royal Highness," I said, relief making my knees weak. "That is all I ask."

"But if you do not"—she lifted her finger—"then my soldiers will take you to prison to await your execution."

"Not trial?" My voice sounded thin in my ears, like someone else's.

"Your cousin's death was not the only crime you were accused of. These are my terms. I suggest you take them. If you do not, I will have my soldiers take you away immediately."

I took a deep breath. "All right."

"Miss Dragović, you may go."

Dismissed, Emilija set a reassuring hand on my forearm, then dipped a curtsy and retreated.

"Follow me." The archduchess led me through a series of rooms to what appeared to be a private suite: instead of the expected portraits and fine sculptures, the walls were covered with quick sketches of landscapes, laughing faces of young men and women. The bookshelves along the walls contained books that appeared to be well read and not merely for show; there was a top hat set carelessly on a corner desk and a sheaf of papers scattered along a table.

Before a closed door, the archduchess stopped and turned. "The archduke is very weak. Please do not try to speak with him. And if he appears to be in any distress, I will ask you to stop at once."

"Yes, Highness." I gripped my hands together, my fingers cold despite the stuffy warmth of the apartments in the early-afternoon sun.

I followed Archduchess Sophie into the room, and only just refrained from gasping. The young man on the bed bore scant resemblance to the archduke I had danced with only a few months before. The rosy-cheeked boy with the laughing blue eyes was wan and pale, his cheeks sunken. His eyes were shut, and I could see the tracing of thin purple veins along the lids. Someone had shaved him, so his cheeks and lip were smooth.

As I approached the bed, his eyes flickered open. "Anna?" His voice was thready, an echo of its former robustness. "I thought you were lost."

At once it struck me how vulnerable I was here—it was easy to be lulled into complacency by the pretty exterior and polished manners of this place, but the archduchess could order my death at any moment and I could not stop her.

Perhaps I was still lost.

"Hush, Franzi," Archduchess Sophie said, moving to smooth the hair away from his forehead. "Miss Arden is come to make you better."

The weak smile he directed at me twisted my heart, because the smile still held affection—still, when I was not at all the woman he had thought me. Still, when I might have been the bearer of the curse that held him bedridden.

"I mean to try, in any case," I said, because I would not lie to him.

The archduchess nodded at me, and I drew nearer, putting my hand over the thin one that lay listless on the bed-covering. Franz Joseph's fingers twitched beneath mine.

I took a deep breath, then closed my eyes. I had broken the samodiva's spells in the cave, but that had been mostly instinctive, and the breakings had been rough. This called for more delicate work.

Finding the skeins of magic wrapped around the arch-duke was not difficult, but the strands did not seem to follow any sort of regular pattern. They wove about one another, knotting, then doubling back. The core of the spell seemed nestled in his heart.

I was not sure where I should begin, which strand would unravel the others. With my inner chimera sense, I plucked at one of the strands of magic branching from Franz Jo-seph's heart. The thread, thick and resilient, did not snap, but the archduke gasped, and his fingers tightened around mine.

I opened my eyes to find him staring at me, pain etched

into the lines of his face. Archduchess Sophie glared a warning at me.

"I'm sorry," I murmured, releasing the archduke's hand. I closed my eyes again and reached for the spell, but new unease made me tentative and slow. My fingers trembled, and I curled them into fists.

I hope you break his heart, Vasilisa had said. What would happen when I unraveled the spell from his heart?

I started instead at the outward fringes of the spell, searching for threads that were looser than others. The weave was not brittle, as so many human-cast spells were. I could not simply snap them. Nor, as I had just discovered, could I pull them loose from the source.

After some trial and experimentation, I found that I could unravel the threads from one another, but this was slow, painstaking work—much like trying to detangle a ball of yarn after a kitten has been through it. I was not sure I was accomplishing anything, but the archduke seemed to breathe easier as I worked.

The afternoon passed into night. A servant came in to light the tapers, and the archduchess asked that two meals be brought to the room.

She instructed me to pause and eat when the food arrived, a simple meal of sliced meat and fruit. The archduchess herself fed Franz Joseph some broth, dabbing at his face with a fine handkerchief when the liquid spilled onto his chin. She did not eat until he had been fed, until I was once more working on the spell.

My head had begun aching earlier; by the time I resumed the spell-breaking after supper, pain throbbed along my temples.

But I could not—would not—stop. Not simply because my pardon hung in the balance, or because the archduchess might be able to halt the impending war. But because as I worked, I could see the lines of pain in Franz Joseph's forehead ease. He had been my friend once, and if I could bring him some comfort, I would.

The spell hung loosely about him now, a collection of threads tied to his heart but no longer woven so densely. If I could uproot them, the spell would fall apart.

I reached for one of the heart strands again, took a deep breath, and tugged gently, as though I were a gardener easing a plant from the soil with the roots intact.

Franz Joseph cried out, a hoarse, broken noise.

I released the strand.

What unholy spell was this? I did not know if I could pull the spell-roots free from his heart without killing him.

I opened my eyes again. Franz Joseph was sleeping, albeit restlessly. The archduchess's eyes were fixed on me, unblinking. Beside her, the light from a brace of candles wavered in the dim room. Beyond, I could see only the reflection of the room in the window—nothing of the stars or the city lights.

"Is something wrong?" Archduchess Sophie asked. She did not seem angry, only concerned.

"The spell is trickier than I had supposed. It is rooted somehow in his heart, and I must figure out how to disentangle it without harming him."

"You will do it," she said. "His life—and yours—depends upon it."

I nodded, nowhere near as sanguine, and took a sip of water from my glass on the bedside table. My doubled soul felt along the lines of the spell again, but this time, instead of trying to force the threads, I simply observed them. I let myself sink into their lines and rhythms. *Please,* I prayed, *let me find something.*

I was no expert, but it seemed that the spell, however it had been powered initially, was fueled by the archduke's heart, his own life force subsumed into the spell that was slowly killing him. As a child, I had watched our gardener attack a mistletoe infestation in some of the trees on our property; I had been shocked to find that a plant I had always associated with Christmas festivities could kill a grown tree if it grew large enough. The gardener had removed the mistletoe by cutting off the entire branch of the tree where the parasite was attached. Even if the spell had a physical presence, I could not cut out Franz Joseph's heart to heal him.

There had to be another way.

If I had Noémi's gifts, I might stop his heart, wrench the spell free, and then start it again—though even Noémi might find that magic too risky.

Wait.

If the spell was fueled by the archduke's heart, there must be *two* parts to it: the first, which attached to his heart, much as the mistletoe grew to employ the tree's own root system for nourishment; and the second, the body of the spell itself, which I could see wrapped around him.

I had been so focused on undoing the body of the spell that I had not seen the possibility of another spell. Once I knew what to look for, I was able to find the first spell: tiny, almost invisible filaments branching off the main fibers to nestle in his heart. I pinched one, and it disintegrated beneath my touch. I pinched another, then another, my spirits lifting a fraction with each one. There were hundreds of the tiny filaments, and I might be at this all night, but I could do this.

"Miss Arden!"

I blinked. The archduchess was standing by the bed, leaning close to Franz Joseph.

"Whatever you're doing is hurting him. He keeps flinching."

I pinched another of the filaments, my eyes open this time and fixed on Franz Joseph. His head jerked.

"I'm sorry," I said. "The only way to get the spell out of his heart is to detach it, tiny root by root. I do not mean to hurt him; that's the spell. But the spell will kill him if I don't detach it—surely a little pain is worth sparing him a greater one."

"Very well." She reseated herself, and I closed my eyes again. Franz Joseph's pain was not the only cost of this spell—each pinch of the filament added another grain to the weight pressing down on my temples.

I lost track of time for a while—the minute pinching of threads occupied my whole focus. When the last of the threads was severed, I opened my eyes to find it was morning: the candle had guttered out, the room was filled with a grey light, and the archduchess was asleep, leaning forward in her chair so her arms rested on the cover of the bed, her cheek pillowed on her crossed arms.

One last mission.

Though I could hardly see for the pain buzzing through

my head, I focused on the strands of spell still surrounding the archduke. I'd destroyed the spell that rooted the curse in his heart; the only task remaining was to remove the curse itself. It hung loose around him, a knotted tangle. But the pinching of filaments had shown me where the thread started. One last time, I reached and yanked at the thread of spell. It unraveled around me in a dizzying spin of color: the released energy from the spell set the pages of a book fluttering beside the archduke's bed.

CHAPTER 8

Anna

After the spell on Franz Joseph broke, everything seemed to happen at once. I shook the archduchess awake, saying only "It's done" before collapsing into a chair, pain tromping through my head as though it intended to take up permanent residence. The archduchess sprang up at once to check on Franz Joseph. A small, perfect circle imprinted her cheek, from the button at her cuff. Seeing that he was resting peacefully, she bustled me out of the room. She rang for a maid, who led me to a bedchamber, and I fell into bed as though I might sleep the hundred-year sleep of a fairy-tale princess.

When I woke again, it was already nightfall, with a soft, enfolding darkness spreading through the room. Someone had left a Lumen light suspended in the air beside the bed, and its blue glow cast a globe of warmth into the dark.

I sat up, then slid out of the bed. I slipped on a dressing

robe (I was wearing only a nightdress, though I did not remember putting it on) and padded barefoot to the door. It opened into a lit hallway, and an imperial guard turned as it opened.

The guard, a middle-aged man with a drooping mustache and paunch, nodded at me. "I'll send word you're awake."

A short time later, a maid brought a tray with a light repast—bread and jam and cheese—and a few minutes after that Archduke Franz Joseph walked into the room.

He came alone, his steps slow but sure. Already, his thin cheeks had regained some color.

He smiled at me and I blushed, tugging the dressing robe tighter around me. Our fraught past had not seemed to matter when he was ill and his mother sat with us, but now I could not help remembering the last time we talked, how we had danced at the ball and he had kissed me. Even if Vasilisa had compelled that kiss through a spell woven into the fairy glamour she dressed me in, the kiss had sealed our sham betrothal. It had promised a future between us.

But that ensorcelled future was gone, obliterated when I fled Vienna and Gábor returned.

What did he mean by coming to my bedroom at nightfall? He might have waited till morning—or given me fair warning. What did he imagine was still between us?

"I've come to thank you," he said, "for saving my life."

"You are welcome," I said formally, stepping back and trying to put distance between us with my words as well as actions. "I am only sorry my breaking the spell caused you pain."

"What is a little pain?" He grinned, moving further into the room. "I feel more myself than I have in months. But you—how are you?"

"I am well," I said, though prickles of discomfort still lingered around my forehead, and I was beginning to sweat at his proximity. "I should be going. Emilija, my hostess, will be worrying."

"I believe my mother sent word to her." He nodded at a small bag in a chair near the bed. "See? Emilija has already brought a few of your things. Please, stay the night. My mother wishes to thank you and offer a formal pardon before the court."

"I thank your mother for her kindness. The pardon I'll accept gladly, but I should rather not do so before the court."

Franz Joseph nodded gravely. "I understand." He reached his hand toward my cheek, as though he might touch me, and I danced out of reach. He sighed and let his hand drop. "I do not mean to offend you. My mother tells me it was the spell that made me imagine I wished to marry you. Perhaps so, but I owe you my life. If you still wish . . ."

He trailed off, and I swallowed a frantic bubble of laughter. He could not truly wish to marry me against his mother's wishes, and I had no wish to marry *him*. In fairy tales, the cowherd always wed the princess after saving her from the spell, but I did not mean to play the cowherd in this story.

"You are very kind," I said firmly, "but no, thank you." I pretended not to see how relief softened his face at my answer.

He stood there for a moment, awkwardly tugging at his collar. "Well, then, good night. Sweet dreams, and we shall see you in the morning."

When he had gone, I went at once to the chair with my bag. Gábor's papers were still within, and the tension knotted inside me eased. I pulled the first paper out, trailing my fingers across the familiar script. A new letter, a short one this time. It began, *"Muri dràgo Anna,"* and this one I guessed at: in Hungarian, *dràga* meant something dear or precious, so perhaps the languages shared this root. (Though it is just possible he was calling me his dragon. Upon reflection, I decided this also pleased me.)

Gábor wrote that Kossuth had recalled him and some of the other Romani soldiers and sent them to march with General Perczel against Austrian soldiers coming in from the west. They had engaged in a mild skirmish, but no one was injured. Gábor ended by relating a humorous account of a new soldier standing guard who had roused half the camp to face an enemy that turned out to be nothing more than a family of foxes. I smiled as I read, though I wished I could hear the story from Gábor and not the thin substitute of his written words.

I reread the letter, lingering over the postscript: "I miss you." Then I penned my own, describing the archduke's curse and my breaking of it: *I hope I have done the right thing. Perhaps now the archduke will hear me and help bring an end to this war before the praetheria can use our own pride against us. Perhaps I might yet redeem myself for all the havoc I caused after the Binding.*

I hesitated, pen poised to strike through that last line.

I had spoken to no one of the uncertainty that roiled inside me at the thought of all my past mistakes, of my secret fear that my chimera magic made me monstrous beyond all hope of redemption.

Would Gábor think less of me if he knew? I took a slow breath. He already knew I was chimera, that I had killed Mátyás once to break the Binding spell. If those had not turned him away, neither would this.

I let the line stand. *Tonight I shall sleep on clean sheets and a soft mattress—a divine luxury after weeks of hard ground or cheap, harder beds. Tomorrow I shall have tea in a porcelain cup with an archduchess before setting off again to find Noémi and Mátyás. But I would trade all the fine beds and all the fine company to be with you in person. This world wears on me like a fine dress after a long illness—it no longer fits properly and makes me grumpy.* I echoed his closing, "I miss you," wishing I were brave enough to write "I love you." But I was not yet ready to commit those words to paper and ink.

I tucked the papers back into the bag and curled up in bed, still tired for all that I had slept most of the day. For weeks I had rested uneasily, half expecting to be captured while I slept. But here—I did not think even Vasilisa would dare storm the palace for me, and the promise of a pardon meant I no longer needed to fear the Hapsburgs. I meant to enjoy this safety, even if I could not do so for long.

I woke to a maid pulling back the curtains and a second maid setting a cup of steaming tea and a plate of toast beside the bed. The second maid helped me dress in the green gown, which someone had cleaned and pressed during the night. I wished I knew who had done it so I could thank them. After caring for my own clothing these past weeks, I would never again be so cavalier about the work done by servants.

A knock sounded at the door just as I finished my tea.

"Come in," I called, standing and brushing a few crumbs of toast from my skirt.

The archduchess entered—followed by two men I had never thought to see again: Count Medem, who had been the tsar's ambassador to Vienna, and my uncle Pál.

I clutched unseeing at the table, knocking my teacup to the floor.

No.

No.

No.

The archduchess marched crisply across the room and handed me a sealed sheet of paper. I took it with numb fingers. "Here is your pardon," she said, "signed and official."

I found my voice at last. "What is going on?"

"You asked me to end the war. I am doing so. In exchange for *you,* the tsar has promised the aid of his army. Confronted by the combined power of Austria and Russia, I do not think Hungary will long resist." She brushed her hands together briskly. "The war will be over before Christmas."

I struggled against the dazed feeling of a nightmare, where I tried to run from a shadowy monster but could only move with glacial slowness. "You cannot give me to them," I said. "You promised me freedom."

"Did I? I promised you a pardon and my aid to end the war, and I have done both."

I wet my lips with my tongue. "That was not what I meant."

"Then you must learn to be more specific. Such a small thing to end the war—I rather thought you'd be delighted."

"Please don't do this." With effort, I refrained from dropping at her feet and groveling. I remembered the Russian delegation in Vienna that spring, which included Svarog, one of the Four who led the praetheria, glamoured as a beautiful blond count. The Russians did not act alone in this decision to aid Austria. I was certain of it. "If you send me with these men, they will only give me to the praetheria, and you will not have stopped a war: you will have given them a weapon."

"My dear child, you're being ridiculous. Your uncle cannot mean you harm, and your obsession with the praetheria is frankly unhealthy."

I looked across the room at Pál. He smiled at me, but there was nothing warm in his expression.

I tried again. "I am a British citizen. I have rights. Lord Ponsonby will not allow it."

Archduchess Sophie waved her hands. "In the eyes of the British government, you have officially vanished. Even your sister does not expect to hear from you again. Who shall ever know?"

Her face was calm, but I caught a glint of light in her eyes. She had failed to make me disappear before, when I had escaped her sentencing. But she would not fail now. This time, I would vanish truly.

"Franz Joseph . . . Emilija . . ."

"They will be told you have gone with your uncle. Nothing to warrant distress in that, is there?"

A great black wave seemed to hang over my head. No matter what I said, the archduchess would not hear me.

"Thank you for saving my son," she said, her voice cold and formal. "You have done this country a great service. This very morning, Emperor Ferdinand is stepping down as emperor, and my son, newly restored to health, is to be the emperor of all Austria. Hungary too, God willing, when the war is over."

While my reeling brain struggled to parse this new information, the Russian count said, "Gather your things, girl. We leave at once."

X

Were it not for the troop of Russian guardsmen surrounding Pál and me, I could almost pretend I was merely a young lady traveling through the country with her uncle. The first day brought us past the black-and-yellow-striped poles that marked the Austrian border. The guards gave us no trouble over our papers, particularly not when Pál pressed a bottle of champagne on them to toast the new emperor when they were off duty.

I could not seem to assemble my thoughts. Every time I lined them up, they toppled like a row of toy soldiers. Franz Joseph was the emperor. I might have persuaded *him* to stop the war when he stood in my bedroom, but instead I had wasted time talking of foolish personal issues. If I had said yes to his halfhearted proposal, I might be empress, my own decree more powerful than that of the archduchess. I had no real wish to be empress, but why had I not said anything to Franz Joseph about the praetheria? Now I was a pawn, promised to Russia in exchange for worsening the war I had sought to end. In a fit of self-righteousness, I had delivered up myself and Hungary in a neatly trussed bundle.

I was not the hero of this story; I was its fool. Perhaps I could crack jokes better than I broke spells.

We continued into Pressburg, where we stayed at a respectable inn. Pál was given the room beside mine, and I watched as he cast wards on the door and windows of my room.

"Do not be so afraid, niece," he said. "You and I have a great opportunity to reclaim some of the glory that should have belonged to our family, if we play our cards right."

"And what does that mean? Help the Russians win? Help the praetheria conquer people and places I love?"

Pál looked cagey, smiling to himself as though he knew something I did not. "Humor the praetheria, yes—they have the potential to be the most powerful players in this little game. And trust me: I have a vision that will take care of everything."

I wrapped my arms around my torso, chilled. As little as I trusted the Four driving the praetheria, I trusted Pál even less. I knew what they wanted; Pál was still a mystery to me. When I did not answer, he only smiled more broadly and left the room.

After that, the days began to blur together. We left the plains behind us and followed winding trails that curled through blue mountains of northern Hungary, between trees waving banners of autumn gold and red. As the road began to climb, I was blindfolded so I could not report on our destination. Had Pál seen my letters from Gábor and known them for what they were? Or was this the sort of precaution they might take with anyone?

Pál was the only one who spoke to me. But I grew to dread his voice: he approached only to tell me of some terrible thing that was happening, some further sign that the war had escalated beyond any one person's efforts to contain it.

It was Pál who told me that Dragović's armies were closing in on Buda-Pest, that the first elected minister of Hungary had resigned, and that Kossuth was to take his place, in defiance of the Austrian government, which had declared martial law over the country. Worse, the uprisings had spread—not only had Croatia taken up arms against Hungary, but now peasants in Romania were revolting against Hungarian nobility.

"Reports of the fighting are terrible," Pál said. "Entire cities have burned. Those who survive the burning have had their eyes put out, their bodies run through with pikes."

He paused—waiting for some show of horror or tears from me. But I would not satisfy him. He might be energized by stories of brutality, but I was not.

After perhaps a week of travel—I had lost track—we halted midday, and my blindfold was removed. We were at a crossroads near some mountain pass. Count Medem approached me for the first time since we had left Vienna.

"This is where you stay, as per my tsar's orders."

He helped me dismount. I looked at the mountains towering around us, at the long, empty stretch of road in all directions. Was I to be left as sacrifice for some great beast? I tensed, prepared to flee as soon as the soldiers were gone.

But Pál stopped beside me. "You will not run," he said, flicking his hands at me, and I found that I could move nothing but my eyes and mouth. My arms and legs were fixed.

We watched the Russian count and his guards disappear along the northeast road with the horses we had ridden. When all sight and sound of their passing had vanished, a pair of men approached us, walking across a field of drying grass.

As they drew near, I recognized the taller of the two: Hunger.

I had been right—I was never intended for the Russians.

"Why?" I asked Pál. "My magic is nothing beside yours—I can scarcely cast a spell. Even my spell-breaking is a mercurial magic."

"I asked for you," Pál said, watching the two men instead of meeting my gaze. "I have plans, and you might prove quite helpful."

"Miss Arden," Hunger said, tipping an imaginary hat. I blinked at him, unable to return his nod, thanks to Pál's spell, even had I wanted to. Which I did not. Hunger did not introduce his companion, a narrow-faced man with curling hair and a pair of twisting horns. After speaking briefly with Pál, they turned and led us back across the field.

Pál released the spell holding me in place. "Do not think you can run from us," he said.

A breeze ruffled my hair, carrying the unmistakable chill

of winter, though the afternoon was yet warm. I shivered and put aside thoughts of escaping. For now.

I retained only hazy details of what followed: a sense of rising elevation, as I had to lean forward as I walked and my thighs burned. I kept my eyes fixed on the curly-haired man and Hunger, who climbed ahead of us.

It was coming on dark when we reached our destination. Some distance up a mountain incline, Hunger held up his hand, and we stopped. Pál disappeared behind a rocky outcropping. The curly-haired man followed.

I took one quick step sideways, but Hunger grasped my arm. His touch burned, hot even through the shirt and coat I wore. He led me past the outcropping to where a dark, narrow gap opened in the rock. *Another cave.* But this one, I fancied, held more than illusions.

Hunger shepherded me into the cave, a roughly shaped oblong that led into another, larger chamber. The others crowded in behind us. Lights hung at intervals along the walls, illuminating the slick rust-brown surface of the rock. The second chamber nearly stopped my breath. Lights shimmered everywhere, but instead of the relatively plain interior of the first room, stone fountains cascaded everywhere: icicles of rock melting from the ceiling onto the floor, rounded tiers erupting from the ground in every shade from burnt umber to russet to gold. I had never seen anything like it.

Praetheria milled about the room, talking in small groups, eating, minding children—some even dancing to a faint piped melody. It did not look like a prison—and then I remembered that the world of the Binding spell had been the most beautiful place I knew; prisons could be exquisite. But beauty could not compensate for lost freedom.

"Come," Hunger said, his voice almost gentle. "Let me show you to your quarters."

"You mean my cell?" Let him call a spade a spade.

He frowned, rubbing his hand over his chin and cheeks. A golden sheen glowed across his face in this muted light. "You will be treated kindly here."

"I had rather I were free to go."

Beside me, Pál spoke for the first time since entering the caverns. "Do not be a fool, niece. You might take your place among the most powerful rulers of the last millennia. Do not waste that chance out of misplaced nostalgia or sympathy. At the end of the day, you have only yourself to rely upon."

Distaste curled Hunger's lip. "You may go, Zrínyi Pál. Anna is tired and no doubt hungry. You may speak with her later." With that, he led me across the crowded room, stepping over a trail of water that glowed silver in the light. We walked through several branchings of the cave system, which was larger than I had initially supposed, and came to a series of smaller chambers. The doorway to each was covered—a mesh of daisies, threads of pearls that chattered in the wind left by our passing, a spider's web.

Hunger stopped before the seventh door, its opening shrouded in mist-grey silk. As he pulled aside the covering, he said, "I trust the accommodations—and the company—will be to your liking."

The room was dim, only a single globe of light hanging

from the ceiling at the center of the roughly shaped space. Two pallets lay inside, facing each other on opposite sides of the chamber. One of the pallets was occupied by a sleeping figure, but at the light streaming through the doorway, the girl turned.

For the second time that night, my heart seemed to stop.

On the mostly silent ride from Vienna, I had had plenty of time to think, to wonder if I would see Noémi if I were, in fact, given to the praetheria. Each time, I had dismissed it as unlikely. Why should they give me an ally? Friendless, I was weaker—and more likely to succumb to their persuasions and charm.

But here she was, pushing her blond curls from her face, blinking sleepily as she sat up, Mátyás's filigree cross still hanging around her neck. Her gaze sharpened, and she threw back her blanket and launched herself at me.

Salt tears bit my tongue as I laughed, clinging to Noémi with all the strength generated by nearly four months' searching for her.

Her cheeks were wet as she hugged me. "I thought I might never see you again."

"Impossible," I said. "I would have searched for you until I was an old crone, too weak to order a carriage."

She laughed, but her laughter was tinged with sadness. Her eyes flicked past me to Hunger, who stood watching our reunion in silence. Something shifted in his gold eyes, and when I looked back at Noémi, she was blushing.

Had he engineered this reunion for me—or for Noémi? I found it did not much matter. For the first time since the archduchess had told me my fate, I was hopeful. If Hunger

106

felt a kindness for either of us, it meant he had a weakness we might exploit.

Noémi gripped my hands in hers. "I cannot deny I am glad to see you. But, oh, Anna, I wish you had not come. They have used me as bait, and now we are both caught— and I'm afraid they will use me as fire to forge a weapon out of you."

CHAPTER 9

Mátyás

I braced for impact as I fell out of the sky. Beside me, Vasilisa screamed imprecations. Bahadır whispered a prayer.

But the impact never came. As we neared the earth, our speed slowed—a spell?—and we came to a stop just before touching lightly on the ground.

Hála Istennek. Relief made my body light.

Vasilisa surged forward, still bound to Bahadır and me by the ropes the samodiva queen had wound around us, and we all nearly toppled. I danced to hold my footing, while Bahadır did the same. The iron-laced net still hung over us like a curse.

"You," she snarled.

I looked up. I'd been so focused on my imminent death that it hadn't occurred to me to look for the source of the net. Which, in hindsight, seemed a glaring mistake.

A towering dark-haired man in copper armor stalked toward us, twin blades gleaming in the sunlight.

Despite the threatening expression on his face and those murderous swords, his appearance sent hope shooting through me.

"Hadúr!" I hadn't seen the war god in months, not since I'd fled the World Tree and the Lady's plans for me to save the world.

Hadúr inclined his head gravely. "Táltos."

Mátyás, I thought. But it did not seem to be the time or place to correct the god.

He turned back to Vasilisa. "You have something of mine. He has not finished his training."

She kicked me in the leg. "This human? I caught him; he belongs to me now. If he needs training, I can do that as well as you."

"I caught you both. By your own reckoning, he belongs to me."

I tugged at the ropes binding me to Vasilisa, looking for looseness or give. It was awkward enough being fought over as though I were a favored toy—or weapon—without being bound to one of the claimants.

The bonds held tight. But though Vasilisa's spell still trapped me, we were no longer airborne, which meant shifting would not put Bahadır at risk of slipping out of the bonds and falling to his death.

So I shifted, my body collapsing inward and downward, a fine layer of fur covering my limbs as I slithered through the ropes. Now mouse-shaped, I scampered out of Hadúr's net and stopped by the foot of the war god. He smiled approvingly down at me.

I whirled around to see Bahadır slide free of the loosened bonds and duck beneath the iron-laced net. Vasilisa was either distracted by Hadúr or did not care that Bahadır had freed himself: she did not react, her focus directed on the god.

I could not see the samodiva queen anywhere—the sky was clear, save for a few distant, raptor-shaped specks that made my mouse instincts twitch. Apparently, the samodiva queen's loyalty to Vasilisa had ended with Zhivka's death and Vasilisa's refusal to punish us.

Something painful twinged inside me at the thought of Zhivka, and I pushed it away.

"You killed my Lady in an ambush," Hadúr said, his rough voice lowering to a growl.

Another twinge; another death I did not want to think about—another death following in the wake of my unnatural second life.

"And now you mean to kill me? Justice cries out for my blood? Really, such an uninspired concept." Vasilisa's voice was flat with boredom, but I caught a sharp edge that pricked me into wariness.

I flattened myself to the ground, just as a terrific shock of energy boomed past me, knocking Hadúr over. When my sight cleared, Vasilisa stood free of the iron-laced netting, her white hair wafting about her head in an electric cloud, her face pale with fury. Behind her, Bahadır struggled upright, then ran toward the nearest copse of trees. I made a mental note: *iron slows but does not stop her.*

Then I realized: the faint prickle of Vasilisa's magic net was gone. Whether consciously or not, she'd released me in order to fight Hadúr. Now was my own chance to run.

Hadúr roared upward beside me, then hurtled through

the air like a breathing cannonball, sunlight fracturing around him. He dropped toward Vasilisa, his twin swords cleaving through the ball of light Vasilisa shot at him as though it were nothing.

Vasilisa fell back, and Hadúr crashed down where she had been standing, his landing sending rumbles through the earth. My paws twitched in the grasses.

Now, I thought. I could fly to Bahadır, and we could escape together while Vasilisa was distracted.

But I didn't move.

I'd scorned the Lady's training, and then my own strength had nearly undone me when I could not control the dragon I'd become. There was more to being táltos than I had discovered on my own: if Hadúr could train me, I would let him.

I still meant to find Noémi, but searching for my sister without clear direction had so far led only to an ambush and our capture. Perhaps there was a way to use my táltos gifts more intelligently to find her.

A fireball scorched the earth near me, singeing my whiskers and shaking me out of my thoughts.

Staying with Hadúr did *not* have to mean I'd invite death right now.

I shot upward, in crow form, and winged my way toward the copse of trees where Bahadır had taken refuge. I settled in the uppermost boughs of an oak.

In the meadow before me, the two near-immortals still grappled. Vasilisa fired spell after spell at the towering god, and each time his sword sliced through the spell as though it were silk. Vasilisa retreated again, throwing up a shield

of fire as Hadúr sheathed his swords in one swift movement and sent a barrage of metal stars spinning through the
air toward her. The stars danced through the fire, drawing
bright ribbons of blood from her arms.

My skin stung with the remembered pain of those same
stars.

Vasilisa flung herself up into the air. "Fine," she said, her
breath coming heavy. "I yield. You can have the táltos. For
now." She turned midair to face the tree where I was hiding. "Táltos, we hold your sister. Train with Hadúr, if you
must. When you've finished, you'll come to us willingly
enough, for your sister's sake."

She vanished in a puff of smoke.

Damn it. I knew it. I launched myself toward the spot
where she'd disappeared, banking as I realized I had no
idea where she'd gone and that I *had* just resolved to fight
smarter.

I fluttered down to the meadow grass, shifting as I landed.
Bahadır emerged from the trees to stand beside me.

Hadúr walked toward us, squinting at me. "The Four
have your sister?"

I nodded.

"We'll find her." His eyes flickered to Bahadır. "Who
is this?"

"My friend, Bahadır." I continued the introduction.
"Bahadır, this is Hadúr, the Hungarian god of war."

Bahadır's eyes went a little wide, but he gave no other
sign of awe. He bowed, briefly, then straightened.

"You look like a soldier," Hadúr said. "Come with your
friend. We'll need good soldiers in this war."

"I'd be honored," Bahadır said. "My father was a soldier. He trained me some before his death."

"Good man." Hadúr looked back at me. "Find something to cover yourself with, táltos."

But as it transpired, clothes were not easy to come by in such an uninhabited region. In the end, I flew overhead in crow form while Bahadır rode the second horse Hadúr had brought with him. He had, it seems, been looking for me.

)(

Riding was not as swift as flying, and I found myself circling back frequently, so as to not outpace the riders. But by nightfall, we had drawn within view of the World Tree, its immense height shooting from the plains like a fountain.

"What is this place?" Bahadır asked as we approached the base of the tree, the horned skull still untouched beneath the trunk. Despite its height, the tree cast no shadow—part of the magic that kept the tree hidden, I suspected.

"The tree has many names: the World Tree, the Sky-High Tree, the Tree Without a Top, the Tree of Life. Any of them will do. The tree is hidden from most humans, for their protection as much as ours. But you are my guest, so the tree is not hidden from you."

Hadúr hesitated, then said, "The way up is not easy; many have found their hearts fail them at such heights. How is your courage?"

"As sound as anyone's," Bahadır said, though he gasped a little as Hadúr's massive arms gripped him and they launched upward. Hadúr did not fly, precisely, but his leap reached heights that no mortal could. He caught the lowest limb of the tree and swung up.

I flew after them, landing near the door of my old room in a hollow in the tree trunk. Hadúr set Bahadır down and told us to make ourselves comfortable while he returned to his forge. The grey ladies I remembered from my previous stay showed up sometime later, though they were not so animated as they had been before.

I imagined they still grieved the loss of the Lady.

)(

It was not quite dawn when Hadúr appeared outside our room. His heavy knock pulled us both from our dreams.

"I have been thinking of your sister," Hadúr said as Bahadır and I emerged, blinking and dry-mouthed, from our beds. He bore a great bird on either shoulder, golden falcons with black wing bands, nearly twice the size of a peregrine. But the falcons were unlike any other bird I'd encountered, and their minds were closed to me. *The Lady's turul birds.* Above us, the shifting branches of the tree revealed tumbling stars in the night sky, but far below, above the *puszta* grasses, the air was still grey, barely lit by a sun that had not yet breached the horizon.

"What?" I asked, my wits still shrouded in a fog of sleep.

Hadúr's face loomed grim before me: his nose a trifle crooked where it had been broken, his dark eyes narrowed beneath heavy brows, a faint scar seaming one corner of his lips. A face that had seen more wars than I could dream of. For the first time, I wondered what it was like to live in the World Tree after the Binding. In the stories, the Upper Realm teemed with gods and other beings. Most of them had died or faded in the Binding, and now it was only Hadúr and a handful of grey ladies and birds rattling around a once-vibrant realm. I peered at him more closely, but he did not *seem* lonely—though truthfully, I could not read much in his expression beyond irritability at my dimness.

"Now that the war has begun, we haven't much time for your training, and I cannot afford to have you distracted by the search for your sister. My sources tell me that the Four are somewhere to the north of us, in the mountains. You may use the Lady's birds to search for her."

"I've sent crows to look for Noémi. None of them have found her."

Hadúr tipped his head to one side. "Crows are very intelligent, but they do not have the same capacity as the turul birds, who bear magic in their blood."

Was *that* why I'd never had much success touching their minds? "But how will they know what to look for? They're not receptive to my particular gifts."

The corners of his lips curled. "You're a shifter. Show them."

Oh. Right. Taking on a woman's form wasn't totally new to me, but something about taking on *my sister's* form smacked of indecency. Concentrating, I shifted my head and face to mimic Noémi's, and then adopted a generic female body, approximately Noémi's height. It would have to do. There was no way in heaven or hell that I was going to think *that* closely about her body. My own clothes hung loose about her smaller frame.

Once the birds had taken a good look and flown away, I shifted back, mildly surprised to find that I was sweating.

"Your sister is very beautiful," Bahadır observed.

"Shut up," I said, by way of thanks.

Hadúr ignored our exchange and led us to one of the broad branches of the World Tree, where I had rebuilt my endurance following my death and rebirth by treading up and down.

Hadúr began slowly, testing the limits of what I already knew, starting with shifting into small, familiar shapes: my crow, a rabbit. The forms grew increasingly complex: a boar, a horse, a man. My human shiftings were not exact, as they depended on my memory, but the more familiar the face, the more successfully I could imitate someone else. Hadúr asked for someone both Bahadır and I knew, to test the likeness.

I picked instinctively, settling into the frame of one of my favorite bandits, who had been killed last summer. But when I spoke, it was with Ákos's voice, and my stomach curled in on itself, as though I'd just raised a corpse. This was a mistake. Beside me, Bahadır shook silently.

"Enough," I said, shifting into my own body again and fighting the urge to retch. "I need a break. And some food."

"Rest is a luxury you will not always have on the battle-field," Hadúr said, but he allowed me to collapse beside Bahadır.

Hadúr snapped his fingers and the grey ladies materialized, bearing trays of steaming pastries.

"Mátyás," Bahadır began, then choked.

"I know. I'm sorry." Ákos had been Bahadır's closest friend; it was unforgiveable of me to spring his friend's specter on him like that.

Following our break, Hadúr ran me through more permutations of shapes, focusing on those not found in this world: a hound with wings, a bear with impervious dragon scales beneath the fur.

The seven-headed dragon hovered at the edges of my thoughts, whispering in my ears, calling to my heart. No matter what grunting approval Hadúr gave my forms, they all felt a fraction off, because they were not the form that truly wanted me. *Or that I truly wanted.*

"Good," Hadúr said as I melted from the bear into a horse with clawed feet. "Again. Faster."

"I can't." Even after my death, there were limits to my shifting. The more fanciful the form, the more energy it took to hold it. *Except the dragon.* That form, alone of all my shapes, energized me. And that form, alone of all my shapes, terrified me.

If Hadúr was disappointed by my human weaknesses, he didn't let on. "Very well. Let's talk of military strategy instead."

I tried to suppress a grimace at the suggestion—strategy generally bored me witless—but did not entirely succeed, judging by Hadúr's raised eyebrow. Time to deflect. "Can you tell me of a táltos's other gifts? I know shifting and some animal persuasion, but Vasilisa said something about a táltos being as dangerous sleeping as awake."

"She meant dream-walking, most like, where a táltos

sends their spirit free of their body during a trance. But you're not ready for that just yet."

Dream-walking. I thought of the times I'd seen Noémi in my dreams and the vision I'd had of the soldiers who attacked my *betyárok* the night before their ambush. These had not been dreams of foresight, the way a Coremancer might dream. These had been real visions, the product of my wandering spirit. I shivered, not entirely easy with the idea that my body and soul could split apart without my conscious will. What would happen if my spirit wandered away and did not come back?

Hadúr had already moved on, summoning the grey ladies again, who produced a set of tin soldiers, half in red uniforms, half in blue, and a table with a contoured surface. Hadúr gave us a short lecture on strategy, most of which I struggled to follow, and then set the red soldiers atop a ridge. "Your soldiers"—he nodded to me—"occupy the high ground." He handed the other soldiers to Bahadır. "How would you proceed?"

Bahadır frowned at the arrangement, then set a small contingent of soldiers before the hill. The others he set some distance away.

"The soldiers will move as you direct them," Hadúr said.

I sent my soldiers down the hill to surround Bahadır's small troop—only to find his other soldiers closing in from both sides.

Hadúr shook his head. "Did you listen to nothing I said? You just fell victim to a classic trap—do not cede the high ground if you do not have to, no matter how easy the victory seems." He waved a hand at me, and a rush of wind knocked me and my soldiers down. "Now you're dead."

"But that's just a standard battle between ordinary soldiers," I protested. "Add Luminate magicians, and things would not be so simple."

"All right. Show me."

I tried again, this time describing magicians who would generate a wall of fire around the soldiers on the hilltop, protecting them from enemy charges, while bombarding the enemy soldiers with cannonballs and Lucifera ground quakes.

"Not bad," Hadúr said.

Bahadır looked thoughtful for a moment, then grinned as he described his retaliation: Elementalist winds circling to slow the cannons and knock their trajectory awry, while also stoking the fire and shrinking it back toward the soldiers it was meant to protect. He paired these spells with Coremancer Persuasion to set my troops panicking within their fire trap and trampling each other.

Hadúr surveyed my soldiers (was it just an effect of the late-afternoon light or were a few of them smoking?) and then laughed. "I think you are dead again, táltos." He clapped Bahadır on the shoulder. "Well done."

I rubbed my temples, which were beginning to ache from the unaccustomed focus. "I think the solution is clear: let Bahadır plan all my battles for me."

"A military leader needs excellent commanders, but you cannot rely on others in battle. Lines of communication are too easily cut, men are too easily killed. It's not enough to be gifted: you must understand what you do."

I glanced beyond the tree branch to the stars spinning in the dark sky that always surrounded the upper branches of the tree. They winked at me, cold and distant. So much seemed to ride on this training: as táltos, I was expected to be a hero, a leader of men. But I was still only Mátyás, whatever my gifts, and I did not know how to be either.

My father had died at his own hand after a loss at cards, disappointing everyone who loved him. I had agreed to die at Anna's hands once to escape that crushing failure, and yet here I was again, trying to exorcise my father's ghost. If I failed now, how wide would those ripples of disappointment reach?

I had promised myself I would stay and let Hadúr train me. It was the smartest thing I could do, under the circumstances. But already I was conscious of an itch, a need to move, to find Noémi, to do anything that might preclude fully becoming the táltos Hadúr expected of me.

$$\rtimes$$

Our days settled into a kind of routine after that: mornings were spent testing, and then stretching, my táltos gifts. Through some experimentation, we discovered that my range for shifting inanimate objects was about thirty paces. Animate objects were harder. I could shift a rabbit at fifteen paces—but nothing approaching the distance at which I had shifted Anna in the ice caves. It seemed my control was greater when real consequences hung on my actions: imminent doom helped me focus.

But when I said as much to Hadúr, he shook his head. "You are not yet ready to try your skills in battle, if that is what you are hinting at. The threat of destruction may help you focus, but it lacks something as a life strategy."

Bahadır laughed, and I mock-glowered at him, which only made him laugh harder.

Afternoons, supposedly to offer me some "rest" from shifting, were spent learning and applying military strategy. Personally, I found the afternoons harder, particularly since Bahadır generally ran circles around my strategies. I can handle humiliation as well as the next man (which is to say, not as well as I'd like)—but I began to suspect Hadúr enjoyed watching my constant defeats.

Some days Hadúr would bring us news of the war, though as I never saw messengers approaching or leaving the tree, I am not sure how he received word. Perhaps the wind carried it to him—I would not put it past either Hadúr or the wind, which had a curious, almost sentient quality as it passed through the World Tree.

He demonstrated the troop movements on a map with animated soldiers. An Austrian general with the yellow-and-black flag of the empire settled into northeastern Hungary, near some of the country's richest mines. Another yellow-and-black army, under General Windisch-Graetz, marched eastward from Vienna, clashing with Hungarian troops only a few hours from Eszterháza.

Dragović laid siege to Buda-Pest. Even with my limited strategic training, I could see these armies closing like a noose around the heart of the country. I remembered how easily Bahadır's toy armies had surrounded and destroyed my own, and I frowned at the map.

The itch was back: it did not seem right to hide in a tree in the midst of peaceful plains while my sister remained missing, while other red-blooded Hungarians fought and died. But I pushed it aside and attended as well as I could to Hadúr. There were still things I needed to learn.

Nearly a fortnight into my training, after exhausting the limits of both my shifting and my animal persuasion, Hadúr finally moved on to dream-walking, a gift I had never manifested before my death. And since dying, I had manifested it only accidentally.

"Dream-walking," Hadúr said, "is one of the oldest known táltos gifts. Dream walkers used their skill to explore enemy battlefields, to retrieve secrets, to find lost things. The best dream walkers could use their spirit selves to leave this plane: some could inhabit the dreams of others, persuading their sleeping selves; others could visit the realm of the dead."

St. Cajetan, save me. "I do not," I said, "intend to visit the damned." Or the saved, for that matter. I imagined they'd be even less welcoming.

Hadúr ignored me. "For this gift to be useful to you, you must exercise conscious control. The first step is to put yourself into a trance."

I must have looked alarmed, because Bahadır said, "Don't worry. I will ensure that no one disturbs your body. No one will shave your head or mustache while you sleep, or paint flowers on your cheeks."

I hadn't imagined any of those possibilities until he spoke. Now I did. "That's very reassuring. Thank you."

Bahadır laughed, and Hadúr sighed. I suppose to someone who had seen millennia, we must have appeared to have the attention span of mayflies.

"A waking trance is not the same as sleeping, though it

may look like it to the outside observer. In a trance state, your mind is actually *more* focused and alert than it is in your typical wakeful state."

"I'm a champion sleeper," I said. "But I know nothing about trances." I was not certain I wanted to. Setting aside my new fear that Bahadır might well shave me while I was entranced, consciously leaving my body to wander where I willed seemed, frankly, dangerous—even mad. But my old nurse would have said, *If it's a goose, it should be fat.* If I was going to train, I might as well do it all.

"Find a focal point," Hadúr said, and I fixed my eyes on a nearby branch of the World Tree that was rustling gently. "Focus all your attention on that point. Think of nothing but that point. *Become* that point."

Some demon inside me prompted me to start shifting, sprouting leaves from my fingertips.

"No!" Hadúr roared. "I do not mean literally become that point. Only direct your thoughts to it."

"Oh," I said meekly. "You might have said as much."

Bahadır smothered a laugh.

"Now focus. Breathe deeply, in and out. Relax your muscles. Calm your mind and hold your focus on that point until everything else recedes. When you engage the trance, explore the surrounding *puszta,* but do not go too far. Dream-walking can be intoxicating, and táltos who have left their bodies for too long have been known to die."

"And you did not think imminent doom was a useful method to focus," I murmured.

Hadúr merely leveled a look at me, one that would have made the strictest of my schoolmasters writhe in envy.

I stopped talking and tried to focus. I was not the scatter-brain Noémi sometimes accused me of being, but holding a singular focus for so long was difficult. My thoughts began to drift: to my already-rumbling stomach, to the warm sun on my skin, to the air currents where a pair of crows tumbled just beyond the World Tree. I wanted to escape *with* my body in crow form, not sit here trying to leave my body behind.

"Focus," Hadúr said again.

I tried. One moment, I was watching the leaves flutter, dark against light, and breathing in time to Hadúr's low counts. Then my focus changed, as when you absently look at an object and your eyesight blurs. Only instead of blurring, everything seemed sharper.

I could see my body as well as the tree above me, a curious mystery of double vision that I solved when I realized I was no longer *in* my body. My spirit self looked at the ground below me, and in the next instant I found myself hovering over it. I turned slowly, the plains sweeping before me in a broad, seemingly endless steppe. I focused on a tree near the horizon—and at once I was moving toward it, soaring across the grasses with an effortlessness I had not known, even in bird form.

It was like riding the thermals as a crow, only unburdened by the limits of a physical body. It was exhilarating. I could see why Hadúr said some táltos forgot to return to themselves—but I was in no danger yet.

I skimmed past the tree, moving faster, until I could see the distant dark smudge of the Bükk Mountains. I thought of the trajectory Bahadır and I had taken with the praetheria, flying in a relatively straight line from the ice cave toward the Hungarian plains, where Hadúr had found us. If the trajectory continued true, Noémi might be somewhere in the Bükk or Mátra Mountains, or beyond that, hidden in the Carpathians. She might even be in Russia, but I hoped she was nearer to hand than that.

It couldn't hurt to search, only for a moment. I sent my spirit soaring northward to the mountains, skimming above the tree line. Viewing the world through my spirit eyes, I discovered that living things gave off a small soul spark, with humans brighter than most. When I encountered such sparks, I slowed and circled closer to the earth. Mostly, I found people clustered around farms and hamlets, and none of them were my sister. Trying to find my sister's soul spark among so many was a fool's errand.

When I reached the mountains, I turned reluctantly back toward the World Tree. The return was faster, my body calling to my soul like a beacon. Reaching the tree, I found the branches lit with a handful of flares: the grey ladies, and brighter than all of them, Hadúr.

Did all praetheria shine so brightly? I didn't know, but I determined to find out. If it were true, then I didn't need to find Noémi, one human soul among hundreds of thousands. I could begin by finding the brilliant lights of the praetheria—and my sister with them.

I settled my spirit back in my body and woke with a shocked gasp, as though I'd been plunged in icy water.

I *had* been plunged in icy water: I was dripping, and there was an empty bucket in Bahadır's hands. He smiled and shrugged.

Hadúr said only, "You were gone longer than is safe for a new walker. Next time, curb your curiosity."

I wiped my wet face with my shirtsleeve (only slightly less wet), and Bahadır helped me stand.

"Are you all right? There's a curious expression on your face."

"I'm fine," I said.

I was more than fine. I knew how to find Noémi.

CHAPTER 10

Anna

Noémi dimmed the light hanging in the small chamber, and I crawled into the bed facing hers. Despite the exhaustion that hung off me, I was not tired.

Noémi was here. She wasn't lost to us any longer. We might both be captive, but her presence felt like a small miracle.

"You were right," I told her. "Mátyás is not dead. Or rather, he *did* die—but he came back."

There was a rustle in the dimness as Noémi sat up, reaching across the space between our beds to grasp my hand. "You've seen him?"

"Yes. I only found him a few weeks ago, but we were searching for you together."

"Why did he never try to find us?"

"I think he believed he would endanger both of us if he did. Instead, he took up with the *betyárok* on the *puszta*.

They called him the King of Crows, and I heard of him even in Vienna."

Noémi let out a gurgle that was half laugh, half sob, and pulled her hand back. "Of course he did." Then she sighed. "He still should have found us. He could not have put us in greater danger than we managed for ourselves."

I smiled ruefully at the darkness, thinking of my own flight from Vienna. "I should like to hear your story."

"I'll tell you soon. Where is Mátyás now?"

"I don't know. He might be here. We were looking for you when we were trapped by praetheria. He helped me escape, but he was gone before I could come back to help him."

Noémi sighed. "I hope he is far from here. This is not a place for humans."

She sounded so certain. What had she seen in these caves? In the dark, I could sense the presence of hundreds of tons of rocks—an entire mountain above me. The air smelled of water and stone and dust. As I thought about the pressure of so much rock, my breath grew thin and labored, and I shoved the thought away.

"And you . . . Are you all right? They have not hurt you?"

Her pillow rustled as she shook her head. "I am not hurt. The praetheria have not been unkind. But it is lonely here, and sometimes I . . . hear things. The praetheria are preparing for war."

"I know." But what was there that I, or Noémi, could do about it? I had already done what little I could—and might as well have done nothing. "We cannot stay here."

Noémi didn't answer.

I propped myself up on one elbow to look across the room at her. Only a little bit of light reached us, from a guard's lantern some distance down the connecting corridor. She lay flat on her back, her eyes staring at the ceiling.

"Noémi? Is escape so difficult?"

"I tried once or twice when I was first captured, but the spell they put on me never let me go far without doubling over in pain. And then I began to feel somehow that I should stay. That I needed to stay. It was that same sureness that led us through the labyrinths in Buda Castle when we rescued Gábor and William; the same sureness that made me believe Mátyás was alive."

I hesitated for a breath. She would not like what I had to tell her. "Are you certain you do not stay because you find Hunger attractive?" I had seen her blush earlier, and I knew how she had looked at Hunger before she disappeared.

"No!" Her voice sliced through the air between us, chilly and sure. *The lady doth protest too much, methinks.* But now was not the time to pursue that. There were other truths that needed telling.

I told her about William's death and then crowded into her bed to hold her while she cried. William had been my friend, and I missed him, but Noémi had loved him, before it became clear that revolution would always be his first love. Perhaps she loved him still.

When she quieted, sobs lingering only as a hiccup in her breathing, I told her about saving Franz Joseph from the spell and the trade his mother had made. In turn, she told me how she had come to the caves.

She had left Vienna to find Mátyás, in the company of Hunger, believing it to be safer than traveling alone.

"Noémi," I sighed, wishing she had trusted me more. I knew why she had not—she believed I had lied to her about Mátyás's death. But she had taken such a risk. "Your reputation . . ."

"What did it matter? Better a ruined reputation than being forced into marriage with the duke of Rohan if I stayed." She reached over to poke me. "And you are a fine one to talk. You also showed up here alone, in the company of strange men."

I blushed in the darkness, wondering if my mother would be pleased or horrified to know that the propriety she had tried so hard to instill in me haunted me yet. "You're right. It was a silly thing to say. But you might have told me about the duke."

"You were too busy trying to save the world."

"I was wrong," I said flatly. "The world does not need my saving. I should have been there for you."

"You're here now," Noémi said, leaning her head against my shoulder, a tacit gesture of forgiveness. She resumed her story, telling me how in a field outside the city, Hunger had shifted to his dragon form and flown her to the *puszta*. For two days, they had searched the plains for a scene that matched the ones she carried from her dreams, with no success. On the third day, Hunger had told her he was needed in Vienna. But instead of leaving her to search for Mátyás alone, as she asked, he had carried her back to a praetherian camp outside Vienna, where he had left her.

"If Mátyás is alive, he will find you," Hunger had promised, and then he had disappeared, and she had not seen him again until a midnight dance some weeks later.

"You were there too," Noémi said, her voice rumbling against my side. "I would swear it was you, though the spell they kept on me would not let me reach you."

And I remembered how I had seen a golden-haired woman my first night in the praetherian camp, after the archduchess had issued her order for my death and Hunger had saved me. Had I not been so shocked by the disintegration of my entire life, I might have recognized Noémi and saved myself months of searching.

Though perhaps, if I had known I was leaving her behind in the camp, I might never have found the courage to escape. *You cannot change the past,* I reminded myself, *only face the future.* Whatever choices I had made, I was here now.

When Noémi spoke again, her voice was heavy with sleep. "I lied earlier when I said I wished you were not here. I'm glad you're here, Anna. It's been so lonely. I was beginning to fear I had lost myself. I do not entirely know who or what I am anymore. But now that you're here, perhaps I shall find myself again."

"Perhaps," I said, very gently, because I did not know how to tell Noémi I was as lost as she was. I had been so certain, going into the Binding spell. I had been chimera, a spell breaker, and though I had been afraid, I had carried with me a sure sense of self. And then the Austrian court had ignored me, the Congress had laughed at me, and the praetheria had betrayed me. I had gone from being a heroine—fêted, loved, respected—to an outcast. Where in all of that was I? Who was I, stripped of all my roles, of all outside opinions? Who was I, alone in the dark, when no one else could see me?

I didn't know.

But I lay beside Noémi, one arm protectively around my cousin, my heart's sister, and listened to her breaths as she slept, until I also fell asleep.

)(

Things did not feel quite so dire when I awoke, though it was odd to wake into the same darkness that I had fallen asleep in. The caves never altered as the world outside did, with the waning and waxing of light marking the passage of days. Someone brought us bread and fresh apples, and then Noémi showed me about the caverns.

"The entrance is spelled to prevent our leaving," she said, "but so long as we do not disturb the praetheria, we are free to wander. I spend most of my days wandering. I offered to help their healers when I first came, but when they did not acknowledge my offer, I stopped asking. I fill the time as best I can, but the days are sometimes slow."

I studied the caves as we walked, looking for potential opportunities to escape. There were armed praetheria everywhere, particularly as we neared the entrance, and though the praetheria in most of the caverns ignored us, I could tell when we drew close to dangerous territory, because all the praetheria stopped their activities to watch us. At night, guards were posted outside our room, and it was not as though we could tunnel through solid rock, even if we knew in which direction to do so. Being underground distorted any natural sense I had for direction.

The second night, I wrote to Gábor, detailed notes about the caves and the number of praetheria and any training I had glimpsed. I was not certain such details would accomplish anything for him in the war, but I felt better for doing *something*. Perhaps, by some miracle, he and his troops might find us. When I finished, I whispered, *"Változz át üres lappá!"* and those damning details I'd written disappeared.

I reread his last letter, another funny observation about one of his fellow soldiers, who could not fall asleep without a complicated ritual that included loudly declaiming poetry. *Even though we are at war, there are hours entire when I forget: when we ride through the countryside and the sky overhead is so blue that it hurts, or the shadows in a grove of trees remind me of a fairy story. Though I am glad you are not here for the drudgery and the dangerous parts, I wish I could share all the beautiful parts with you. And I think, somehow, that even the drudgery would be transformed, were you here.*

It might be the prettiest compliment he had paid me. I read it again, running my fingers along the line. I wanted to save the words, but it was too dangerous—if someone found the letters and realized what they were, I might lose them. Worse, they might pose a threat to Gábor. I read the letter a final time, then whispered the charm to obliterate it.

In the morning, Noémi and I resumed our explorations. The caves extended for miles, well past the rooms settled by the praetheria, though guards prevented us from venturing into the unexplored depths. The caves had their own austere beauty: gold and russet icicles of stone hanging from the ceilings, towers of stone thrusting up from the ground. One of the caverns even held a small lake, where praetheria could occasionally be seen rowing a small boat.

I knelt at the water's edge. Fairy lights lined the walls of the cavern and reflected off the black surface, but beyond the occasional ripple, the lake revealed nothing.

I trailed my fingers in the cool liquid, and Noémi yanked me back, her face pale. "Don't touch the water. There is something that lives here—I don't know what. It doesn't seem to disturb the praetheria, but Hunger warned me that it might not be so kind to humans."

Remembering the creature who had nearly buried me underground in Prater Park, I shivered. I dried my fingers on my skirts, and we went back to the main chamber.

Whispers stirred through the crowd gathering there: someone was coming. New praetheria arrived several times a day and seldom engendered so much interest. Who could it be? We had not seen Hunger since my arrival—perhaps he had returned from whatever business had taken him away.

A woman crowned with fiery Titian hair emerged from the antechamber, flanked by a pair of praetherian guards. My uncle Pál scrambled in her wake. The samodiva queen.

I scanned the darkness around her, looking for the company I had last seen her with: Vasilisa, Zhivka, *Mátyás*. But no one else followed her.

My heart began to hammer. I grabbed Noémi's arm. "She's alone," I said. "Perhaps Mátyás escaped."

"Or perhaps he's being held elsewhere. Or he did not survive your rockslide. It would not be the first time you have killed my brother."

I cast her a sidelong glance, unable to read her tone. Was this some black humor? Or had she still not entirely forgiven me?

She went on, "That woman is one of the Four. She is more powerful than she looks, and commands near absolute loyalty here."

I looked at the samodiva queen again. *One of the Four.* I ticked them off on my fingers: Vasilisa, Hunger, the four-headed Count Svarog in the tsar's court, and now the samodiva. I knew who they all were now—perhaps Gábor and the Hungarian soldiers could use that knowledge.

Hunger fought free of the crowd to stand by the samodiva queen. He bent his dark head to hers, her red-gold hair a brilliant contrast to his. Pál inched nearer to them, as though he would make himself part of their conversation. Why was he here? What did he hope to gain from his alliance with the praetheria? If they won, they'd have little use for humans to help them rule. I glanced at Noémi, but she was not looking at Hunger. I could not tell if she was deliberately ignoring him or if she had not yet seen him. Her eyesight was still uncertain, and the dimness of the caves could not help.

Before we could approach them, the queen swept away, trailed by the two guards and Pál. Hunger caught sight of us and joined us, a slight smile on his lips. His golden eyes were unreadable.

"What news does the queen bring?" I asked.

"Some that would please you, some that would not." The smile broadened.

I pressed my lips together in vexation. Hunger still spoke in riddles.

"He won't tell you," Noémi said, her fingers tightening around my forearm. "Won't or can't, I'm not certain."

"Then tell me this: is Mátyás well?"

"Your cousin is alive."

Noémi's grip on my arm eased.

"Where is he?" I asked.

But Hunger only shook his head, a light glinting in his eyes that might have been amusement. "A word of warning before I go. The samodiva Zhivka died on her return to these caves, and her queen blames Mátyás. She was not granted retribution, and so she might seek vengeance against one or both of you. She has only just returned from other business, else I would have spoken sooner. I have told her she is not to touch you, but be wary."

He bowed again and then disappeared.

Zhivka was dead?

I had known Zhivka for only a few weeks, but I had liked her—liked her subtle wit and her bright smile. Even when she had betrayed us, I had not stopped liking *her*. She had put family above friends, but I found I could not fault her for that. Had not Mátyás and I done the same, when we went searching for Noémi instead of trying to fight a war?

It seemed impossible that she was dead.

Even more impossible that the samodiva queen held Mátyás responsible. I thought of how Zhivka had teased

Mátyás and how he grumbled at her but enjoyed her teasing all the same. He would not willingly have hurt her, not for all her treachery.

Noémi touched my arm lightly. "Anna? Are you all right?"

"I'm all right," I said, but the thought of Zhivka's death lingered with me, a disquiet ghost.

CHAPTER 11

Anna

For seven nights after the samodiva queen's return, the queen and her sisters occupied the largest of the caverns and danced.

They danced around a fire, their movements shaping the flame to mimic Zhivka's form: a lick of fire for her hair, a spurt of light where her smile would be. The song of their grieving echoed through the cavern and stole into the side chambers, imbuing the rock itself with sorrow.

For seven nights, everyone else in the caves—human and praetherian alike—was banned from the big cavern. We knew of their dancing only from their songs, from fragments shared by those who caught glimpses as they passed.

On the eighth night, everyone was invited to a vigil in Zhivka's honor, the last rite of remembrance before her spirit was bid a final farewell.

When Hunger told us of the vigil, I refused to attend. "The samodiva queen cannot want us there."

"This vigil—truly, more of a dance—is for Zhivka, not for the samodiva queen. Where you might offer a eulogy of words to the dead, the samodiva offer dance and fire. You do not have to participate in the dancing, but your absence would be seen as a dismissal of her death."

Hunger brought us gowns to wear, as neither of us had anything fitting a formal ceremony. The dress I had arrived in—Emilija's dress—had lost its claim to finery somewhere on the road to the cave. My new gown was black like night, shot through with threads of silver stars. Noémi's was a wash of gold and crimson, like fire-made-silk. I held my frock against me and remembered the last time I had let a praetherian dress me: Vasilisa had glamoured a gown and a mask for me to wear to the archduchess's masquerade, and everything had fallen to pieces.

I put on the dress, wondering as I did what price I would pay for this night's finery.

Musicians were already playing when we arrived, a haunting elegy that swirled around the stone pillars, that curled in my ears and twisted my heart. I paused at the entrance to the cave, my hand gripping Noémi's, and closed my eyes. The music caught me up, sweeping me back to the first time I had seen the Binding spell that had held the praetheria captive for a thousand years—a world so lovely that it hurt, even now, to think of it.

I should not be here.

For weeks after going into the Binding, I had yearned for it, like an opium addict kept from laudanum or pipes.

That yearning had been a bruise on my heart, a limb I had not known of until I lost it.

Standing at the entrance to the cave, that same yearning filled me, and I feared it. I was prisoner here, and the music put me in danger of forgetting that, of falling—again—for the hard-edged beauty of the praetheria. The first time I had been so seduced, I had broken the Binding. The second time, I had been betrayed. I could not let there be a third time.

And yet . . .

I moved into the stone chamber at Noémi's gentle tug. The samodiva were already dancing, a dozen or more women with hair like flames: a dozen shades of crimson and gold, even the pale blue of a candlewick. Sparks trailed from them as they danced, weaving in and around one another, brushing hands as they passed, a bright flame lighting at each touch. Each brightness flared against my heart—mourning for Zhivka, whom I had not known well, for something bigger than us both that passed just out of my reach.

Eventually, the samodiva broke apart and gathered onlookers into their dance. There was no distinct pattern, no steps that I could tease out, but there was a rhythm to the movement all the same. The samodiva continued to pass their sparks to their new partners, who held a flame like a star in their palms before the light guttered out.

A light extinguished, a soul snuffed.

After the onlookers passed through the samodiva, they began to dance with one another, swirling in and amongst the rock spires. A griffin stepped in time with a filmy-winged woman; a cockatrice danced with a tree-man; a faun danced with a melusine, her tresses still damp and trailing water on the floor.

Beauty and brutal strength blurred together as the music rose and fell. Where did one end and the other begin? The praetheria—most of them—were as dangerous as they were lovely. Was that danger part of their beauty? Or that beauty part of their danger?

I could not watch the praetheria dance and wish them dead, even if their survival meant the destruction of my world. No one watching the samodiva mourn their lost sister could doubt the depth of feeling driving them. I could not hear their music and hope to conspire against them. Surely there was room in our world for this realm splayed vivid and raw before me?

A praetherian bowed before us—a tall, willowy creature with skin like night and batlike wings. Murmuring something soft to Noémi, she drew her into the dance.

I stood alone, watching the spinning pairs, the faerie lights shining in my cousin's golden hair. Noémi passed from the bat-winged creature to a samodiva, and Noémi too held a bit of light in her hands before moving on. The inchoate longing I'd felt since entering the room grew, making my heart ache.

"Would you dance?" Hunger asked me.

A beat of hesitation—*Is this wise?*—and then I held my hand out. His touch was warm, not burning, but as he drew me into the whirl, the longing thickened in my throat until it might choke me. All the things I wanted but did not know how to reach for seemed to flicker before my eyes: I wanted the war to end bloodlessly, with everyone happy; I wanted this somber vigil in the caves to be nothing more than a dance. I wished my father were here, to tell me how to go on and so I could watch his scholar's eyes brighten with appreciation at this splendid room. I wanted to be spinning in Gábor's arms, not Hunger's, and face a future with no question more pressing than how we should spend our lives together.

Could a person die of wanting?

The music shifted as we whirled through the cavern—a roaring, burning beat that seemed to ignite the chamber. Illusory fire flickered between the dancers, stirred up by the energy of our tapping feet. The samodiva queen watched me, her face torn by grief.

Hunger held me close and turned us through the crowd, spinning me until the room seemed to spin with us. When we slowed, he reached up to tap the pulse at the base of my neck. "Your longings call loudly tonight."

"You bring out the worst in me."

A ghost of a smile crossed his lips. "I wish you would curb them. I can do nothing for them, and they will only bring you pain."

"I did not think you cared particularly for my pain."

"Because I make hard choices does not mean I feel nothing," he said, and my heart gave a curious little twist.

"Why do you persist in this war?" I asked.

"What other choice do we have? We will not be made prisoners again."

"That does not mean you have to slaughter us."

"Us?" Hunger peered closely at me, his golden eyes bright. "Which 'us' are you speaking of? The Austrians, who drove you from them with a death sentence? Your family, who does not seem to understand you? The Hungarians, who do not listen to you? Why are you so determined to take their part against us? They do not stand on moral high ground here."

Words tangled in my head, on my tongue. "Some of them are my family, my friends. Most of them are innocent. They should not suffer because those in power have made poor choices. I cannot believe there are no peaceful ways for your kind to live among us."

"Our kind," Hunger echoed, "as though we are something wholly different from you. We love, we laugh, we bleed, we die. We bear children, our hearts break. Most of us were innocent too, but that did not stop *your kind* from sentencing us all together. And you—*chimera*—what makes you human rather than praetherian? Not your double souls. Are you so certain, when the dust settles and your scientists finish drawing their charts, that you will not be labeled praetherian and damned with us?"

I stumbled over the uneven flooring, and Hunger caught my arms. This time his touch did burn, a heat that pulsed through my sleeves and into my very bones. Was he right? Did my double souls make me something other than human? Where was the line dividing human from praetherian? Did such a line exist, outside of an idea generated by humans who wanted to define themselves against something else, something other? The samodiva queen shared more in common with me than with the shrubby creature who had tried to bury me alive in Prater Park; I shared more with Hunger than I did with the Russian tsar.

When the song ended and Hunger bowed to me, my curtsy was perfunctory, my thoughts still tangled. Another praetherian asked me to dance, a courtly old man with rosy cheeks and a long white beard who might have been a human grandfather, were it not for his eyes, red irises rimmed in gold.

Pál found me next, and he pulled me rather stiffly into another movement of the dance. For all his sartorial neatness, Pál was an indifferent dancer.

"Vasilisa will be returning soon, to train you," he said.

I looked away from the amusement in his face, fixing my eyes on the fires flickering around the room. "Trained to do what?"

"To be chimera, my dear. To fight."

"I don't want to fight," I said, tugging free of his grip. The other dancers swept around us, the only still spot in the room.

At this, Pál laughed. "Of course you do not. I did not, either, when I was young. But I learned that only by embracing my gifts could I embrace my destiny. My fate leads me to splendid things, as will yours, if you do not resist it."

"Then why does Vasilisa come to teach me, and not you?"

He pursed his lips as though he had bitten into something sour. "The praetheria do not entirely trust me, though I have proved my worth many times over."

"I do not trust you, either." I walked off, shaking, and took refuge away from the crowd where I could catch my breath and find Noémi. I needed someone familiar, someone safe.

Catching sight of her across the cavern, I picked my way along the rim of the chamber, only to find that Noémi was not alone. Hunger was with her, his back toward me.

He held both her hands in his, and she did not pull away.

Something about their position, the way they held themselves separate but with their heads inclined toward each other, suggested I ought to retreat and give them space. But I could not seem to move my feet.

Hunger released one of Noémi's hands to cup her cheek as though she were a dandelion globe: something beautiful and ephemeral that might escape if he breathed too hard.

Her eyes flickered shut, and she leaned into his touch for the briefest moment before drawing away, recalled to herself.

"I cannot do this," she said.

"Cannot do what?" Hunger asked, his voice low and sweet enough to draw my own heart from me, and I was not the one he spoke to.

"I cannot care for you. Cannot . . ." She stopped.

"Cannot or will not?"

She lifted her shoulders. "Does it matter? You hold me here as a prisoner, to force my cousin—and perhaps my brother—to fight with you against people and places I love. How can you in good conscience ask me to love you against my own interests, against my own heart?"

"I have no good conscience," Hunger said, and Noémi's lips curved into a reluctant smile. "Do I disgust you, as a praetherian?"

Noémi straightened, her nose flaring in indignation. "You know little of me if you have to ask that."

"I know your heart. I know your inflexible honesty. You may be the only person—human or praetherian—who always dares speak truth to me. I find it quite charming."

Noémi looked away, but she could not hide the blush stealing into her cheeks. "You do not disgust me. But if you care for me at all, let me go. Let Anna go. Stop driving this war."

"That I cannot do. Not for you, not for all the world."

Noémi froze for a moment, pain flashing raw across her face. When she pulled free, Hunger did not follow her, but stood, stiff and straight, as the crowd swallowed her. I whirled and stumbled back the way I'd come.

My heart ached for Noémi. She had a gift for drawing suitors who loved her, but loved their own cause more. First William, now Hunger. There might be honor in putting principles above people—had not Gábor done the same?—but that did not make the pain of being sacrificed any less. At least with Gábor, I knew this sacrifice for a temporary one that would end with the war. Noémi had no such assurance.

I had lost my taste for the dance, which was likely to continue past dawn. Instead, I made my way back to our holding cell.

Noémi lay on her bedding, her face turned toward the rock. I hesitated for a moment, wanting to comfort her. But her posture suggested she wanted to be left alone, so I would honor that for now.

I sat on my own bedding and rifled through my bags, tugging out the well-worn pages Gábor had given me. I needed his words to ground me, to funnel my still-spinning emotions into known channels. New words were scratched across the sheet. His normally neat writing was cramped and uneven, witnessing some great agitation.

My dear Anna,

I scarce know what to write. My friends and fellow soldiers lie dead behind me.

So many, Anna. I cannot unsee them. Their voices echo in my ears.

We engaged the Austrians when we should not have—our position, backed against a forest where the Austrians could take cover, was not good. But Kossuth sent word to attack (though he is not a military strategist), so attack we did. Our soldiers were outmatched almost at once, flanked on all sides by the enemy. The soldiers we might have met. But Lucifera traveled with them, and the handful of Elementalists on our side, with their illusions and wind and storms, could not undo the Lucifera spells, which dropped boulders on our troops, deadlier than cannon fire, and which folded the ground around entire companies.

We are regrouping and making our way to safety as best we can. Most of us are on foot, and the weather is turning.

May God hold you more securely than He has me.

I read the letter again. Where was Gábor now? Was he injured? The cramped cave seemed to fill with the sights and sounds of the fighting outside Buda Castle, after I'd broken the Binding—the bitter tang of smoke and blood, the sharp cries of the wounded and the staccato of gunfire. I swallowed down bile.

I scrawled something in return, some wish for his safety and suitable expressions of horror. But my words were attenuated and thin. What were mere words in the face of devastation and grief? What were words when action was needed and I could do nothing?

If I had been there, instead of dancing with the praetheria, perhaps I could have broken some of the Lucifera spells that decimated his army. Perhaps I could have saved someone. When Mátyás and I had decided to follow Noémi instead of Kossuth's army, we—I—had put Noémi before Hungary, before Gábor. And that choice, like so many of my choices, had borne bitter fruit. Had I known then what I knew now, would I have made a different choice?

It was useless to speculate. I could not go back and undo the past, or my choices. The only way forward was to keep moving.

I closed my hands into fists and then relaxed them.

I loathed feeling trapped.

CHAPTER 12

Mátyás

The difference between a man and a rat may be the quality of their cages.

My current cage was particularly fine—the broad green expanse of the World Tree, caught between the vault of sky and the spreading plains—but I felt no less trapped than a rat in a laboratory.

It had been nearly a week since I had dream-walked in search of Noémi and discovered the trick of locating the praetheria by their glowing soul sparks—nearly a week in which I had failed to make any progress in finding her. Hadúr kept me so busy with training during the day that at night I collapsed into my bed, exhausted—too spent even to dream.

Was I a man or was I a mouse? I had come to Hadúr willingly enough, to learn what I could of being táltos. I had not bargained on trading away my freedom in the process. I was not an apprentice, with a contract to earn out. Neither was I a prisoner. But Hadúr insisted I was not yet ready to join the armies, and he gave me no leave during which to find Noémi.

The itching to act deepened, burrowing into my heart and sending roots rippling through my body. Surely, I'd learned enough by now.

"I need a drink," I told Hadúr, at the end of another endless strategy session.

"I've a very fine *pálinka*—" Hadúr began, but I cut him off.

"In a *csárda*," I said. "Where such alcohol is meant to be drunk. Not in a tree. Bahadır, are you coming?"

Bahadır looked startled. "I don't drink."

"I know that." There was a reason I'd never invited him drinking before. "But I could use the company." If I abandoned Hadúr, I could not also abandon Bahadır—at least, not without telling him why I was going. If he chose to stay, that was his business.

Hadúr must have caught something of my intention in my voice because he offered to come with us.

"The point of drinking in a *csárda* is to drink with ordinary men. If you come, you'll rather spoil the purpose. No offense meant."

"If you meant no offense, you would not forbid me to join you," Hadúr grumbled. "Go. I hope you give yourself a headache."

I grinned at him. Now that I'd made up my mind to leave, I found I'd rather miss Hadúr. His irascibility reminded me of my uncle János, though the war god was far more formidable.

Once Bahadır agreed to come, I launched myself out of the tree, shifting into crow form as I tumbled through the air, letting my clothes flutter to the ground around me. Bahadır followed more sedately, using a pulley system he'd rigged, a kind of cage attached to ropes and wheels that let him ferry himself up and down. I'd have rigged a pulley myself if the only alternative was being carried in Hadúr's arms as he leapt up and down from the tree. (Of course, I'd also have crashed to the ground and died, so perhaps it was as well I could fly.)

I was still collecting my scattered clothing when Bahadır reached the base of the tree. Luckily for both of us, he carried the coin purse, or I'd have been collecting coins too.

"I could have brought those for you," Bahadır said, fixing his gaze across the *puszta* and not on my semidressed person.

"I know," I said, finally locating my trousers caught on a bush some dozen yards distant. "But this was more fun."

"I think someone needs to explain to you what 'fun' means."

We walked to the nearest *csárda,* a mile or so distant. The small taproom was not much to look at: a packed-dirt floor, a soot-stained hearth, and broken windows stuffed with straw.

After the first drink, I bespoke a room from the owner of the *csárda,* and Bahadır looked at me.

"What are you doing?"

"Moving on. It's time. My sister is still missing, the Austrian army continues to encroach upon Hungary, and I do nothing—I whistle and twiddle my thumbs on the top of a tree."

"It's not nothing," Bahadır said. "You're preparing."

"I've done enough preparing. At some point, a man has to act."

"Or act too soon and prove himself a fool," Bahadır muttered into his tea. Lifting his eyes to mine, he asked, "Are you certain you are not running?"

The question stung. If I wished to run, I'd stay hidden in the World Tree. "Are you certain *you're* not? You have not faced your father's killers."

The blood drained from his face, leaving his brown skin chalky, his scar lurid across his cheek. My words had been a low blow, and I knew it, but I could not recall them.

"If I returned to Scutari, I would surely be killed, and there would be no one to help my mother and my sister." He set his teacup on the rather sticky surface of the table and stood. "At least I know what I am afraid of. Do you?"

He swept deftly through the crowd and out the door of the taproom into the soft darkness. I stared after him, wanting to call him back but finding the words sticking in my throat.

I took another swig of *sör,* but the taste had soured in my mouth. *Damn and blast.* So much for sleeping in the dubious comforts of the *csárda* while I dream-walked in search of Noémi. Bahadır would doubtless report back to Hadúr that I'd gone off, and I had no desire to be hauled back to the tree like a recalcitrant schoolboy.

Bahadır had, at least, left the coin purse for me. I paid our tab, then left. The air outside was crisp, carrying the hint of the coming winter. I'd overheard an old man in the bar claim that this winter would be long and fierce. I hoped he was wrong. The cold did not agree with my complexion.

Outside the village, I shifted to a crow again, stooping to pick up the coin purse with my beak but leaving the clothes pooled on the ground behind me. I'd need to purchase a horse—and new clothes—as soon as I could put distance between me and Hadúr.

The night was clear, and despite the weight of the purse dragging on my beak, I enjoyed flying, riding on the air currents and sweeping below the stars. I didn't have a clear destination—only *away*—but as the night wore on, it was clear that "away" meant back to familiar habitations, west across the *puszta* toward Buda-Pest. Below me, the farms and pastures and wild prairie slumbered.

A couple hours into my flight, my attention snagged on a mass of dark shapes below, lit by sporadic fires. Curiosity being one of my besetting sins, I dipped lower for a better look. The mass proved to be a camp full of soldiers bearing the yellow-and-black standard of the Austrian royal family, with the double-headed eagle snapping in a brisk wind.

I scrambled to make sense of their location *here,* well past Buda-Pest. Either the city had already fallen to Austrian soldiers or the soldiers pursued a different quarry. I knew from Hadúr's lectures that if Buda-Pest were in danger, the government would have to relocate—the most logical choice was Debrecen, across the plains from Buda-Pest, as the second-largest city in Hungary and easily accessible to Buda-Pest by the newly completed railway line from Vác.

Still considering, I circled over the camp. It did not seem to matter whether this army chased Kossuth and the rest of the rebel Hungarian government from Buda-Pest to Debrecen or was bent on some other errand. An Austrian army this deep into my homeland was no friend to me.

And I had an idea.

I found a promising farmhouse not far from the army's camp, landed lightly on the ground, and shifted. The farmhouse was abandoned—likely a temporary response to the army's proximity—and I found what I was searching for in one of the bedchambers: the skirt and blouse of a peasant woman, and a kerchief to tie over my hair. I shifted again, with a mental apology to Noémi, whose face I borrowed, and donned the clothes. I slipped on a pair of boots, adjusting my feet so the boots fit and did not rub, then walked toward the camp.

As I had anticipated, a pair of guards stopped me at the perimeter. "What do you want?"

I adopted what I hoped was a dulcet expression—something Noémi would never adopt herself—and said, in broadly accented German, "I should like to see the general. I've urgent news for him."

My plan was brilliant, if simple: distract the general and other ranking officers with a diversion, then set fire to the cannons and supply wagons, hobbling the army's forward momentum.

The older of the two soldiers, with a greying mustache, said, "General Windisch-Graetz is not to be disturbed by the likes of you, but I will carry a message."

I batted my eyelashes at him. "I'm sorry, but I must deliver the message direct to him."

The second soldier, a young brown-haired man with patchy sideburns, leered at me. "I've a notion what 'message' you wish to deliver. I'm off watch in an hour, if you'd rather deliver it to me."

Good lord, what a pig. I fought to keep the revulsion from my expression. Did Noémi face such comments? Then: had *I* delivered such comments to a woman? Let a crow pluck out my eyes if I ever did so again.

The older soldier cuffed him.

"Please, sir, it truly is urgent," I said, ignoring both the crude soldier and the turmoil his comment stirred up. "It concerns Kossuth Lajos."

"Kossuth, eh?" The older soldier looked interested. "I'll see if the general's adjutant is still awake. That's the best I can promise." He glared at the younger man. "Keep watch until I get back. If you mess this up, I'll feed you to the cook's mongrel dog."

As luck would have it, the adjutant was taking a dictated letter for General Windisch-Graetz, and I found myself ushered into a tent before the general himself: a tall, spare man with steel-grey hair. His eyes were piercing. "Yes?"

"I beg pardon for disturbing you," I said, dropping an awkward curtsy. The adjutant and a middle-aged woman, fiddling with something in her lap, both watched me attentively. "I thought you should know that Kossuth Lajos is at this moment not five miles from here, meeting with a Hungarian outlaw called the King of Crows. He means to offer the bandit pardon in exchange for his support of the war."

Those piercing eyes grew sharper at the mention of the King of Crows, as though he recognized the name. I fought down an irrational flicker of pride.

"How do you know this?" the general asked.

155

"My father helped arrange the meeting. He fancies himself a patriot, but I am loyal to the emperor."

The general inclined his head. "Then I thank you for your service. We will deal with this at once." He turned, not to the adjutant or the older soldier who had escorted me but to the middle-aged woman in the corner of the tent. "Frau Schreiber?"

The woman stood, smoothing her navy skirt. "He lies."

He? Fear stabbed through me. There was a crawling sensation in my head, as though an insect scuttled across my brain. Damn it, the woman must be a Coremancer. No one else would have seen through my shifting.

I braced myself to run, but the adjutant hissed something, shaking his fingers at me, and the ground beneath my feet was suddenly porous, sucking my boots in with a slurp.

Perfect. A Coremancer *and* a Lucifera. I'd landed myself thoroughly in the suds this time. *Here lies Eszterházy Mátyás: He had an idea.*

"Who is he?" the general asked, still watching the woman.

"A shifter—the form he wears is real, not a glamour."

"And is Kossuth, in fact, nearby?"

"No closer than we already knew him to be, fleeing on the railroad." The woman took a couple of steps nearer, peering at my face. "Interesting. About one thing he did not lie: the King of Crows was nearby. He stands here, in fact."

"The outlaw magician?" Windisch-Graetz asked.

I'd overstayed my welcome in this conversation: time to disappear and execute the second stage of my plan.

The Coremancer shouted, "He's shifting!" just as I began to change, and the adjutant shouted too, and a wave of earth came crashing over me, burying me in the soil beneath the camp.

The crow I'd been shifting to choked on the dirt, and I flailed useless wings against the ground. Another shift, and I wiggled through the dry soil as a plump, pinkish worm— *not* my favorite creature, but at least I could breathe and move freely. The coin purse I'd borrowed from Bahadır was buried in the ground beside me, but that was the least of my worries at present.

I had a few moments while they thought I was still trapped. If they meant to capture me and not simply kill me, they'd be retrieving me in a moment.

Casting my mind out, I found a brace of hunting owls nearby. I urged them closer to the camp, close enough to shift, and then the light, feathered bodies began changing. Through our mental link, I could sense the shifting from the owls' perspective: the pale brown wings hardened, taking on a scaly sheen. The broad heads narrowed, lengthening above their shoulders.

The first owl hooted in alarm, and a spritz of fire emerged. It tried to flee, and promptly careened into the other dragon.

I swore again. In my rush, I hadn't taken the time to calm the owls, to project my plan into their brains. Now, instead of foiling the Luminate magicians as I'd hoped, I'd have to exert all my attention to soothing two crazed owl-turned-dragons.

The second dragon crashed to the ground and emitted a

gout of flame, which tore through the camp, setting fire to tents and scattering soldiers and horses alike. Not the supply wagons I'd intended, but a decent distraction.

Only now, the camp was roused, alarm bells ringing and shouts filling the air. I tried to nudge the first dragon toward the supply wagons and the second toward the cannons, hoping to set them alight before the soldiers were organized, when my body went flying upward and I found myself suspended by a spell, limp and pink before the general.

The Lucifera adjutant had rallied.

"Let me crush him, sir," the adjutant said, "like the worm he is."

Whoops. I shifted again, launching myself through the air before my wings had finished forming.

But I'd misjudged the adjutant's spell, which held not only my worm self but my crow self fixed in the air. I felt as though I'd flung myself against a brick wall.

"Can you stop the shifting?" the general asked, a tightness to his voice the only sign of his annoyance. Despite myself, I was impressed: his camp was burning and his evening had doubtless not gone as intended, but he still did not raise his voice.

The crawling feeling in my brain was back, scuttling through my memories of shapeshifting, making the crow shape in my head fuzz and blur. In response, my crow self fuzzed and blurred, and I lost my hold on the owls, which, returning abruptly to their own forms, winged away as fast as they could.

"Who and what are you?" the general asked, ignoring

my nudity much better than the rather prim Coremancer, who would not look at me.

I didn't answer. I could tell him I was an Eszterházy, which would doubtless earn me better treatment in whatever passed for a camp prison—and possibly some clothes—but what was the point? I didn't intend to be prisoner long. The Coremancer couldn't stop me shifting indefinitely, though at present I had nearly reached my limit. Hunger clawed at my empty gut.

The general shook his head in disgust. "Take him away. Perhaps he'll feel more talkative tomorrow."

The Lucifera adjutant used his levitating spell to move me out of the tent. The cool night air pricked every exposed hair on my body. I wanted to rub my arms for warmth and cross my legs to cover myself, but I could not move: the adjutant had added an Immobility spell to the Levitation.

I was well and truly stuck—at least so long as his attention and his spell did not waver.

The burrowing hunger in my gut seemed to deepen, bringing a tug of longing. Miles away, I could feel the World Tree, its vague sentience sharpening to alertness at my attention. It called to me, whispering a shape to my mind, a beast out of fable to guard the heart of the tree.

No.

And perhaps it would have ended there—my will set against the tree's more inchoate nudging. But the adjutant, acting as though my presence was a personal affront to him, was not content to float me through the darkened camp. Instead, he had to draw attention to my humiliation, sparking Lumen lights along our path, calling to any soldiers he could see. He let the Levitation spell drop, so that my immobile body dragged and bumped across the cold ground.

As the gathering soldiers laughed and hooted, something in me snapped.

The shape I'd been fighting boiled up in me, swelled, and burst forth like a savage bloom.

CHAPTER 13

Mátyás

I came back to myself in fits and starts, like patterns seen beneath a guttering lamp.

First there was a memory of blood, of shouting and screams cut short with the satisfying crunch of bone.

Then flying, first as an enormous, sleek, multiheaded beast whose full stomach pointed to a satiation I could not bear to think of. Then as a crow, streaking across the *puszta.*

I woke sometime in midmorning, my head pillowed on my bare arms, drool pooling in the corners of my mouth. There was blood underneath my fingernails, and the memory of blood still coated my tongue. I was sick in a nearby bush, and then sat, spent, in the thin sunlight of late fall. I should have been cold, unclothed as I was, but the only thing I felt was a vast, crawling exhaustion.

What had I done?

I'd sworn I would not take the dragon form again—and yet in a moment of weakness, a burning flicker of shame, I'd given in to it.

If my initial, ill-conceived plan had not succeeded in impeding the army's movement, I had bloody well succeeded now.

So much blood.

I tried to tell myself I'd struck a blow for Hungary's independence. I tried to tell myself this was war and casualties were an inevitable side effect.

Anna had told me that her branch of the Eszterházy family was mostly Coremancers: that gift had clearly skipped me, because I was a terrible liar, particularly to myself.

I thought of Bahadır's final words in that squalid *csárda*. He'd accused me of running, of not knowing what I was afraid of.

He was wrong. I knew what I was afraid of.

This is what I was afraid of. Of destruction without redemption—of becoming monstrous like my father. There was no glory in the shambles he'd made of his life, of all our lives.

I'd always thought I was afraid of disappointing those around me, as my father had disappointed me. When the Lady first tasked me with using my táltos gifts to save Hungary, I had fled because I was afraid of disappointing her, of disappointing everyone who trusted me.

But what if it was more than that?

What if it was not failure that frightened me but success? Perhaps I hadn't left Hadúr's training because I thought I had learned enough; perhaps I had left because, deep down, I feared learning too much. After all, a small man can have only small failures. A powerful man will have powerful ones.

A táltos can leave half an army decimated in his wake, with no one to stand against him—not even himself.

Bahadır was not wrong about me running.

In the searing light of this new realization, I saw the shape of my past differently. I'd spent so much time running. I'd run from my father's death, hiding my grief in games and drink and pretty girls. I'd run from the Lady's offer to train me, fearing that my power would make me a monster. I'd even run from Kossuth and the war, looking for Noémi instead. I wasn't wrong to put Noémi first, but I had done so to avoid a different responsibility.

I didn't want to keep running.

Not from the war.

Not from myself.

Running hadn't saved me—and it sure as hell had not saved the army I'd left ravaged behind me. Running hadn't even let me find Noémi.

With this new filter, I saw that my father's death was not a disappointment because he failed but a disappointment because he ran from his challenges—his bankruptcy—instead of facing them.

Only once in my life had I stood my ground: when Anna entered the Binding and I had agreed to die to destroy a spell. I'd died in fire and pain—*but I had also been glorious.*

Maybe it was time to stand again.

On that victorious note, I pushed myself to my feet—and promptly stumbled over a half-buried root and collapsed to the ground again. I gave up on standing—literally, not metaphorically—and shifted back to crow form.

My wingbeats were steady and sure, slicing through the air above the *puszta* as I made my way back to the World Tree.

※

Hadúr did not seem particularly surprised to see me again, which rather spoiled the effect of my triumphal return. Bahadır said only, "I'm glad you're back."

"No more running," I said.

Hadúr summoned us both to his tactical room, where colored swaths of soldiers still sprawled across the maps of the regions. I wondered if his diagrams had shown him anything of my slaughter of Windisch-Graetz's army. I would never know, because Hadúr drew the story out of me as surely as a fisherman with his rod. At the end of it, Bahadır looked grave, but Hadúr only grunted.

"You were a fool to take on an army alone, táltos. That dragon of yours can be a powerful protection to this country, to the World Tree, but only if used well. If unchecked, that hunger will drive a monster that cannot ever be fed."

I didn't say anything. What could I say? I had been a fool.

"But your story tells me a couple of important things. First, I have been unjust to keep you from searching for your sister. The needs of the war compel me until I have a hard time seeing beyond that: I forget the urgency of individual human needs. So, we will do better.

"Second, we have neglected some aspects of your training: among them, protecting your mind from Coremancers and other magicians." Then he clapped his hands, and nothing more was said about my rogue behavior.

And yet, after that, the texture of the training changed. Perhaps it was that Hadúr granted us both a little more autonomy in what we studied, even soliciting our feedback. Or that he wove tactics for finding Noémi into our routine. In any case, those new trainings left me feeling more a colleague than a mere student.

Hadúr taught both of us to guard against Coremancer attacks by building our mental control: envisioning a wall around our thoughts and letting nothing escape. "Coremancer art thrives on weak regulation of thoughts and emotions," he said. Not surprisingly, Bahadır was better at this than I was.

When I'd begun to exhibit a little more control, Hadúr taught me how to walk into dreams.

"Dream walkers of old possessed two different skills: sending their spirit abroad in the physical world, and sending their spirit into the dreams of others. With the first skill, your spirit moves through an environment you already know. Walking in dreams is both easier and harder: easier, because you do not have to travel so far, but harder, as dreamscapes can be unfamiliar and dangerous. Far more táltos walkers have lost themselves in dreams than in the physical realm."

That did not sound particularly promising.

Hádur tapped his fingers together, a surprisingly refined gesture for a man of his bulk. "In the first form of dream-walking, you send your spirit into the physical realm while you are in a trance—not a true sleep. In the second form, you send your spirit into dreams while you sleep truly, retaining only enough control of your dreaming mind to recognize that you dream, and to step outside it.

"All dreams exist in a world apart from our physical world, one that coexists with it but does not map perfectly across it. As you step out of your own dream, you should be able to see the dreams of others swirling around you as bits of mist that solidify as a sleeper dreams. I am not a dream walker, so I do not perfectly understand the practice, only the theory."

He took a sip of brandy from his glass, then wiped his hand across his mouth. "You might have more luck finding your sister in this fashion: I am told that the dreams of familiar souls appear brighter to the dream walker."

In the days since I had returned, I had tried several times to find Noémi by sending my spirit abroad, but I had seen no sign of the praetherian soul sparks. I'd finally concluded I was looking in the wrong places, or the brightness of Hadúr and the grey ladies had something to do with the World Tree, not praetheria in particular.

Hadúr had me practice by giving both myself and Bahadır sleeping drafts. Before swallowing his, Bahadır gave me a sidelong look and muttered, "Am I a miserable friend if I hope you fail at this? I'd rather not have you stomping through my dreams."

I grinned at him. "That's only because your imagination falls short of the splendor of dreaming of me."

"Oh, I can imagine that just fine," Bahadır said. "It's only that I prefer sweet dreams to nightmares."

Then Hadúr made us drink drafts—I think to shut us up. Falling asleep was easy; dreaming, easier still. But it was not until I was halfway through a pleasurable dream of cards, where every hand I touched came up lucky, and gold spilled across the table, that I remembered I had a task other than sleeping.

Step outside the dream. My first effort involved my dream self high-stepping like a dancer who had lost his cue. I decided perhaps I was trying too hard and let my consciousness drift.

And then I was outside my own dream, floating in a featureless grey space, with bits of mist strewn around me, just as Hadúr had said. I didn't see anything particularly bright that might be Bahadır, so I snagged the mist nearest me, and found myself, in an eyeblink, in another dream.

I didn't know the dreamer or the landscape of the dream—a reddish desert where the sand swirled into impossible monoliths and cathedrals of wind and dust. The dreamer trudged across the sand, oblivious to the wonders taking shape around him. There was nothing in the dream to keep me, so I attempted to drift out, as I had from my own dream.

But drifting out didn't work, so I trailed the dreamer across the sands until a powerful gust swept us both into the sky and the dreamer awoke with a start. Finding myself back in the grey lands again, I pinched myself awake.

This dream-walking would take some practice.

※

Hadúr found us at breakfast a couple of mornings later. "There's something you should see." Following him to the strategy room, we saw that the colored armies of Hungary's enemies had shifted: the yellow armies of Austria spread across the plains and cut down from the northern mountains in a wide swath of gold. The red Russian armies came in from the east to meet them, with Dragović's blue Croatian soldiers still holding the south-central part of Hungary.

In the southeast, where Hungarian white had been holding her own against Romanian purple, a new influx of Russian red covered the region. A smattering of Ottoman soldiers (green) showed up for the first time—worried, Hadúr explained, by the Russian presence.

Bahadır fingered one of the Ottoman pieces but said nothing. I suspected he thought of his mother and sister, at home in Scutari.

"The war is intensifying." Hadúr picked up a white Hungarian piece and set it down on a point perhaps 60 kilometers northwest of us. "And the Hungarian armies are not unified: Kossuth has appointed a Polish general, Dembiński, to lead the armies instead of General Görgey, a move that has not endeared Kossuth or Dembiński to the troops. Dembiński is moving the armies toward Eger, hoping to draw the fighting away from Buda-Pest and Debrecen, where the government has re-formed."

I stared at the map, at the sea of colors. Everywhere, Hungary was surrounded, only the barest scattering of Ottoman green indicating possible allies.

"It's time," Hadúr said. "Hungary needs us."

X

Hadúr, Bahadır, and I set off on horseback the next day, following the silver ribbon of the Tarna as it flowed out of the north. My mount was even-tempered enough, but I missed Holdas, my ugly white horse, who had disappeared when Vasilisa captured me. We passed by a handful of military camps and small villages interspersed with forest before we spotted the spires of Eger in the distance: a pair of towers fronting the yellow dome of the basilica; another pair of church towers just off the main square. Rising above all this was the castle where Hungarian forces famously withstood a vastly superior Turkish army in the sixteenth century.

Rumors followed us, whispers that the Austrian army was not far behind.

Though Eger was not a large city, it took us some time canvassing soldiers in the town square before someone could direct us to Dembiński, currently visiting a clergyman in a well-appointed house near the basilica.

The manservant who opened the door did not seem inclined to let us in—and I'll grant the sight of Hadúr in full copper battle armor was alarming. After I discreetly passed him a few coins, he became much friendlier, even sending for a servant to hold our horses. Casting one last, uncertain look at Hadúr, he admitted us to the house and went to check if Dembiński would see us.

Dembiński came out, wiping his mouth on a napkin. We'd interrupted his lunch.

"What is it? It had better be important." His eyes

caught on Hadúr and traveled slowly up the copper armor, lingering for a beat on the spreading ash tree engraved on the chestplate. "Who the devil are you, sir?"

"Hadúr." The glint in the war god's eyes might have caused a lesser mortal to quail, but Henryk Dembiński was clearly made of sterner stuff. Or perhaps, being Polish-born and -bred, he simply didn't recognize the Hungarian war god.

"I suppose you've come to enlist?"

"I've brought a táltos," Hadúr said, and Dembiński's demeanor shifted. Where he had been irritable and bored, he grew intent.

"Eszterházy Mátyás," I said as Dembiński stared at me. His gaze swept Bahadır. "And the rest of you?"

Amusement curling his lips, Hadúr said, "I've some military training."

"Bahadır Beyzadi," Bahadır said. "My father was a military man."

"We could use trained recruits," Dembiński said. "The soldiers Kossuth sends me are raw as new-hatched chicks."

He led us back to the dining room. If the clergyman hosting Dembiński seemed put out at the sudden enlargement of the party, he said nothing, only beckoned for new places to be laid. The second man at the table, with his neatly trimmed facial hair and round eyeglasses, was Görgey Artúr—the general who was to have led the army before Dembiński showed up. I wondered if he resented his rival.

Unlike Dembiński, Görgey clearly recognized Hadúr's name, though his expression suggested he believed Hadúr to be an imposter laying claim to the god's name rather than the actual god.

Like Dembiński, however, he was interested in me.

"Táltos, eh? What can you do?" Görgey asked.

"Shapeshifting, animal persuasion, some dream-walking," I said.

"And when you are in the dream state, can you hear what is said around you?"

I nodded.

Görgey sat back in his seat, eyes shining. "But this is excellent! Coming by good intelligence in this campaign has been my Achilles' heel. Either the riders I send out do not return or they return with information that is outdated by the time they arrive. Or worse, wrong altogether."

The talk moved more generally to strategies for the upcoming campaign, and I applied myself to my lunch, falling into a pleasant food haze—from which I was rudely pulled by a soldier darting into the room and announcing that fighting had been reported at Verpelét, some eight miles distant.

"Impossible!" Dembiński said. "The Austrians cannot have reached us so soon. It is too soon!"

"But there is cannon fire. I heard it myself," the soldier said.

"Only some distant thunder," Dembiński insisted.

Görgey sprang up and dashed to the window: the skies outside were clear. He flung open the window, and the sound came, undeniable. Cannon fire.

"Damn and blast," Görgey muttered.

"It is too soon!" Dembiński repeated, looking vexed, as

171

if someone had just spoiled the surprise of a party he had planned. Standing up, he asked for a carriage to be brought round at once.

The clergyman looked uncomfortable. "I'm sorry, sir, but I have no carriage to offer you. No horses, either, those being conscripted for army use."

Dembiński whirled around to Görgey. "How came you here? By some vehicle, yes?"

"Yes," Görgey said. "But—"

"Have it sent for," Dembiński said, over the top of Görgey's objection.

When the "vehicle" was drawn up before the front steps, I understood Görgey's hesitation. He and his chief of staff had traveled to Eger in a hay cart, pulled by a sluggish old mount.

Dembiński eyed the cart, still piled full of hay, with revulsion. "I am commander in chief of the armies of Hungary. I cannot arrive at the battle in that. I will wait for a more suitable carriage to be found."

Görgey said, "That might be hours. Meanwhile, your men need you."

"You can borrow my horse," Bahadır said as the servant approached with our horses.

"Ah. Excellent," Dembiński said, selecting Hadúr's horse, and missing entirely Hadúr's grim expression.

I don't know why Hadúr did not simply overrule Dembiński: perhaps he was still taking the measure of the man. In any case, Hadúr took his seat beside the cart's driver, who looked at him with terror, leaving Bahadır and Görgey's chief of staff to settle into the hay.

The two generals mounted, I followed suit, and we cantered along the road to Verpelét. Dembiński continued to bemoan the early arrival of the Austrian troops. The decisive offense he had planned would be ruined entirely by early action.

Görgey curled his lip at Dembiński's ongoing complaints, though he took care not to let Dembiński see it. Sidling close to me, he said, "This state is the moral agony of a braggart, who, having pretended to be a strong swimmer, is now seized with mortal fear lest he should be drowned, because the water into which he has ventured happens to reach up to his neck."

I don't know if Dembiński heard Görgey, or only marked his attitude, but he stiffened and said, "I came to Hungary entrusted with the supreme command over all the Hungarian troops. I have met you with kindness, because I know that it must mortify a Hungarian to serve under a non-Hungarian. But you reproach me for my orders, instead of obeying them!"

Görgey stiffened in turn. "I obey every order that serves the interest of my country."

The two fell into an uneasy silence after that. While I was glad of the quiet, I could not help thinking: *With such men as allies, we make our enemies' job easier.*

At length, we came to a group of standard bearers holding aloft the tripartite flag of Hungary—red, white, and green.

Dembiński pulled up. "Is the battle ahead?" He nodded down the road.

One of the men shook his head. "Not here. In Kápolna."

After some frustrated hemming and hawing, Dembiński opted to follow the road to Kápolna. But when Görgey and I made to follow, he stopped us. "No. Go south; make sure the troops there hold their position along the river and keep the Austrians from advancing."

Görgey thinned his lips at the command but turned his horse without a word.

It was dark by the time we reached the banks of the Tarna River. The army was still in position, so Görgey delivered his message to hold their place, and we returned to Kápolna under cover of darkness. All told, the journey had taken upwards of three hours—a singular waste of time for a general to carry a message that any foot soldier could have done, that *I* might have delivered in crow form in a fraction of the time.

What was Dembiński playing at?

When we finally found him, he was asleep in a farmhouse he had commandeered. The hay cart had arrived at the farmhouse too: Hadúr was studying maps near a low-burning fire and casting derisive looks at the sleeping general. It was Hadúr who told us that Bahadır and Görgey's chief of staff had been dispatched with orders for outlying army corps.

"I'd best be off," Görgey said. "I'd hoped for further word from Dembiński, but my troops can't wait." He glanced at me. "Will you undertake to ride to Richard Guyon's troops and have them advance as soon as may be possible?"

It was sometime past midnight, and I yearned to curl up in a corner of the room and sleep, but I had asked to be part of this. "Richard Guyon?"

"An English gentleman, of a French family," Görgey said, as though a foreign nobleman fighting for Hungarian independence were an everyday thing. I thought of General Dembiński's Polish blood—and my friend William, who was Polish-Scottish. Perhaps it was.

I debated carrying the message as a crow or riding on horseback. As the distance was not far, I decided it was better to arrive fully clothed than have to scavenge clothes, and so I mounted up once more.

When I reached the camp, it was quiet, with only a pair of sentries awake to mark our arrival.

I slid down from my horse, stumbling a little in my haste. "I'm here to see Guyon."

"Colonel Guyon is asleep," the sentry answered.

"Then wake him," I said. "I've urgent dispatches from General Görgey."

The sentry saluted, and I followed him through the camp. I had the disquieting sense of walking through a graveyard, the pale canvas tents as tombs, the sleeping bodies as corpses not yet buried.

The sentry ducked into a large tent near the center of the camp. A moment later, a young man emerged, already dressed, though it was not yet dawn. The ink smudges on his fingers suggested he'd been writing.

"Gábor!" The exhaustion of the late night vanished, burned away by the surprised joy at seeing my friend.

I held out my hand, and Gábor clasped it firmly. "Mátyás! How came you here?"

"Bearing dispatches for Colonel Guyon," I said.

"Have you found Noémi?"

"Not yet—but I've come to realize the war cannot wait until I find her."

"She's with Anna," Gábor said. "In a cave somewhere in the mountains, held by the praetheria."

Surprise, joy, relief, and alarm washed through me, tangling in an uneasy mixture. I'd forgotten about the letters Anna wrote Gábor. "Are they all right?"

He looked grave. "As well as can be expected, when they're held prisoner."

A second man emerged from the tent, yawning and rubbing at his dark beard. Gábor introduced us, and I relayed my message.

"Advance?" Richard Guyon echoed. "You'd best go rouse the men, Kovács. And have fortification sent around. The men will need it." He retreated back into the tent.

Gábor sighed. I cast him a sharp look. "Fortification?"

"Liquor—whatever we have most to hand. Guyon is a firm believer in the value of a stiff drink for bringing up courage."

"Does it work?"

Gábor's lips quirked with what might have been a smile. "They certainly seem less frightened, if not more agile."

I smothered a laugh—and then, as memory slammed into me of students drinking in Café Pilvax just prior to our aborted revolution, any urge to laugh died. Some of these men might not see another sunrise. Let them have their drink.

I trailed behind Gábor, watching him set a wave of men rippling out to wake others.

The sun began to rise, the faintest hint of grey in a black

sky. A good chunk of the camp still lay dreaming, undisturbed by the growing commotion around them. I thought of Görgey's admonition to advance as soon as possible.

This was taking too long. In the forested area along the fringes of the camp, I could hear songbirds. *Perfect.* A few nudges, and a host of songbirds descended upon the camp. They made an ungodly chorus: tweets and chirps and fractured songs. Muffled—and not so muffled—swearing was soon added to the mix. The camp was stirring now, fully awake. I sent the songbirds away with a mental thank-you.

I might have saved myself the effort: an hour later, the camp still had not budged. Soldiers were grooming horses, mending uniforms, and taking down tents. But Guyon had not reemerged to take charge, to order the men to line up and begin marching. What was the man doing—preparing for a dance with a debutante at a ball?

The sun was up now, the sky a pale blue with a golden horizon.

"Shouldn't we be moving already?" I asked Gábor.

He shrugged. "Guyon is a good man, but he will not be rushed."

I thought of Dembiński and Görgey, facing the Austrians at dawn. Would an hour make a difference? Perhaps two? How long did it take for the tide of a battle to turn? Despite a lifetime of being fed heroic battle stories, my ignorance was daunting. And the slowness was like an itch I could not reach: so much hung on this war, and yet Colonel Guyon could not be bothered to drive his men in response to an urgent summons; Generals Görgey and Dembiński squabbled with one another and with Kossuth;

everywhere was inefficiency and disorder. How were we supposed to defeat the Austrians, much less the praetheria in turn?

At last Guyon emerged, his hair neatly combed and his beard newly trimmed, and the troops began to gather: infantry in lines, the cavalry mounting up.

This was my cue. "I'd best get back," I said. "I'll look for you when this is over."

Gábor reached out to clasp my hand, his fingers sure around mine. This was not his first battle. "May God keep you safe."

CHAPTER 14

Anna

It was difficult to track the passing days inside the caves, where the light was always steady and the temperature always cool. It had been early fall when I came to the caves; the mountain leaves were just starting to turn when the Russian soldiers gave me to the praetheria.

A few mornings after Zhivka's vigil, Hunger brought some of the last fall leaves turning on the mountain: a handful of reds, golds, and burnished bronze.

"I thought you might like the colors," he said, handing them to Noémi.

"How can you do this?" I asked. "How can you be kind to us and yet keep us prisoner?"

He shrugged, his gold eyes glinting in the dim light. "I do little enough. Your work will be easier if you do not hate us."

I wanted to say, *I do hate you.* But the words wouldn't

come. They would not be true, in any case. I feared what the praetheria could do, but I could not hate them, not after swirling through the measures of that dance, the sheer beauty of the praetheria catching my heart with tiny hooks that would not release me. In Vienna, I had seen the praetheria in shades and gradations, just as I did the humans around me. Hunger's betrayal of me had wiped all that away, a wash of shadow that colored everything I thought I knew. But now I was seeing those shades again: the giantess whom Noémi and I often encountered with her children, who always had a kind word for us and whose laughing children were even taller than me. A tiny, gnomelike creature who knew my weakness for sweets and smuggled us bits of honey or sugared breads whenever he passed our way. A young man with golden hair and a blazing smile—a sun deity before the Binding spell had drained much of his strength—who pulled tiny stars out of the air and left them littered behind himself like bread crumbs in a fable, and who had given us a handful of such stars to brighten our cell.

And Hunger, bringing us leaves from the mountain because he knew of Noémi's fondness for pretty things. I resented those leaves, because they cracked the defenses my careful, practical cousin had built around herself. Noémi deserved true happiness, not the false cheer of a bit of brightness, delivered with a smile.

In his letters, Gábor urged me to try and escape, to bring the Hungarian army the precise location of the praetheria. He had been recalled from Perczel's army and sent by Kossuth to join General Görgey's troops in the north, to report on Görgey, whom Kossuth did not entirely trust. But I could no longer see the praetheria simply as an enemy to be fought. Some of them would feed gladly on the turmoil and bloodshed their war stirred up. But most wanted only to find a place in a world that had little use for them.

The praetheria had brought me here as a weapon, something they hoped to turn against the human armies, against my own family and friends. I was not willing to be a weapon, and I was finding myself increasingly unwilling to be a spy, either. The details I provided in my letters to Gábor shifted from descriptions of the caves and estimates of the number of praetheria to stories about the praetheria as individuals.

How could I choose human or praetherian when each side held part of my heart and choosing would mean setting my heart against itself? I could as soon set my dual chimera souls against themselves.

So I did nothing, chose nothing, and stayed in the caves, suspended in indecision.

On bleak days, I asked myself why it mattered. This was not my war. I was no soldier; I had no gifts or allies powerful enough to shift the future. Noémi taught me a Hungarian proverb once: *Egy fecske nem csinál nyarat.* One swallow does not make a summer: one person alone cannot change things. What I did or did not do would change nothing.

On those days, it was tempting to stay in the caves, where my needs for food were met, where I did not have to make hard decisions. And the longer I stayed, the more insidious and seductive the feeling grew. Perhaps this is how mortals like Tam Lin were lost in faerieland. What began with a trap ended as a willing imprisonment—a gentler cage than whatever choices faced them in the real world.

But I could not stay motionless forever. Not choosing was still a choice—and one I was increasingly unwilling to make.

〉〈

Noémi set her winning hand at whist on the floor of our room with a small crow of triumph—and the cards caught fire as soon as they touched stone.

Both of us scrambled to our feet, Noémi patting at a scorch mark on her skirt where one of the cards had landed.

Laughter rippled out behind us, causing us both to whirl around.

"Most excellent," Vasilisa said, her smile wide. "I do like that lurch of fear."

I smoothed out the scowl forming on my brow. "What do you want?" I had not seen her in all my weeks in the cavern, and I had begun to think that Pál was mistaken (or malicious) when he threatened me with her training.

"So hostile," Vasilisa said. "And I came only to see how you are getting on."

"I'm fine. Where is Mátyás?"

"The táltos boy? He's safe."

"That isn't what Anna asked," Noémi said, drawing close to my side.

"Isn't it? It's what she meant, though."

"Is he here?" When Vasilisa's smug cat-smile only deepened, I clarified, "In these caves?"

"Not in these caves, no. But near to hand."

Her answers were maddeningly ambiguous. I could not tell if she meant he had escaped or was being held somewhere nearby.

"If you've come only to annoy us, please leave."

She tutted at me. "I'm afraid I cannot do that. I've been charged with making something useful out of you."

Charged by whom? Pál had brought me here, but I could not tell what role he played in the praetherian plots. From his servile attention to the praetheria, he seemed more commandee than commander in these caves, but I could not imagine he would be content to remain in that role forever.

"I've no intention of fighting for you."

"You were eager enough once."

Witness, Vasilisa had told me that spring, and I had done so—revealing the mistreatment of the praetheria to the entire Congress and spilling my own guarded secret (that I had broken the Binding) in the process.

"That was before you betrayed me, before you threatened the people and places I loved."

"As your kind has threatened mine?"

I looked away from her fierce glare. "I will not be a weapon," I said, but more quietly.

"You already have been," Vasilisa said. "And will be again. The only question is for whom—and whether you will do so willingly." She reached out a delicate hand and set it on Noémi's shoulder. Noémi went rigid, sucking her breath in, as though in pain. "Such a curious paradox, don't you think? That humans are at once so powerful and so fragile. So vulnerable."

Her hand slid around Noémi's throat, and the blood drained from my cousin's face.

"Let her go," I said, bracing myself to pry her hand away if necessary.

Vasilisa did not move. "There are ways to persuade you to help us that go beyond words. Your love for others makes you weak—your sister, your cousins, that Romani boy. Each of those is a weakness we will exploit, if we must. This is not a civilized war, played between lordlings who recognize a truce and send their troops forth only in daylight. We fight to survive, and we will use whatever means we can."

She released Noémi, and while the color returned to Noémi's cheeks, my heart sank. I had delayed too long, and my indecision would now cost us both. Until we could find a way out of the caves, I would have to play along.

"All right," I said, gripping my hands together. "What must I do?"

"Practice," Vasilisa said. "You've so much potential, and yet you keep it locked up like a miser."

The words she gave me the first time we met circled around my head. *What you could be, Anna Arden, if you were not afraid!*

She was not wrong. I *was* afraid. I had broken the Binding spell because it had seemed to be the right thing, but I had not anticipated the changes it would bring in its wake. How could it be right for one person—for me—to hold so much responsibility? How could I trust myself not to abuse my gift? How could I trust myself to see beyond the immediately personal choices that called to my heart, to know what damage I might unleash?

It was safer to be small.

"And what am I supposed to practice?"

"Breaking spells, for a start," Vasilisa said. "You still do not cast spells reliably. And there are other things you might do." She picked up a singed card from the floor. "Creation itself is a kind of spell. All living things at their heart are held together by soul stuff, which is the source of magic. Even this card is a result of making—a kind of magic—creating something new where it did not exist before. And what can be made can be unmade."

She held the burnt card out to me, and I took it. "See if you can feel that bit of creation in the paper."

I meant to feign following her directives, but with the flimsy card in my hand I grew curious. *Was* there some spark, even in this small bit of paper? I sent my inner sight out cautiously, as though the card might catch fire again between my fingers.

Nothing.

Vasilisa gave off the faint bone-buzzing I'd come to associate with spells, but the card gave me nothing. Neither did Noémi, who had retreated to her pallet.

"Perhaps it was too much to hope that you could sense it," Vasilisa said. "Your human senses are so often confined by what you believe to be true, rather than what is true. Try this instead: imagine that the card is a spell and attempt to break it."

Would Vasilisa know if I only pretended to break the spell?

I closed my eyes, but did nothing, and a moment later, fire surged up my arm. When my eyes flew open, I found Vasilisa pinching the skin at my elbow, the slight prickle of her spell following in the wake of the pain.

"Do not toy with me. I have not the patience for it. I'll stake your cousin out on the top of the mountain and leave her for the vultures to find."

Taking a deep breath to steady myself, I thought of papermaking: grinding down wood to fibers to make pulp, pressing the pulp into fine pages. I closed my eyes and pictured that transformation as a spell nestled inside the card, the almost invisible net of magical lines woven together. I imagined pinching those threads, just as I might a real spell.

A faint pressure built between my fingertips, and I opened my eyes just as Noémi gasped. The card I held had crumbled, a few fibers caught between my fingers, the rest in a pile at my feet.

I dropped the fibers I held and wiped my fingers on my skirt, as if they were somehow filthy. My heart pounded in my throat. There had to be some other explanation for what had just happened—Vasilisa's fire had not quite gone out, and poking at the card with my mind had caused it to disintegrate.

Because the other possibility—that I had somehow *unmade* the card, somehow undone the process that created it—was unthinkable.

My temples began to throb, prelude to one of the headaches that inevitably followed spell-breaking.

Vasilisa crouched, ran her finger through the bit of dust, then stuck it in her mouth. When she straightened, she was smiling. "Good," she purred. "Most excellent."

She left us both staring, dismayed, at the pile of fibers on the floor before Noémi thought to sweep the debris aside.

)(

Some days later, Noémi and I were prowling through the caverns when a commotion in a side chamber drew our attention. I was distracted, watching for Vasilisa so I might avoid her, and would not have noticed the crowd had I not seen Hunger racing toward the praetheria, his golden eyes blazing with something that might have been fury. Or fear.

"Let me through!" he said, and the crowd parted for him. I grasped Noémi's arm and pulled her behind him.

A small clearing in the center of the rocky chamber held a pair of praetheria. One was dark-haired, with brown bat wings folded behind him and two sand-colored curving horns springing from his forehead like a ram's. His mus-cled chest gleamed in the dim light. Beside him, coming scarcely to his waist, crouched a second praetherian, who looked the way I imagined the Greek god Pan, with furred legs and a curling crop of hair. A cloak of bark and leaves clung to him, giving a rather shrublike impression. He seemed oddly familiar, though I did not remember having seen him in the caves before.

In front of both praetheria was a soldier, sunk to his waist in solid rock, still wearing the high plumed shako hat favored by most of the military orders. He wept a little.

Noémi's grip tightened on my arm. "Anna," she whispered, "is that—?"

"Shh." I remembered, with sickening clarity, the shrublike praetherian who had tried to suck me into the ground at Prater Park in Vienna. Was this the same creature? He did not look the same—the bark that now covered only his cloak had then covered all his limbs—but his appearance might have been illusion, like nearly everything else that night.

"Chernobog," Hunger said, and the horned praetherian looked away from the soldier. "You were told not to attract human attention yet."

The praetherian's lip curled. "And who shall miss one soldier in wartime? Soldiers disappear all the time. You cannot keep us confined to these caves for weeks without offering some entertainment."

Electricity sparked in the air between them, some challenge that I could not quite decipher. Hunger's lips tightened. Then, on a long exhale, he said, "Don't make a habit of it."

Hunger turned, nearly bowling Noémi and me over. His face changed, shifting from resigned to grim. He put one arm around each of us, shepherding us out of the chamber. "Come away," he said. "You do not want to see this."

And as the soldier's cries became screams, then abruptly cut off, I pictured the rock closing over the soldier's head as he struggled to breathe. I pulled out of Hunger's grip to be sick behind a cluster of stones.

Noémi's cheeks were wet when I rejoined them.

"How could you allow that?" she asked.

Hunger's face went blank. "I am not a master of these folk. I lead, but they follow willingly or not at all. If I command too much now, when there is nowhere to lead, I might lose them altogether when I must lead."

I tried to parse his words. Did this mean the praetheria were not so unified as I had first supposed?

"Lead them where?" Noémi was asking. "Against human soldiers? Against our friends? You have a choice, as much as the next creature. You do not have to fight this war."

Hunger studied her face for a long moment. His eyes seemed sad. "I have made my choice." He bowed abruptly, then walked away, leaving us to make our way back to our room in silence.

I thought of Borbála, telling Marina she would always choose her. I wanted that for Noémi—someone to wipe out the memories of everyone who had chosen something else instead of her: her father, who had shot himself; Mátyás, who had died in the Binding spell for me and then stayed in the *puszta* instead of finding her when he was reborn; William, who loved his revolution. I, who had failed her so completely that she had run from Vienna with Hunger.

And Hunger.

Had we not been surrounded by praetheria who would have stopped me, I would have run after Hunger and scratched his pretty face with my bare hands for adding wounds to the invisible scars Noémi already bore.

Since I couldn't hurt him, I watched Noémi instead. But there was nothing in her carefully blank gaze to read.

I woke that night to stillness, the quiet broken only by Noémi's soft breathing and a faint dripping somewhere, the endless stream of mineral-laced water that produced the vast stone sculptures of the caverns.

Something was missing.

It took me a moment to identify it, but when I did, I sat bolt upright: the low murmur of voices between the praetheria who guarded us.

"Noémi," I said, just as a brilliant flare lit the opening of our small chamber, a hungry flame licking up the curtain Noémi had hung. Ash rained down on the stone floor.

The samodiva queen stood just beyond the disintegrating curtain, fire dancing up and down her arms.

I rubbed the prickling gooseflesh on my own arms beneath my nightdress. Hunger had warned us to be wary, but nothing had come of his warnings and I had forgotten them. Too late now. Across the room, Noémi sat up with a gasp.

"My sister is dead," the queen said, "and her death is still unanswered. You are blood kin to the man who killed her."

"My brother is not a killer," Noémi said.

I spoke at the same time, my words crossing Noémi's. "Mátyás wouldn't have killed Zhivka, not deliberately."

"He set bees on us, unprovoked, and she died from the stings."

"Oh," Noémi said, her healer's mind moving more rapidly than mine to grasp the implications. In a much smaller voice: "Oh. I am so sorry. That is a terrible way to die."

"Surely it was an accident," I said. "Why must her death be answered?"

I did not see the hand moving before a thin whip of fire lashed across my cheek.

"I will ask the questions. You are prisoner here, not me."

I rubbed the burning welt on my cheek. There must be something that would satisfy the queen short of our deaths.

"Hunger will not be pleased if you kill us," Noémi said.

This seemed to give the samodiva queen pause. She frowned, her beautiful mouth pinched. "It is true the spell breaker might still be useful. But you are his full sister, and it might be better for Hunger were you gone. His attachment to you is a weakness we cannot afford."

The queen's body lit as though she were flame, and she advanced on Noémi. I cast out my inner sense, searching for the source of the fire, but the samodiva queen cast no spell—the fire was simply an extension of herself.

She shot a blast at Noémi, who rolled off her bed to the stone floor. Her bedroll ignited behind her.

I screamed, scrambling to put myself between the two of them.

The queen tossed a second volley of flame, but a barrier of ice flashed up between Noémi and the fire. The ice turned, sizzling, into steam, and the fire died.

"Stop!" my uncle said, his voice commanding. "These two are my kin. If you kill them, I will challenge you myself."

The queen let her fire fizzle out. "I cannot let my sister's death go unanswered."

Pál opened his hands, revealing two palms full of honeybees. "A sting for a sting," he said. "Pain for pain."

The samodiva hesitated. It was not what she wanted—
I could see as much in her eyes—but she seemed reluctant
to cross Pál. Again, I wondered precisely how my uncle fit
among the Four. "All right."

Pál lifted his hands, and the bees flew toward us. The
first one reached me, stinging almost at once: a hot dagger
slash across my cheek. The others settled on me, dozens of
featherlight legs followed by burning points tattooed over
my body. Noémi cried out. I must have done the same, but
I didn't notice: the pain stitching across my skin blotted
out everything else.

It is a sad truth of bees that when they leave their stinger
behind, they die. When the tiny bodies had fallen to
the ground, the samodiva queen gave a short nod before
swinging around, her white skirts trailing behind her as
she left us.

Noémi gasped, rubbing her hands over the angry welts
across her skin. My arms were bubbled and red.

Pál twitched his hands, and the bee corpses disappeared,
along with the stinging spots across my body, although the
pain lingered.

"How—?" Noémi began.

"Illusion," I said.

Pál bowed. "I could have driven her away, but she would
have come back. This way she finds herself answered, and
she might leave you alone. However, you should not forget
that you are prisoners here, not guests, and this makes you
vulnerable." He cast me a sly glance, his oddly pale eyes
gleaming. "Or you can swear allegiance to me, and I will
keep you safe."

Gooseflesh rose on my skin. I knew—more or less—what the praetherian aims were. But Pál was a mystery to me, opaque and dangerous. "No," I said.

"Very well," he said, pleasantly enough. "But remember: you are not safe here."

CHAPTER 15

Anna

The day following our confrontation with the samodiva queen, Vasilisa inspected the bare rings drilled into rock where the curtain to our cell had hung, then looked at me. "I am sorry you were disturbed last night. Some of us," she said, her voice dripping disdain, "allow personal feelings to compromise our larger goal."

I wondered if she meant Hunger as well.

Vasilisa drew me into the corridor to practice breaking spells. She cast a few halfhearted spells at me that I broke easily, but when she asked me to unmake a ring she'd brought, I could not do it. The ring remained a stubborn, immutable circle of gold in my palm.

"You are too much in your head," she said. "You think too much of what will happen, and then nothing does."

"I don't want to unmake anything."

"But you will, because this is your fate and you cannot outrun that. Sooner or later, it will claim you."

I don't believe in fate, I thought. We made our own fate through our choices. But I said nothing, and Vasilisa swept away, grumbling to herself.

)(

I wrote to Gábor of my sessions with Vasilisa and of Hunger bringing leaves to Noémi. *I don't know what to make of it all. I wish I could see what larger vision their actions fit.*

Gábor wrote back that evening.

> *I do not have to be a Coremancer to read Hunger's actions: he admires Noémi. Vasilisa's goals are less clear. Learn what you can from her, but be careful. The praetheria are not our friends, however charming they might be.*
>
> ~~*Though I do not think you need to study to unmake things—you unmake me every time we speak.*~~
>
> *Sorry. That sounded better in my head. I meant to give you a compliment, to defuse the strength of my imperatives. I don't mean to tell you what to do, only support you.*
>
> *Let me try again.*
>
> ~~*The curve of your smile is sharper than a winter wind.*~~
>
> *Not that. You are neither frigid nor sharp.*

The ink broke off with a jagged edge and a smeared line, and then, in a different hand: *Like a well-tuned violin, you bring forth sweet music under a master's touch.* The line had been crossed through with a heavier hand than the previous ones, and I had to hold the paper to the light to read it.

When the meaning penetrated, my whole face ignited with heat.

My apologies. One of my Romani fellows mistook my frowning expression as a plea for aid. Perhaps: You might break a thousand spells and a thousand hearts, but you cannot break me—I am already in pieces before you.
It's fortunate for me that I'm a better soldier and scientist than poet, though rather unfortunate for you.

I laughed, as I suspected Gábor had meant for me to do with his increasingly absurd compliments. He continued, more seriously:

I wrote last time that Kossuth had sent me to the Army of the Danube to watch General Görgey. I think Görgey may have his own suspicions of Kossuth, and of me, because he has sent me to assist General Richard Guyon instead. You'd like Guyon, not least because he's an Englishman. We're off to stop the Austrians from advancing through the northern mountains and claiming the mines. I mean to watch for the praetheria as we travel: with any luck, I'll find you as well. I miss you. Go with God and in good health.

I read the letter twice, then a third time. I tapped the paper, the words of the Vanishing spell on my lips. But I didn't speak them. Gábor's lightheartedness warmed me like a charm in winter, and I was reluctant to erase it. In England, I had counted laughter cheap: something to fill hours of boredom. I knew better now. Laughter kept the darkness at bay. Some days, it was all we had.

I kept the letter. I might need that laughter again.

)(

"A challenge! A challenge!" The words seemed to ricochet through the winding chambers of the caves, carried by hundreds—thousands—of praetherian voices. Underneath and around the German and Hungarian that I understood were dozens of other echoes, some languages I recognized and others I did not.

I set down the book I was reading and looked at Noémi. "Should we investigate?"

She shook her head. "What if it's another soldier?"

I swallowed hard at the memory of the boy in the shako hat, entombed beneath the cavern floor. Noémi and I had avoided that branch of the cave ever since.

I picked up my book again, but the words blurred together. The chanting was growing louder, more insistent. Whatever this was, it was bigger than the soldier.

I put the book down and stood up. "I can't ignore this. What if it's something that might affect us?"

Noémi sighed and slipped a long needle back into a fabric sleeve. "Your curiosity is going to get us both killed someday."

I grinned at her with a lightness I did not feel and slid my arm through hers. "Or perhaps it will save us."

We followed the chanting to its source, in one of the larger caverns with a roughly level floor. Praetheria were clustered all around the edges, clinging precariously to stone icicles, perched on top of rocky mounds, the larger praetheria lifting the smaller ones for a better view.

I could see nothing but a sea of heads and backs, which meant that Noémi, who was both shorter and had poorer vision, saw even less.

I tapped the arm of a praetherian near me, a tree-creature with green barklike skin and curling antlers who stood several heads taller than me. "What is going on?"

"A challenge," the creature rumbled, eyes fixed forward.

"For what? Between whom?"

At my new questions, the creature looked down at me, warm brown eyes widening. "You are not one of us."

There were a few humans aside from Noémi and me among the praetheria, but not many. Most of the others had come as romantic partners to the praetheria. A few, like Pál, sought whatever influence they could find. "No," I agreed.

"We have not had a challenge since long before the Binding broke, when the Four won their places at our head by defeating all comers."

"Who is challenged?" Noémi asked, her voice suddenly taut with worry, her arm tense against mine.

"The samodiva queen," the tree-creature said, and Noémi relaxed, almost imperceptibly. "Here," the creature said, sweeping us both up and setting one on each shoulder. I steadied myself, one hand grasping an antler, and the creature rumbled. Was that laughter?

Now we could see the floor before us, a tightly ringed opening where two praetheria faced one another: the samodiva queen burned bright—I could feel the waves of warmth radiating from her even at this distance—but her flames obscured her opponent. Hunger and Vasilisa stood at the edge of the ring. The last member of the Four, Count Svarog, was not present. I supposed he must still be with the Russian tsar. Pál stood near Vasilisa, a pleased smirk on his face.

"Chernobog," Hunger said in a loud voice that carried through the room, "state your challenge."

The challenger shifted position, and I could see him more clearly: the horned praetherian who had buried the soldier in rock.

"The queen has proved herself weak and unfit to be one of the Four: she let a valuable resource escape, as grief for one of her sisters compromised her."

Was he talking about Mátyás? But if he had escaped, then why was Vasilisa not also at fault? I glanced from the samodiva queen to Vasilisa and guessed that Chernobog deemed the queen the weaker of the two.

"Grief is not a weakness," Hunger said. "We have all grieved for the praetheria hounded and hunted by our enemies."

"If we are to attain our former glory, we cannot afford such grief," Chernobog said. "And it is my right as a member of this company to challenge the queen."

"You understand that if you lose this challenge and survive, you will be cast from us," Vasilisa said.

"I am not afraid."

Hunger turned to the samodiva queen. "Zhena, do you accept this challenge?"

I'd never heard anyone say her name before.

"I accept." The queen's voice rang clear and bright and unafraid.

The creature beneath us murmured, "The queen has not been challenged in a very long time, and she has used much of her strength mourning her sister. I think she will find this battle much harder than she expects."

"Then begin," Hunger said.

The ring around the queen and Chernobog widened as the spectators moved back to give them space. Chernobog billowed upward, his physical body growing even as a pair of softly furred bat wings unfolded from his back. The samodiva queen stood her ground, but the fire wreathing her seemed to brighten. A ripple of desire swept through the audience, a craving so dizzying that I nearly fell from my perch and only the steady hand of the creature below me kept me upright. The circle around the contestants tightened again as the praetheria pressed forward, drawn closer to the samodiva queen.

Chernobog laughed. "Your glamours may work on humans and weaker folk, but they do not touch me."

The glamour vanished. I had not even recognized it as a spell until it was gone: I felt as though someone had doused me with cold water. My body, which had been flush and warm, was now chilled and empty.

A ring of fire sprang up around Chernobog, high enough to mask all but the tips of his horns. He laughed again. "I am the king of hell demons. Do you think a little fire will daunt me?"

He vaulted through the flames, a clawlike hand extended

before him to grasp the samodiva's throat. He thrust her backward, the crowd parting before them, to slam her body against a stalagmite nearly as wide as she was. She clawed at his fingers, her flame rising white-hot around her. A few of the praetheria nearest her fell to the ground, overcome by the heat. But though Chernobog flinched, he did not release her.

The samodiva kicked at him, filmy wings sprouting from her back and batting furiously at the air. Chernobog ignored her blows and pushed her back against the rock, her feet and legs seeming to melt into the stone.

No. I knew how this ended.

Flames soared around the samodiva, heat so intense that I flinched away. Every bit of water from the room seemed to evaporate, leaving the air like sawdust in my lungs. Beside me, Noémi coughed.

Chernobog roared: this heat touched even him. His wings unfurled, stirring a great wind through the caverns, but the flames only swirled higher. I thought for a moment he would release her: the scent of cooked flesh filled the air where the samodiva's fire seared his skin. But he just grunted and pushed deeper, and the flames were slowly extinguished. The samodiva queen was buried in the rock, only a fragile bit of wing dangling from the stone.

For a long beat, nothing happened. The room was still, everyone's attention focused on the rock where the samodiva was buried. Bright lines like lightning splayed out from the center, and then the stone burst, crumbling like a pot left too long in a kiln.

The samodiva queen was blazing with rage, and the

wave of heat radiating from her knocked the assembled praetheria back a pace.

She shot a fireball at Chernobog, who sprang upward, the sweep of his wings sending air gusting around the cavern. He broke a spear of rock from the ceiling and hurled it down at the queen, who dodged and flung herself up to join him in the air, her filmy wings gleaming like sunlight.

A second volley of rock caught the queen on the shoulder and crumpled one of her fragile wings. She tumbled down, landing with a sickening crunch on the stone floor below. Someone cried out.

Before she could rise, Chernobog had landed beside her, a great taloned foot lashing out to stomp on her throat. He reached down and wrenched her head to one side. The accompanying crack resounded through the chamber.

Chernobog lifted his foot away and scooped up the queen's body. He rose into the air with her limp form dangling from his grip like a small, fading star. The samodiva's radiant fire trailed away, unfocused and lost, dissipating into smoke.

The samodiva queen—Zhena—was dead.

She had seemed so powerful, threatening us in our room. And fearless as she demanded restitution for Zhivka's death. How could someone with that much fire and life die so casually, her neck snapped as though she were a defenseless child?

The samodiva queen had driven Zhivka to betray us, but she had not been without compassion, to judge from her care for her sisters and her grief over Zhivka. Chernobog, who tormented soldiers for entertainment, had none. If he took his place among the Four, they would never relent.

Chernobog descended from the cloud of smoke like an Old Testament god, reeking of brimstone. The samodiva queen still hung from his hands, but all her brightness had gone out. He flung her corpse at the feet of Hunger and Vasilisa, and a dismayed murmur from the crowd broke out at his blatant disrespect.

"I told you," he said. "Weak."

If Hunger was troubled by this turn of events, his calm face showed nothing of it. "Your challenge was successful. Welcome to the Four." With a murmured word to Vasilisa, he lifted the broken body of the queen and walked from the room. Vasilisa, Pál, and the praetheria nearest Chernobog clustered around the horned god, presumably to congratulate him on his win.

The tree-creature set us both on the floor. He accepted our thanks with a sad nod, and we fled the chamber.

Back in our room, we were silent for a long time, lying on our beds and staring at the rock ceiling. Again, I thought of the sheer weight resting quiescent above us, the layered earth that could crush us in a moment.

At last, Noémi spoke. "I told you I felt we ought to stay, that there was something I was called to do or observe in these caves. That feeling has vanished. Maybe I only imagined it—I don't know. But I do not think we can safely stay here any longer."

"No," I agreed. "We need to get out."

And then what?

The praetheria would certainly attack, particularly with Chernobog goading the Four. My weeks in the cave had given me some idea of the scope of the battle facing the human armies—it would be far larger and far deadlier than any of us had suspected. I had already told Gábor some of this, and he would have passed word on to Kossuth. If we got free, we should have to warn the Austrian and Russian armies as best we could. The human armies could hope to face the praetheria only if they stopped fighting each other.

And yet, for a hale human army to face a prepared praetherian army seemed like a recipe for disaster—a battle where no one won and everyone lost. Emilija told me that a good soldier fought not for the sake of fighting but to end the fighting. I did not want to win a war but to end one.

But how?

In the last months I had been hungry, hunted, cast out from everything I knew. My ego had been stripped bare, and I saw myself for what I was: a rash, foolish girl who had believed she was more important than she was. A girl like that had nothing to offer a world at war.

One swallow could not make a summer.

And yet . . .

Perhaps it didn't matter whether *I* could do something or not. Perhaps what mattered was the trying. Before he left for war, Gábor had told me, "I might die whether I choose to fight or not, and I would prefer an active death."

I might achieve nothing. But I had rather try and fail than not try at all. Vasilisa and Pál seemed to think I had some worth as a weapon—enough that Vasilisa had hunted me, that Pál had intrigued to catch me. Even if I could not (yet) see how breaking spells might help me end a war, I would try. One swallow could not make a summer; one soldier could not win a war. But a dozen soldiers acting together might turn the tide of a battle.

Alone, I could do little enough. But I would not be alone.

Together, with my friends, we might achieve something that mattered.

We just had to escape first.

CHAPTER 16

Anna

After Chernobog's defeat of the samodiva queen, the atmosphere in the caverns shifted. The praetheria who had been kind to Noémi and me began to avoid us, as if our presence made them uncomfortable. The giantess no longer spoke to us, though she might acknowledge us with a terse nod. Those who had been indifferent took to "accidentally" jostling us as we passed or laying snares for us, and more than once Noémi and I found ourselves in a tangle of bruised knees and wounded dignity, sprawled on the cavern floor. Hunger was the only praetherian who appeared to seek us out. Even Vasilisa stayed away for a few days.

"Perhaps," Hunger said, coming upon us after one such tumble, "you ought to stay closer to your room. Or wait for me or Pál to come with you."

"That's kind of you." Noémi's blush belied the dignity in her tone. "But we do not need your escort."

"No," Hunger agreed, reaching down to help her rise. "But you might find it more comfortable. You might even enjoy my company."

He did not release his grip on Noémi's hands once she was standing, and her blush deepened. She mumbled something, and Hunger, his eyes brightening with delight, said, "I quite understand if you find me too much. You would not be the first woman overwhelmed by my manifest charms."

This outrageous statement seemed to restore Noémi. "Oh, do go away," she said crossly.

Hunger laughed and let her go.

Our prowls through the caverns were not random: we were looking for possible escape routes. But beyond the unexplored depths of the caves where no one went, there appeared to be only one exit. It was always well guarded, and we were never alone. If Hunger or Pál did not trail us, a guard did.

Vasilisa found us on one of these rambles. Chernobog lurked behind her, horns casting pointed shadows across us. The few nearby praetheria, after a swift glance at the pair, found urgent business elsewhere.

Vasilisa flicked her gaze at Noémi. "Miss Eszterházy, you are not needed. I suggest you return to your room."

With a murmured apology to me, Noémi disappeared. Vasilisa led Chernobog and me to a smaller chamber nearby, empty of praetheria though rich with configurations of stone. I bristled at her assumption that I should simply follow her—but really, what choice did I have?

Perfunctorily, she had me demonstrate my basic skill,

tossing a spell at me that I broke—if not easily, then at least competently enough.

"Is that all?" Chernobog asked. "For all the trouble you went through to acquire the girl, I expected something more."

"She can unmake things too, though she is unfortunately blocked at the moment. We are working on it."

"And time? Can she unmake the past as well?"

Vasilisa's eyebrows shot up, though she masked her surprise quickly. "I was not aware that was a chimera gift."

He grunted. "Was speculated as such. The only chimera I met did not live long enough to attempt it."

I was not sure which part of his statement was more alarming: that chimera could unmake the past or that the only chimera in his company had not lived long.

Chernobog watched as Vasilisa ran me through a few more tests: a painful spell that set every nerve in my body screeching until I snapped its source; an ice-bear illusion I shattered only after the bear knocked me to the ground; a net that tightened around me before I unraveled it.

Chernobog broke off a club of stone longer than his arm and held it out to me. "Unmake this."

"I can't unmake stone," I protested. The rock was not fabricated, as the card had been.

He passed the stone from one hand to another, running one finger along a trail of water. As though he had plucked my thoughts from my mind, he said, "But this is not the original shape of the stone: millennia have gone into its formation, drop by drop. What can be made can also be unmade." He pointed it at me as though it were a saber. "Try."

My shadow self rumbled uneasily. I had shifted the stones beneath the foundations of Schönbrunn and had set an avalanche to block the entrance to the ice caves. I had not *unmade* the rock, precisely, but I had broken it down, had loosed the bonds that held the particles of stone together.

I took the rock from Chernobog, equal parts repelled and drawn by the prospect of unmaking. *Could* I do it? Should I do it? The questions seemed two entirely different things.

I set my fingertips on the end of the stone lance and closed my eyes. I could not sense anything to indicate a spell, no buzzing, no frisson along my bones. I tried, as I had with the avalanche, to picture the minerals in the stone loosening their bonds, but the slight shudder beneath my fingers might have been imagined.

My head began to pound.

"Try harder," Chernobog instructed.

A weight settled across me, like a fine misting of rain. My eyes flashed open. Chernobog had not moved, but his shadow flowed toward me, cloaking me, spreading tendrils around my throat. My shadow self uncoiled and spread, liquid and hot, through my body, burning at each point across my skin where it met Chernobog's darkness.

"Chernobog . . . ," Vasilisa said, a note of warning in her voice.

"You coddle the girl too much," he said.

I tried to draw back, but his shadow followed me. Worse even than the burning where his shadow touched me was the sense that the shadow had somehow crossed the barrier of my skin and was spreading, like ink in water, through my doubled souls. My more ordinary soul shriveled, drawing back before the creeping darkness of Chernobog's reach, and the shadow soul swelled into ascendancy.

She had been ascendant before, in times of high emotional tension, including when I broke the Binding—but she had always been part of me, rooted in my core. But this boiling power was not me.

If I reached out now, the stone lance would crumble. But what else might unravel with it? My soul?

Months before, in Vienna, Vasilisa had told me I could cast spells only if I would join my souls. I could not allow Chernobog's pollution to spread further: he was driving my souls apart, engorging one and starving the other.

I closed my eyes again, concentrating not on that encroaching shadow but on my two souls: there was a quietness at the very center of my mind, away from the turmoil rocketing through my body. I clung to it, dragging my consciousness of my souls with me.

My souls were not separate from me: they were me. When I breathed, I did not provide air to just one; when I slept at night, my souls slept too. It was only my mind that kept interfering, kept dragging up my double-souled chimera self as if I might forget I was monstrous if not reminded. What had Vasilisa told me? That I was too much in my head?

I took a long breath and let my mind ride on the inhale and exhale. I pushed deeper, trying not to think, trying only to feel that calm. In that center, I held my two souls, and instead of smashing them together, instead of severing them, I embraced them both.

A wave of warmth washed over me, a bone-deep sureness.

"Lumen," I whispered, casting one of the few spells I knew. But I directed the light not to the chamber around me but toward the darkness inside of me.

Chernobog's shadow pulled away so quickly that it left a burning line to mark its passing. Chernobog cursed, and I opened my eyes to find him snarling. Or perhaps grinning? His lips pulled back around his teeth, but I could not read the expression in his eyes.

Stars spangled on the edge of my vision in time with my pulse. I inhaled.

His arm shot forward, his fingers curling around my throat, as he'd done to the samodiva queen. Before I could exhale, he had propelled both of us across the room, slamming me against the wall and knocking the wind from me.

His eyes were cold and flat. Did he mean to kill me? Surely Vasilisa would not let it go so far.

My head pounded, joined now by throbbing aches all through my back. Chernobog's shadow wrapped around me again, joining his fingers at my throat.

I couldn't breathe. My vision, already sparkly, began to fuzz at the edges and darken.

The rock behind me began to soften and melt as he pushed, my shoulders pressing into stone.

I remembered how he had tried to bury the samodiva queen in rock, how he had smothered a soldier in stone, and my body flushed with ice.

His fingers loosened as the rock swallowed my ears, then

my cheeks. My legs, kicking wildly, were still outthrust before me.

"Unmake this," he whispered, pulling his hand free. The words rumbled through the stone around my ears. I caught a wild, desperate breath as the rock closed over me.

There was a small pocket of air before my face, but it was not enough. Already the blood felt heavy and sluggish in my veins.

The darkness inside the stone was absolute.

I could not move.

How long would it take for me to die?

Don't panic, I thought. *Too late,* I thought.

I didn't know how to unmake rock.

But maybe I could break it.

With my inner sense, I sought out the fissures in the rock, the nearly invisible seams crisscrossing the layers of stone. The rock had not always existed in this form: some of it had been grains of sand, compressed to stone over the years. Crystals had formed in pockets.

"Be yourself," I whispered. Not an unmaking but a making of sorts—a return to its original form. The rock around me began to crumble an infinitesimal bit, and I could move my fingers.

This tiny success spurred me onward. I nudged my souls together, driving them toward the fissures I'd widened. I didn't know a spell for cracking rock, and I was no Lucifera in any case. But Vasilisa had told me once that spells were not necessary if the will was strong enough, and I had nothing now but will.

"Break," I whispered, and a crack like cannon fire

boomed around me. The wall of rock erupted. I tumbled backward, landing on my rear in another chamber of the cavern, to the immense surprise of the praetheria gathered there. I scrambled to my feet and dusted off my skirt, trying to control the trembling in my hands.

The pain thundering through my head was almost blinding.

"Anna?" my uncle asked, rising from his seat at a table where a game of cards was in process. "What on earth are you doing?"

"Chernobog put me in the wall," I said, as though that explained everything. Perhaps it did.

Pál frowned. "You would be wiser to humor the Four, child."

I started to shake my head, stopping when the pain only intensified. "I could not do what he wanted." But I had done what I needed.

His frown deepened. "Then you had best pray, child. Because if they do not find you useful, they will not keep you here. And they cannot afford to let you go."

The agony in my head reached an exquisite pitch. I stopped caring what the Four might do to me. If they killed me, at least my head would stop aching.

"The Four can go to hell," I said, taking a sliver of pleasure from the shock on Pál's face. "I am going to my bed."

X

I slept for hours, a blessedly dreamless sleep, and woke to an empty room. My bag lay open in the center of the floor.

213

For a moment, I blinked at it, uncomprehending. Then I scrambled from my bed, jarring my knees against the rock floor as I dug through the bag.

Gábor's letters—both spelled sheets of paper—were gone. What had he written last? Something about heading to the northern passes to head off the Austrian army and protect the mines. And I had not erased the letter because I wanted to remember the part that made me laugh.

Nausea rolled through me. I wanted to weep. The praetheria knew where Gábor and the Hungarian soldiers were heading. They knew I had means of writing the soldiers. What else might they know?

Noémi ducked back into the room. "You're awake!" She registered the look in my eyes and dropped to the ground beside me. "What's wrong?"

"Gábor's letters are gone. Along with the last message he sent me."

Noémi knew as well as I what that meant.

"Oh, Anna." She reached a hand toward me, then let it fall. "Hunger told me what happened with Chernobog. I have never seen him so angry."

"Were you with him just now? When someone snuck into our room and stole my letters?"

Her blue eyes narrowed. "Don't blame me—your keeping the letters made them dangerous, not my absence. Are you in pain? I can lighten some of the bruises."

My entire body ached, including my head, though the worst of that had subsided with my rest. But I was not about to let Noémi heal me. I deserved to feel some pain for my own stupidity.

214

"I'm fine." I stood up, wincing at the movement.

Noémi put her arm around me, her own irritation forgotten as her healer's instincts kicked in. "You're not fine. Someone put you in solid rock."

"I'm a fool."

I was worse than a fool. I'd put Gábor in danger—and I'd proved Chernobog right. *Unmake this.* Chernobog's voice echoed in my head. He'd pushed me into the wall to goad me into action, and I'd acted. I had not unmade the rock, not precisely, but what I had done was destructive magic all the same. What kind of chaos could such unmaking unleash on the battlefield? Breaking spells alone had made me monstrous, had given me a gift and a responsibility beyond what I trusted myself to bear. If there was more to being chimera than spell-breaking, what might I become in following those gifts?

Terror curdled in my heart. It did not bear thinking of.

"Anna, look at me," Noémi said. "Whatever they hope to make of you, that does not have to define you."

She put her arm around me, and I curled into her, laying my head on her shoulder, comforted by her warmth and her pragmatism. Only a few people could look at me as she had just then, as though they could see all of me and did not flinch from it but loved me still. Gábor had that same gift.

What you could be, Anna Arden, if you were not afraid.

I had promised myself I would try to end the war. Making myself small, flinching from my powers because I did not like who they made me, would not help me—would not help any of us.

If my friends could see what was monstrous in me and still love me, still believe in me, I could do no less.

"We cannot stay here," I said.

"I know," she said, smoothing my hair. "I know."

)(

Our particular stretch of the caverns was often deserted, indifferent praetheria deterred by the presence of the guards. But word must have spread of the strange human girl who fell through walls, because a steady parade of praetheria streamed past our cell that morning. Eventually, Noémi and I gave up attending to them and turned to our own pursuits. If we were boring enough, they would lose interest.

Most of the praetheria slowed outside our room but did not stop. Midmorning the next day, a pair of praetheria stopped and stood staring at us. I did not look up from my book, though I read the same line three times without comprehending.

"Anna?" one said at last, and I looked up.

The lidérc grinned back at me.

I sprang up and would have hugged her, save a last-minute awareness that the guards—two Valkyries this time—were watching and might wonder at the unaccustomed familiarity. I looked closely at the lidérc's companion, which was not easy: her edges blurred a bit, and my eyes wanted to move over her without stopping. A glamour, I realized, and once I knew that, I could see the girl beneath the spell: a sturdy girl with two brown braids and a red-lined mantle.

"Emilija?" I kept my voice low. "How did you come here?"

She made a face. "It was some time before we realized you were no longer at the palace, and longer than that before we discovered what had happened to you."

"It was the new emperor who told us you were gone," the lidérc said. "A week or so after his coronation, he came to ask if we knew where you were, as he knew we had come with you to the city."

His mother had not told him. I huffed a short laugh. Somehow, I was not surprised. Franz Joseph would not have been party to the trade that had been arranged between Her Royal Highness and the Russian court. "What did you think had happened to me, when I did not return?"

The two women exchanged a look, and I wondered at this new friendship. Emilija and the lidérc had scarcely known each other when I left them in Vienna. Yet they had come all this way together. For me.

"We thought you were busy with the new emperor, enjoying the luxuries of the palace," Emilija said. I read beneath her polite words: *We thought you had forgotten us.*

"I didn't forget you," I said. "I had no choice."

"We know that *now*," the lidérc said. "Which is a lucky thing for you."

"The Russian delegation was not hard to track," Emilija said, "once we knew to look for them. But after they passed the fortress at Komárom, they disappeared."

"Magic," the lidérc said.

Emilija shot her another look. "Anyway, it was some time before the lidérc could find a praetherian who knew of this place and could give us directions. She glamoured me, and here we are."

"Your timing is excellent," I said. "We need your help to get out of the caves." If they could sneak in, they could sneak us out.

"We supposed as much," Emilija said. "If you could get out, you'd have done so already."

"The sooner, the better," the lidérc said, shivering.

I raised my eyebrows in question. I'd not thought the lidérc afraid of anything.

"A human mob cornered me in a cave once. And instead of coming in to flush me out themselves, they sent an Elementalist to flood the cave, to wash me out."

I pictured the horror of water rising all around me, pressing me against stone walls. "How terrifying. We'll leave as soon as we can."

⋈

We waited until dawn, when most of the praetheria slept. The guards who had taken up their watch a couple hours earlier had been drawn away by the lidérc's magic before Emilija came to fetch us.

"Come quickly," she said.

Noémi and I were already dressed, and we brought nothing with us—our missing things would give warning sooner than our absence from our room. Gábor's letters were the only things it pained me to leave, but the lidérc had searched for them the day before, using her glamour to gain access to private chambers denied to Noémi and me, and had turned up nothing. I could only pray that Gábor wrote nothing incriminating, and that he would stop writing when I did not reply.

I hoped he would not pay for my carelessness.

I hoped he would forgive me my forced silence.

I glanced down the empty corridor. Some distance away, a light pulsed like a star. Even though I knew what it was—a projection of glamour, like the one the lidérc had used to draw away the satyr—it still tugged at me. Noémi took an unwitting step toward it, and I pulled her back. "It's only the lidérc."

We crept down the silent passageway. At the branching of a pair of caverns, Emilija pulled us into a crevice. Our movement dislodged a few bats, which dove low over us before flying off, and Emilija swore softly.

We waited for some time, breathing shallowly, until the lidérc joined us. She did not tell us what she had done to occupy the guards after drawing them away, but a satisfied smirk graced her face. She cast a glamour over the three of us—I felt the faint tingle as it settled—and we set off.

Abandoning the need for silence in favor of speed, I led the others through the tangled cave system on a round-about passage that would avoid the most densely occupied caverns. Most of the chambers we crossed were empty of praetheria at this early hour, though I tensed whenever we passed someone. The lidérc unfailingly greeted each pass-erby with a nod or a word, and I held my breath, waiting for them to see past our glamour, waiting for them to call her out as a stranger. No one did.

Sometimes the way was easy, the path worn clear by many

feet or the cave sufficiently wide and even. Sometimes we struggled, hugging close to the walls and watching our footing carefully as the elevation lifted and plunged.

We edged around the lake, its rippled surface black in the dim light. I caught my foot on a loose rock and had to sidestep to regain my balance. My shoe splashed into the shallow water at the lake's edge.

The lake erupted, a dark shape vaulting like a geyser above the water. The creature was enormous: long fins like oars and a narrow snout with dagger-sharp teeth. I scrambled away, and the teeth closed on empty air.

An echoed shout rang through the cavern. *My shout,* I realized, seeing the horrified looks on the other girls' faces. What if we'd been heard?

"Run!" Emilija hissed, and we ran.

We made it through the caverns to the scree near the exit without being stopped. As casually as though she were going to fetch supplies from the nearby forest, the lidérc marched toward the guards. We followed close behind, so the noise of our passing was covered by hers, so her glamour could stretch to fit us all.

"Good hunting," said the nearest one, a stocky man with skin like the midnight sky, a constellation of lights pulsing just below the surface.

"Thank you," the lidérc said.

Noémi's face was green-tinged as we emerged onto the mountainside, and I squeezed her hand reassuringly. The sky was the pale grey of dawn, and I turned my face toward the light like a parched creature toward water. I had not seen the sun in so long.

The rich smell of pine needles and decaying leaves was exhilarating after the rock and water smells of the caves. This was how freedom smelled. How it tasted.

Emilija nudged me, and I remembered our urgency. I scrambled down the slope behind her, drawing Noémi with me.

We were out. Another mile or two and we might be far enough away to breathe easily.

We did not make it a mile.

We did not even make it a score of steps before a shadow draped across us. I glanced up, thinking (hoping) a cloud had passed across the sun. But the figure hulking above us was no cloud; it was a giant, and Vasilisa was perched on his shoulder like a bird.

The giant's fingers closed around me like the steel bars of a trap.

CHAPTER 17

Mátyás

Perhaps the tardiness of the Hungarian armies was catching. I returned from Guyon's camp to find Dembiński still in the farmhouse, surveying maps over a low table and blustering to Hadúr. "Dammit, where is Görgey? I need him on the right flank. Bloody fools are already retreating; the Austrians forced a river crossing during the night."

"You sent him to cover the left flank," Hadúr said, his voice deceptively gentle.

"I need someone to cover the ridge at Kerecsend," Dembiński continued, as if Hadúr hadn't spoken. "Someone who will not run the first time a bullet whistles past his ear. We have to hold the heights: if we must retreat, as seems likely, that's our best hope for fending off the Austrians long enough to get across the bridge before we're cut off and surrounded."

"Guyon is coming, sir," I said as soon as Dembiński paused to draw a breath.

"About damn time." Dembiński did not seem to mark the hypocrisy as he stood up from the table and rolled up the map he'd been studying. He pointed the map at Hadúr, then at me and Bahadır. "You three—take charge of the heights. Those are Colonel Klapka's men, but he's gone haring off to Eger after the rest of his army."

Hadúr nodded once. His stolid face betrayed nothing of how he felt at being ordered about like a common foot soldier, let alone by a general whose orders seemed at cross purposes. Then we grasped our weapons, mounted our horses, and rode to war beneath a pale November sky.

We found the ridge easily enough, a long, gradually rising prominence culminating in a steep drop-off in the north. The southern side was wooded, offering decent coverage for the troops.

Well, such troops as they were.

We arrived just as Austrian cavalry ruptured across the field before the ridge. They could not be meant as a serious attack—no seasoned commander would send cavalry to attack soldiers hiding amid the trees. But no one had told our infantrymen as much: a whole stream of them came running down the south side of the ridge, bursting from the wood like startled pheasants.

As the soldiers poured toward us, Hadúr muttered something. Glancing back, I saw that he'd dismounted, so I reined in my horse. Chin tilted heavenward and eyes closed, Hadúr unslung the great longsword he wore at his hip and plunged the tip into the ground.

A shockwave radiated out from that point. My horse sidestepped uneasily, and the men running toward us stumbled.

"Men of Hungary!" Hadúr roared. "Hold your ground!" The men stopped running. A thin, reluctant awe curled around my heart, and I rubbed the cross I wore. I was not much given to worship, but there was something in Hadúr's call that spoke of older times, when both men and gods seemed greater than they did now.

"Go back up the ridge. Hold your position. If you die, let it be with honor—not spitted on the point of my sword for cowardice."

More frightened of Hadúr than the cavalry, the soldiers climbed back up the ridge. We followed, leading our horses on foot. Already the cavalry had pulled back, with the Austrian infantry marching across the field in their place. Hungarian sharpshooters fired down on them.

Now that there was no turning back, I was light-headed, almost giddy. The battle scrolled out before me like a hand of cards—a bit of luck, and I could turn the cards to my advantage. Or I might be flattened by them. The risk tapped a familiar, seductive drumbeat along my veins.

Beside me, Bahadır stared across the field. What did he feel? Was he calm, his training granting him assurance and serenity? Or was he, like me, aware of his heartbeat ratcheting up, of the hum of excitement thrilling through him? Probably he had more sense.

A bombardment of Austrian rockets began, smoking propellants firing over the heads of the advancing infantry to land on our ridge. Hadúr urged the Hungarian infantry to meet the charge, but daunted by the bursts of rocket fire, they held back.

But what the infantry refused, Bahadır took upon himself, creeping to the tree line, where he had a vantage over the valley below, and firing his gun at the advancing foe. He had run from a fight once, fleeing from the men who killed his father and would have killed him. But in the months I had known him, I had never seen him run (well, save once, but Ákos had made him do it). I suspected his father's ghost goaded him, as mine did, though to better purpose.

When I moved to join him, Hadúr stopped me. "You're táltos. Don't waste yourself on military arms—use what gifts you have." And then he stomped off, to try to re-form the infantry into something resembling order.

Since my death, my being táltos had been drubbed into my brain as though this were some incredible gift that would save Hungary. But standing on an unremarkable ridge in the middle of a battle, I lacked the faith of Hadúr and the Lady.

Most of my gifts seemed flimsy things here. I might summon an army of crows to attack the advancing soldiers, but they'd be slaughtered by rifle fire. I might disorient the enemy horses, but what of the infantry? I might send my spirit into the enemy camp to discover their plans, but who would protect my body on this ridge while I dreamed?

The dragon shape nudged at me. Yes, I might shift. But I had little control in that form—I could as soon destroy my allies as my enemies.

Another form would have to do. I shucked off my clothes and shifted, picturing a griffin I'd seen in the Binding spell: the forequarters of an eagle, the hindquarters of a lion. Flexing my wings, I lifted above the trees, then circled above my own troops once, twice, getting used to the feel of this new form.

Then I dove down toward the infantry, who veered out of my way, shrieking. A handful turned and ran. One hardy soldier stopped and took aim: I dropped low and snatched him up with my sharp claws and lifted him, screaming, into the air. At a sufficient height, I flung him back toward his fellows, and three of them toppled beneath his weight like a set of children's toys.

The soldier did not rise. I suppressed a pang of guilt. This was war: I could not afford to feel sorry for each soldier I killed.

I flew a few more circles above the troops, evading their attempts to shoot me down. The stray bullet that grazed my wing did no more than sting. The infantry began retreating before me. I could hear whooping behind me and caught a glimpse of a few of our soldiers clambering down the ridge to give chase to the fleeing enemy.

Then a *whoosh!* and a sudden burst of heat, and the ridge exploded in flames. The men coming down the hill writhed in agony, their cries hoarse and terrible.

A pair of Elementalists had caught up with the infantry. I could see them just beyond the Austrian troops, their hands weaving an intricate spell.

I might trap their hands in an iron-laden vine—most Luminate could not cast spells without their rituals—but it was hard to hold the griffin form in my head *and* catch the pair of them at once. I concentrated on the first magician, but the vines had scarcely begun to twine around her feet when a ball of fire nearly knocked me from the sky.

Fire licked up my right wing, leaving my wingtip blackened and smoking. Awkward, listing hard to the left, I faltered over to the shelter of the trees beyond the burning ridgeline. I shifted back to my own form, gasping at my arm, the raw red patches on my fingers, the burns bubbling along my wrist. The tips of my middle and pointer finger appeared white and did not hurt at all, which was a bad sign. *If I'd taken the dragon form, I'd not have burned.* I pushed the regret aside and found my discarded clothes near Bahadır.

My friend abandoned his vantage point to inspect my arm. "There's a medic back among Guyon's troops—you need to get this treated."

I shook my head. "Not yet. Just find something clean to wrap my hand in. I'll have a healer look at it tonight."

Bahadır's eyebrows drew together in exasperation. "If you do not die first of stupidity. Sit—you look pale. I don't want you fainting."

"It's your magnetic presence," I murmured, sitting obediently. "I can't help myself."

Bahadır laughed, as I had meant him to. He cut a strip of linen from his undershirt and wrapped it around my fingers and wrist. I wished Noémi were here, her cool fingers lifting the burn from my skin.

But the war hadn't stopped while Bahadır tended my injury: a crackling noise drew my attention to where smoke billowed from the trees. Soldiers were retreating around us, coughing at the acrid fumes. A wind—Elementalist-driven?—had picked up, sending the flames back toward us.

I staggered to my feet. "We've got to hold the ridge, or the others will be cut off."

"I'm not sure we can," Bahadır said. "Not without risking more lives than is sensible."

Hadúr's voice roared across the crackling fire. "Retreat! Head south and east toward the Kerecsend bridge!"

"Can you walk?" Bahadır asked, taking a half step toward me.

"It was my arm that burned, not my legs," I said, but as I moved, the trees spun around me and pain radiated from my hand to my shoulder. Bahadır put his arm around me, supporting me as I walked.

We reached the bottom of the slope to find the Hungarian army in disarray: infantry and cavalry mingled together, rushing aimlessly through a muddy field.

"Toward Kerecsend!" Hadúr's voice carried over the troops, his words calming the chaos and shaping it into a sluggish eastward drift.

A curious lifting sensation pulled at the top of my head, as though a hot-air balloon were attached to my scalp.

Bahadır's grip tightened. "Mátyás, look at me."

I tried to, but I had trouble focusing on his face. His dark eyes seemed to swim. I kept marching, my legs moving somehow independent of my body.

"You're going into shock," he said. "You need to lie down."

At that I laughed—a pure, silvered bubble of delight. It seemed so perfectly ridiculous. Of course I should lie down in the middle of a retreat. Why not ask for a down pillow and a glass of wine while I was at it?

I tried to object, but the words must have faded somewhere between my tongue and the air, because Bahadır did not appear to understand. Instead, he guided me back toward the base of the slope, where he settled me in the shade beneath an oak tree. He pulled out a canteen and wetted the handkerchief he carried, dabbing it across my face.

Initially, the coolness was welcoming: but moments later I was shivering, my entire body convulsing.

Bahadır eased me out of the shadows into the weak sunlight, then shrugged out of his own coat and draped it across me.

"You should go," I said, trying to gesture at the retreating soldiers. Bahadır ignored me. "I'll be fi—" I broke off, my attention caught by a wavering spot perhaps a hundred feet from us, like a heat haze somehow concentrated in a single location. The shimmer grew denser and darkened, and then a narrow hole opened above the grass.

A Lucifera-made portal.

Austrian soldiers poured through the opening in strict precision, heading toward our unwitting soldiers. A lumbering mechanized flying creature the size of a small boat followed them out of the glimmering slit, all jagged edges—some misbegotten cross between a wolf and a raven, rendered in metal. Our soldiers would never cross the river before the Austrians cut them off. Hadúr was too far away to warn; any outcry would only draw attention to our suddenly vulnerable position. Bahadır dragged me back behind the tree, and I tried to swallow air but only gagged at the sudden thickness in my throat.

Bahadır clapped his hand across my mouth. "Hush."

I couldn't breathe. I clawed at his hand with my good

fingers, and he released me at once. I had to draw Hadúr's attention. I thought first of my crows: they were uncommonly smart, with an uncanny ability to recognize and remember human faces. I'd known a woman near Eszterháza who had found herself constantly bombarded by crows when she dared pass by the local church for having once had the temerity to throw a rock at a roosting crow.

Still, I hesitated to call them. I remembered the carpeting of bees and wasps that had met my call for aid against Vasilisa. I did not want to add crow carcasses to those already strewn across the field.

A murder of crows.

Heh. (Sometimes my amusement was wholly inappropriate to time and place.)

An idea sparked, and I reached out to the vultures already circling the field. Obedient to my nudge, a handful swooped low over the field, drawing tightening circles around Hadúr until he swung around, irritated, to swat them away . . . and saw the army closing on his soldiers.

Hadúr sprang over the heads of his troops, his sword sweeping through the air before he landed with a thunderous boom. The soldiers around him tumbled in widening ripples, like grain mowed down by a scythe. I'd never truly seen Hadúr fight. He was in his element, light glinting off his copper armor like some unholy blood-infused halo. But there was no magic to his movements, only a grace and strength born of millennia of training: an exquisite, violent dance.

The Austrians stopped marching and turned the force of their military on Hadúr's single figure, a copper flame in the field. The mechanical monster that had followed the soldiers out of the portal fired a steady volley of shots at Hadúr. The thing's aim was off, but it was only a matter of time before it got lucky or whoever had control of the mech adjusted it.

I caught one of the circling vultures again, urging it to come near enough for me to shift it. I thought of my disastrous shifting of the owls and opted for a griffin this time. With an odd, muffled squawk, the bird ballooned outward, listing wildly as it struggled to adjust to its new form. I sent the griffin toward the mech, drawing its fire away from Hadúr.

The vulture-turned-griffin was only meant to tear the mech with its claws, but instead, it collided with the metal monster, and both mech and griffin tumbled to the ground. The mech exploded, knocking surrounding Austrian soldiers down like a house of cards. The griffin didn't rise, and the smell of burnt flesh wafted across the field. *Damnation*. I should have chosen a dragon again.

Hadúr fought on, and belatedly his own troops stopped watching open-mouthed and went to his assistance. Worn from the shifting and its failure, I let my attention slip, my burning arm fracturing the reality before me.

Time slowed, an oddly luxurious slowness where everything imprinted itself on my memory. Then it raced, so fast I could hardly grasp my own movements, let alone other details. Always, I could see Hadúr at the limits of my vision, dancing like fire across dry grass. Bahadır disappeared at some point, when he was certain I would not move. I may have slept for a while.

Here lies Eszterházy Mátyás: He died as he lived, asleep when it counted.

By the time I could walk again, it was late afternoon, sun streaking across the field in low, thick bursts. The battle still ground on. Bahadır returned and forced me to eat some bread and wilting cheese.

"We've got to get you out of here," he said. "The only way out is through."

With Bahadır's help, I staggered toward the field, skirting the worst of the fighting.

We hadn't gone far when a grey-green fog began creeping across the meadow, a curiously heavy miasma. "Cover your face," Bahadır said, pulling a handkerchief up to his nose just as the fog reached our feet.

I put my kerchief over my nose, but not before I caught the odd, almost floral note of the mist. At once, a weight seemed to drop onto me, and I sagged to my knees, only Bahadır's arm around me keeping me upright.

We could never hope to win this war. Better to lay down our weapons now and escape with some honor.

I was reaching for the gun holstered at my side when Bahadır interrupted me. "It's a spell, Mátyás."

I blinked. In the shifting mist, the battlefield looked less like a charnel house and more like a scene from a fairy story, a fight of words and distant, hazy wounds, their edges worn away by time. A spell to set us all doubting. Coremancer work.

But the mist was insidious: even knowing that my doubts were (mostly) magic-driven, they still settled heavily on me, echoing my true uncertainties. Around me, I could see soldiers faltering, some falling to their knees, others throwing their weapons away.

I watched a boy, barely old enough for the fuzzy mustache he sported on his lip, drop his bayonet at his feet only to stare, a moment later, at the saber piercing his middle, blood blooming across his linen shirt.

We had to get rid of the mist. I sent my táltos sense out, reaching farther than usual, as the battle had driven most of the avians away. But they responded within moments: slowly at first, in ones and twos, then in a growing wave.

The birds soared over the battlefield, blocking out the intermittent sunshine: cormorants and cranes, egrets and herons, goshawks, osprey, harriers and owls, even a handful of swans. All the great birds of the northern plains and mountains, swooping low over the battlefield, the flapping of thousands of wings churning up a wind that stirred the miasma and then, slowly, sluggishly, began to disperse it.

The birds were not immune to cannon and rifle fire, and I saw several plummet from the sky, my heart snagging with each fall. But enough lived to drive away the mist before I sent them wheeling back to their homes, the gratitude in my heart a tiny spark I clung to as the battle resumed.

The battle near Kerecsend ground to a halt at nightfall, each side licking its wounds.

Thanks in part to Hadúr's ferocity and the dispersal of the mists, the Hungarian armies were able to cross the Tarna River before the Austrians cut off their retreat. After dark, bobbing Lumen lights moved across the field: volunteers looking for survivors among the dead.

The raging inferno of pain in my arm made me dizzy, but I was still standing, which was more than I could say for some. The pain was matched only by the twisting in my gut, the aftereffects of too much magic and too lean a larder.

When Bahadır finally dragged me to a makeshift field hospital, I almost wished he had failed: the smell of blood and offal surrounding the small, crowded tent overwhelmed me. The hospital was full to overflowing; overworked doctors, nurses, and volunteers struggled to stanch the worst of the wounds. My burns seemed insignificant in comparison. I was about to give up when we ran into Gábor among the volunteers.

He led us away from the tent to a less crowded spot on the field outside, though we couldn't escape the cries and groans of the wounded. He unwrapped my bandage with surprising gentleness, then hissed at the red and raw skin below. "You should have had this seen to earlier."

"It was on my list," I said. "Right after 'Don't die.' "

Gábor gave me a level look that said my weak attempt at humor was not appreciated, then took a damp cloth and pressed it gently against my skin. He lifted my burnt hand in his and closed his eyes, and the round stone in his ring began to glow. The white tips of my fingers turned black, then angry red, and I found I could feel them again.

It was not an improvement. I sucked in a breath.

Gábor released my hand to wind another bandage around it and my forearm. "You'll not lose the fingers, and so long as infection does not set in, I think you'll live. Make sure the bandages are changed frequently."

"Thank you. It hurts like the devil, but I am grateful."

"I wish I still had some of Guyon's brandy for you. You ought to sleep if you can."

Something cold touched my nose, featherlight. I held out my left hand, and a pair of snowflakes landed on my wool sleeve, perched in pristine perfection for a moment before melting.

Bahadır and I found a patch of grass near a banked fire—no pitched tents tonight—and curled close to each other for warmth. My body ached with exhaustion, but the pinching cold and the abominable throbbing in my arm kept me awake. I reflected, ruefully, that this might be the first time in my life that my sleeping superpower failed me.

Sometime after midnight, I gave up. Bahadır was asleep, twitching uneasily at some dream. The flurries earlier had dissipated, and the clouds overhead had broken apart to reveal stars. I stood up, wrapping my dolman closer about me and blowing on my fingers to warm them. In the distance, I could still hear the low moans of the wounded.

"Mátyás."

I whirled around to find Hadúr stumping toward me, a bandage wrapped around his shin.

"Good battle?" I asked.

His lips twisted. "A fool's battle. Dembiński may be a hardy soldier, but if all his battles are fought thus, the Austrians will need little to destroy our armies." He shifted, rubbing the back of his neck. "Come with me. There is something I must show you."

Curious, I followed, and my breath formed a cloud in the crisp night air. We walked past sleeping men; others, restless as I had been, sat talking softly around fires or sharing bottles of something that offered more warmth than the dying flames.

Hadúr led me back across the river to the field where the Austrians had surprised us with a portal. He kindled a small light, for which I was grateful, as I did not relish the idea of stumbling over dead bodies in the dark. What did he mean to show me?

In the distance, I could see pricks of light from the Austrian encampment.

At length, Hadúr stopped. The field immediately around us was unnaturally quiet, the tumbled bodies still. "As táltos, another of your gifts is speaking to the spirits of the dead. It can be a useful gift, particularly in wartime, when you can glean information about enemy movements."

I glanced around at the bodies with fresh alarm, feeling a wash of relief when no ghosts materialized. "You want me to—what? Interrogate the newly dead?" It seemed sacrilegious.

"Most spirits linger in our world for only a short time after their death, from a few minutes to a few hours. You do not need to *interrogate* any newly dead tonight—but see if you can speak with them."

I was not sure which part of his speech was most alarming: that *most* spirits did not linger or that I did not need to interrogate them *tonight*.

"To talk with them, you'll need to put yourself into a trance: you cannot see them with your physical eyes, only your spirit ones. I'll watch your body, see to it that no one buries you or robs your body."

Was that flattening of his lips meant to be a smile? He stood, waiting expectantly, so I sighed and lay down upon the ground, taking care to find a spot that was not already occupied or covered in blood. I tried not to think too hard about what I was doing.

I settled into the trance, my spirit self lifting away from my body as casually as I might peel away my shirt at the end of the day. My spirit looked around the battlefield, trying not to notice quite how much my body looked like the other corpses.

A flicker of movement caught my attention, a faintly glowing outline of a young man, hovering over a body nearby. By the uniform, an Austrian. His mouth was moving, but I could not make out the words.

I drew closer, and the words resolved themselves into the familiar cadences of the Lord's Prayer: *"Führe uns nicht in Versuchung, sondern erlöse uns von dem Bösen."*

Lead us not into temptation, but deliver us from evil.

What did he make of this battleground, his bloody body unmoving before him?

"Excuse me," I said in German, and the boy startled, making the sign of the cross. But then I hesitated. What did one say to the dead? "I'm sorry for your loss" might be taken as mockery.

"Who are you?" he asked, relieving me of my crisis. "A ghost?"

I winced a little. Did he not realize he was himself a ghost? "A spirit," I answered. "But not dead." Wait. That wasn't quite right. Dead . . . but *not* dead? Reborn? I kept the clarification to myself. Best not frighten the boy further.

"This was not supposed to happen," he said. "I was supposed to go home. My Dorothea waits for me. My Mutti. My brothers. Is this hell? It is not heaven."

"A battlefield," I said. "Near Kápolna."

"Can you bring me back?" he asked, drifting closer. His eyes were wide, unblinking. He reached for me, but I danced away from his grasp.

"That isn't in my gift," I said. At least, I did not think it was. I should have to ask Hadúr about the old stories.

The boy abandoned his attempts to reach me and lay down on his body, his spirit sinking into the flesh. "Try," he said, but it was only the spirit that spoke. The corpse's lips remained twisted into a grimace.

My spirit self knelt beside the body, curious. (My *damned* curiosity.) I thrust out that inner energy I used for shifting, for animal persuasion. "Live," I whispered. "Be whole."

Then I rocked back, expecting the spirit to pop back out of the body. Only demigods like the Lady had power to bring back the dead.

The boy reared upright, gasping, his lungs making a horrible gurgling noise. I saw then what I had not seen before, that gunshot had ripped a huge hole through his chest. His eyes opened wide, and he reached one hand toward me.

But of course, he could not see me now, not without my body. His face clenched in a paroxysm of pain, and he drew a few more grating breaths.

St. Cajetan and all the holy saints. The boy was dying again—I had put him back in his body, but I could not undo the damage he'd sustained.

I reached out, grasping a gossamer bit of something that might be spirit, and yanked. The ghost flew out of the body. At once, he began weeping.

"I lived. I lived. Why did you kill me?"

"You were dying and in pain. You would not have lived much longer in any case. Would you rather suffer so?"

"I lived," he repeated. "What are you? Demon? Devil? I lived."

He returned to muttering the Lord's Prayer, interspersed with sobs of "I lived."

I retreated to my own body, the boy's murmured cries pinching my spirit ears until, mercifully, I woke, gasping. I looked at Hadúr. "I'll be *damned* if I ever do that again."

CHAPTER 18

Mátyás

The battle near Kápolna staggered on, each day a prolonged repetition of the one that preceded it: soldiers
battering one another with swords, rifles, cannons, and
magic. I fought where I could, but more judiciously than
I had that first day, saving my magic for things that could
help: a pair of dive-bombing crows to distract a cannoneer
at the crucial moment of aiming his weapon; bees to sting
the lips and tongues of magicians so they could not speak
their spells; lines of cavalry horses that would not stand
their ground.

The Austrians slowly tightened their noose around us,
but they seemed in no hurry to strike the killing blow.
Perhaps they still hoped to drive us to surrender. Hadúr
grumbled about military mismanagement: "Dembiński is
a fool, trying to bludgeon his way through the surrounding armies."

Then came word that Dembiński was injured and had

retired to a neighboring inn to recover. He summoned the nearby commanders and their adjutants to attend on him: General Görgey, General Guyon, Colonel Klapka.

When Hadúr caught wind of the meeting, he found me and Bahadır. "Come. We're going."

Bahadır said, doubtfully, "I don't believe we've been invited."

"Invitation be damned. This has gone on long enough."

Hadúr had no trouble locating the inn. He had a little more difficulty persuading the guards at the door of the taproom they'd commandeered to allow us entrance, but he marshalled the voice that had made troops fall in line in the field, and it seemed to work just as well. The guards let us in.

Görgey nodded at me and seemed more amused than irritated by our interruption. General Guyon did not seem to recognize us, but Gábor, sitting beside him, smiled. The others appeared variously mystified, annoyed, or outright angry at our appearance.

Dembiński bristled. "What the devil do you mean by this, sir?"

Hadúr, copper armor clinking around him and glowing with curious intensity in the dim light, strode to the center of the room. "I mean, *sir,* to put an end to this foolishness. You are destroying this army quite as effectively as the Austrians might wish."

"Who says so?"

"I say so. And before you question my authority again, let me remind you that I am Hadúr, the *Hadak Ura,* Hungarian god of war."

There were a few raised eyebrows at that, but not as

241

many as I'd expected. Hadúr in full glory was quite convincing.

"Starting now, I am commanding this war."

Dembiński began, "But Kossuth—"

"Kossuth has no more notion how to run a war than have you. A good leader knows better than to disrupt a successful operation, and I might have been content to merely take orders if you'd given orders worth following. But you have not."

Dembiński finished his thought with more firmness. "Kossuth appointed me, and I will not step down until I hear the order from him."

The man had courage, I'd grant him that.

Hadúr looked around the room, his eyes settling on each general and staff member in turn. Most of them quailed before his gaze. Gábor, I noticed, did not; nor did General Görgey. "Which man among you is going to tell Kossuth that the god of war offered to lead your armies and you turned him down?"

No one answered.

Hadúr smiled and settled atop a table. "I thought not. Our first task is to break free of the Austrian armies surrounding us and regroup."

In rather grim terms, he laid out the current situation of the war: we were surrounded by Austrians and the Russians were on the march. At best, we might delay our surrender a few weeks. We needed reinforcements. Kossuth's emissaries to France and England had failed: France was embroiled in her own war, and English armies were occupied with putting down praetherian insurrection in the countryside.

Hadúr looked at me. "I want you to take messages to General Perczel and General Bem. Have Perczel bring his army up behind the Austrians in the northeast. Have Bem bring his troops up from Transylvania to meet us."

He made no mention of the praetherian threat, and I wondered at the omission. Did he have some larger plan to address that, or was he at present concerned only with the survival of Hungary? He was the god of war. But like the Lady and other demigods who had been trapped in the Binding, he was technically praetherian. Which loyalty goaded him here? His loyalty to Hungary—or to the praetheria?

It took me all night to reach General Perczel, flying as a great horned owl and carrying the letters in my talons. I arrived just as dawn broke, shifted in the woods beyond their camp, and stole a coat and trousers that had been left on a line to dry. Görgey's seal on the letter from Hadúr was enough to buy me entrance to the general's tent, but Perczel looked harried, so I made my report brief and handed over the letter. I snagged some breakfast from a nearby pot, returned the purloined clothes, and set off again, a crow for the daylight hours, the remaining letters in my beak.

General Bem was harder to find in the mountains of Transylvania, but I tracked his troops down at midmorning on the following day. Unfortunately for me, I ran afoul of a pair of scouts just outside the camp as I was shifting.

They stared, open-mouthed, at me in all my naked glory. Flushing a little, I turned so I was presenting my backside.

"Luminate!" said one, raising his gun.

"Don't be daft," his fellow said, knocking the gun aside. "There's magicians on our side too. Find out what he wants before you shoot him."

"I've messages for the general," I said, waving the letters in the air above me.

At this, they both looked perplexed. Finally, the second soldier said, "Best find you some clothes, then." The first soldier disappeared, and the second kept me company, his eyes carefully averted. I began to feel amused, and by the time the first soldier had returned with some clothes, I was downright cheerful.

General Bem, another borrowed Polish commander, was not quite what I had expected. His round face shone at me beneath a receding hairline, like Mikulás arriving with toys for children, but his eyes were keen. "My soldiers say they found you naked in our woods, and yet you've come bearing letters from Görgey?" His Hungarian was faintly accented.

"Yes, sir," I said. The letter was from Hadúr, but I didn't correct Bem: there was a second letter from Görgey explaining the change in leadership. "I shapeshift, but, alas, my clothes do not make the transition with me."

"How very enterprising. A useful skill, that, in wartime."

"Not always so useful for fighting, sir," I said.

"There are many ways of fighting," Bem said. "Not all of them involve weapons. You serve no one by belittling yourself. Do you fly, then?"

I let my grin surface at the longing note in his voice. "Yes, sir. Would you like to try it?"

And that is how I came to shift a decorated general in the Hungarian army and spent the better part of an hour teaching him to fly as a crow does, riding the air currents and tumbling through the sky. When I released him at last, his eyes sparkled above rosy cheeks.

"That was splendid— I'm afraid I don't know your name."

"Mátyás," I said.

Bem's aide-de-camp was waiting for us when we returned, and as soon as the general walked into range, he began castigating me for taking the general away so long— until he got a good look at me.

"Eszterházy Mátyás, on my life! I heard you were dead."

Petőfi Sándor, the militant poet who had driven us to revolution and rallied the people to storm Buda Castle, stood before me. He was no friend of Kossuth's, but he was, as ever, a patriot. He'd lost his neat appearance— neither his mustache nor his clothes were as well kept as I remembered—but his eyes blazed as brightly as ever.

"I was," I admitted. "A goddess brought me back."

"Now, that's a story I should like to hear sometime," Petőfi said. "But how did you come here?"

"He brought me a message," General Bem said. "And then he taught me to fly."

"Of course he did," Petőfi said, laughing.

"Have you ever been a crow?" General Bem asked. "Marvelous. Simply marvelous."

Bem sent an adjutant to fetch us some food. As the shifting had begun to take its toll, I did justice to the food, to the adjutant's awe and Petőfi's amusement. Petőfi plied me with questions about my life since the Binding, and I told him about becoming the King of Crows.

"Well, naturally," the poet said. "Once one has lived and died a revolutionary, what is left but banditry? I shall write a poem for you."

I laughed. "My exploits need no poems, thank you very much."

As I rose to leave, General Bem said, "Fly safe, young man. You've a position in my army anytime you choose."

"Thank you, sir."

"And should you die in battle, I'll write a rousing epitaph for you," Petőfi declared. " 'One thought torments me, that I might die in a pillowed bed. . . . *Isten,* do not give me such a death!' "

There was something in his recitation of his own poem, a ferocity that made the bright day suddenly dark. I shivered, touched by a premonition I scarcely understood, and launched into the air.

)(

When I arrived back at camp, the battle was still raging. I fought off exhaustion to join the others, and when the fighting slowed enough for me to stumble back to my bedroll, I did not so much fall asleep as cannon into it.

When I dreamed, it was of the battle: of bodies rising from the ground to continue fighting, of spells whistling through the air that I could not dodge. It was a relief when I remembered I did not have to stay inside the nightmare. I let myself drift outside the dream, to the grey realm of dreamers.

I watched the haze of sleepers as they coalesced and thinned, then took shape again. A particularly bright mist caught my attention: something about the red and gold swirling in its depths seemed familiar.

My fingers closed around the mist, and I slid inside the dream almost at once.

There was no battlefield here but a ballroom filled with glittering chandeliers and gleaming gold leaf on the walls. The edges of the room fuzzed away into nothingness. Couples whirled around me, mostly with indistinct faces, but a few I recognized: a pair of students from Café Pilvax in Buda-Pest, my uncle János, the soldier girl I had helped rescue.

At the center of the room, Anna twirled in Gábor's arms. I drifted through the crowd as orchestral music swelled. When Anna lifted her face to receive a kiss, I tapped Gábor, who dissolved, and stepped into his place.

"Is *this* what you dream about?" I grinned at her. "I'm flattered."

Anna drew back in alarm. "I wasn't dreaming about—"

I took pity on her blushing confusion. "I've been looking for you and Noémi for weeks. Hadúr has taught me how to walk through dreams."

"So this is real? Not part of my dream?"

"Not unless you want it to be."

She ignored my comment. "Are you safe? Where are you?"

"Somewhere near Eger. Technically, we're on a battlefield, so 'safe' might be relative, but I'm well enough at the moment. Where are *you*?"

"In the mountains somewhere, in a cave."

"And Noémi?"

"I don't know. We tried to escape and were caught. I haven't seen her since then. Is Gábor with you?"

"Not *with* me, but I've seen him."

"You must tell him that my letters were stolen, that he can't write to me." Anna stopped, head cocked, as though she was listening to something I could not hear. "I've got to go. Find me again, please."

"I will," I promised, and her dream disintegrated around us.

CHAPTER 19

Anna

My visitor came unannounced, heralded only by a growing globe of light against the darkness.

It had been a week, maybe more, since our attempted escape—it was hard to gauge the passage of time in the new cell where I was kept. The space was smaller than the room I'd shared with Noémi, the walls rougher and colder. Instead of a bed, I had a blanket. I was always cold. Meals were brought and cleared away in silence at odd intervals by unfamiliar praetheria. I spent the rest of the time in darkness, filling the space around me with terrified imaginings: that the others had been killed, that the praetheria already marched on the Hungarian armies. I had tried, more than once, to recapture the same Breaking spell that had plunged me through rock after Chernobog had entombed me, but either the cell was spelled to prevent such an escape or I was not sufficiently in possession of myself.

Even Vasilisa had not come to gloat.

It was Hunger who came, walking easily down the uneven stone corridor leading to my cell. I gripped the bars fronting the entrance to my alcove.

"Where have you been?" I asked, my voice rusty from disuse. It was not what I meant to say.

"Occupied," Hunger said, gold eyes gleaming. He sat down on the floor outside my cell and surveyed me. "Are you all right?"

I didn't answer him: he could see that I was well enough. "Where is Noémi? Emilija? The lidérc? What has been done to them?"

"Noémi is secured elsewhere. The others escaped."

I released a slow breath. *Thank God.* "Noémi is well?"

A broad yearning stole into his face, before Hunger wiped it away. "She's unharmed."

"You should let her go."

Again, that flash of longing. "I cannot."

"Cannot or will not?"

He did not answer. He rubbed his hands across his eyes, a very human gesture of exhaustion. But I would not feel sorry for him. "You were meant to be a guest, to be encouraged to help us of your own free will."

I snorted. Not ladylike, but there was no book of manners for behavior in a prison cell. "Your idea of persuasion is a funny thing. What was supposed to win me over: Watching a soldier be buried alive? Seeing the samodiva queen die? Being entombed by Chernobog? I confess, it's hard to choose amongst so much charm."

"At least you retain your spirit. Hold that. You will need it."

I peered at him. Beneath the gold sheen of his skin, there were circles under his eyes, a chalky pallor that had not been there before. "You cannot approve of what is being done here—you cannot have meant for someone like Chernobog to take the samodiva's place."

"What has happened is done. There is no going back from it."

I could not quite read his flat tone. Did he regret what had happened? "No—but you might choose a different way forward. It's not too late to stop this war. Please, let us go. We can help you—"

He cut me off, standing in a fluid movement. "You cannot stop this. It is too late."

The silence falling behind his retreating footsteps was a living thing: heavy, feral . . . and lonely.

)(

I was dreaming of Mátyás spinning me through a ball-room when footsteps sounded outside my cell, tugging at my consciousness. I told Mátyás to find me again and was already swimming out of the dream when a guard yanked the bars open and hauled me upright.

Just beyond the guard, Vasilisa stood in a frilly white gown, as though she were attending a society fête. Beside her, Pál nodded. "Bring her."

The guard dragged me through the corridors and chambers of the cavern. When my sleep stupor wore off, I tried to ask what was happening, but Pál waved his hand at me. "Hush," he said, and I could not speak.

We reached the entrance of the cave, and the guard pulled me through.

Noémi waited in the fading light outdoors, Hunger beside her. After the initial rush of joy at seeing her alive and unharmed, I was swamped with dread. The praetheria had not brought us here to set us free.

Hunger shifted, his dragon form stretching long and sinuous in the gathering dark. We were each bound, and Pál shoved me into a saddle fastened to Hunger's back and tied my hands to the pommel.

When Pál stepped back, Vasilisa wrapped her arms around him, and they rose into the air. Hunger's great wings fluttered, and he lifted as well, his powerful claws closing gently around Noémi. I winced. I had flown in Hunger's claws before, and it was not comfortable. Not that being bound to his back was a great improvement.

Even in my fear, I could not help relishing the feel of wind against my skin, seeing the stars emerge overhead like so many diamonds, the nearly full moon gleaming like a pearl. I had missed this sight.

The air at this height was frigid, much colder than the cool temperatures of the cave. I shivered, wishing I'd worn something warmer. (A ridiculous wish: I had nothing warmer.)

We did not fly far. After only a few minutes, we began to descend. Hunger settled slowly, releasing Noémi before landing firmly on the ground. She stumbled a little, and Vasilisa drew her away while Pál helped me down. Hunger shifted back to human form, his suit so well fitted it had to have been glamoured.

A short distance away, a troop of soldiers sat on their horses, unnaturally quiet save for the soft whuffling of their mounts. The soldiers wore the high shako hats of Hungarian hussars, and for a moment, my heart bounded. *We might be saved.*

But only for a moment, until my searching eyes took in the horned figure of Chernobog standing near the horsemen. Peering more closely at the soldiers, I saw some were too attenuated and oddly jointed for humans. These were praetheria, dressed as Hungarian soldiers.

Chernobog stalked toward us. "There is a small unit of Austrian soldiers not far from here, mostly new recruits sent to join the main body of the army. We strike at midnight—hard, fast, without mercy."

My skin crawled. Was this it? The beginning of the end?

I sidled closer to Noémi, and no one stopped me. Her very human warmth was comforting, though she smelled—as I'm sure I did—of sweat and unwashed flesh. But why had they brought us here?

We waited for some time, silent and uneasy. Above us, clouds crawled across the sky, blotting out the moon and stars.

Chernobog gave the order, and the soldiers rode out, the underworld god following them like a plague. A pair of horses were brought forward for us to mount: Noémi and Hunger on one, Pál and me on the other. I tried not to cringe when Pál put his arms around my waist; it would only amuse him to know how unsettling I found him.

The battle was fully engaged when we arrived, if a bit lopsided—Austrian foot soldiers trying valiantly to fight back against praetheria on horseback. Most were not even in uniform, untucked shirts and missing trousers suggesting they'd been roused from their sleep. A few fled, running pell-mell toward the uncertain shelter of trees in the distance.

I tried not to watch the battle, though Pál kept our horse turned that direction. It was enough—too much—to hear the clang of metal on metal, the bursts of gunfire, the gurgling cries of the dead and dying. I swallowed bile in my throat.

At length, a white flag of surrender was raised, and the Austrians threw down their weapons. The praetherian soldiers in Hungarian uniform circled around them.

A pair of Austrians were brought forward, boys not much older than I was. Chernobog snapped his fingers, and they began sinking into the ground, their startled cries turning to genuine screams as they were buried alive.

"Stop playing with them," Vasilisa said. "There must be nothing here that suggests our presence—the Austrians must blame the Hungarians for the atrocities, not us."

"Human Lucifera can do as much—and no one will find their bodies to know." Chernobog shrugged. "It shall be as you wish." The ground closed over the two unfortunate boys, cutting off their screams.

Another soldier was tugged forward, less willingly than the first two, obviously fearing to share their fate. This one was older, a touch of grey in his beard and at his temples. An officer?

"Unmake his eyes," Chernobog said, snapping his fingers at me.

What? I jerked in the saddle, sure I had heard wrong. But Pál had not given me my voice back, and I could not ask. My uncle dismounted and pulled me down, dragging me to stand before the frightened soldier.

I stared at him, my heart thrumming in my throat. He looked to be my father's age. Did he have children waiting for him at home? A wife? Friends?

"His eyes," Chernobog repeated, watching me idly, as though he'd asked me to pass the salt at dinner. "We did not bring you here for your amusement but to see if you have the strength and stomach to do what's necessary when needed. If you do not obey, we will hurt your cousin until you do. It would be a shame if she died."

I glanced back at Noémi. Her shocked expression told me she had heard Chernobog's threat. Hunger stood beside her, his fists tight and his golden eyes dark with anger. He must have known what Chernobog planned. If he cared for Noémi at all, how could he let her be used so?

Perhaps, like me, he had no choice.

I turned back to the soldier. His eyes were not worth Noémi's life. But how could I do this?

Eyes were not a manufactured thing that could be un-made, returned to its component parts.

When I hesitated, Chernobog nodded back at Vasilisa—who lit Noémi's hair on fire.

Noémi's mouth opened in a silent scream. Horrified, I whirled on Pál, whacking him with my bound hands. *Stop,* I mouthed. *Stop!*

Pál waved his hand, and the fire winked out.

I returned my attention to the soldier, my heart thudding

painfully against my ribs. He watched me, wary, horror at the sudden spurt of fire still reflecting in his eyes.

I had to try. God help me, but I had to try. The next time I failed, they might kill Noémi.

Shaking now with both nerves and cold, I closed my eyes and called up my shadow self, hovering just beneath my consciousness. She came swiftly, trembling just as I was. I reached out, trying to feel for some sense of magic, some thread or spark that I might break.

Nothing.

I glanced behind me at Chernobog, watching with unblinking eyes. At Vasilisa, her face lit with unholy amusement. At Hunger, whose face told me nothing at all.

Back to the soldier now, terror making my hands clammy. What if I could not do this?

And what if I could?

Both options made my stomach roil.

Again. Desperation made my shadow self stronger, but my questing senses felt nothing they could grasp. I sent my second sight in the direction of his head, twisting in the same gesture I'd use to break a spell, hoping—fearing—to snag something.

The soldier fell back with a cry, hand clapped to his ear, where blood poured out.

A wave of revulsion knocked me to my knees, and I vomited. As repeated heaves racked my body, I thought, *I cannot do this. I cannot.*

Pál must have sensed this, because his hand was on my back, warm and unexpectedly gentle. "I think you ask too much of her. This magic is beyond her."

"Then kill the girl," Chernobog said.

"No." Hunger's response was swift and sure. "If you lose your leverage against Anna, you lose her—she won't be moved by threats against herself. Don't waste her cousin on something Anna could not have done in any case." I wondered if the others heard the thread of desperation running under his rational words.

I sat back on my haunches, spent and shivering. There was vomit in my hair and on my clothes, and I could not get my hands free to wipe it off.

I did not care.

With one long look at Noémi, and then at Hunger, Chernobog turned back to the soldiers. "Kill them all," he said. "And not gently. Put out their eyes, rip open their stomachs, peel back their skin. Leave their bodies in a state that will horrify the Austrians who find them."

He stalked forward and plunged his own clawed fingers into the eyes of the soldier before me, who fell, screaming.

My stomach wrenched again, and I doubled over, dry-heaving. I tried to block out the sounds of the slaughter that followed, but by the time it had ended, I was curled in on myself, weeping as though I might never stop, great gasping sobs that shook my body. The tears froze on my cheeks.

Vasilisa tugged me upright, not ungently, and murmured, "It would not hurt so much if you cared less."

She slid one arm around me to help me back toward the horses. The praetherian soldiers had already dispersed, melting back into the nearby forest.

With a resounding crack, one of the great trees fell,

narrowly missing Hunger. He jumped back, cursing, and the earth beneath him shook, knocking him to the ground.

The earth beneath my own feet was steady. I whipped my gaze around to see Pál, his fingers flickering with another spell. A thousand droplets of water seemed to emerge from nowhere and arced through the air to encase Hunger in a film of ice.

Hunger shifted, and the ice burst in a thousand tiny fragments, like glass. They glittered on the dried grass around him, and Hunger's great dragon turned to face Pál.

"There has been no challenge issued," he growled.

"I am not praetherian." Pál flicked his fingers and a circle of trees lifted to the air, roots and all.

Chernobog said, "You do not deserve the dignity of a challenge. You've grown soft, my old friend." He stalked to Noémi and grabbed her by the hair, shaking her to demonstrate the source of Hunger's weakness.

Distracted by Chernobog's movement, Hunger did not dodge fast enough. The trees plummeted down, smashing along his curved spine, across his neck.

Hunger roared, and a gout of flame surrounded Pál, who did not flinch. The fire burned itself out against Pál's faintly luminescent skin. *Pál had planned this.* He had known before he arrived how this night would end, and he had come spelled against dragon fire.

I reached out to snag Pál's protective spell, and Vasilisa grabbed me, shattering my concentration.

"Do not make this worse," she hissed, and something cold burrowed against the sensitive skin of my throat: her nails, sharp as any dagger.

"You put him up to this," Hunger said to Chernobog,

evading the spear of ice Pál flung at him. "The praetheria will not thank you for betraying me."

Chernobog laughed, his hand still tangled in Noémi's hair. "The praetheria will follow whoever is strongest, as they always have. And the strongest"—another shake for emphasis—"is no longer you."

I jerked away from Vasilisa, and her nails tore at my skin. Locked alone in my cell, I'd filled some of the empty hours practicing what few spells I could remember: a Lumen light, a basic Fire spell. My failure-to-success rate was staggering, but I'd gritted my teeth and tried all the same. While Pál was distracted, I snapped the spell preventing my speech and whispered, *"Adure."*

I flung the fire-lighting spell at Pál.

But the shape of the spell didn't hold; it fizzled as it left my fingertips. Before I could summon my will again, a weight crashed into me from behind, knocking me to my knees. Vasilisa glowered down at me, a look that could shrivel a full-grown tree.

"If you interfere in this fight, Chernobog *will* kill you. All my hard work to bring you here will be undone." She appeared to consider for a moment. "Perhaps *I* will kill you and save him the trouble."

Hunger sprang forward, his teeth and claws closing over the spot where Pál stood—*had stood.* A glimmering archway marked the opening of the portal Pál had shaped.

Hunger's long, serpentine head darted around, searching for Pál's new hiding place. My eyes swept the clearing, skipping lightly over the soldiers' bodies, before searching the trees. Pál had disappeared.

Not for long, though: he dropped out of the sky onto

Hunger's shoulder, a long, wicked blade gleaming in his hands. He plunged the blade into the base of Hunger's neck and then vanished again.

Hunger roared. His dragon's strength and fire were a poor match for an opponent he could not find. He flexed his wings, once, twice, stirring up a windstorm that snagged my hair and whipped it into my eyes.

A great longing poured into me, as though my heart had pushed its way free of my breast and hung vulnerable before me. The yearning tugged me forward, stumbling, but Vasilisa wrenched me back. Noémi broke free of Chernobog, as desperate as I was to reach . . . what? It hardly seemed to matter, only that I reach Hunger, that I put a stop to the terrible, pleasurable need tearing through me.

I found myself weeping without entirely knowing why. As though everything I loved, everything I hoped for, had vanished in a blink.

And then Noémi was plucked up, flying through the air like a rag doll before landing with a soft *whump* on the ground before Hunger.

I scrambled to my feet, sprinting across the clearing. Noémi lay unmoving, the breeze stirred up by Hunger's wings lifting a tendril of golden hair from her head.

Hunger's reaction was instant, faster than conscious thought. He shuddered down to his human form and knelt on the ground by Noémi, any mindfulness of his own danger lost in his concern for her. Pál's dagger was still lodged in his upper shoulder.

Before I could reach them, Pál appeared beside Hunger,

the shimmering line of his portal bright behind him. He whipped the dagger from Hunger's back and drew it, in one smooth line, across his neck.

Blood bloomed like a shadow across his throat, and Hunger fell.

CHAPTER 20

Anna

Hunger's body fell across Noémi, who began to stir. He lay across her knees like a discarded coat, dark blood spoiling his fine linen shirt. Noémi sat up, rubbing at her head.

Then she saw Hunger.

Her cry rang out in the still air, full of ravaged grief. She gathered the praetherian in her arms, his blood marking an uneven pattern across her throat, across the pale dress she wore.

Pál glanced at me and lifted his hand to silence her again, but Chernobog waved him away with a laugh. "Let her scream. There's no one here to care."

The horned god rose into the air, his bat wings nearly invisible against the night sky. "Bring the girls," he said to Pál and Vasilisa, then flew away.

Pál marched toward Noémi, who made a tiny gesture with her fingers. The faint buzz of a spell brushed past me, and Pál slumped to the ground.

At that, Vasilisa raised her hands in the air: a sign of truce. "You needn't fear me, healer. But we must work fast." There was a leashed fury in her voice—the same anger I'd witnessed when we first met, when we'd seen a praetherian shot at a society ball.

We? What a complicated net of alliances this night's work was exposing.

Vasilisa snapped her fingers, and a light hovered above Noémi, enough to see how very still and dead Hunger looked, his neck gaping like a cruel grin. She turned her burning eyes on Noémi. "Can you heal him?"

"You watched him die," Noémi said. "You *let* him die. Why do you want me to heal him now? You might have prevented his death."

"And I might have lost everything else I have worked toward these past years. Chernobog meant to bring down Hunger—if not now, through Pál, then through some other means. Hunger was already lost. Had I fought alongside Hunger, I would have declared myself Chernobog's enemy." Her words were hard, furious.

"You and Hunger together could have defeated Pál and Chernobog," I said. Vasilisa was afraid of nothing and no one.

"And at what cost? The praetheria cannot afford infighting, cannot afford to show disunity among the Four. And Chernobog was not wrong—Hunger *was* weakening. This does not mean I want him dead." She fixed her eyes on Noémi again. "And so I ask, can you heal his body?"

"I—I think so."

"Then do so. By all the gods I have known and loved, we might yet salvage something from this night's misery."

Noémi worked slowly but efficiently, murmuring spells over Hunger. First the interior ligatures and vessels sealed, then she walked her fingers across the gaping line of his throat, and it closed up. Though I wanted to kneel beside her, to offer her my support, I held back, afraid that even with my improved control I might inadvertently spoil her spells. As she worked, I marveled at her strength: were that Gábor, I'm not sure I could have done what she did, even with her gifts.

Wordlessly, Vasilisa handed Noémi a wet cloth (though where she had obtained it, I didn't know, as she hadn't left our side). Noémi wiped the cloth across Hunger's face and neck, blotting the blood from him with a gentleness that betrayed some of her heartbreak. Now that the spellwork was done, grief was creeping across her face, showing in a hollowness of cheek, a wet sheen to her eyes.

By the time she finished, Hunger looked as though he was sleeping, though his stillness belied that.

"Can you bring him back?" Vasilisa asked.

Noémi shook her head, tears starting to slide down her cheeks. "That is not my gift. I have only done so once—but it was a different death. Not so"—she gulped—"violent."

"The Lady might have brought him back," I said, my own pain driving me to be cruel. "Unfortunately, you killed her."

Vasilisa did not move, but her spell-fire lashed across my cheek, and my head snapped back.

"Will you give us a few minutes?" Noémi asked, her voice steady despite her tears. "To say goodbye?"

Vasilisa hesitated the barest moment, then nodded. She

retreated to the edge of the clearing: far enough to give Noémi some privacy but where she could still see us.

When Vasilisa had gone, Noémi's composure broke. She curled her arms around Hunger's head.

"I did not want to love you," she said, and then her voice dissolved into sobs.

I had no words to give her, nothing that could make this disaster less than it was. We had lost the only ally we had in this place—and Noémi had lost even more. I sank down beside her and wrapped my arms around her, hugging her tight as my own tears fell, as though a tight grip might hold at bay, for a moment, the tide that threatened to wash us both away.

God, help us, I prayed, though my prayer felt trapped by the clouds above us. Snow was beginning to fall, heavy and thick.

And then, *Mátyás, where are you?*

If ever there was a time for my cousin to find us, it was now.

CHAPTER 21

Mátyás

I caught the last wisp of mist from Anna's dream as she woke, and it pulled me outside the dream realm. I didn't understand how—I scarcely understood the mechanism of dream-walking as it was; I'd have to ask Hadúr. One moment I was inside Anna's dream; then I was standing in the grey realm, grasping her dream as it faded; then my spirit was standing in the real world, tugged by that wisp of a dream across space.

Reddish-brown rock walls surrounded me. Before me, the bars of a cell stood open, and an unfamiliar praetherian dragged my sleep-slurred cousin from a tiny alcove. She looked tired and drawn, as she had not seemed in her dream.

A guard pulled Anna through the twisting cave, following Vasilisa and Anna's uncle Pál. I trailed them, emerging at length beneath a star-strewn sky. And then everything

266

else faded, because Noémi stood before me. Not the girl I'd seen in dreams, but my sister, in the flesh. Like Anna, she looked worn, but whole. I drifted over to her and set my hand against her cheek, though I knew she couldn't feel it. *Noémi.*

Impossible as it seemed, I'd found them. (It would be more ideal if I knew *where* we were, but that was a minor annoyance I could solve as I found my way back to my body.)

I followed the cadre of praetheria and watched, appalled, as they slaughtered Austrian soldiers. I could not stop them: I would not abandon Anna and Noémi to raise a useless alarm. (The carnage would be over before any alarm had effect.) And I could not work magic so far from the anchor of my physical body. When I tried to rouse some roosting crows to distract the horned praetherian's attention from Anna, they merely twitched in their sleep.

Then the fighting was over, and I breathed a sigh of relief—only to see Anna's uncle attack one of the remaining praetheria, a golden-eyed man in a neatly tailored suit, incongruous in this place of blood. It took me some time to place him, as I'd seen him just once before: he'd helped Anna kill me in the Binding.

Then he was dead, and my sister went to pieces.

Damnation.

I went immediately to Noémi, tried to brush the tears from her cheek. But of course, insubstantial as I was, I accomplished nothing.

"Táltos?" The smooth voice jerked me backward. I'd been so focused on Anna and Noémi that I'd not noticed the ghost materialize beside me. Superficially, the spirit resembled the body on the ground, but the eyes gazing at me blazed with light.

I stuck out my hand, more from habit than any conscious decision. "Eszterházy Mátyás. I don't believe we've been formally introduced, though you killed me once."

"Hunger." He did not take my hand, and I let it drop. It had been a pointless gesture anyway.

I scrambled for something to say. "Dying is the worst part. It gets better after that."

He raised one eyebrow at me. "The Lady brought you back," he said. "You were not dead for more than a moment."

"Six months," I said, and immediately wished I hadn't. I sounded asinine.

"You might bring me back," Hunger said.

"I put a man back in his body once. He started dying again immediately. And just a short time ago, I was unable to rouse crows. I can't do what you ask."

"Your animal persuasion is not rooted in the same part of you as your shifting or your spirit-walking. It requires more physical grounding for the animals to recognize your call. But for this—your sister healed my body, and I do not think I will die again immediately." Hunger looked much more thoughtful than I imagined I'd be in a similar situation. "If you'd be so kind."

I'd told Hadúr I'd be damned before raising the dead again. Well, likely I already was.

"I can't promise anything," I said. "You'll need to put yourself back in your body."

Obediently, Hunger lay down, his spirit melding into the contours of his body. With the same prayer I'd whispered over the boy, "Live, be whole," I sent my inner sense questing toward the body. The shifts were small ones: from an inert heart to a working one, muscles contracting and pumping again. Lungs expanding, pushing oxygen into the blood.

Hunger choked and sputtered and sat up. Noémi looked at him as though the sun had risen after she thought the whole world had ended. I glanced away. The expression on her face—tender, intimate—was private, meant for one person alone, and most definitely not for her brother.

A kick of triumph fizzed through my veins.

I was táltos, and I had made a man live again.

The triumph was chased almost immediately by a bracing terror. *And who am I, to bring a man back from the dead?* What arbitrary whim of fate (or God—I would not put it past Him. Or Her) had decreed I was to have such gifts rather than the next man or woman? A gift that could be blessing and curse alike?

That I could bring a man back did not redeem my failures: it only made the capacity for them greater.

Damn and blast it all to perdition.

I blinked—to clear my head more than anything, as my spirit body did not need to blink—and focused on the scene before me. Noémi had wrapped her arms around Hunger and was sitting practically in his lap. The longing radiating from his eyes as he returned her embrace made me blink again. He stroked her hair with infinite gentleness.

"Did you do this?" Anna demanded of Noémi.

Noémi shook her head wordlessly.

"Mátyás put me back. He's here, in spirit only." Hunger glanced across the clearing to where Vasilisa was already approaching. "We need to go now."

Anna followed his glance. "But Vasilisa wanted us to save you."

"Vasilisa's allegiances are . . . complicated. We have a very old friendship, and while she will not betray me to Chernobog, she will not let you go free, either." He looked back at Anna, gestured to the snow falling thick around them—snow I could see but not feel. "She cannot abide running water—that might slow her."

Anna seemed to gather something significant from his words, because her face took on an intent expression and then the snow stopped drifting. A sheet of water poured from the sky in its place, blocking Vasilisa's advance only twenty paces away.

"The water won't hold her for long," Hunger warned. "Táltos, you must shift them now."

My hesitation lasted only a heartbeat. I might fail—but I had brought a man back from the dead, and I would not fail now for lack of trying.

I started with Anna. At this distance, shifting felt less like the fluid run of water and more like pushing through packed snow—difficult but not impossible. A few moments later, a crow fluttered up from the ground.

"Quickly!" Hunger said. The wall of water was nearly gone, turned to steam by a volley of fire.

I turned to Noémi. Before she had finished shifting, Hunger transformed into a sinuous dragon, and he rose with Noémi's crow into the air. The water wall evaporated, and Vasilisa plunged through it.

She looked up at the retreating shapes, and though I knew she had power enough to pull them back to earth with her net, she only smiled. *Complicated allegiances, indeed.*

With the girls aloft, I sent my spirit after them. I knew from Hadúr's testing that I could not maintain transformations beyond a certain range: if a rabbit-turned-crow got more than a quarter of a mile from me, the shifting reverted. And that was while I was anchored in my body. I needed to stay close enough to Anna and Noémi to maintain their crow shapes.

I was perhaps a hundred feet from the clearing when something jerked me back like a tether. Then I felt it: the nearly invisible weight of one of Vasilisa's nets.

"Welcome back, táltos," she said, still smiling at the sky. "Don't worry about your sister and your cousin. They won't get far without you."

CHAPTER 22

Anna

Flying was glorious: the rush of wind past my beak, the blood pumping through my featherlight body, the rhythmic flutter of my wings, the lift of an air current beneath me. If this is what Mátyás felt when he shifted to crow form, why did he ever come back?

Relief made me giddy. For the first time in weeks, the heavy weight of stone did not hang over my head, the constant uncertainty of my future did not gnaw at my heart.

I cut through the dark night—and I was free.

Then a hiccup in my flight: abruptly, I was heavy and sluggish, falling through the air rather than floating. I waved my arms, but the motion that powered my flight was worthless without feathers and hollow bones.

The hiccup lasted only a moment before I was back in feathered form, my heart beating double-time. What had happened? Had Mátyás released our shifting shapes—or had we perhaps outpaced him? I slowed a little and caught sight of Noémi diving toward some shrubs below.

I was still a good twenty feet above the ground when I lost the crow shape altogether.

My throat constricted around a scream as I fell. Every experience of falling flicked through my head: trying to soar over the estate pond as a child, crashing into the Binding spell when Lady Berri created her portal, dropping from the air outside the barracks in Vienna. I'd been lucky so far—but how far could I press that luck?

Four times might be too much.

A great *whoomph* and I landed sooner than expected, against something firm but not hard. Great leathery wings were raised around my head, and my dazed senses parsed this: Hunger had caught me. He settled on the ground a moment later, and I slid from his back to collapse in a heap on the cold grasses. The stars spun overhead, and I drew in a ragged breath.

Chills pricked gooseflesh along my skin. My feathered shape wasn't the only thing I'd lost in shifting. My clothes were gone as well. I should have guessed as much—I'd seen Mátyás shift, after all—but eighteen years' drilling in modesty asserted itself: I yelped and crossed my arms, trying to shield as much of myself as possible from the night air and from Hunger—and from anyone else who might be passing.

Hunger had already shifted, scrambling to the tree where Noémi clung precariously to the upper branches. He was fully dressed, a trick Mátyás could stand to learn.

"Let go," Hunger said. "I'll catch you."

"I can't," Noémi said. "I'm . . . naked."

"So much the better," Hunger said, and I could hear the smile in his voice. But from Noémi's indignant cry, this was not the right response. "Devil take it!" he said. "That's not what I—that is, I *did* mean it, I think you're lovely however you're dressed or undressed. But if it makes you uncomfortable, I'll find something. Hold on."

I craned my head to see Hunger pluck a few strands of grass and weave them together. Under his fingers the weaving grew, pulling in shadows from the night around us until he had a length of fabric that rippled like lake water. He threw the cloak up at Noémi, and then tossed a second one to me. It fell over me like the airiest of silks. I wrapped it around me and sat up in time to see Noémi drop from the tree into Hunger's arms.

Noémi called Mátyás's name a few times, but there was no response: no shifting, no other signs that he'd heard us.

"We need to keep moving," Hunger said. "We escaped too easily."

"You think Vasilisa let us go?" Noémi asked.

"I think Vasilisa is willing to let Chernobog and Pál believe I am dead, but I know her. She is only toying with you."

I wanted to find a place to sleep until my body was drunk on it. Dawn was not far off, and I'd not slept much before the guard had awakened me. Whatever had happened to Mátyás, perhaps he could reach me in my dreams. But sleeping would have to wait until we were safe—or in what passed for safety in this world.

)(

Without Mátyás to shift us, we made our way on foot. Hunger offered to carry us, but I thought a dragon flying in daylight might be too conspicuous, and Noémi vetoed it on grounds that he was still recovering and could scarce bear his own weight, let alone ours. She fretted about the small magic Hunger used to power our cloaks, so as soon as we came within hailing distance of a settlement, Hunger disappeared.

He returned a few minutes later with blouses, skirts, and a pair of hooded woolen cloaks, and I did not ask how he'd procured them—or how he had come to guess my size so well. I ducked behind a tree to scramble into my new clothes, and the magic cloak I'd worn reverted to a few dried strands of grass.

We did not speak of what had passed the night before: the attack on the soldiers or Pál's betrayal or Hunger's resurrection.

Near midday, we stumbled across a farmhouse where a pig slaughter was under way. I knew from Noémi that such were common as fall turned to winter: the snowstorm we'd stumbled through had left fainter traces in the valley than the mountains we'd fled but still enough to prompt the household to action.

We had no money to offer the farmer or his wife—and no time to offer labor in exchange—but Hunger smiled at the woman, and we were each given a bowl of savory pork stew alongside crusty bread. I watched the others work as we ate: wrapping the cuts of meat; grinding the excess into sausage; preparing thick, fat-ribboned slabs of *szalonna* for storage against the winter.

Their kindness, as much as the warm food, sustained us as we moved on.

We sheltered together that night in a rough lean-to made of dead branches stacked together. Noémi and I both gravitated toward Hunger's radiating warmth, and I tried to ignore the discomfort of sleeping so close to a man who was not a relative—a man who had seemed to be, until the previous night, my opponent, if not my enemy.

Sometime in the black stillness of middle-night, I woke, chilled. Hunger was gone, and Noémi was curled in on herself like a small child.

A heartbeat of panic: Had he abandoned us? Betrayed us?

Then my eyes adjusted to the thin moonlight, and I saw Hunger standing a little distance from our shelter. Without looking at me, he lifted a hand to gesture me to silence. I stood and, stepping as carefully as I could, joined him.

"What is it?" I whispered.

He didn't answer, but I heard it anyway: the thin, far-away howl of a wolf. Then a second call to answer it, closer. Much closer.

"Vasilisa?" I asked. There were still wolves in these mountains.

"I think so."

I had not seen Vasilisa's wolves since she had set them on me and Emilija just before Mátyás found us. I had severed her bond with the wolves, and they had fled from her while she cursed at me. She must have reharnessed them—or collected new ones. I shivered, tugging my stolen cloak closer about me.

"Stay here," Hunger said, and with a peculiar lunge, he shifted into his dragon self and lifted into the air. A few minutes later, the orange glow of fire lit the night, and the smell of singed fur filled the air. A pained whimper echoed off the frozen trees. He said nothing when he returned, only shifted back, his black scales shrinking down before melting into the trousers and coat he wore. I woke Noémi, and we moved on.

⋊

Some hours later, well into morning, we found ourselves gaining on a small group of women, most young, led by a girl in a distinctive red cloak, with twin braids down her back.

Exhaustion forgotten, I ran toward them, throwing my arms around Emilija, who stumbled back at the sudden assault. She stiffened under my embrace, then relaxed as she recognized me and returned the hug. Beside her, the lidérc grinned at me.

"You're safe!" I said. "But who are all these with you?"

"Emilija has been collecting them," the lidérc said.

"I have been *recruiting* them," Emilija corrected. "A motivated woman makes as good a soldier as a man."

"But for whom?" I asked, thinking of Emilija's father leading the Croatian armies across Hungary.

"For *us*," Emilija said. "I was in those caverns with you; we cannot let the Four take over our homes." She caught sight of Hunger behind Noémi, and her hand went to the butt of a gun at her hip. *Where had she found* that? She'd been as penniless as we were when she left the caves—and as poorly armed. "What is he doing here?"

"The Four have driven him out," I said.

Emilija did not remove her hand. "What guarantee do you have that we can trust him?"

"You have none." Hunger smiled slightly. "Save perhaps this: is there not a human saying that the enemy of your enemy is your friend?"

"The enemy of my enemy might still prove my enemy," Emilija said.

All pretense of humor dropped from Hunger's face. "I would sooner die than bring harm to Noémi. Beyond that, my goal has always been to save the praetheria. I committed to a path I thought most likely to win them security, but that path is lost now. Ordinary praetheria will be little better off under Chernobog's rule than under the Hapsburgs'. I will do what I can to help you end this war if you, in turn, will help me find a better solution for the praetheria than these so-called sanctuaries."

Emilija studied him for a long moment, then let her hand drop from the gun. "You have my word. But I will be watching you, praetherian."

Hunger bowed. "I would expect no less, soldier."

It was midafternoon on the fourth day following our escape when we finally reached an outlying arm of the Hungarian armies. Emilija's recruits were better-provisioned than we were, so we did not starve, though I was growing tired of unadorned bread.

The troops were not hard to spot: long columns of worn, grim-faced men carrying limp standards. They were spread across multiple roads, reaching for miles across the plains. We quickened our pace until we'd reached the trailing line of soldiers.

The men's eyes flicked over us. The lidérc kept her pointed teeth sheathed, her feet booted, and her eyes downcast.

"The Austrian armies are pursuing: this is no place for women. Go home." It was a boy who spoke, dirt grimed into the creases around his eyes. He looked my age.

Emilija threw her cloak back to expose her gun. "I'm a Red Mantle. I daresay I fight better than you do."

His eyes widened, this time with a grudging respect. "And the rest of them?"

"We're looking for General Richard Guyon," I said, naming Gábor's commanding officer before Emilija could get into an argument.

"Guyon?" The boy picked at his ear and glanced toward an older red-haired man who'd stopped to watch our approach. "That the division that was ambushed in the mountains?"

The man nodded. "Austrian soldiers waited for them just outside a mountain pass, damn near murdered the lot. What's left of them is up ahead of us."

What's left of them.

My heart seemed to stop. Had Gábor made it out?

"Well, then, they'll need new recruits," Emilija said cheerfully.

I could not seem to breathe. I felt again that cold shock of horror I experienced when I'd returned to my room to find Gábor's letters gone. Gábor had told me that Guyon's troops were in the Bükk Mountains, approaching a pass. He didn't name the pass, but there might have been enough identifying information for someone like Pál to get word to the Austrians.

The lidérc slid into place beside me. "Anna? You look as if you've just seen someone die."

I forced my lips to move. "Gábor was with Guyon's division."

Noémi drew close, took my hand. "Don't despair yet. Maybe he still is."

But as we cut south across the fields, to skirt the soldiers clogging the road, all I could hear was the hissing echo of my words: *was, was, was.*

⚜

It was near dark when we reached Guyon's division, tents already springing up, soldiers huddled around a handful of fires. I pulled my cloak tighter against the chill and tried to remember to breathe.

Richard Guyon proved to be a dark-haired man with a rather long nose, with his left arm in a sling. He was standing just outside a tent, receiving some briefing as we approached, so we waited until he was done speaking. The private leading us stepped forward.

"This young woman has a message for you, sir."

Guyon surveyed me somewhat skeptically. "Yes? Be quick about it, young lady. I've a war to fight."

His Hungarian sounded like mine, with the accent of

his English homeland. I'd known he was English—Gábor had said as much in his letters. But finding a fellow countryman in the midst of a war was like coming on a rose blooming in December: an unlooked-for gift. A piece of home. My throat constricted, and all the words I'd practiced abandoned me. *Where is Gábor? Will you help us end this war?*

"Well?"

"I've brought you some soldiers, sir," Emilija said, gesturing to the women behind her.

"Can they fight?"

"As well as most of your men, I'd wager." Emilija raised her chin.

The tent flap lifted behind the general, and a young man emerged, already speaking to Guyon. But as his eyes took us in, his words fell away.

"Anna," Gábor said instead, a smile breaking across his face: sunlight after a rainstorm, light fractured into a million colors.

My heart swelled, lifted, burst—too full to stay neatly confined behind my ribs. "Gábor."

He was here. Whole. *Safe.*

The terrible weight I had carried for the past hours lifted a fraction, though I should have to reckon later with my guilt for all the men who were not here, who were not whole or safe.

General Guyon raised his eyebrows. "You know this woman, Kovács?"

Even in the pale light of the lantern I could see Gábor was blushing. My own face felt warm, but I did not care.

Gábor was here. *Is,* I thought. *Not was.* I could withstand any embarrassment for that, any pain.

"We are friends," I said in English. More than friends.

Guyon's eyebrows lifted even higher. "You're English. And a lady too, I'd swear, though I've never seen one with such a haircut—or in such a place."

I dropped a curtsy. "Lady Anna Arden," I said. "My mother is Hungarian." As though that explained everything—my short, unruly hair; my sudden appearance in the midst of a Hungarian war.

He puffed out a breath. "Well. You'd best tell me how else I may help you."

I need to apologize. . . . No. There was no time for that.

I switched to Hungarian for the sake of the others, who did not all speak English, though it was harder to find the words after the brief stint in my mother tongue. "We've brought a warning. The Russian army does not fight alongside Austria, not entirely. They fight in collusion with a praetherian army, which is biding its time, waiting for our own forces to weaken before attacking. I do not know what the praetheria have promised Russia, but I do not trust them."

"Galicia," Hunger said, stepping forward. "The Four have promised the tsar Galicia in exchange for his aid—and the safety of the Russian people. Austria and Hungary have no such promise, and if the plan unfolds as intended, the praetheria will establish a stronghold here and then spread out across Europe, into the Mediterranean, and on-ward."

Beneath the shadow of the hat he wore, Hunger's golden

eyes looked ordinary and brown. If I did not know him for praetherian, I would never have guessed it.

"These are serious claims—but how do I know they are true?"

"I believe Anna," Gábor said. "As long as I've known her, she's been a woman of integrity."

I pressed my lips together, swallowing the words that would betray my damnable mistake that destroyed much of Guyon's army.

"We've been to the caves where the praetherian army prepares," Emilija said. "We were held prisoner there and only recently escaped. I am Emilija Dragović, a Red Mantle and the daughter of Josip Dragović. I would not abandon my father and my army without good cause."

The lidérc stood back, her gaze lowered. But the line of her neck was taut: she was not comfortable here, surrounded by human soldiers. I made a mental note to ensure that one of us stayed with her.

General Guyon tugged at his beard. "You'll need to speak with Hadúr and Görgey."

It took only a few minutes for Gábor to gather horses for our small group: Noémi, Emilija, the lidérc, Hunger, and me. Emilija's recruits stayed behind with Guyon's men. Emilija fretted at leaving them, but Gábor assured her that they would be given food and a place to sleep.

As Gábor led me to my horse, he tugged at my short hair with one hand, then rested his fingers against my cheek. I caught his hand and pressed my lips into his palm. Everywhere our skin touched seemed to spark.

"I should not be so happy to see you here, in the middle of a war," Gábor said with a soft laugh. "But I am. I worried when your letters stopped coming."

An angry red line peeked out just above his collar, and I tugged the fabric down, fingering the welt as it crawled across his collarbone before disappearing beneath his shirt. He laid his hand over mine. "I'm all right."

"But others aren't." I swallowed. "Gábor—your letters. They were stolen from me when you were in the mountains."

"But you erased them?"

I looked at him, stricken. "All but the last."

A long moment passed. He didn't say anything, only nodded shortly and cupped his hands to help me mount. Once I was safely astride, he backed away, not letting his fingers linger a fraction longer than necessary.

My heart ached, guilt compounded by a new fear. Gábor must hate me for what I'd done. Once the initial joy of seeing him whole had faded, I'd thought I would no longer need to fling inky words across the distance between us, trying to span it with paper and pauses and imperfect thoughts. We would have spoken words, looks, touches— perhaps even kisses.

I hadn't considered that there might be worse distances between us than the ones bridged by paper and ink.

He led us under the faint sliver of a waxing moon. Noémi kindled a blue Lumen light to supplement the meager illumination from the sky and sidled her horse beside Gábor. "Have you seen Mátyás?"

284

Gábor frowned. "I've not seen him for several days. He was with Hadúr."

An hour or more passed before we found Hadúr, talking to one of the captains. Mátyás had mentioned him a time or two as a Hungarian demigod, but I was still unprepared for the reality: the hulking size of him, the dark curling hair, his sheer physical presence. Or the copper helm he still wore, dented and smeared with blood.

He turned to us, scowling. But the scowl lifted when he recognized Gábor, and his lips curved as his eyes rested on the lidérc. He inclined his head gravely. "Well met, sister."

"Sister?" I echoed.

The lidérc shook her head. "Not literal sister," she said. "A sister of the heart. And your question betrays a good deal of ignorance."

Gábor introduced us, adding, "We've come for Mátyás. And to talk about the praetherian threat."

Hadúr nodded, as though the request did not surprise him, and led us to a quiet stretch of the camp, where a small fire burned before a tent, identical to the hundreds of others scattered nearby. Bahadır was stirring something in a pan over a small fire, and he sprang up as we approached. His eyes flashed across us, lighting with recognition and then lingering on Noémi.

"You must be Mátyás's sister. And you are a healer? Perhaps you can help him."

"Why does he need a healer?" Noémi asked, whitening.

"Let me see him."

Bahadır pulled back the flap of the tent to reveal Mátyás, resting on a cot, his chest lifting and falling with shallow breaths, his face still.

285

"He's been like this for five days," Bahadır said. "We have carted him behind the army and given him broth, but I am afraid he cannot sustain this for long."

Five days: since the night Hunger was killed and then brought back. Since the night Mátyás's shifting broke and we fell out of the sky.

Noémi knelt beside Mátyás and ran skilled fingers across his pulse, checking beneath his eyelids, listening to his breath. She lifted her head to look at Hunger. "There is nothing wrong with his body: why will he not wake?"

But it was Hadúr who answered. "There has always been this danger for a táltos who traveled: that he might go too far from his body, that he might overextend himself and not find his way back."

I tabulated all the things Mátyás had done that night: found me in a dream, followed me out of a dream, brought Hunger back, shifted Noémi and me to escape. Was this the cost of his work?

I wanted to be angry with Hunger for asking Mátyás to bring him back, for pushing Mátyás to shift us instead of fighting Vasilisa, and thus risking all of us, but I couldn't. My own mistakes had been costly enough: I had no right casting more blame.

"You think Mátyás's spirit is lost?" Noémi asked. "How do we find him?"

"Another walker might find him," Hadúr said. "But there were never many of those."

"Then we must find one." Noémi turned to Hunger, her eyes pleading. "Can you . . . ?"

But Hunger shook his head before she'd finished speaking. "I cannot do what you ask. Nor, I think, can anyone here. You will have to pray your brother finds his own way back."

X

Morning came all too early, with sharp-edged frost creeping across dull earth. My muscles ached from too many nights spent sleeping on cold dirt and not in a proper bed. Noémi did not appear to have slept at all: she'd spent the night beside Mátyás, trying to feed him the broth Bahadır had made.

"No change?" I asked.

She shook her head.

Later that morning, we were summoned to a council of war. Noémi and Bahadır stayed behind to tend Mátyás, but the rest of us followed Gábor to a large tent at the center of camp where Hadúr held court. Gábor did not look at me, and my heart twisted. *You deserve this,* I reminded myself.

The tent was already crowded with military men, though I recognized only a couple: Richard Guyon and Kossuth Lajos, the provisional head of all Hungary. He was smaller than I imagined, a medium-sized man with a neatly trimmed chestnut beard and confident demeanor.

Hadúr reported to the assembled men what we had told him of the praetherian plans, along with their possible alliance with Russia.

A thin general with a pointed beard said, "How do we know this report is true? What proof have we?"

Hadúr indicated me, Emilija, and the lidérc. "These

young women have been to the praetherian camp. They've seen and heard the preparations they warn us of."

Pointed-beard scoffed. "Hearsay. No doubt they're telling a tale to make themselves important."

"I'm a soldier," Emilija said, her hands fisting in her lap. "Not a silly society gossip. I do not make false reports."

"You're Josip Dragović's daughter? Your father leads armies against us even now—such stories might only be a ploy to frighten us into surrender."

"You might lack a sense of honor," Emilija said, her eyes flashing. "But I do not!"

Goaded by the man's doubt, I added, "I broke the Binding spell and helped free the revolutionaries trapped near Buda Castle. Will you tell me also that I am not a patriot, that I am only telling a tale?" A few faces lit up at this, but several men whispered to each other, and the whispers did not seem happy.

Hunger said, "Until a week ago, I was a leader among the praetheria. I am here now only to stop a war. You should believe these women—and do so before the winter solstice, when the power of many praetheria reaches its peak."

Those nearest Hunger shifted away from him, dismay and repulsion creasing their faces.

"You're praetherian," a man with rounded glasses said, surprised. "You might have been planted as a spy."

Beside me, the lidérc curled her booted feet beneath her seat and pressed her lips together. My heart hurt for her. She had come here in good faith, believing that the Hungarian army might want the same things she did—

security, an end to this war. But all they had shown was mistrust of everything she was: woman and praetherian. I wanted to stand and shout at the room, but the memory of my disastrous confrontation with the Congress in Vienna kept me quiet.

Another military leader, with broad red cheeks and curling hair, turned an accusatory finger on Hadúr. "You claim to be a god of war—but you were locked away in the Binding, same with the other praetheria. Who's to say that you are not setting us up for betrayal, even now? Perhaps you and this golden-eyed monster are working together."

An uneasy murmur ran around the room.

Kossuth sighed and rubbed his temple. "I have heard reports that you are a formidable warrior, and doubtless your military expertise exceeds mine. But your methods of seizing control of this army are highly unorthodox—if not treasonous—and I am not at all certain we can afford to let you stay. At the least, your aims may not be congruent with those of the Hungarian government."

Hadúr's lips thinned to a grim line. "If you do not believe me, I will not force my aid on you. If you are content to see Hungary destroyed, so be it. I cannot help a people who will not see their own danger."

In dismay, I watched him leave the tent. If Hadúr abandoned us, how would we persuade the others to stop this war?

The man with glasses—General Görgey, I think— looked at Kossuth. "You are making a mistake."

"It is my mistake to make," Kossuth said crossly.

"It will cost all of us."

A breathless messenger darted into the room. "General Haynau has broken the siege at Komárom," he said. "The Hungarian armies in the west are in disarray, retreating toward us, and Haynau pursues them."

Beside me, Emilija hissed.

Komárom had been one of the last freestanding strongholds in western Hungary: for it to fall meant a definite blow for our armies. But I did not understand what had put the strain in Emilija's face. "Who is Haynau?"

"The Hyena of Brescia," Emilija said, drawing her lips back in a snarl. "An undisciplined sadist who gives a bad name to all military men. He's not one of your old-school gentleman generals. Haynau fights to win, and he is merciless."

A gust of air whirled in behind the messenger. It smelled of ice and snow. It smelled of death.

Kossuth glanced from the messenger to General Görgey. "Find Hadúr. Bring him back." As Görgey slipped from the tent, Kossuth waved at Hunger. "Put that one under guard."

Two soldiers flanked Hunger, who stood unresistant, only his eyes hard. I doubted the guards could hold him against his will.

Görgey returned a few minutes later, alone. "Hadúr is gone."

CHAPTER 23

Anna

It took nearly a week for General Haynau, the Hyena of Brescia, to reach us: a week of flat-out retreat across the *puszta,* praying for General Bem or Perczel or another of the Hungarian reinforcements to reach us before Haynau did.

Hadúr still had not returned, and I could not help feeling we were marching not away from but toward some cataclysm. At least Mátyás still lived, though he had lost too much weight. His clothes hung from him, and Noémi fretted at his increasing pallor.

The lidérc returned from hunting one evening to find Noémi, Emilija, and me huddled together for warmth in our makeshift camp; the generals had decided nighttime fires might betray our location too easily—as though the crushed vegetation in a wide swath on either side of the road we followed had not already signaled our whereabouts.

The generals had also decided that setting and striking tents took up valuable time, so we were to sleep under the stars. This ruling, of course, did not apply to the generals themselves. Mátyás slept in a cart nearby, covered with as many blankets as we could spare. Bahadır was gone: he'd disappeared not long after Hadúr, and no one seemed to know where. I did not think he'd abandon Mátyás lightly, so one of the generals must have given him orders.

The lidérc carried a brace of hares slung over one shoulder. "I've got news," she said, and we clustered around her, even though news those days was invariably bad. She poked around the campsite. "Where is the fire? This cold bites into me like a fene."

A fene egye meg. Let the evil spirit eat it. Mátyás had been fond of that particular epithet. I hoped he'd live to use it again.

"No fires, remember?" Emilija said.

"I could warm you," Hunger said, joining us. The lidérc snorted. His imprisonment had not lasted long, but a guard trailed him at all times.

"You only wish you might." She glanced around at her audience. "So, my news: Haynau is not alone."

The lidérc took a bite of the rabbit leg and swallowed. I swallowed too, reminding myself that not everyone needed—or even liked—the taste of well-cooked meat. The lidérc's eyes lingered on me, as though she could sense my discomfort and was enjoying it.

Or maybe her gaze lingered for a different reason. "Franz Joseph, emperor of all Austria, comes with him."

I lay awake for a long time that night. It was cold, just

as the previous night had been. And the night before that. But somehow this cold cut deeper, grating against my bones despite the blankets cocooning me. I shifted, worry for Mátyás and the dilemma confronting us eating at my thoughts: we could not stop the praetheria without the cooperation of the human armies, but the human armies would not believe us. I thought of Franz Joseph, likely sleeping before a fire—perhaps even in a bed. If I could get a message to him, would he listen?

Tiny flakes of snow freckled my cheeks, my closed eyelids. I turned to my side and pulled a blanket over me so it covered my face.

I fell asleep at last, after I had given up on sleep entirely, and tumbled into a dream of home. I was back in England, with my parents and James and even Catherine, who set a round, rosy bundle of a baby in my arms. Everything was safe and comfortable and known. When I woke, it was to find my eyelashes sealed shut with ice, the remains of my tears frozen tracks across my cheeks.

X

Gábor found me a day later, at dusk. I had seen him only briefly since the council of war: he was busy as Guyon's aide, and I could not leave Noémi for long, though I knew Hunger would help her tend Mátyás. But Noémi waved me away as Gábor approached, telling me fresh air would be good for me.

"Will you walk with me?" he asked.

I searched his face, trying to read if he was still angry at me for what I'd done. I deserved the anger, but I did not like how it hung between us like the winter snow: an icy, formidable barrier.

"Of course," I said.

Gábor steered me toward the edges of the camp, where we might have some privacy. Hooting followed us but quickly faded away. He made no move toward me but walked in tandem beside me, his arms swinging. His fingers closed, then opened, then closed again. My eyes drifted to the fine line of his jaw, now covered with a short beard. He had always been clean-shaven before. I wanted to touch it, feel the thick hairs rough against my fingertips, but I did not dare.

"I'm sorry," I said. "I never meant for anyone to be hurt—I only wanted to keep a part of you with me."

Gábor turned to look at me. "Men died, Anna. Some of them were my friends."

"I know." I was used to being chastised—by my mother, by my governess, even by Ginny and Noémi. But it hurt more coming from Gábor, because his good opinion mattered more. I felt a sudden sympathy for Emma, from Miss Austen's novel, standing before Mr. Knightley. I only wished I had her assurance of a happy ending. "I would undo their deaths if I could—I would give up my own life if it would change anything."

Gábor sighed, the stiffness going out of him. "I don't want that. Besides, if we are going to assign blame, I deserve some of it for writing details of our location when I should have been more discreet. Anyway, I did not come to upbraid you but to tell you that General Bem is close, at last. And that Petőfi Sándor is dead—killed fighting along-side Bem as they withdrew from Transylvania."

I caught my breath. I had not known the poet well, but he had always been so vivid, so full of life. He had yearned to die in battle, and so he had—much as I might wish it otherwise. I remembered his pretty young wife, whom I'd met at a ball in Buda-Pest. Did she know?

"They're going to turn the army around," Gábor said. "General Görgey believes that if we act quickly enough, we can surprise the Austrian soldiers before reinforcements reach them. With Bem's aid, we'll be equally matched."

I rubbed my hands against my arms, where the crisp air pricked gooseflesh beneath my woolen sleeves. Now that we were alone, I found I did not know what to do or say. The words I wanted to say—a lifetime of words—clotted in my throat. I could not seem to disentangle the ones that would do what I wanted them to: cut through everything that separated us. The heart was only an organ of muscle and blood, beating in my chest. How was I—or anyone—to translate its longing into action or language with any fluency?

Gábor took my hand, and we walked into the gloaming until all the sounds of the camp died away on the air. We talked of little things and big things, of Emilija's training any woman in camp who would join her, of Mátyás, his cheekbones jutting like ships from his hollowing cheeks. Gábor fell silent, his eyes fixed on the far horizon, where only a rim of gold remained. His hand slid from mine.

"What is it?" I asked.

"I—" He began, broke off, began again. "Guyon sent

me to talk to some new recruits today, to persuade them to stay. And I did it. They will stay now, whether they wished to or not."

I didn't understand the tightness in his voice, as though it pained him to tell me. "But surely we need them?"

"Yes, we need them." His voice was grim. "But, Anna, I used a Persuasion spell."

"But . . ." I recoiled a fraction before I caught myself. Persuasion was Coremancer magic, and Gábor had shown no sign of it before. Of all Luminate gifts, Persuasion troubled me most: my mother, my sister, my uncle Pál, and Archduchess Sophie had all used their Coremancer gifts to fit me to their idea of what I should be.

"It's come on gradually, since the Binding. I didn't realize what I had until the war had begun, when Kossuth sent me as a government commissioner to help recruit soldiers, then to watch Görgey. I thought at first that it was only that I had a gift for talking, that in wartime my eloquence mattered more than my race." His lips twisted ruefully. "We have a saying, 'Among the *gadže,* a Rom's only defense is his words.' I thought that's all they were: words, powerfully spoken."

He fell quiet, and the silence stretched between us. I waited.

"I think I wrote you about the Romani men who joined my first division. They approached us, wanting to join up as soldiers. The lieutenant who met them cursed at them, told them that they were only good for carrying bugles and drums, and we had enough damned minstrels already. I couldn't help myself: my anger boiled over into words. I told the lieutenant to stop speaking, to apologize at once. I told him that any man—or woman, for that matter—who wanted to fight should be allowed to join, and it was our privilege, not theirs, that they did so."

He laughed a little and rubbed his forehead. "To my shock, the man did. Apologized profusely, showed them where to get uniforms. And nothing more was said until later, when I heard his friends ribbing him about giving in to me. One said it must be a Romani curse, and the others all seemed to agree. I realized that the burning heat in my veins had been magic, not merely anger—but of course the magic that becomes a 'Luminate gift' when found in the nobility becomes a 'curse' when someone like me wields it."

I had not heard this bitterness from him in a long time. Why had he never told me of it before? I took his hand again and did not wince when he gripped a little too tight.

"They knew Kossuth had sent me, so no one dared confront me directly. Instead, I found a dead mouse in my boots, and my soup at dinner was salted to the point that it was inedible. I was glad when Kossuth recalled me a week or so later and sent me to Perczel. I convinced the commander to let the Romani men go with me—I didn't dare leave them with that division, and Perczel was much more appreciative of willing bodies."

He caught my eyes again, his own hollow. "Though given the disastrous battles that followed, I'm not sure I did them a favor."

I traced his fingers between mine. "Their deaths are not your fault. You did the best you could with the information you had."

But was that true? I'd done the same when I broke the

297

Binding—and yet, on sleepless nights, I could not help question whether the war, the praetherian threat, could have been avoided if I'd done nothing. If Herr Steinberg had killed me outside the Binding in Eszterháza, perhaps the only thing on the plains this December would have been herds of cattle, making their placid way through the frostbitten grasses.

"Why didn't you tell me before?" I asked.

"I couldn't find the right words in a letter. And then I did not want to see you look at me differently. The Coremancers you have known have been . . . difficult."

I gave a half laugh. "True."

"Of all Luminate gifts, this is the last I would claim," he said. "I don't want this magic. All my life I have seen the damage that compulsion brings in its wake. People don't like to be forced, by magic or by physical threat. I think of what I could do as a Coremancer, how I could change the laws governing the Romani, and I am tempted—more than I like to admit. But if such laws are won by magic, will they hold? Will people be more resentful if they find they've been Persuaded into better treatment? And what if I cannot stop there? What if I use the gift for my own gain? I don't want my words to be a weapon."

"Words do not have to be a weapon," I said. "They can be a balm too."

I hesitated. The words hovering on my tongue could not be recalled once spoken. But Gábor needed them, and that need was greater than my pride. "I love you," I said, giving him the truest balm I knew.

I wrapped my arms around him, and after a heartbeat

where I began to question everything, he settled his around me, and dropped a kiss against my temple. *"Me tut kamav."* He dropped a second kiss on my hair. "I love you."

"Me tut kamav," I whispered back, and his eyes widened with such joyful surprise that I wished I knew more Romani, to envelop him in words that reminded him of home. I should have to learn. "I wish I had something better to offer you than my flawed gifts."

He ran a finger down a strand of my hair that had worked loose. "All of us offer flawed gifts alongside the true ones. Your gifts do not define you; you define your gifts. If you cannot see your courage and compassion, I can. But I don't love you for your good qualities or your bad ones. I love *you.* Love doesn't differentiate like that."

I smiled at him, gratitude for his goodness—the unspeakable gift of his *love*—suffusing me with warmth despite the cold night. "I think you answered your own fear: you may have a Coremancer gift, but that gift does not define you—you shape that gift. And because you are thoughtful and honorable, you will shape that gift in thoughtful and honorable ways."

His eyes were very soft as he smiled back. "Thank you." Then he bent his head toward me, brushing his lips against mine, and we did not talk again for some time.

I had never been so sharply aware of my own body. Culture and the religion of my childhood had trained me to see it as a mere thing to be ornamented, a vehicle to move my eyes and my mind through the world. But now I saw my body as something infinitely more, as matter that both desired and was desired. Even in my brief flirtation with

Freddy back in England, I'd never felt like this: as though the whole world were centered in the places where our skin and lips touched.

Was it the war and the awareness of my own mortality that made me feel this physicality so acutely? Or was it that seeing myself through Gábor's eyes—as someone worthy of love—freed me to acknowledge my own feelings?

The light around us shifted, long blue shadows swallowing the last of the early winter's day. It was past time to go back—both Gábor and I had other responsibilities. But I didn't want to go. I didn't want to lose him again, even if it was only to another camp. I didn't want to face the battle and its aftermath—the uncertain grind toward an equally uncertain future.

I willed the moment to stretch out indefinitely. Once, I had thought I wanted everything my world had to offer: a place among the powerful, important work, respect. The war had chiseled all that away from me, honing my wants until they remained few and bright: a breath of peace, my family, Gábor.

"What if we didn't go back?" I asked. There was no one to stop us from walking away from this war.

His eyes closed for an instant: veins drew purple tracings across his eyelids. Was he pulled to this vision, as I was? His eyes opened again, dark in the fading light.

"Is that really what you want?"

Yes. I sighed. "No. Of course not."

Because how did one live in the aftermath of a tragedy? No matter how beguiling the possibility of flight, guilt would poison everything between us. "I just want you to be safe. I want us all to be safe. I want the war to be over."

I wished someone could promise me that we would survive this, that everything would come out right in the end. But there were no promises, not here, not now. Perhaps not ever.

"I know." Gábor held my hands to his chest, where I could feel the thrum of his heartbeat against my knuckles. "We're doing the best we can."

What if that was not enough? That uncertainty loomed before us like a chasm. One misstep, and we'd all fall. I rose on my toes to kiss him, meeting his ache with my own aching. The kiss we shared was frantic, nearly wild, as though we could will away the war and our own shadows with the heat between us. When we broke apart, our lips were already chilled with the early-winter air, our breath coming white as fog between us.

X

The lidérc helped me slip away later that night. We borrowed a pair of horses, and her glamour hid us as we moved past bivouacking soldiers. The winter's chill deepened as we rode, clouds above us blotting out the moon and the stars but withholding snow for now.

"Thank you for helping me," I told her.

"I am not doing this purely for you—the sooner this war ends, the sooner I can go home."

She almost never spoke of home, only of a mythic mother who had not survived the Binding.

"Where is home?"

She was quiet for a moment, weighing her answer. "There's a curve of the Duna River where the hills capture and hold the summer light, not far from Pécs. That is where I would go, were I free to go anywhere."

I pulled my cloak tighter around me. "It sounds heavenly. I've begun to wonder if I shall ever be warm again." Or safe.

"You would be welcome to visit," the lidérc said, her voice diffident.

"If we get through this war, I should be honored." I hesitated a moment, because the lidérc was guarded about her past, but curiosity goaded me. "You've come a great distance with Mátyás, and then with Emilija and with me. None of us are praetherian. Why do you help us?"

She was silent so long that I began to think I'd offended her, and she would not answer. Then, "It's not just about you. Or about me. If the praetheria are to survive, if humans are to survive, then we have to find a way to live together without fighting. Also"—a rare flash of her pointed teeth—"Emilija has more sense than most humans. And Mátyás was kind to me."

"And me?" It was a foolish question, fishing for a compliment, and I regretted it as soon as I'd uttered it.

"You amuse me," she said, her grin growing wider.

I started to laugh, then choked it back, remembering our need for secrecy and speed. She might have said much worse.

I'd expected to travel for some time, as Haynau's army was some four or five miles behind us. But we had not traveled half that distance when we began to encounter foot soldiers in full uniform, followed by mounted cavalry. It was an hour past midnight.

We pulled off the road into the shelter of a copse. The lidérc's glamour would hide us, but only so far—if the soldiers bumped into our horses, the glamour would not suffice to convince them they'd felt nothing.

The soldiers carried muted Lumen lamps, casting only enough light to reveal their footing but not enough to be seen at a distance. A cannon rumbled past us.

The soldiers were moving into place for a nighttime assault.

I swallowed a curse. I might have lost my only opportunity to speak to Franz Joseph. Once battle was engaged, he'd be much more difficult to reach. And what of the soldiers sleeping behind us? "We should warn the armies."

"They'll have sentries to give warning faster than we can reach them," the lidérc pointed out. "What about the emperor?"

"We can't reach him now," I said, gesturing at the waves of soldiers.

The lidérc smiled again, a curiously feral smile. "*I* can reach him. If you can point him out to me, I can guarantee he will come speak to us."

I'd nearly forgotten her other gift, for luring travelers. For some time, we watched the passing troops in silence. I began to despair that we'd missed the emperor—how could we recognize one individual soldier in the dark, amidst all the others?

But then a standard bearer rode by, the Hapsburg crest snapping in the breeze. And just beyond him, in a pristine red-and-white uniform, a young man with a familiar bearing.

"I think that's him."

"You *think*?" The lidérc raised her eyebrows at me. "Well, we shall know soon enough."

She drew her hands together, then opened them, like a flower blooming. A coursing light rested just above her palms, a swirl of white and gold and traces of peach. She drew her hands away, and the light hung suspended.

None of the soldiers looked toward us, save one. Behind the standard bearer, the mounted officer nudged his horse out of line. A few of his men shouted at him, and when he didn't turn back (or even respond), a handful rode after him.

The first time I'd seen this part of the lidérc's gift, I'd been overwhelmed by the ferocious draw toward its light. This time, I felt none of that, only a mild amusement that it gathered Franz Joseph so surely while leaving everyone around him untouched. When he came within hailing distance, the lidérc let the light wink out.

She gave me a tiny shove. "Tell him to send his men back."

I stumbled away from the trees, feeling a trifle foolish, and called, "Franz Joseph, please send your men back. I mean you no harm: I'd just like a word."

"Who are you?" Franz Joseph squinted into the gloom before him. Without the lidérc's light, neither of us could see much.

"It's Anna—Anna Arden."

Even in the dimness, I could see Franz Joseph stiffen. He shouted back at his attendants to halt, then slid down from his saddle to walk toward me.

He was very trusting, this young emperor. I might have slit his throat before his attendants could reach him—if I were the throat-slitting sort.

"What are you doing here?" he asked. His shoulders relaxed as he came close enough to see my face, his hand falling from the hilt of his sword. Perhaps not so trusting, after all.

"Your mother gave me to the Russians, in exchange for their cooperation in the war. The Russians, in turn, gave me to a praetherian army, who are waiting out this war to establish their own rule over us."

"That's ridiculous," he said. "My mother would never act in such underhanded fashion."

"When I found Anna," the lidérc said, stepping forward, "she was being held in caves by a praetherian army."

He shook his head. "You must have misunderstood. Your uncle—"

"Yes. My uncle sold me too." I rubbed my cheek, which was beginning to feel numb from the constant cold wind. "If you won't believe me, don't. But you need to know that a praetherian army is waiting for us—perhaps waiting for this very battle, where you crush us and then they crush you."

He shook his head again. "They haven't the strength for that. Not when the Russians are—" He cut off, perhaps realizing he had said too much.

"The Russian tsar is under the thrall of a praetherian lord," the lidérc said. "If you think they will spare your army, you are mistaken."

"What would you have me do?" he asked, his voice

filled with the plaintive cadence of a young man who has had too much laid upon him, too soon.

"Your Majesty?" one of his attendants called, nervous.

Franz Joseph held up his hand. "A moment more."

"Stop this war. Call off Haynau. Tell your other generals to withdraw. Revoke the Congress's decision to sequester the praetheria and call for a new Congress," I said.

"I can't do that."

"You're the emperor," I said. "It's not a question of ability, only will."

"Very well, then. I *won't* do that."

Despair washed over me. Until that moment, I had not realized how much I had counted on Franz Joseph saying yes.

The lidérc said, her voice soft and laced with iron, "Then you will lose this war."

Franz Joseph ignored her. To me he said, "You shouldn't be here. It's not safe for a woman. I can give you safe passage back to our camp, and we can make arrangements for you to return to Vienna."

Abruptly, I missed Gábor, who would never patronize me so. "It's not safe for anyone," I said. "And I will not be coming with you."

The emperor's men called again, and with a tightening of his lips, as though he wished to say more but refrained, Franz Joseph turned and remounted his horse. I wished I had the words to make him listen: it was not the Austrians alone who would lose this war—we all stood to lose, human and praetherian alike.

CHAPTER 24

Mátyás

Awareness returned in fits and starts: a scrap of color here, a shadow there.

I scrambled to collect the bits, to fit them into a pattern that might tell me where I was and how I came to be there.

An impression of heaviness, an inability to move my body.

Am I drunk? The patchy memory fit, as did the feeling of heaviness. But I did not remember drinking, only swirling through a dream, and then shifting (twice?) to a crow.

I made a point not to drink and fly—that never ended well.

I was missing something. I closed my eyes, struggling to capture the elusive thread, though my current location was completely dark.

Memory slammed into me, and my eyes flew open again. I'd helped Anna and Noémi escape, and something had gone wrong.

Vasilisa . . . a net.

And then I'd lost the shifting, lost Anna and Noémi. Again.

But where was I now? I could see nothing with my spirit eyes, only an endless blankness. Without a body, I could not feel anything tangible. I cast my inner sense out, hunting for some sign of life. I found bats clustered, not far distant, sleeping upside down.

Sleeping in a cave.

My proximity to the bats suggested I was also in the cave—probably the same one where I'd found Anna. Was I suspended in the rock walls? That would explain the blankness.

I'd passed through rock before in spirit form, though I didn't care for the sensation of my soul stuff separating to find minuscule gaps in the rock. But now, no amount of straining would let me ease through—when I reached too far, my entire spirit caught fire with pain.

The rock I could not see (or, technically, touch) pressed in on me, smothering me until I could not seem to draw enough air—a ridiculous sensation, given that my spirit had no lungs to speak of. But the feeling of being buried persisted, growing heavier and more insidious with each moment that passed.

Hadúr had not said much about what happened to spirit walkers who did not return to their bodies, but I did not imagine it could be good. If nothing else, without awareness, I'd have limited access to food. My body would waste away, my muscles atrophy.

If I could not find a way to escape, my body would die.

I didn't know what would happen to my spirit then, but I did not want to find out.

CHAPTER 25

Anna

Following our failed conference with Franz Joseph, the lidérc and I took a circuitous route back to camp to avoid the Austrian soldiers covering the roads. I listened for the sounds of battle as we approached the camp, but there was nothing. Only the wind whispering in the trees, the call of an owl somewhere in the distance.

We looked at each other and urged our horses faster through the fields.

There was no movement in the rearward camp. But there were bodies everywhere, tumbled across the blood-iced grass like detritus left in the wake of a massive storm. Haynau's army had reached Klapka's troops and mowed over them. These dead had been surprised in their bedrolls, slaughtered while dreaming. Where were the sentries who should have given warning of the army's approach? Bribed to silence—or dead, most likely.

The metallic tang of blood and frost was heavy in the

air; I fought a rising gorge. If we had turned back when we first encountered the soldiers instead of pressing on to talk—fruitlessly—to Franz Joseph, could we have prevented this? Saved anything?

The lidérc must have read my misgivings in my face, because she brought her horse close to mine and touched my hand. "If we had tried to give warning, they might have killed us too."

"Might" was small comfort to the dead.

The wind carried the sound of fighting to us now: the dull roar of cannon fire, the rattle of bullets.

Oh, God, I thought. *Mátyás.*

The cart that carried him was slow, following at the rear of Guyon's troops, somewhere in the middle of the combined armies. Every night had found us at the fringes of the camp. How long would it take the Austrians to reach him? To reach Noémi?

I spurred my horse forward, and the lidérc followed. The Austrian army stood between us and the Hungarian soldiers, and we could not ride straight through them, much as I wished to. Instead, we skirted the field of dead, trying to keep our distance from the worst of the fighting. But we could not entirely avoid pockets of violence. The lidérc's glamour still held, keeping the soldiers from challenging us, but twice she was forced to use her light-lure to draw soldiers out of our path, and once I broke the spell on a fireball headed toward Hungarian soldiers. I was too slow to catch the released magic, though, and the fireball fell apart in a rain of sparks that hissed when they hit the frozen ground.

We reached Guyon's camp just before dawn, light

311

staining the dark sky above the horizon. Chaos reigned everywhere. The cart we had used to carry Mátyás lay tossed on its side, one wheel broken. But of Mátyás and Noémi, there was no sign.

They couldn't have gone far: Noémi could not easily carry Mátyás's weight, even thin as he was. I spun around, and my gaze snagged on a shelter some distance from us, a circular structure made of reeds bound together, the typical refuge of shepherds during the summer months. One side had collapsed, but it was the nearest thing that might offer a hiding spot.

When my horse got close, Noémi appeared in the entrance, brandishing a gun. When she saw who approached, she lowered her weapon with a long sigh.

"Anna. Thank God. We've got to get Mátyás somewhere safer."

With the three of us working together, we managed to shove Mátyás onto the back of my horse. I mounted behind him, and the lidérc pulled Noémi up with her. We found a village a half mile or so from the fighting, a few watchful souls standing at the end of the main street, their faces turned to the distant boom of cannon fire. Noémi's coins bought a bed in the home of one of the villagers who had not yet fled. I waited to see her and Mátyás secure before the lidérc and I headed back toward the battle.

"Stay," Noémi said. "You're not a soldier."

"But the lidérc is," I said. "And they will need help tending the wounded." I was a poor fighter, but I had two hands, and I had been learning how to work in the field hospitals when I was not helping Noémi with Mátyás. Besides, I needed to know what was happening if I was to have any hope of ending this war, slim as that hope was.

I found the hospital almost at once, a tent set up some distance from the fighting. The lidérc did not stay but saluted me before riding toward the battle to look for Emilija. And then I had little time for speculating, because the work of the hospital demanded my attention. I fetched cloths and washed them out again and pressed them to wounds that never seemed to stop bleeding and held the hands of dying men and women.

There were so many of them.

My hands grew red with blood, rubbed so deep into the pores of my skin that I gave up trying to rinse it out. I had not worn gloves in months: I took a grim amusement in thinking how Mama would react to the toughening of my once-soft hands.

By the time darkness fell, I was wavering on my feet. I had not slept in nearly two days. One of the nurses noticed and told me to get some sleep. I had not gone ten steps from the tent when someone grabbed me, wrapping strong arms around my waist.

After shouting and jabbing an elbow in my assailant's gut, I realized it was no strange soldier but Gábor. He released me, holding his hands before him in a gesture of truce. His hair stood up around his head; his eyes were wild. "I couldn't find you. I've been all through the field, and I could not find you. I thought—" He broke off.

"I'm fine," I said, slipping my arms around him. "Only tired. I helped Noémi move Mátyás to safety and came here. How bad is it?"

313

"Bad enough," he said. "The Russians have cut off General Bem, crushing our armies between them and the Austrians. General Görgey has called an emergency meeting with the surviving generals this evening. No doubt he will have new information for us then."

I yawned, and Gábor caught it from me. "Tell me after I've slept," I said, and Gábor agreed.

)(

I dreamed I was back in the caverns again, once more sealed inside rock by Chernobog, but this time I could not seem to break free. When a pale hand thrust itself through the stone, I took it gratefully, my dream self finding no incongruity in a disembodied hand pulling me through rock where my own efforts could not.

Emerging from the stone, I found myself in a room of glass and crystal, silver threads of light catching on the faceted stones and refracting into a thousand tiny rainbows, a thousand gleams of fire.

The hand released me. I looked left, my thanks fading on my tongue as I saw who had pulled me through.

"You're welcome," Pál said, his pale eyes bright with amusement.

I scrubbed my right palm along my left arm, trying to wipe away an uneasy sense of grime. Even if my own subconscious had called him there, having my uncle in my dream felt like a violation.

"Wake up," I whispered, willing my exhausted self to perk up.

"Waking up won't help you," Pál said. "When you dream again, I will find you. You might as well hear me out now."

A great chill enveloped me, as though someone had ripped off the blanket covering my sleeping self. "You're a dream walker."

"I'm a bit of everything," Pál said, smiling. "And you, dear niece, should curb your lamentable habit of stating the obvious. My being a dream walker has nothing to do with the point. . . . Well, perhaps a little."

He paused for a moment, long enough for gooseflesh to prickle on my dream arms.

"I have your cousin Mátyás. His spirit is trapped in rock walls, much like the ones you've dreamed of."

Cold fear pinched my heart. Pál continued, "I imagine he is dying in the real world, wherever you have stashed his body. That is not uncommon when walkers wander so far that their spirits cannot return."

Licking lips that were suddenly dry, even in my dream, I asked, "Why are you telling me this?"

"Because I would like to propose a trade. You—or him. His body, that is. Give me either of the two, and I will release his spirit. Chimera or táltos—I'm not picky. I'd prefer you, of course, as I think you're more manageable, but I'll take either. Blood calls to blood, you know, and you both share mine."

I thought of what Pál and the Four might accomplish with me, with my uncertain spell-breaking. I thought of what the praetheria might accomplish with a táltos, and my blood froze. "Me," I said. "You may have me, if you release Mátyás."

Pál told me, briefly and concisely, how I might make the trade, and vanished.

The crystal room imploded, shards of ice raining into my face.

I woke, gasping.

There was ice on the tips of my lashes—but these did not contain the salt of tears.

Overhead, a half-moon shone over the frosted field. It was December 17, four days until solstice. A Sunday, though any religious observance had been largely abandoned as the battle wore on.

It didn't matter.

It was the end of the world.

)(

I found Gábor pacing outside a tent at the center of a hasty encampment and told him of my dream.

"What will you do?" he asked.

I let myself have a heartbeat to think how I loved this about Gábor: his willingness to let me make my own choices, even when it was dangerous.

"I will make the trade," I said. "What choice do I have? If I do nothing, Mátyás will die—and I will not be the cause of his death a second time. If we give them Mátyás's body, and they find a way to use him as a weapon . . ."

"Perhaps there is another choice. Perhaps—" He paused, staring at something behind me, his brow knitting together, then lifting, as though the sunlight had broken early.

I turned around. A large man strode through the camp, a

blue Lumen light illuminating his way, casting deep plum shadows across his copper armor, across the horned helm he wore. *Hadúr.* Behind him, scrambling to keep pace with the war god's long-limbed stride, came Bahadır. The Turkish boy carried a banner I had never seen overhead: a gold ash tree emblazoned on a green field.

Hadúr nodded at us as he came and then entered the tent. Bahadır followed him. Gábor and I glanced at each other, then hurried inside behind them. No one stopped us.

The generals appeared to be in the midst of an argument, which broke off at Hadúr's appearance.

General Görgey spoke first. *"Hála Istennek."* He removed his spectacles and rubbed them against his shirt, then replaced them with a long sigh. "We could use your help, *Hadak Ura.* The Austrians have us penned in on all sides, and our situation is dire. We thought we'd lost you after our intemperate speech earlier."

"A wise man"—Hadúr glanced at Bahadır—"urged me to put aside my pride. He reminded me that wars are not won by lone heroes. Rather, wars are won by soldiers—a hundred men and women working together. We will win this together, or not at all."

Hadúr raised his chin and swept his glance around the tent. Even those who had protested his presence earlier were rapt with attention: Kossuth, the general with the pointed beard, the commander with the broad red cheeks. Desperation made an excellent persuasive tool. "I will help you end this war, but only on my terms. We will not fight to win a battle against the Austrians or the Russians—or against the praetheria, who are even now mobilizing

317

against you. We fight to win a future for human and praetherian alike. We fight not to kill but to win an opening for parley. The only way to open negotiations is to make the war too costly to continue."

My heart began burning. *This*—this was the answer I'd sought, a way to end the war and create a space for negotiation.

There was some discussion among the generals when Hadúr paused, but it was not as lengthy or heated as I'd expected. The generals had the look of drowning men who had unexpectedly been thrown a rope to save themselves and were doing everything in their power to cling to it.

At last, Kossuth stood. "We accept your terms."

"If we win, the praetheria must be given a place in Hungary—not driven out," Hadúr warned.

Kossuth nodded. "We are prepared to discuss terms."

Hadúr walked to the center of the room and stabbed his finger into the map displayed there. He began to lay out a strategy for holding off both the Austrians and the Russians.

"And the praetheria?" someone asked.

"The best way to kill a snake is to cut off its head," Hadúr said. "The praetherian armies are driven by the Four—currently, three—who lead them, and if their leadership falls apart, their armies might be more willing to discuss terms.

"These three will not be easy to stop, though. Each is immensely powerful and has honed that power over centuries, and they will be well protected behind their troops. We might lure them out with a challenge, if we have any

318

praetheria willing to issue one, but they will not accept such challenges from human soldiers. If it comes to it, I can challenge one, but that leaves two unaccounted for."

Vasilisa's voice whispered in my head: *And you— chimera—what makes you human rather than praetherian? Not your double soul.*

"Might I do it?" I asked. When everyone turned to look at me, I flushed. I knew what they saw: an indeterminate young person in a soldier's trousers and shirt. I did not look capable of taking on anyone in this room, let alone one of the remaining Four. My magic was largely defensive: breaking spells, not launching them. I did not truly believe I could face Vasilisa, Svarog, or Chernobog—but it was the only thing I had to offer.

Hadúr was not unkind when he said, "I don't think so. They would tear you apart."

He had not said I was too human—but his answer was clear. *No.*

"Then might Mátyás, as táltos?" I asked.

The grim lines in Hadúr's face deepened. "He might—if he were not dying."

I told them of Pál's proposed trade, how we might get Mátyás back.

"Is this trade part of the praetherian plan of attack?" Görgey asked.

"Undoubtedly," Hadúr said. "I would be loath to lose either of you."

"It doesn't have to be a loss," Bahadır said, speaking for the first time. "We can use this." He blushed under the combined scrutiny of the generals, just as I had, but

319

continued undeterred. "We can send you into the praetherian camp armed with something that looks innocent but can prove destructive. A kind of Trojan horse."

Gábor's eyes lit with interest. "What did you have in mind?"

"A chemical compound of some kind. The praetheria will be watching for iron weapons and for magic. Hmm . . . does anyone in camp have a Bologna stone?"

The generals looked mystified. Gábor spoke up. "It's a stone that glows after being exposed to sunlight: some people use it for light in the absence of magic. Or for luck."

Guyon said, "I think there is one such among my troops. I'll ask."

As Hadúr set everyone to a task, Gábor turned to me. "The praetheria would not go to so much trouble if they meant to kill you. We will get you back, I swear it."

There are fates worse than dying. Gábor looked worried enough that I did not voice the words, only squeezed his hand reassuringly before he left with Bahadır to find a Bologna stone (though what they meant to do with it, I had no idea).

My heart quailed from the task before me, but I could see no way around it, only through. Surely the others carried fear with them in equal measure as they set about their work. I took a deep breath to steady myself, then went to find Noémi and warn her of the trade to come.

X

The village was quiet when I approached. A pair of self-appointed sentries along the western edge nodded to me as I rode in. Clouds scuttled across the sky, revealing and then concealing a half-moon, alternately lighting the frosted landscape and plunging everything into shadows.

I found the house where Noémi had taken Mátyás, tied my horse near a watering trough behind it, and then slipped inside. Mátyás was asleep beside the fire, and Noémi sat in a chair near him. I halted on the threshold.

Noémi wasn't alone. And it wasn't the kind widow who owned the cottage sitting beside her, but Hunger.

I watched as Noémi ceremoniously handed Hunger an empty basket. He took it from her and inspected it, and I nearly betrayed my presence by laughing at the stupefied expression on his face.

"What is this?" he asked.

"Have you been gone from Hungary so long that you've forgotten?" Mischief glinted in Noémi's eyes. I hadn't seen that look on her face in a long time—I could forgive Hunger nearly everything for bringing that light back to her eyes. "A village girl can reject a courtship by presenting her suitor with an empty basket."

Hunger looked up, an answering gleam in his eyes. He set the basket aside and moved his chair closer to Noémi's. The laughter faded from her face. "Do you mean it?" he asked.

"It's only a folk custom," Noémi said, playing with her fingers. "I can't very well reject a courtship that has not been offered."

The gleam in Hunger's eyes deepened. He took one of her hands and lifted it to his lips, pressing a kiss on each knuckle. I knew I should leave, but I could not find the will to move. "I've offered you that courtship in a dozen different ways, a dozen different words. Each time you said no."

"How could it be a true courtship when I was kept imprisoned by you, by the other praetheria? How could I possibly say yes, when I might always wonder if I'd said yes for love or because I felt driven to it? It was not fair of you to ask me." Noémi did not draw her hand away, despite the sharpness of her words.

Hunger huffed a soft laugh. "My truth teller. You are right, of course. I should not have asked you then—I should not have held you prisoner so long. You were a convenience at first, a way to draw Anna and Mátyás to our cause. And then, by degrees, I began to see that I did not want you to leave, that I would make any excuse to be near you, to see you, even if I wronged you with those excuses. I was afraid I would lose you—and when the war began, that fear was replaced by a deeper one, that you might be hurt, even killed. You were safer in the caves."

"You should have let me go," Noémi said, but she did not seem truly angry, and with her free hand she brushed the curls away from his forehead, then rested her palm against his cheek. "I could have given you my love freely, had I been free."

"I am sorry," Hunger said, raising his eyes to hers, and I caught my breath. I had never heard him apologize before: this golden-eyed sárkány with the indomitable arrogance of a dragon-turned-man. "I understand now that I have hurt you, and I wronged you." He glanced at the basket, overturned on the ground beside him. "Am I too late, then?"

Noémi was silent for a long time. From a shelf near the fireplace, a clock spoke softly: *tick, tick*. The fire crackled in the grate. Mátyás's chest rose and fell beneath a blanket. "Not too late," she said at last. "But it is the wrong time, all the same. When this war is over, when we are safe, ask me again."

Hunger cupped his hand beneath Noémi's chin and studied her for a moment. When she did not pull away, he leaned forward to set a kiss, petal-soft, against her lips.

Heat flushed my face, and I was not even the one receiving the kiss. How was Noémi still upright?

That brief flash of desire must have betrayed me, for Hunger swiveled around. "Anna!"

I stepped forward into the circle of firelight and told them why I'd come.

CHAPTER 26

Anna

The trade was set for the following night, at an hour past midnight.

At dusk, Noémi and I drove a cart into camp, with Má-tyás, unmoving, behind us. Gábor was already waiting for me.

"I have something for you," he said, and I followed him to where trampled fields lay quiet beneath the gathering dark.

He fished in his pocket and removed a small polished stone with bands of brown and gold threaded through rus-set. "It's a hope charm," he said, holding it in his palm. "If you cup it in your hands and say 'Hope,' it should give you a rush of warmth. It's a Coremancer spell I haven't perfected yet, so I don't think it will work above once, but I couldn't let you go wholly alone into the praetherian camp."

"It's beautiful." I took the stone from him, feeling the

warmth of his fingertips brushing mine, and slid the stone into my pocket. But the new weight was a reminder of everything I'd been trying to forget. My breath caught. "I am not certain I can bear this," I whispered. "I am afraid. I don't want to leave you."

"Then don't go." Gábor wrapped his arms around me, and I leaned into him, letting the tension that had been building in my body ebb out of me. "Mátyás would not blame you."

"But Noémi will. I'd blame myself too. I have to go."

A sigh, long and slow, escaped from him. "I know it." He shifted his hold on me, so we stood facing each other. His eyes were bright. A sliver of moonlight danced along his cheekbones, caught against his lips.

I leaned up for a kiss. He caught my shoulders with his hands. "Wait. I want to say something." He took a deep breath. "I've been waiting for the perfect time and place— but I'm starting to see that there is no perfect time or perfect place. I might lose my whole life to waiting, and I'd rather have an imperfect happiness now than the hope of a more perfect one later."

Snow began to fall, a sifting light as flour.

Gábor pulled me closer, erasing any space between us. His heartbeat matched mine. "We might neither of us survive this war. All we have is tonight. I offer you everything I have: my heart, my soul, my life, if you want it. I cannot give you the life you were raised to, but I think I can make you happy."

I drew back a little, searching his face. "Are you asking me to marry you?"

He raised one shoulder, a lopsided shrug, and grinned at me. "If you want me to."

"*This* is not the life I was raised to," I said, gesturing at the fields around us. "But here I am."

He tilted his head. "Is that a yes?"

I thought of Noémi, putting off her happiness with Hunger until the war was over. Until it was safe. But living itself was not safe: there were no guarantees given to any of us. "Yes," I said, so there was no misunderstanding. *Yes.* It was a promise to myself, to our future, should we live to claim it. "But for now"—I lowered my eyes demurely—"I should like you to kiss me."

I could feel his grin against my mouth as he complied. Then his kiss deepened, and it was not so much kiss as prayer, a sacred caesura in the infinite *now* that stretched between us.

Gábor spread his woolen mente on the ground beneath us, tugging me close, not as though I were something fragile but as though I were something infinitely precious. His touch grounded me, and despite the cold night I was warm and flushed, and exactly where I wanted to be.

)(

Midnight came too early. Noémi's voice, cutting through the chill night air, dragged us back to the present. I stood, finger-combing my hair and tugging my shirt straight. The gesture seemed oddly irrelevant: what did it matter if I was untidy if I was surrendering to the praetheria? Gábor retrieved his mente from the ground and slung it around his shoulders, then offered me his hand.

He did not relinquish my hand when we joined the others, not until a horse was brought for me to mount. Then he lifted me into the saddle, his fingers lingering around my ankle. I smiled down at him, our secret joy rising like a balloon inside me. I pushed away the impending dread curling around the edges of my thoughts: I'd have to face the reality soon enough.

Bahadır brought me a metal canteen and a sachet of salt. "When you're ready, add water to the contents of the container, and then the salt. The mixture will create a tremendous heat, enough to detonate gunpowder or anything explosive, without recourse to fire. But do not mix them before they are ready or they might injure you."

I put the sachet in my pocket and hooked the canteen on my belt, feeling as though the contents might explode anyway, without water or salt.

Our group was small: me, Gábor, Hadúr, Emilija, and the lidérc. Noémi and Bahadır rode with the light wagon that carried Mátyás's body. I did not see Hunger, who was still maintaining the fiction for Chernobog that he had died. I suspected he was somewhere nearby anyway. Where Noémi went, he generally followed.

The meeting place was some miles from the army's campsite and the battlefield, a swath of *puszta* not yet touched by the war. Emilija had scouted the field earlier, to ensure that no hidden armies lay in wait. As we rode, the residual warmth of my time with Gábor ebbed away, leaving me cold and afraid.

Morning was only a few hours off, and the dawn it brought would be grim. The probable future scrolled across my mind: the Russians coming in a relentless wave, the praetherian army darkening the horizon like a tide of locusts, the few Austrian mechs launched against them crushed like children's toys.

I shook myself. It was no good borrowing fear from something that had not yet happened. I had to stay focused. Make the trade for Mátyás . . . resist Pál . . . set off my explosive . . . escape. Ideally in that order.

The lidérc drew beside me as we rode. "Don't be afraid, Anna."

"How can I not be? I am giving myself to people who do not care for me."

The lidérc shook her head. "I don't mean Pál and the Four. Anyone with sense would fear the trade you are making. I have been watching you a long time. I saw a girl who *was* fearless, breaking the Binding spell. Now I see a woman who doubts herself, who bottles her gifts away as though they were a fire that would burn her. But fire is not always bad. A contained fire can do much good: it can warm a house, cook meat, bring light." She reached out to touch my hand, an unusual gesture from a creature who kept to herself. "Don't be afraid of your gifts. You do no one a favor by making yourself small."

A flicker of warmth kindled in my heart at her words. I tried to hold on to it as we approached the field where four silhouettes made an uneven line across the starlit horizon: Vasilisa, Pál, Chernobog, and Svarog, the four-headed golden-haired god I'd last seen with the Russian tsar.

Dismounting from my horse, I patted its rump to send it back to the others. Noémi hung a Lumen lantern in the cart above Mátyás. She adjusted his blanket, then looked up and blew me a tiny kiss. Hadúr and Bahadır bowed, and Emilija offered me a military salute. Gábor made no gesture, only watched me with unblinking eyes, the weight of his gaze like a caress. I studied my friends, fixing the picture of them in my heart until I could not bear to delay any longer. I turned away and began to walk, and the lidérc fell in step beside me.

"You needn't come with me," I said.

"This is my choice," she said. "Weeks ago, you asked me for my name, and I told you that you had not earned it. But I want to give it to you now, so you can face your battle knowing that I believe in you." She paused, and I paused too, fixing my eyes on hers. "My name is Ildikó— for 'battle.'"

Ildikó. She fell back then, letting me walk forward alone, but her name hummed in my ears, her gesture of faith bolstering my flagging courage.

For Mátyás, I thought, and did not let myself dwell on what would happen after the trade.

Halfway between my friends and the praetheria, I halted. I would go no farther until the praetheria released Mátyás.

Pál began the intricate gestures of a spell, and I braced myself, half expecting a trap. But the bone-deep buzz of his spell passed harmlessly over me, and then someone shouted behind me. I turned to see Mátyás sitting up beneath the blue glow of the lantern. Noémi scrambled into the wagon to hug him. Pál had released Mátyás's spirit, as promised.

A moment's relief rushed over me, quickly sucked away by growing dread.

Time for my end of the bargain.

The walk across the remaining length of the field seemed weirdly both endless—as though I would relive that walk forever in my nightmares—and requiring no time at all. When I drew close, Chernobog stalked forward and grasped my arm, dragging me back to Vasilisa, who seized my other arm.

With her free hand, she gestured in the air, and a shape erupted from the ground behind Svarog: a griffin, its great wings raining dirt on our exposed heads. I didn't know if Vasilisa had hidden it in the ground or merely conjured it. Perhaps it didn't matter: the beast soared toward my friends, its flight both beautiful and terrible.

Another shout, and I squinted across the field. Mátyás had collapsed in Noémi's arms, as limp and unmoving as he had been only minutes earlier.

I jerked my arms but couldn't dislodge either Vasilisa or Chernobog. "What's happening to Mátyás? Why are you attacking them?"

Neither answered me.

A golden light appeared to the left of my friends, a low, pulsing glow that seemed to hum across the open space. The lidérc's lure. The griffin wavered, shifting its course to meet the light.

Svarog pounded a stave into the ground, and the earth trembled. In the distance, my friends tumbled like pins, and the lidérc's light winked out. The griffin corrected course, winging toward Mátyás and Noémi. Hadúr launched himself into the air, a movement that was closer to flying than leaping, and swung his great sword at the winged beast. The griffin screamed at him and dodged, swerving around the war god to plunge toward Noémi, who stood over Mátyás's body with a dagger gleaming in her hand.

The griffin's talons slashed at Noémi, who cried out, then collapsed like a punctured balloon. Even from this distance, I could see the dark streaks furrowed across the bodice of her pale dress. The griffin crowed, a horribly echoing sound in the sudden stillness, and then it sprang aloft again, carrying Mátyás's limp body by his arms.

Noémi. I nearly dislocated my shoulders trying to wrench free, but Vasilisa and Chernobog held me fast.

Hadúr knelt on the cold grass, his arms crossed on the hilt of his sword, the tip of the blade resting in the dirt. Why did he do nothing, when the griffin was carrying Mátyás away? But then the clouds overhead opened, releasing bolt after bolt of lightning. Hadúr stood and raised his sword. His copper armor drew the lightning, and he wrapped it around his blade as one might wrap wool around a distaff.

Then he pointed the sword at the griffin, and lightning arced over the beast's head, creating a crackling barrier before it. The griffin shied back, and Hadúr leapt, catching its rear leg. Bahadır and Gábor ran forward to help him.

But the flying creature snarled and snapped his beak at Hadúr's arm, and the god of war fell back to the ground with a thud. He shook himself, then sprang up once more, pounding toward us. His longsword glittered, still crackling with unused lightning.

The tight grip on my right arm loosened, and Chernobog thundered across the ground to meet Hadúr.

"Stop!" Gábor called, infusing his voice with all the Persuasion of his Coremancer gift. I froze. Beside me, Vasilisa stilled briefly. Chernobog hiccuped in his run, brushing through the compulsion as if it were a cobweb.

He collided with Hadúr as a continent might, with a bone-jarring crash that shook the world to its core. But my focus was not on them. I peered through the darkness, willing the activity around the wagon to resolve into something that made sense. My mind kept replaying the moment when Noémi fell, those terrible slashes across her body. Hunger joined Emilija and the lidérc, who were fussing over Noémi, and ice ran through my body: he would not have revealed himself unless something went calamitously wrong.

The griffin landed beside us, dropping Mátyás in a crumpled heap before him. Svarog snapped his fingers, and a richly carved cart—a chariot, really—appeared out of the gloom, drawn by three horses. Svarog lifted an unresponsive Mátyás into the vehicle, then mounted up, driving the horses before him.

What spell had Pál cast? He had not released Mátyás's spirit. A Lucifera's telekinesis, moving Mátyás like a puppet to trick us into thinking Mátyás was whole?

I wanted to go to Mátyás; I wanted to run across the field to Noémi, but Vasilisa held me fast. She wrapped her arms around my waist and hoisted me into the air. When I began to struggle, she whispered, "I'll break every bone in your body if you fight me now, and I'll enjoy doing it. You don't need to be intact to be useful."

I stopped fighting. Below us, Chernobog slammed his

shoulder against Hadúr's raised shield. Lightning still crackled along the horned god's raised wings, evidence of Hadúr's last attack. A fireball lit just beside Hadúr, and his attention slid, only for a fraction of a second, but it was enough. Chernobog slid a pronged pike beneath Hadúr's shield and through his copper breastplate.

Hadúr dropped his sword and stumbled back, gasping. The ground opened beneath him, earth slurping at his legs, then sides, then neck, as though it were a living thing of insatiable appetite. When only Hadúr's head remained visible, Chernobog sauntered toward him, twirling the war god's sword through his fingers. Cracks radiated from the ground where Hadúr struggled to break free, but I did not think he had enough time.

I closed my eyes before I could see the sword come whistling down.

The last of the ancient Hungarian gods, a casualty not of war but of treachery.

Disaster upon ruin upon calamity.

From this vantage, I could see Noémi, spread like a doll on the floor of the wagon. Hunger rocked her body as she had once rocked his, her blood staining his clothes as his had once stained hers. A cry rolled out across the night, of longing unfulfilled, of a devastation that threatened to unknit every muscle binding my bones together. I had known that Hunger could draw desire with a breath; I had not known he could also do its inverse, that his grief could drive despair like a poison through my blood.

The night air skirled past me, cold and sharp. Chernobog sped ahead of Vasilisa and me on velvet wings, still crowing about his victory. Vasilisa did not once look back, though she must have felt Hunger's unfurling.

But I did. I craned my head back until I could see nothing of the blue light hanging beside Noémi's body. I watched until darkness swallowed all my friends.

I knew what Hunger's grief meant.

Noémi was dead.

CHAPTER 27

Mátyás

After a prison of stone, my body was a strange thing: flaccid and soft, vulnerable. I felt as though I might lift off the earth at any moment, untethered. I'd been trapped in the rock so long that time had begun to blur and morph, and then at once I was free, my spirit drawn irresistibly to my body, a compass pointing north.

Only . . . my body did not seem entirely to fit me, like a favorite pair of shoes left behind on a long vacation that no longer know the swell and shape of one's feet.

I tried to sit up, but the muscles in my stomach did not want to cooperate, and so I lay on the ground, gasping like a beached fish. Where was I? Brightness burned against the horizon, and I turned my head away from it, the light stinging my still-sensitive eyes. The air swirling around me was cold, bitter with frost and winter wind. Not in the caverns, then. Dawn?

"Hush," a woman's voice said, light fingers stroking my shoulder. Not Anna or Noémi. A thin warmth seeped from her touch, radiating from my shoulder through my body. I could feel some of the strength returning to my arms and legs, and after a few moments I pulled myself upright. My stomach muscles gasped and strained at the effort, but they did not betray me, as they had before.

I blinked, the spots of light and dark in my vision finally cohering as I adjusted to the growing brightness of morning. Thin, gruel-like clouds smeared the winter sky above the horizon.

Two people sat watching me—the pale-haired woman, Vasilisa, and Pál Eszterházy, who was some sort of cousin to me, but I'd never bothered to untangle our precise relationship. He'd never merited that much of my time. Maybe I should have paid more attention.

"Can he fight?" Pál asked.

"He can stand," Vasilisa said. "I do not think he should attempt holding a gun or a sword. The Healing is only a spell—it's not true healing, and the strength it grants will wear off eventually."

"Here, boy," Pál said, addressing me. "Can you shift?"

"I daresay," I drawled. "But I'm not in the mood to oblige you."

"It doesn't matter," Vasilisa said. "We'll know soon enough."

※

The praetherian army moved out with the dawn, a great regiment of creatures. With Vasilisa, I watched as the front line thundered past: gnarled mountain giants; a bull-headed minotaur; a phalanx of tree-men, their bark-skinned arms wrapped around one another; a pair of stonelike guta, their inhuman strength palpable even at a distance.

They were followed by creatures fleeter but no less terrifying: the jointless shadows of the fene; a group of samodiva, their glamours shimmering around them, flames trailing behind them like wings; a pale-faced Fair One, her lips already stained dark with blood. Though some held weapons and some did not, all were deadly.

They streamed past in dizzying numbers.

When the foot soldiers were well under way, a second wave sprang to the sky: gold-and-black-banded dragons; griffins; a winged unicorn; a battalion of helmeted Valkyries, riding flying horses.

Beside me, Vasilisa began shifting: her slim figure broadened, her limbs grew denser. Her lovely, unlined face seemed to collapse in on itself, wrinkles spreading like ink across parchment. The cloud of pale hair darkened and thinned, until only a few scraps clung to an age-spotted scalp.

I pulled away in surprise, and Vasilisa misread my movement.

"I repulse you, do I?" she asked, cackling. "Good. I feared my pretty face wouldn't be enough to strike terror into the hearts of men. Behold me in all my glory." She cocked her head to one side, considering me. "Do you know me now, boy? Your cousin never did."

I stared at her, my eyes running over her stooped shoulders, the wiry hands, and the curving nails. I caught at scraps of memory, stories told by my nurse, and tried to fit them together. She looked like a witch from a fable, a tale told at bedtime to give children nightmares. But she wasn't just a tale, she was the original nightmare.

She rattled a pair of items in her pocket, the mortar and pestle she always carried. The fragments of memory knitted together. "Baba Yaga," I said.

"Smart boy," she said before stepping forward to wrap her arms around me and lift us both into the air. As we rose, she said, "I've got you spelled, as before. Try to shift and I'll let you drop to your death in my magic net." She laughed again, a sound like bones grinding together. "And off to war we go."

From the air, I could see the *puszta* unrolling beneath us. The praetherian army spread across it, an irresistible tide. Beyond them, I could see more lines of soldiers, reaching to the horizon and heading west. Whose soldiers? Surely not ours, or they'd be marching to meet us or away, but not parallel. How much had I missed in my rock tomb? Was the war nearly over or just beginning? And my friends— where were they now? Were they safe?

We flew for a long time—a dozen or more miles, as the crow flies, though much more slowly, always keeping pace with the armies marching below us. We flew until the sky was dark with smoke and the horizon was lit by flashes of gunpowder, the ground rocked by cannon fire and magic spells.

We set down just as the first wave of praetherian soldiers crashed into the human soldiers. The screams carried clearly across the open plains.

"I won't fight with you," I said.

"Won't you?" Vasilisa—Baba Yaga—asked. "You are not quite human yourself, táltos. How do humans who know what you are look at you?"

"My friends do not care."

"Ah, but I do not ask about your friends. Your friends are mostly outsiders: Anna, the Turkish boy, the lidérc. I mean the others, the same ones who have driven the praetheria out of their towns. When they see you, do they see a Luminate soldier, using a magic they understand? Or do they see a monster, a dragon with a hunger as deep as the world?"

I flinched, and she laughed.

"I knew another of your kind once. Not quite as you are, with your crows and your multitude of shapes. But a man who could become a dragon, a dragon who could become a man, a creature who forgot, over the centuries, which came first and where the line began and ended between being human and not. I think you have met him: he loved your sister."

Hunger. A sudden terrifying moment of clarity: was *this* why Hunger had taken his name? That yawning need that overcame me in dragon form?

"Will your Eszterházy name protect you, if humans know the truth of you?"

I scarcely heard her: another ripple of understanding shook me. "*Loved* my sister? Did Hunger die of his wounds after all?"

Vasilisa shook her head. Her voice, when she spoke, was a gentle rumble. "Your sister. Noémi is dead."

The cold air swirling around me seemed to harden, a

339

rim of frost coating my eyes and nose and throat so I could not catch my breath. Noémi? Dead? Impossible. It was *my* epitaph that was supposed to grace a misbegotten headstone, not hers.

Here lies Eszterházy Noémi: She died a death not meant for her.

No. She must be wrong. My spirit shifted, still not quite comfortable in my body, and I had a peculiar double sense of being both within and without my own skin.

Vasilisa's eyes were dark with something that might have been pity. "I am not wrong. Will you still fight against us, on behalf of those who caused your sister's death? There are only a handful of people you love in this world: your sister is gone, and your cousin fights with us."

She nodded and looked away, and I followed her gaze. Anna stood beside her uncle a hundred feet away, her face pale in the morning light.

Anna saw me looking and waved. "Mátyás! You must—" But her voice cut off, snatched away by a wind that sprang up between us.

"Let me speak with her." About Noémi, about this strange changing war that I did not understand. How had Noémi died? I could not imagine that the Hungarian army would turn on her, not when her gifts of healing were so needed at the front. And yet Anna was here, fighting with the praetheria, as Vasilisa said. What had happened while I was locked in my rock cage? What changed?

"Later," Vasilisa said. "Anna has a task that you must not disrupt, just as you have yours."

"And that is?"

"To end this war."

I turned to look at her full on. Her eyes, half buried in creases, were steady and calm.

"Not to fight it?"

"Do you think we want this fight? Do you think we rejoice in bloodshed? Once, maybe. They called me Baba Yaga, but a *baba* is only an old woman, and sometimes a midwife. Sometimes new life comes baptized in blood. I would see life at the end of this war, not death."

"Then why bring the war at all?"

"Should we have let the Hapsburgs and the Congress send us all away? Should we have made ourselves weak so you could continue to live as you always have, ignorant, oblivious?"

"Of course not—"

"Your people were bringing us a war whether we wished it or not. If we did not want to be hunted down, we would have to fight. The only way to win a place for ourselves in your world is using your weapons: power, intimidation, blood. If we want to be taken seriously, we must show ourselves a threat."

"But if you are seen as threatening, won't that just confirm everything humans fear about you? They'll simply combine armies to fight against you."

"And so we must show ourselves too powerful to be taken down. We must show ourselves powerful enough that humans will be glad for a cessation of war, glad to give us the small boons we ask: a place of our own, to be left in peace. Even as we speak, the sisters of the Morrígan are bearing down on London, an army in their wake. Ireland is burning behind them. The Melusina are offering a truce in the midst of the civil war in France. Farther north, Fenrir has been released, and wolves ravage the northlands.

"We can draw this out, long and bloody. Most of your friends will die. . . . Or you can help us and end it now."

I frowned at her. "I thought you wanted to build a new world for the praetheria. I thought you wanted to make yourselves demigods."

She raised one hoary eyebrow. "And where did you hear this? From us?"

"Anna said—" I broke off, trying to remember what Anna had said. The praetherian threat had always seemed so present and real.

"Because a thing is threatening does not make it evil. All we ask—and it is not so much—is a place of our own."

I fell silent.

Noémi had already died in this war. For a moment, I was frozen, trapped by old memories: Noémi at Christmastime, giving me all her candies from the tree until I was sick with the excess of sugar. Noémi, shrieking as I left frogs and salamanders in her bed. Noémi, mothering me when I had no one left to do so.

Noémi. I swallowed an unaccustomed tightness in my throat.

Surely it was better to end this war, before more lives were lost in the long, bloody unraveling.

Vasilisa continued, "It is not enough for you to fight with us. Your tricks and shapes can be useful, yes, but they are not powerful enough to end this. You must take your táltos shape, the dragon that guards the World Tree."

"You can't want that," I said. "In that shape, I'm beyond control—mine or anyone else's. I might kill you and the armies that follow you." *Monstrous.* The word echoed in my head.

"As to that, I have some experience with dragons. I think I can help you control your hunger." She set a hand on my shoulder, surprisingly heavy, given the fine bones and sagging skin. "Because a wolf has sharp teeth and instincts to kill does not make it a monster—it makes it a wolf. An old woman with a gift for witchcraft is not a monster, unless she chooses to base her craft on blood magic." Her smile was tinged with irony. "A táltos with a deadly shape is no monster, unless his choices make him so. To kill to end a war: is this monstrous? Some might call it merciful."

She had come uncannily near my own thoughts. I shivered a little in the cold air.

I had shied away from being the táltos the Lady asked of me, because she could not promise that I would not lead men and women to their deaths. Vasilisa did not ask that fatal leadership of me: she asked me only for myself. I might live or die, I might bring others to their deaths, but I would not be haunted by the deaths of those who followed me.

"And besides," she added, more prosaically, "your human body is dying, all those weeks untended by your spirit. The dragon form can heal all that."

Still I hesitated. The arguments Vasilisa presented were logical, compelling. I wanted to believe her. But there was something I was still missing. How had Anna come to join them?

"And Anna?"

"Your cousin has always sought to end this war. When she found that the human generals would not listen to her, she came back to us."

I scratched my chin. That did sound like Anna.

Vasilisa sighed. "You make this decision difficult, but it is not so hard. It is what your sister would want—for you to heal, for you to live. As a healer, she would want this war to end quickly: a nice, clean wound, not a long tear that invites infection."

She was right. Noémi would want me to do what I could to end the war. A little death and destruction now was better than a prolonged devastation. "Very well," I said.

I bowed my head and closed my eyes. I could not see the World Tree from here, but I could sense its power, its roots stretching deep into the soil of the *puszta,* grounding an old magic into this world. That magic called to me, even as I let myself fall into that familiar form, even as my body sprouted upward, even as a moment of bright agony cleaved my head apart, seven snaking necks branching from my trunk.

The ravenous hunger was back, driving me even as the shift took hold. A need as deep as the *puszta* was wide, a chasm as endless as the sky.

CHAPTER 28

Anna

As a child, I sometimes pictured the end of the world, as a speculation to while away a rainy afternoon or after listening to a particularly vivid sermon on the book of Revelation. The scene before me now—winged beasts descending from the sky, a field black with smoke, grasses red with blood—echoed those old visions and amplified them with details I had not thought to imagine: the way the wind carried the smell of burnt flesh, the cold prickle of snowflakes falling from a deadened sky.

My cousin, shifting into a seven-headed beast.

He did not quite fit the biblical account: he was black, not red, and bore no crowns—an irrelevant detail that my brain seized upon as if it were somehow important. As if it might somehow make sense of the destruction before me.

As if, by concentrating hard enough on minutiae, I might forget that Noémi was dead.

Noémi had always reminded me of her biblical namesake, the Naomi who had inspired such loyalty in her daughter-in-law Ruth: full-hearted, faithful, hardworking. *Intreat me not to leave thee, or to return from following after thee: for whither thou goest, I will go; and where thou lodgest, I will lodge.* Noémi. All those shared days and nights at Eszterháza, in Vienna, in the caverns among the praetheria. She had been the best of friends. She had been my sister. And I should never see her or speak to her again.

My eyes stung, my throat grew tight. But I could not indulge in tears. Not here, not yet.

Screams tore across the sky as Mátyás lumbered forward. Cannons fired at him, but the cannonballs bounced harmlessly off his skin. An Austrian mechanized monster lifted into the air, droning toward him, and he batted it out of the sky. It fell, crumpled like a scrap of paper.

I had never seen Mátyás's transformation into a dragon, though he and Gábor had told me of it. I had thought they were exaggerating.

They weren't. He was terrible and beautiful, as all great beasts are, and I could not see any sign of my cousin inside him.

"Ah," Pál said, rubbing gloved hands together. "It is time."

The look he turned on me was measuring, indifferent, and the cold air nipping at my cheeks seemed to coat my insides as well.

"Time for what?" I asked, stalling.

"For your part, and mine."

"I do not see how I have any part in this."

"I know your gifts better than you know them," Pál

said, his ice-blue gaze never leaving mine. "Who told you that you were chimera? Who told Vasilisa what you might do? Who sees the future scrolled out as clearly as a historian might see the past?"

What had he seen of my future? It was one thing to suspect oneself a failure, or perhaps a monster. Far worse to have suspicion confirmed. And what if it was neither of those things? What if his vision showed me as I had so long yearned to be: powerful, important, heard?

Pál must have read something of my thoughts in my face. "Let me show you something."

He pulled a small ornamented mirror from a bag at his side, and breathed on it, so that steam covered the surface. Tiny specks of frost dotted the edges.

Shapes began moving beneath the fogged glass. Emilija first, standing with her women soldiers before an army. Of the standards waving above the army, I recognized three: the black and yellow of the house of Hapsburg, the red and white of Croatia, and her father's own flag. *Emilija faced her father's army.* A gout of Luminate fire erupted around the women, and when the smoke cleared, only one still stood. She was not Emilija.

I saw Bahadır die, pinned on a long pike, in company with a group of Hungarian soldiers, surrounded by Russians they had meant to surprise. The lidérc, carrying a green banner emblazoned with a gold ash, caught between an Austrian soldier and a green-skinned troll. She would not have named either her enemy, but that did not stop them from killing her, one firing a gun as the other brought down a metal-studded cudgel.

Another ripple. When the fog cleared again, it was

Gábor's face mirrored back at me, his eyes gone cloudy, his cheeks spattered with blood.

"Stop," I said, pressing my hands against my stomach. "I don't want to see any more." But terrible as the images were, I could not look away. These deaths, of people I loved, deserved a witness.

The mirror moved farther afield, to giants roaming through the streets of Vienna. One stopped before the Hungarian embassy. A woman ran out, cradling a child: Catherine and Christopher. The giant stomped his massive foot down.

Another ripple, and London materialized: my parents, cowering together in my mother's sitting room, a woman with a cloak of crow wings and a bloody sword raised above them. James, sitting at his desk at school, his cheek on an open book as though he were sleeping, a spear protruding from his back.

I dropped to my knees and vomited. After wiping my mouth, I demanded, "Is this true? Or only an illusion to scare me?" *Pray God, let it only be an illusion.*

"How do you think this war should end?" Pál asked. "Your friends are outmatched at every turn. There is no way in which you win. No way except mine."

My shoulders sagged. How could I have hoped, even for a moment, that there would be any other ending to this story? My friends and I had been powerless to change the trajectory of the war, though we had tried. Had we been other than what we were—older, more educated, more connected, more powerful—could we have changed anything? Here, on the brink of failure, I was haunted by questions.

I thought I knew what it was like to feel powerless, to see all of society arrayed against you. I'd known it when Herr Steinberg closed in before the Binding broke, when I had no assurance I was doing anything other than bringing death upon us.

I'd felt it standing before the archduchess, when all my will was not enough to keep her soldiers from dragging me away, when all the moral right I could claim was not enough to keep her from pronouncing a sentence of death on my head or a lifetime of captivity on the praetheria.

But this powerlessness was absolute: I had no conviction of right to carry me through, no hope that something better than I might outlast me. No hope that my friends might succeed where I had failed.

Was it because I was the wrong age and the wrong gender to have a real voice? But Joan of Arc had been only a girl. Queen Victoria had been only a girl when she ascended to the throne.

Perhaps it was some failing unique to me. Some flaw in my makeup . . . my chimera blood.

"And what is your way?" I was not curious, only resigned. A cold, colorless voice fading into a landscape of frost.

"It's better if I show you. You'll need spirit sight for this, that same sense you use to distinguish spells. Sometimes it's helpful to close your eyes, so that the physical world does not interfere with your spiritual sense."

I closed my eyes, but there was nothing, only the dull red of the inside of my eyelids. Even my inner sense for spells, which felt magic as a buzzing along my bones, seemed blunted.

"Here, let me help you," Pál said, putting a hand on my elbow. A light stream of magic fizzed through my body, and my eyes flew open. I shook him off, my heart thumping.

"Calm down," he said. "I won't hurt you. I'm merely amplifying your own ability to see."

He left unsaid the fact that he could force me—his magic and physical strength were both greater than my own—but it hung between us anyway.

I closed my eyes again, gritting my teeth against his magic. I took a deep breath and blew it out between my lips. A touch calmer, I focused outward.

And, abruptly, there it was: the whole of the battlefield laid out before me in glimmering lights and threads, a weaving of such complexity and loveliness that it eclipsed any previous idea I might have had of beauty. Like sunrise, shafting through dew beaded on a spider's web—magnified a million times. Like light on the curl and foam of waves, the opalescent hue of an ocean breaking across a shore, everything beautiful and bright and dark all rolled into one.

A memory stirred, of a hazy summer afternoon and Gábor and his sister Izidóra trying to teach me to sense magic in the world around me. Was *this* some of what they saw?

The memory sent a savage pang through me, an intense longing for Gábor and, a beat later, for Noémi, who had helped me hide those secret meetings. But that same longing set the vision trembling, and I pushed it aside.

"What is this?" I asked.

Pál's grip on my elbow tightened. "You know that magic

comes from the energy of soul stuff: all of the living world is woven together by threads of power. Creation, time itself, all the names we give to the physical world to shape our understanding of it—at their core, they hold magic. We can follow these threads forward in space, as we do now, or forward in time, as I did when I showed you your friends' fates.

"But we can also follow these threads backward in time: neither time nor space are linear in the ways we usually understand them."

I kept my eyes pinched shut. "It's lovely, but what does it have to do with me, with this war?"

"Skilled magicians manipulate this field of magic all the time, whenever they cast spells. Most can only sense a few of the lines and weaves, those pertaining to their particular expertise. Elementalist"—his fingers dug into my elbow as certain threads and lines lit up in turquoise and green—"Coremancer"—the greens faded, replaced by pinpricks of purple across my inner vision. "Most can't hold this complexity in their heads, so they do not even try. They simply call up what they need through their spell rituals and their will."

"But you can hold it," I said.

"As can you," Pál replied, "with my aid. Some of that skill is in your blood. Some of it is chimera—the extra soul stuff inside of you makes the task less arduous for your other senses."

"If magic happens when people shift these lines," I said, "what happens when I touch something?" The vision still shimmered before my closed eyes, but I caught my breath, afraid that even by breathing I might unwittingly destroy something.

"Creation is of a much tougher warp and weave than you fear. It takes skill and training to manipulate those lines and patterns, as you should know. You cannot destroy it by brushing against it. Or by breathing."

And there it was again: the subtle, intrusive reminder that I could not keep him out of my head. I shivered, and the vision wavered.

I opened my eyes, blinking at the frosty landscape before us, and pulled away from Pál. Mátyás was only a dark smudge in the distance now, though the terror following in his wake was almost palpable.

"In the normal way of things, magicians draw from the weave only a little at a time, their power spread more or less evenly across the world. But war . . . war wreaks a splendid destruction. All the working and unworking of magic, concentrated on the battlefields. So much death and release of soul energy, violating the regular rhythms of birth and death. All of this destabilizes the weave, weakens its connections, making it easier to rework, to change the fabric of space and time. Why do you think prodigious social change is so often precipitated by violence? I know this; the praetheria know this. Their new world will be birthed by blood and broken spells.

"But it does not have to be so." He caught my elbow again, turning me to face him. "I have made no secret of my ambitions, not from you. In another life, I should have been born to rule, my Luminate gifts my divine right. But in this world, I was only a secondary child of a secondary family, and I could not carve my way alone. I needed this war to destabilize the weave of creation so I could shape it, needed praetherian support to secure you and drive our world into this war."

I ran my tongue across my lips, my mouth dry. The moisture froze almost at once. How fitting that the world should end in ice. "Why should you need me, if your gifts are so great?"

"I cannot undo spells without great effort—but you can. If you can unmake a spell, you can unmake a moment in time. You can remake the world."

A rhythmic pounding sounded in my ears: I could not tell if it was cannon fire from the battlefield or the blood suddenly thrumming through my head.

"Isn't that dangerous?"

He ignored me. "Think of it. We could go back only a few generations, set an Eszterházy on the Austrian throne instead of a Hapsburg. Such a small change, and I would inherit an empire. You'd be born to power too—you'd have the voice you've always wanted. We could set the praetheria free from the Binding, just as you did, but take steps to see that they are integrated into society, not barred from it. We could prevent this war entirely. Your cousin Noémi need not die—nor my mother."

Grandmama. An old ache flared like a bruise against my heart.

"You cannot know that. If you change one thing, you risk changing everything."

"I've spent years reading the patterns of the future and the past," he said. "I know *precisely* what changes to make.

Fewer than a dozen small breaks in the pattern, and we can build the world you've always dreamed of. A safer, fairer world."

"This cannot be what Vasilisa and the others meant for you to do when they let you lead me onto the battlefield."

Pál smiled, a curious half twist of his lips. "Not precisely. But if they failed to divine my true intent, that is their problem, not mine. What do you say to my plan?"

"What will happen to my family?" His future had shown them at the mercy of other praetherian armies.

"Where we lead, others will undoubtedly follow. We can ensure their safety."

I gnawed on the inside of my cheek. I wanted that world. To have Noémi back, whole, alive, happy. And Grandmama too? I could undo their deaths, the deaths of all those men who died in the mountain ambush after I lost Gábor's letter. In that world, there would be nothing to divide me from Gábor, nothing to threaten the people and places I loved. Where moments before I'd been nearly undone by powerlessness, my uncle was offering me a world where I would never need feel so again.

I looked at my hands, callused now in ways they had never been in my life as a lady. My hands—like myself—were ordinary now, not remarkably pretty, not exceptionally smart, not unusually brave or strong.

But I could be extraordinary.

I could take the power Pál offered and undo the order of the universe. I could remake my world.

For one breath, I let myself imagine this. I let myself feel what it might be like to know myself unmatched, to hold the heart of history in my hands.

But only for one breath, because how could I be sure of Pál? I did not believe he could wield that much power without being corrupted by it. How could I be sure of myself?

"I'd have you to advise me," Pál said gently. "I trust your heart. You would see to it that I did not step out of line—after all, without you, I cannot hope to achieve this. It would be your world as much as mine."

But if I remade the world, it should be my *world, not Pál's.*

The sudden, vicious possessiveness of the thought startled me and recalled me to myself. Such absolute power was dangerous: to me, to Pál, to everyone.

Much as I wanted a world that was safer, more just, it could not be *my* world. Or Pál's. We'd been brought to this battlefield by people attempting to create the world in their own image, to benefit themselves and those like them. The Luminate had done as much, when they imprisoned the praetheria. The Hapsburgs had done the same, building their empire on the backs of Hungarians, Bohemians, Poles, Serbs, and more. And even my beloved Hungary, when she declared independence, had done so at the expense of the Croatians and Romanians within her border. And now the praetheria threatened to do likewise.

It was the tendency of living creatures to do so: like gathering to like.

It did not mean it was right.

If I built a world in my image—no matter how just and splendid and fair I believed it to be—how could I know what weaknesses I had brought with me? I might make myself an archduchess—an empress, even—but at what cost?

I had broken the Binding spell without fully understanding what I did, and though I had brought good into the world with that decision, I had also brought pain. Whatever I hoped to become or do, I did not yet have the resources to decide the fate of my world.

Hadúr had said the war would not be won by a hero acting alone but by all of us acting together. I did not believe our peace could be bought singularly, either.

I could not do what Pál asked.

At that decisive thought, cold threaded my veins. Pál was watching me, his eyes inscrutable. What had he heard of my frantic spin of questions, my resolve? I thought of Noémi and tried to let that inevitable wash of grief flood my thoughts so Pál could not read them.

"All right," I said, trying to buy time. "Show me what it is you need."

I closed my eyes again, and Pál took my hand. I tried not to recoil from the feel of his bare fingers against mine. The glimmering lights appeared again and then began to spin as Pál pulled us back through time. He paused, a few moments later, and I watched as a knot of darkness brightened with a tiny flare.

"Noémi," he said, and I wished he would halt there, wished I could study how to unpick the threads that had closed off that brightness, so the flare would keep burning. Could I undo just her death and not the rest?

But he was already moving, spinning through days, weeks, months. I could not follow the pattern anymore; my head began to ache. If Pál could not rework the past without me, I could not do it without him, and the further back we traveled in vision, the more my certainty grew that it was not enough to refuse to help him—I needed to stop him.

One swallow did not make a summer, or one soldier a war, but a single soldier could perform the task before her. A single swallow could be glorious, carrying ribbons of light in her wings as she soared through the summer sky.

I weighed my options. I had the explosive mixture Bahadır had given me, but nothing at hand with which to detonate it. I could not physically overwhelm Pál. And if I tried to unmake anything vital, like his eyes, as Chernobog had tried to force me to do in that gruesome attack, Pál would catch me before I succeeded. I didn't think he'd kill me outright—his plan rested on my ability—but he was not above torture. Or killing those I cared for. England was not far enough away to protect my family, not when Pál could make a portal as easily as breathe. And everyone else I loved was here, somewhere in the miles of *puszta* around us.

Worry made my thoughts dull and cloudy. I needed clarity—I needed hope. My free hand curled around the stone Gábor had given me, my lips shaping the word "hope," so that Pál could not hear it. The warmth that flared through me was immediate and calming, and a memory stirred in its wake.

A few weeks earlier, after a particularly bloody fight, I'd spent the night beside Noémi in a field hospital, stanching wound after wound, some pouring more blood than the body could bear. She had told me how blood had to clot to slow its flow, to heal, but knots of blood could make their way through the veins of a recovering soldier and kill him just the same.

Blood was a vital element but not an obvious one. We might notice our heartbeat, pumping blood through our bodies, or the lift and fall of our lungs. But who thought of blood when it was safely wrapped inside one's skin?

Before the spinning vision of the past began to slow, I had already begun: using the same inner sense that I'd used to undo the curse surrounding Franz Joseph, I reached out to Pál. I was not sure what quality of the blood made it clot, so I concentrated instead on the flow of liquid through his lungs. When I had asked the stones above the ice caves to shatter to form an avalanche, I did not need to know each seam that made them up; I asked only that the stone accelerate its natural progress toward decay. Nudging the blood toward clots was a similar kind of unmaking—not asking blood to be anything other than it was, only asking a particular function of it.

I did not think this was the unmaking Chernobog envisioned me capable of.

The main danger was that Pál might read my mind before I finished. While part of me attended to the unmaking, the rest of me concentrated on his Vision spell, trying to recapture that initial feeling of hope and possibility I'd felt when he presented his plan.

The whirling lights of Pál's Vision spell stilled at last. "Here," he said. Using light to guide my inner eye, he teased a few threads from the pattern so I could see them, then explained how I was to swap two threads, snapping them just as I might a spell, after which he would rework them into the whole, beginning our rewrite of history.

I could not tell if my attempt at clot-forming had worked; Pál seemed unmoved. I needed to stall for time, so I reached for the threads he showed me, intending to let my own ineptitude prevent me from actually breaking the weave.

Beneath that focus, my second soul whispered to his blood: *clot, clot, clot.*

Before I could touch the vision threads, Pál backhanded me with his free hand. I reeled, the lights of the pattern disappearing as our connection broke.

"You are one of the few members of my family, of my own blood, and yet you attack *my* blood?"

I froze, my hand against my cheek. Despite all my efforts to hide them, he'd heard my thoughts.

He whispered a spell, and as its edges brushed me, my blood felt as if it were dissolving. Whatever I'd succeeded in doing, Pál had just undone. "I promised to elevate you to glory—and this is how you repay me? By trying to kill me? I should leave you for the ravens, to peck your eyes out, you ungrateful wretch."

He reached for me, and I scrambled back. His eyes had always been eerie, unnaturally pale, but now they reflected a deadness that frightened me more than all his inscrutable moods had. "Perhaps I don't need you, only your second soul."

I stared at him. He must be mad. "You can't have either of my souls."

"Why not? You only need one. In the general way, a

soul divorced from its body is no use to me, as the separation kills the body and thus the soul loses its vitality. Except, of course, for a táltos. Perhaps if I fail with you, I'll try again with your cousin."

He advanced again, and I turned on my heel to run, but some invisible spell snaked around my ankle and yanked me to the ground. Frozen dirt and blood filled my mouth.

Pál tangled his fingers in my hair, splaying them across my head and digging the fingernails into my scalp. I bit back a yelp. He murmured something, and agony exploded across my body, burrowing under my skin and burning through my veins.

And at my core, in the place where I kept my souls, a fissure erupted. Fire cleaved between them, and my second soul, my wild shadow self that I adored and feared in equal measure, peeled away.

I screamed, a raw cry that rose to the clouded sky and fell away, muted. This pain echoed my agony when we broke the Binding spell, when Mátyás had shifted my second soul away from my body so I could draw the spell into me. I had thought that pain would kill me: only Hunger's grip, siphoning away the worst of it, had kept me upright until Mátyás could release my second soul back to me, until I could shatter the spell.

But this pain—Pál had not been gentle in stripping my soul away, as Mátyás had been. And Hunger did not stand beside me to blunt its edges.

I writhed on the ground, every nerve ending in my body sparking. The gaping hole at my core seemed to spread, as though someone had run a sword through me and carved away half my body. I could not breathe.

Pál stood over me, considering, his body blocking the weak light that filtered through the clouds overhead. "It's a pity I cannot kill you now without rendering your soul worthless."

His footsteps moved away, and I pushed myself upright, gritting my teeth at the black stars swimming in my vision. A small cluster of soldiers fought near us—Russians and Hungarians, from the look of it—and Pál swept his hand at them. They froze instantly, ice creeping from their boots to their belts, from their hands to their cheeks. They toppled slowly, like a child's dominoes left ignored on a table.

A crawling despair washed over me. I had tried to stop Pál and had failed—worse still, he had stripped from me the last strength I possessed.

Who was I, if I was not even chimera?

The intensity of the pain had settled into a massive ache throbbing in my muscles and bones. I slid my chilled fingers into my pocket and brushed against Gábor's stone. "Hope," I whispered. There was no rush of warmth this time: Gábor had warned me the stone would not work above once. But I found his words, curled like a treasure box in my mind that needed only to be opened: *Your gifts do not define you; you define your gifts.*

I was Anna Arden before I knew I was chimera; I was Anna Arden still. The Four had talked so much of unmaking, but I did not believe it was truly possible. You could not take a thing out of existence, only change its form. For all the times I thought my old self gone, she was still here, only transformed. Even with my chimera self stripped away, I was still here.

I had gifts and flaws together, and there were people in

the world who loved me. I might be in pain, I might be half-souled, but I was not nothing.

I struggled to my feet, swaying as I rose. I scanned the battlefield and found Pál not far distant. He was not moving swiftly—rather, he seemed to be taking his time, tossing casual spells like flowers at the surrounding soldiers, and smiling when they fell. I lifted a sword from one of the frost-covered soldiers with a murmured apology.

Pál was not looking for me to follow him, and he did not see me as I drew closer. His pride might be his sole weakness, but it was a weakness I could use. He had clearly forgotten that, single-souled, I could cast the spells I struggled with as chimera. Vasilisa had taught me I did not even need to know the spell ritual if my will was strong enough.

My will was adamantine.

"Fall," I whispered, drawing together every scrap of power I had and pushing it toward Pál.

I caught my uncle midspell. The ground buckled beneath him, and his spell deteriorated in a burst of fire before him. He fell backward, his head *thunk*ing against the frozen ground. Ignoring the pain that spiked through my feet with each step, I ran forward, the sword heavy in my hand.

I did not know any killing spells—and did not think I had the will for one, in any case—but I knew the bite of metal. I'd felt it when I stabbed Mátyás; I'd seen it in the blow that had felled William, the thrust that killed Hadúr. While Pál lay still on the ground, groaning at the red, bubbled skin on his face, I rammed the sword into his gut, angling up toward his heart. A killing blow, I hoped. One that he could not undo or counter with any number of powerful spells.

Pál's eyes flew open. "How—?"

I stood over him, blocking the light from his face, as he had blocked it from mine. "Not all power lies in spells or doubled souls," I said. "I am Anna Arden, and I will have my soul back."

CHAPTER 29

Mátyás

The dragon seemed to swim across the field, long muscles coiling and uncoiling, the seven heads sinuous and sleek. Ice crusted the field beneath its clawed feet, but it neither felt the cold nor cared. Its singular focus was filling the ravening emptiness inside it.

Screaming heralded its march across the battlefield, and the dragon followed the sound, drawn less by the noise than by the sense that each thin cry unfurled from a warm body, a mouthful (or two) that would take a minuscule edge off the aching that drove it.

Threads of magic spun around the beast, trying to halt its forward motion. It shook them loose, their power spinning harmlessly into the air around it.

The dragon was unleashed, and it was hungry.

CHAPTER 30

Anna

I watched Pál as he lay dying. It did not take long—a matter of minutes, though it felt like hours, his bloody fingers scrabbling uselessly at the hilt of the sword, his breath dissolving in curses. The flat grey sky, shedding bits of snow, revealed nothing of the passage of time.

I could not break the spell holding my soul to him, but before he stopped breathing, the spell snapped and my second soul winged back to me, slamming into me with the force Noémi's hound had used to knock me to the ground the first time we met. (My second soul had the same exuberance too.) I kept my feet, but only just.

A long, shuddering breath, and then Pál was still. I knelt to brush his eyelids closed, then sat down beside his body. He had tried to kill me the first time we met. He had led the Circle to us at Eszterháza, and the Circle had killed Grandmama. He had killed Hunger, and only Mátyás and Noémi's quick work had saved the sárkány.

But he was still my mother's brother, still the man who had been a frightened child when the Circle made him into a weapon. Still the child my grandmother had mourned most of her adult life.

As I knelt beside his body, a litany of my dead ran through my mind: Grandmama. Lady Berri. William. Zhivka. Petőfi Sándor. Hadúr. Pál. Noémi. I curled my arms around my knees and began to cry. For the dead, whom I could not bring back, and for the living, who could not escape the bloody reach of this war.

When I'd spent myself, I stood and wiped the tears from my cheeks. A few drops had caught on the ends of my short hair and hung—frozen salt diamonds.

In the aftermath of Pál's death I felt oddly untethered. My uncle's death seemed so cataclysmic, and yet little had changed. The battle still raged. I might still lose everything.

But I had won myself back. That was something.

I looked around once more, assessing. In the distance, the black mass that was Mátyás wreaked havoc on the human soldiers.

How had he come to fight for the praetheria? What had Vasilisa told him? Partial truths, I guessed. Enough to make him trust her. But he was fighting for the wrong side, burning energy in battles that might yet destroy us.

One soldier, I thought. *One task.* I could not end the war alone, but I could do this one thing.

I had a glimmer of an idea, but no assurance it would work. Closing my eyes, I pictured Gábor as I had seen him last, as I walked away from him toward the praetheria. I thought of the trees and fields around Eszterháza, the heartbreaking hominess of a stork settling in to roost, a heron picking through the reeds. I pictured England—my family's home in Dorset. My father, hunched over some bit of obscure scholarship. James, racing between the house and the stables.

Noémi.

I knit all the longing together and pushed it outward: an invocation and plea.

Would it be enough, in a battlefield rife with desperation, with a hundred thousand hearts beating with hope and terror and need? I shuffled through my mental pictures again, holding them until the pain of absence was unbearable.

Long minutes passed. A cold wind picked up, biting my cheeks and stirring the hair of Pál's corpse behind me.

A flicker of movement: a birdlike shape where no birds flew (save the vultures circling high above). The flicker swelled, and Hunger stood beside me.

"What?" he asked, rather ungraciously.

I faltered. The only time I had seen him look worse was when he was dead. Dried blood (Noémi's?) crusted his cheeks, and his eyes were hooded and haunted. I guessed that Noémi's death was replaying through his head as it was through mine.

His gaze fixed on a spot behind me, his dark brows drawn together in a frown. "Is that Pál?"

"Yes."

"Good."

I did not turn to look at Pál. "I need you to help me stop Mátyás."

When Hunger didn't say anything, I plunged on. "I

know you're grieving Noémi—we all are. But she would want us to channel that grief into action; she'd want us to stop Mátyás before he tears himself apart. We still have a chance to salvage this."

Hunger looked back at me and bowed his head. "As you wish."

If he did not sound enthusiastic, he had not said no, either. I'd accept that.

He shifted with the ease of someone long accustomed to it, then lowered his torso so that I could scramble astride his back. I'd sat thus before, though the last time he'd been fitted with a saddle to anchor me. I leaned forward, my belly against the knobbled spine of his back, and knotted my arms around his neck.

He lifted with a rush, the cold wind roaring up to meet us. We soared over the battlefield, following the smoking, groaning ruins of the armies. The devastation rocked me: had it only been this morning that the praetherian army marched out? A miasma of fear rose from the dead and dying, from the living trying to scuttle back beyond the reach of a powerful, deadly army.

We landed a short distance from Mátyás. The appearance of a second dragon—even if he only had one head instead of seven—set up a renewed chorus of screaming and soldiers scrambling to get away. Even the praetheria gave the two dragons wide berth.

One of Mátyás's seven heads reached out to snag a fleeing soldier, snapping him in half.

Hunger swelled to meet Mátyás, increasing his size by half, and my grip on his neck loosened. I slid backward, my heart catapulting into my throat, before finally lodging against his shoulder blades, where his wings sprouted outward. He folded his wings back around, anchoring me.

"Mátyás!" Hunger called, and the dragon before us stilled, the seven heads pulling back in unison to eye us. Dragon faces are not particularly expressive, but I imagined this one was surprised. I doubted Mátyás had met anything yet to stand against him in dragon form.

"Mátyás," I echoed, craning around Hunger's shoulder to look at my cousin. "Please stop—come back to us!"

Dragon muscles tightened beneath me. "I'm not sure he can hear you: he's consumed by the hunger of that form. He's drawing power from the World Tree, but that power was intended to protect the tree, not destroy life, and the longer he uses this shape to destroy things, the more he erodes the deeper connection."

Hunger's answer was curiously specific and set a warning jangling along my veins. "How do you know all of this?"

Mátyás hissed, and two of the heads struck forward. One narrowly missed Hunger's neck—and me behind it—the other latched onto Hunger's upper arm. Hunger clawed the head away and released a gout of fire, and all seven of Mátyás's heads screamed. "Because the hunger that goads him—I know it. What he is now, I was once—a táltos defined by the shape I wore."

Hunger.

I nearly lost my grip in surprise—only the leathery wings folded around me held me in place. I'd thought he took his name from his role in the Four, a black-humored nod to the human legend of the Four Horsemen. I'd never thought to wonder at his past: he seemed so much a creature out of story, a legend born onto the pages fully formed.

"How did you learn to control the hunger?"

He snapped his teeth at Mátyás. "I didn't. The World Tree calls this shape forth from táltos when it needs a protector. But I was young and brash and arrogant, and instead of becoming a dragon to protect the tree, I sought only to feed my hunger. And so eventually a hero—I've forgotten his name—arrived and drove me out of the tree, because that's what heroes do. Exile broke my connection to the World Tree and the hunger."

In Grandmama's stories, it was always the simple farm boy who defeated the dragon. Was Hunger still bitter, all these centuries later?

Two great wings unfurled behind Mátyás, lifting him from the ground. His wingspan blotted out cloud-filtered light, plunging us into shadow. Then he dove toward us, claws outstretched.

He was fast, but Hunger was faster, and he flung us to the side so that Mátyás's clawed feet pounded the frozen dust instead of us. Mátyás lumbered around, his airborne grace lost on the ground. Hunger snaked his long neck forward and his jaws closed around the throat of one of Mátyás's seven heads, snapping it. While that head dangled uselessly, the other heads roared. Hunger danced back, out of reach, his sleek black limbs far more graceful than my cousin's.

"I don't think exiling him to break the connection will work."

"No," agreed Hunger. "We need to remind him who he

370

is inside that devouring hunger. See if you can talk to him.
I'll try to keep you safe."

I wriggled downward, through the protective enfolding
of Hunger's wings, and let myself drop to the ground. The
impact knocked my breath away, and it took a moment
for me to collect myself and sprint out of the way of the
lumbering dragons.

I slipped around Hunger, to the no-man's land between
the two clashing dragons. My heart climbed into my
throat, beating frantically.

But I wasn't alone.

Bahadır stood beside me, his breathing heavy, as though
he'd just run a great distance.

"What are you doing here?" I asked.

Mátyás sprang into the air, and Hunger followed, driving him back. I danced out of the way of a swinging tail.

"I saw Mátyás across the field and came to join him. He
gets lost in this form: I thought I might help him."

"You're a good friend."

Bahadır turned a smile on me that was more a grimace
than an expression of mirth. "I'm a terrified friend." He
sucked in a breath. "I ran when my father was killed by the
sultan's men. I was a child; I could not have done anything
then. But I will not run now."

Dragon fire scorched the earth in front of us, and we
both jumped.

"When Zhivka brought him back, she touched him and
spoke his name. Maybe if we can get his attention . . . ?"
Bahadır said.

Mátyás landed with a thud, his fanged mouths lashing

371

out at Hunger, who settled beside him, interposing his bulk between Mátyás and a handful of soldiers who watched us. We tried shouting his name, but Mátyás seemed fixed on Hunger and ignored us. I tried to creep closer, to touch him, but his tail came sweeping round and caught my ankle, throwing me to the ground.

"Do you still have the canteen and salt?" Bahadır asked.

"Yes." I'd added water to the canteen before Pál brought me to the battlefield but hadn't found occasion to use it.

"Good." Bahadır dashed away, returning a moment later with a barrel of black powder that he'd rescued beside an overturned and abandoned cannon. I handed him the canteen, then the salt. He dumped the salt into the canteen, screwed the lid back on, and shook it rapidly. He set the canteen in the barrel, put the cover back on, and then flung the barrel at Mátyás.

His aim was impeccable. The barrel struck the joint between two of Mátyás's waving heads, then exploded: powder and wooden debris and scraps of canteen metal screamed through the air.

The six remaining heads froze, then turned their focus on the two of us. Six heads, twelve eyes, innumerable sharp teeth.

Well. We had his attention now.

"Mátyás!" Bahadır yelled. "It's Bahadır. Your friend."

Bahadır poked me, and I echoed him. "Mátyás! It's Anna. Your cousin."

The six heads swayed a bit, but they did not attack, and I stepped toward the beast. *Zhivka touched him.* Behind me, Bahadır began talking about Ákos and the other bandits, about their time together on the plains. A great shudder rippled through Mátyás, but he did not strike. I took another step. Two more.

Hunger crouched beside Mátyás, watchful, his muscles coiled in case he needed to spring into action. Bahadır kept talking and I kept walking, and still Mátyás did not move. But when the Turkish boy stopped to draw breath, one of the six heads drew back. Hunger launched forward and intercepted the striking head, but a second and then a third head snaked around him, mouths open, fangs glistening.

I dodged between them, throwing my arms around Mátyás's foreleg. The skin was smooth like a polished opal, and warm. This close, I could see that the scales were not all black, but luminescent, with touches of turquoise and emerald and amaranth swirling in their depths.

"Mátyás!" I shouted again. "I love you—even this part of you, that you hesitate to name. This dragon is you, but not all of you. You are cousin and brother and nephew. Bandit and soldier, táltos and spirit walker, dragon and crow. You are Mátyás, the King of Crows."

A breath of heat against my face: dragon's breath.

I closed my eyes, pressing my cheek against the smooth scales. I did not want to see the moment Mátyás decided to eat me.

"You are King of Crows," I whispered again. "Mátyás, *Rex Corvus.*"

The heat withdrew, icy air encircling me once again.

I opened my eyes.

One of the great heads was still lowered, staring at me,

but the black eyes were no longer flat. Something like recognition glinted in them.

"Anna?" The voice sounded as though it came from somewhere very far away, small and unused. Then the name was picked up by five more throats, and my name reverberated in the air.

I sagged against his foreleg. "Mátyás."

The scales began to shrink beneath my cheek, and I released my grip. The seven heads melted into one, the great body collapsed into a smaller one, without scales. When Mátyás stood before me again, I hugged him. Bahadır clapped him on the back. He was still too thin (and too naked, but I was trying very hard not to notice that), but the color had returned to his face, and he looked infinitely better than when I'd seen him last.

Hunger shifted too and came to stand beside me. Naturally, he was impeccably dressed: fitted striped trousers and military-style dolman with silver frogging. He handed Mátyás a cloak. "Someone must really teach you how to shift without losing all your clothes."

CHAPTER 31

Mátyás

I took the cloak from Hunger and swung it around my shoulders. It was a damned sight more pleasant than the cold-pricked skin I'd worn earlier, though I'd need to supplement it with additional clothes soon.

Remembering what Vasilisa had told me, I peered at Hunger. "You were táltos?"

Hunger sighed. "A long time ago. I've kept the dragon shape because it suited me. If there were other shapes, I've since forgotten them. I was never as good at shifting as you appear to be."

We stood in an odd bubble of quiet, the battle having spun away from the fighting dragons; it had not yet returned to envelop us. Hunger told me a short version of his story, how he had been driven from the World Tree and lost the intense hunger. "That is not a tactic I would recommend," he said.

"With practice, you'll get better at managing the hunger," he continued. "Stay close to the World Tree; it will help you remain grounded. Nothing will fill the hunger completely, though. A being that is completely satiated loses its edge, and you will need that edge, as táltos and protector, now that Hadúr is dead and no one is left to tend the World Tree. You have to learn to live inside the hunger and longing. Let it goad you without destroying you. Better still, learn to cultivate it in others, as I have done. I find it infinitely preferable to rouse desire in others than be ravaged by it."

I lost the last part of his speech. "Hadúr is dead?"

"Chernobog killed him, just after Noémi died," Anna said, handing me a pair of trousers. There was only a slight speckling of blood below one knee, so I pretended not to notice and slid them on.

Noémi, Hadúr. And the list would no doubt grow before this battle was over. As a child, I had gone swimming with my family one summer at Lake Balaton. We got caught by a surprise storm, and as the wind churned up waves, one crashed over me. I saw it just before it hit, but I could not move away fast enough. The ground went out beneath me, and I floundered in darkness, unsure which way was up. I could feel my grief now, poised like that wave. But I could not let it crash. Giving in to grief in that moment felt too much like running—a way to avoid the responsibility before me.

If I died in this war, I wanted to die with my eyes open. I wanted to die trying. For so long, I had thought my father's failure came from disappointing us, from not being the man we believed him to be. And so I had been careful to set expectations low, so I would not disappoint, so I would not be my father.

But my father had not disappointed us when he lost the family fortune at cards—we might have lived through that. He had disappointed us when he left us to bear the shame alone.

There was no dishonor in failure, so long as I tried. My mother used to say that everyone is the blacksmith of his or her own fate; I would be the smith of mine.

"Vasilisa said we needed to convince the assembled armies that peace was more costly than war," I said.

"Vasilisa holds words cheaply," Hunger said. "She told you whatever she thought would best twist you to her will. The praetheria, under the three who drive them now, are not looking for peace."

"I think she's right, though," I said, "about convincing the others. But we need an army."

There were four of us: me, Bahadır, Hunger, Anna. Wait—a figure was crossing through the smoke-covered field toward us. Gábor made five. Anna ran to him, throwing her arms around him with such energy that he staggered.

Bahadır pulled a crumpled bit of fabric from his shirt. He shook it out: a gold ash tree on a green field. "We have Hadúr's standard." He tied it to the end of his rifle and raised it above his head. The wind caught it, whipping it out smartly. "General Görgey and the Hungarians know to come to our aid when we raise it. The lidérc has been recruiting praetheria, and Emilija is trying to persuade her father."

"Will that be enough?" I asked. The battlefields I'd seen

in my hunger-maddened state were chaos: Austrians and Russians and Hungarians all fighting one another and fighting the praetheria. Even I had seen that much.

"There might be enough soldiers on these fields—human and praetherian alike—who do not want this war," Hunger said. "If we can rally them."

Anna was looking intently at Gábor. "You could help," she said.

Gábor pressed his lips together. "You know how I feel about Coremancer gifts."

Anna said slowly, "I don't think persuasion always has to mean coercion, or even manipulation. Your words can be an invitation—they can open a place for understanding, for negotiation."

She hesitated, but Gábor picked up on her unspoken words. "And we are desperate." He sighed. "I will try."

He made his way to a wagon near an overturned cannon, abandoned in the swiftly moving current of the war. He clambered aboard, so he would have some vantage point over the flat battlefield. He held himself still for a moment, his face pensive. Then he called out, "People of Hungary, Austria, Russia, Croatia, and the provinces! Praetheria! If you can hear me, I beg you to listen."

His voice carried across the field, a voice that I felt as much as heard. When had he developed Coremancer abilities? I had missed too much.

"This war needs to end. We are destroying one another—and for what? Because we hope to prove our own superiority? To indulge our arrogance?"

As Gábor spoke, the weight of the war felt like a tangible

thing, pinning me to the ground until I could scarcely move.

"We look to end this fight, to restore peace not just for humans but for praetheria as well. We look to forge a new world. If your heart responds to this plea, then join us. Whoever you are, whatever you are, we will find a place for you."

The piercing weight of the war was followed by a sharp longing to throw that weight away. Did Gábor know how powerful his magic was? I did not feel forced or coerced— but a singing had taken up in my veins, a warming sureness that fighting alongside him was the right and inevitable path.

The reaction to his words was not immediate, though the fighting stilled around us as he spoke. When he finished, there was a sluggish stirring of men and women taking up their weapons again, resuming their fight.

But not all of them.

At first singly, then in pairs and clumps of soldiers, people began pulling away from the battle. Hungarians mostly, at first, because Gábor had spoken in Hungarian. But the pull of his words transcended language, and after the Hungarians came a few Romanians, a handful of Croatians.

And praetheria.

A giantess, who seemed to know Anna, because she nodded at her and then searched the ground around her, frowning—I realized she was looking for Noémi too. A pair of Valkyries, who did not look at any of us but came to rest beside Gábor anyway. A tree-man, looking so like the tree-man I had accidentally killed in our bandit camp that my heart twisted. A Fair One, similar to the one I'd reluctantly saved from a mob months earlier. A cluster of samodiva, their glamours burning bright around them. I told them I was sorry about Zhivka, and they brushed their hands against mine in silent acknowledgment.

There were others whom I did not recognize, and still we were not many—several dozen, perhaps a hundred—but more than I had hoped for.

"But who shall lead all these soldiers?" Bahadır asked.

"You," I said. "You always did think circles around me when Hadúr taught us strategy. You were born to lead." It was true: Bahadır had an instinct for groups that I had never had, even when I led my *betyárok* as the King of Crows. Thank St. Cajetan, we did not all have to lead to contribute something of value.

Bahadır's cheeks darkened with the praise, but he seemed pleased.

"I'll help," Gábor said. "I make an excellent adjutant."

While the soldiers continued to gather around us, waiting for instruction, Hunger said, "We need to cut the praetherian army off at its head—we need to eliminate or neutralize the three praetheria who lead them. Chernobog will not refuse a challenge. His pride is his weakness; he believes he cannot lose."

"*Can* he lose?" I asked.

"Maybe," Hunger said, shrugging. "You ought to pray it's true, because you are our best hope of challenging him. Otherwise, he will hide behind his minions, and we don't have enough numbers to overwhelm them."

One of the Valkyries said, "I will come with the táltos.

If he fails, I will challenge Chernobog myself." Her sister murmured agreement.

"And Vasilisa and Svarog?" Anna asked.

A young man joined us, struggling to the front of our makeshift army. His hair blazed gold, even in the muted light from the overcast sky, and a string of lights hung around his neck like stars. "I can take Svarog."

"And you are?" I asked.

"His son."

Others of the praetheria, including the tree-man, offered to join the young man, should he fail. It seemed Svarog was not quite so feared among the praetheria as Chernobog, which should have terrified me. Instead, that familiar thrum of a calculated risk buzzed through my blood.

Hunger insisted on facing Vasilisa himself. He turned to Anna. "Will you come with me?"

I saw the fear in her face: the widened eyes, the pale cheek. Anna swallowed once and said, "Very well."

Alarm penetrated through my cloud of energy. "You can't mean for Anna to fight her?"

"Not alone," Hunger said. "But she's chimera, and she has faced Vasilisa before."

"It's all right," Anna said. "I need to do this. Besides, you cannot offer to challenge Chernobog and then lecture me for a similar choice."

Abashed, I said, "You're right. I'll wish you good luck instead."

We were all going to need as much luck as we could get.

Our little group began to disperse—the young man, with a handful of praetheria heading out to find Svarog;

Hunger, shifting to carry Anna away; Bahadır and Gábor, already discussing how to use their small numbers to their advantage.

I looked at the Valkyries. They were both taller than I, even unmounted, and they still would not make eye contact, instead fixing their gaze at a point above my head. It was disconcerting.

"So," I said. "Do you know where Chernobog is?"

The taller one inclined her head, then both of them mounted their flying horses and took off. I borrowed a nonflying horse and did my damnedest to follow them.

Chernobog was not hard to spot, once we drew close. He let lesser praetheria lead the charge, but he was not far behind, towering above the soldiers as he spitted them casually on a longsword or shoved them down into the ground, the dirt swallowing their screams as it closed over their heads. I had seen him fight once before, when I followed Anna and Noémi in spirit form: he was brutal, vicious, nasty.

I tamped down a brief flare of panic.

The Valkyries landed beside Chernobog as I galloped forward, and he swung toward them. "You would betray your own kind?"

"You betrayed us first. We might have won peace if you had not brought this war."

I wasn't sure if that was accurate, but it sounded good.

I took a deep breath. Now or never. "Chernobog!" I called, hoping my voice did not sound as thin to the praetherian as it did to my own ears. "I formally challenge you as one of the Four." Three? I swallowed my correction, lest it make me look more ridiculous.

382

Chernobog's lips curled back over his teeth, and he slammed his sword at me. I yelped and dove out of the way, toppling off my borrowed horse. The tip of the sword scored my hip, leaving a burning line in its wake.

"Does this mean you accept?" I called up, already shifting to something better equipped to withstand his attacks: a bear, with a decidedly non-ursine scaly hide beneath the fur. I swiped, throwing all the strength of my powerful new body into the movement, and caught Chernobog's arm with my claws.

His sword clattered to the ground, and I kicked it away. He did not even glance down. Instead, he twisted his arm so that he caught my wrist, his own curved claws stabbing through the fur and scale to draw blood. Then he shoved my arm up behind me, and something cracked.

A sharp pain shot through my arm, and I growled, pushing forward to close my jaws across his shoulder. Instead of releasing me, he thrust downward. The ground beneath my feet opened up and I fell, my jaws snapping shut around air. Earth closed over my head.

All the nervous energy that had buoyed me evaporated. I shifted, trying not to remember the weeks I'd spent similarly immobilized in rock, the suffocating weight of dirt all around me. As a mole, arrowing toward the surface, I could breathe easier. I thought of creating some ancient wyrm, a blind creature with thousands of teeth that could erupt from the ground below Chernobog. But I couldn't be certain I'd emerge in the right spot, or that I'd be able to hold a shape that could both dig *and* surprise the horned god.

As soon as I hit the surface, I shifted—this time into

a long, ropy serpent that coiled lightning-fast around Chernobog's legs, swooping up his hips to pin his arms to his sides. I fought the urge to send a call to an avian army to help me. Hunger had been quite clear: a challenge must be fought alone, or my life was forfeit.

The horned god was powerful, but my serpent was nearly his equal, and for a moment I thought I might hold him long enough to wrap a final coil around his throat and mouth and squeeze the breath from him. I did not think it would kill a near-immortal, but it would slow him long enough for me to come up with another idea.

Chernobog wrenched an arm free and sliced a claw down the soft underbelly of my serpent form. Hissing in pain, I dropped at his feet. The dark god plucked me up and flung me into the air. I shifted in mid-arc to an ancient creature I'd seen in a book: a cat with long saber teeth and powerful claws. As I fell back to the earth, I aimed those teeth at the horned god's face.

He twisted his head to meet me, and instead of teeth closing around exposed flesh, a gleaming horn caught my stomach, ripping upward. He tossed me on the ground, where I curled around my wound, the shock sending me back into my human form.

Blood gushed across my skin, steaming in the frigid air.

I was weakening, not just from blood loss. The flesh and blood I'd consumed that morning in dragon form had long since burned away; my stomach, where it did not sting from the gaping wound, was knotted around itself in a hunger nearly as fierce.

Why had the Lady believed my táltos skills might save

the world? Truth was, my skills were a damned poor substitute for actual strength in battle. My animal persuasion, my dream-walking, my shapeshifting—none of that would save me.

That left only the dragon.

I'd nearly lost myself to the dragon three times. Bahadır and Anna between them had brought me back the last time: would a fourth time prove mastery or my final undoing?

I didn't have much choice. As a rock erupted from the ground beneath my already injured hip, I shifted upward, the ravening hunger rising with me.

A whirlwind of dust and stone gusted up around us, cutting us off from the others. Chernobog hurled a dagger at me, but it bounced harmlessly off my scales. Shadows like smoke slithered around the two of us, branching off from Chernobog's shadow. They slid up my scales, burrowed between my teeth. They called to the hunger inside me, and it swelled in response. As the hunger grew, the edges of my awareness fuzzed.

No. I fought against the shadows, but they were insidious and everywhere. Chernobog swung a sword at me, and I barely managed to parry it with my claws. The bloodlust followed the hunger, whispering how exquisite it would feel to feed that lust. But if I lost myself now, I did not trust myself to possess wits enough to win this challenge—or to come back to myself when it was over.

What had Hunger said about owning this shape? The dragon was born of the World Tree, called into being to protect it. It was in the branches of the tree that I first found this form. The tree was still some distance from us, perhaps thirty miles, too far to see, but I could feel its presence as a kind of steady thrum in the earth beneath me. Hadúr had said once that the roots stretched for miles below the *puszta*. Did they stretch this far? I dug my claws into the dirt, trying to concentrate on the tree as I parried another of Chernobog's attacks. *There.* I could feel the root system, nearly invisible filaments stretching through the *puszta,* resting beneath my feet. I drew on that grounding, a slow rush of warmth washing through me, and the shadows fell away.

The horned god hissed, his wings unfurling behind him as he lifted into the air. I matched his movement, my heads darting forward at once. Two of the heads caught at a wing, tearing a long rip down the center. Off balance, Chernobog fell, hitting the ground with a thump that shook the plain.

I dove, landing on top of him and pinning him down.

The earth opened around us, a deep fissure. As we tumbled down, the fissure sealed over us. I knew a moment of panic as the darkness enveloped us; in response to my slackened vigilance, the hunger nearly overwhelmed my awareness.

I pushed back both the fear and the hunger, thrusting my heads forward to slash and bite, my claws to cut and gouge. Chernobog reciprocated, his claws scrabbling for purchase against my scales.

We seemed to fall a long time. Molten earth spouted up around us—called by a lord of the underworld? The heat against my skin manifested as pressure: it didn't burn, not yet, but if we were to be surrounded by the stuff, it might cut off my breath, burn my throat, sear my lungs.

With heads and claws, I seized Chernobog and pulled him toward me, beating my wings as much as I could in the cramped space to slow my fall. Two heads grasped his horns, and the centermost head closed around his throat. His pulse pounded between my teeth, a siren call to my hunger. His claws scraped against my exposed neck and my belly. I ignored the spreading pain.

For a heartbeat, I hesitated. If I answered that hunger now, what did it make me? A hero? A monster? Vasilisa's words flitted through my head, that a wolf is not a monster for having teeth and claws. And Hunger's: you have to live inside the hunger. Let it goad you without destroying you.

Destruction was the flip side of creation. If Chernobog lived, he'd drive the praetherian armies to destroy everything I'd known and loved in the world. If he died . . . we might have a chance to create anew.

My jaws snapped shut, teeth piercing the pulsing vein, blood filling my mouth, my throat. The hunger blazed up again, and I nearly lost myself. There was a fierce bliss in this, abandoning sense and coherence to need. I rode the cresting wave of hunger, biting and tearing, until a wing brushed against one of the fine, exposed filaments of the World Tree roots.

I came back to myself: to the part of Mátyás that belonged to the dragon. Or to the part of the dragon that belonged to Mátyás?

Beneath my teeth, there was no pulsing blood to draw out my hunger. Chernobog was dead, or near enough.

I dropped his body, letting it fall to the fires below. Then I shifted one more time, to my old familiar crow, and flew up through the ravine, breaking the crust of the earth at the top like a hatchling erupting from its shell.

)(

The Valkyries were fighting with other praetheria when I emerged.

I shifted back to my human self, shivering beneath the light fall of snow. *Damn and blast it all.* I needed to learn how Hunger shifted without losing everything.

The taller of the two, with long red braids, skewered an elfin man with deer antlers, then turned to nod at me. "You fought well, táltos."

Her sister, with a cloud of dark hair around her brown skin, ran her horse against two squat, bearded creatures and added, "May all your fights be so prosperous. Should you die today, we will find a place for you in Valhalla."

"Um, thank you." I was acutely conscious that I was still naked, with no weapon to speak of, and two human soldiers were racing toward me. I tugged a jacket off a dead soldier and borrowed his saber.

The dark-haired Valkyrie blocked the soldiers while I wrapped the jacket around my waist.

My kingdom for a horse. I cast my animal sense out, looking for an unmounted beast. A moment later, a white horse cantered up to me. It bore no bridle, but it trotted straight to me and whuffled at my cheek. I froze. I knew this beast. It was Holdas, my own brute of a horse that I had thought lost long since, when I'd been captured in the Austrian ice caves.

I swung up, and Holdas whickered a greeting.

The red-haired Valkyrie turned a sly look on me. "Death comes riding on a white horse. Now I know for certain the world is ending."

I laughed and raised my sword. "No, it's beginning. *Hajrá!*"

CHAPTER 32

Anna

I did not recognize Vasilisa when Hunger set down behind her: an old woman with exultation lifting the lines of her face, a pack of dire wolves before her laying waste to any soldier who stood against her. Then she turned, tossing a bolt of lightning into a knot of soldiers, and I saw the old woman I had carried out of a prison in Vienna. She shot green-tinged fire at us before Hunger's forelimbs had settled on the ground. Hunger roared, his answering fire sending up a conflagration before us.

"Vasilisa!"

She fluttered her eyelashes at him, a grotesque mockery of a young girl's flattery. "Yes?"

"We need to end this."

"No, *you* need to end this. I need do nothing of the sort." One of her wolves tore out the throat of a soldier, sending blood spraying across the accumulating snow, and she clapped her hands together.

"You let me escape," Hunger said. "You encouraged Noémi to heal me when I might have died. I cannot believe that you truly want this war."

"Why?" Vasilisa flung a small shower of rocks at us, and Hunger raised his wings over my head to protect me. "Because we are old friends and I did not want to see you killed in such shabby fashion does not mean I want peace. You have grown weak and sentimental. This is what too-close association with humans brings."

"I am not sure," Hunger said slowly, his dragon voice low and rumbling, "that love, what you call sentimentality, is always weakness. I am coming to think it might save us. In any case, I have lost my taste for war. This one has cost me too much."

I remembered his keening grief when Noémi died, and my heart contracted.

"These people do not love us," Vasilisa said.

"We've given them no cause to," Hunger said.

"And they have given us no cause to love them," Vasilisa said, hurling a tiny starlike light at me. I did not dodge in time, and it lodged in my shoulder, sending a rippling pain through my body.

It occurred to me that though she was attacking, she was not trying very hard to kill us—and she was listening.

"You're right," I said. "We have treated you terribly. The Binding was a mistake, and we have only compounded it since you were released. But I—" A surging emotion choked my throat. "I released you in good faith. I wanted things to be better for you, for us. I failed—we all failed. I have lost people who were dear to me, whom I cannot get back. The praetheria have suffered losses too. But we can do better—all of us. Maybe we don't deserve the chance, but we might come to. I witnessed for you when you asked me to, and it nearly cost me my life. I'm asking now: please, give us a chance to do better."

"*Please,*" Vasilisa mimicked, her voice dripping scorn. "Your language is filled with such insipid words. No, we have already given you too many chances."

"If you will not agree to stop fighting, then you leave me no choice." Hunger dug his claws into the earth, and the ground fractured before him. "I formally challenge you, as one of the Four."

Vasilisa froze for the barest second, then smirked. "You forfeited your spot among the Four when you died at the hands of a human. No, I will not accept your challenge."

"You cannot refuse a challenge!" Hunger barked at her, sparks from his tongue dying tiny deaths on the grass before us.

"I just did. I did not save your life to kill you myself. Besides"—Vasilisa gestured at the fighting around us— "you have thrown your lot in with humans; you are scarcely praetherian anymore. And who should witness for us? Not your little friend here."

She flung another of her tiny stars at me. This time, instead of dodging, I cast out and caught the thread of the spell, snapping it before it reached me. The energy dissipated in a small burst of heat. She tugged at the wispy hair clinging to her scalp. "Your pet human offers better sport than you."

A pair of Vasilisa's wolves sprang forward, teeth bared, and Hunger hurled himself at them, his wings stretched taut.

The moment Hunger moved from my side, Vasilisa waved her hands around the clearing, and a transparent bubble settled over the two of us. Hunger tore away from the wolves and threw himself against the faintly gleaming barrier, but it held.

His claws and teeth scrabbled fruitlessly at the shield, and even his dragon fire couldn't mark it. The wolves snarled and slunk around the perimeter.

"What you could have been, Anna Arden, if you were not afraid," she said sorrowfully. "You could have been remarkable, fighting alongside me. You could have held the world in your hands."

"What do you want?" I asked, not taking my eyes off her, off the hands she held quietly before her.

Her eyes lit and she bared yellowing teeth in a fierce grin. "I want to see what you can do, before I kill you." Her hands blurred with motion and a dozen sparks streaked through the air toward me.

I broke the spells fueling two of the sparks, but the rest latched onto me like so many electrified leeches: encircling my wrists, hanging from my throat, my thigh. Vasilisa gestured again, and each spark exploded, a miniature lightning storm that scorched the flesh beneath it and sent black stars streaking across my vision. Pain screamed through my body and my knees buckled.

Vasilisa cackled. "How can you fight me when you cannot even *stand*?"

I closed my eyes for a brief moment, trying to rally. My chimera souls roiled inside me, frantic and uncertain. I pushed them together, searching for the unity that would let me cast spells, but everything was so unsettled. Electricity crackled in the air near me, and I threw myself to the side, my eyes flying open.

The lightning left blackened veins on the ground, melting the light cover of snow.

I had faced Vasilisa before. The only time I had been mildly successful had been when I had used her own magic against her. As she began casting another spell, I braced myself. When the spout of green fire left her fingertips, I reached out to snag the spell. But instead of letting the broken magic escape, I gathered it to me, shaping it into a blade that I pushed back at her.

Another shock of green fire knocked the blade aside. "Better," Vasilisa said approvingly. "But you cannot surprise me with a trick you have used before. Indulge me. Show me what you can do, and I will make your death quick. Painless."

My mind raced. It had been Vasilisa who had told me months before that I could not cast spells unless I embraced who I was. Knowing I was chimera was not enough—I had to love that self too, the good and bad together. Did I?

Most days, I knew myself too well. I knew when I was cowardly, when I was hateful, when jealousy curdled in my gut. I knew when doubt colored everything, when I did not trust myself or my own mind. It was hard to love that girl, hard to see past her flaws.

My fingers curled around Gábor's stone, still, improbably, safe in my pocket. If I could not embrace myself, perhaps I could borrow from others. I thought of how Gábor looked at me, seeing my shadows and loving me anyway.

I thought of Noémi, who had been my friend, though I did not always deserve it. Of my father and James, who believed in me, even when I failed. Of the lidérc, who was funny and faithful and no monster, despite what her appearance suggested. My friends and family had shown me that you do not have to be perfect to be worthy of love. The best love was given as a gift, unearned.

Vasilisa clapped her hands together, and a ring of green fire erupted around me, constricting me even as I drew breath. The heat tore at the inside of my nose, scraped down my lungs.

I shut my eyes against the flame, twisting the thread of the spell so it snapped.

Who was I, when everything else had been stripped away? When I could no longer hide in smallness or behind any pretensions to greatness? I could feel my two souls pulsing inside me: two steady lights, human and monster both. And what was a monster, but something we did not understand?

I would *not* be afraid.

I called for my souls, and they came, rising in a twin wave, a wash of power that did not delineate where one began and the other ended. I drew on that magic, filling myself till every inch of skin tingled. An echoed memory of breaking the Binding spell flitted across my mind, but I pushed it away. I needed a true spell now, not merely a breaking.

Or did I?

Unmake this. The praetheria—and Pál—had not sought me because I could craft spells but because I could unmake them. I had broken the curse Vasilisa left for Franz Joseph in my kiss, though it had rooted deep in his heart. Pál had wanted me to unmake the weave of the world.

I could try to cast a spell against Vasilisa, who had a millennium of experience with magic to draw from.

Or . . .

Unmaking was not a dissolution of self but a transformation. Vasilisa's identity came almost wholly from her magic: could I unmake that? An idea glimmered, but I had to ward off Vasilisa's attacks while I prepared it.

When Hunger, Noémi, and I escaped from the caves, I had slowed Vasilisa by unmaking the snow falling around us, returning it to water. I did the same now, gathering the snow on the ground around us and drawing from the pulsing energy in my souls to send a thin veil of water whirling around her: a miniature cyclone that would hold her—I hoped—for just long enough. She hurled an impressive arsenal of curses at me; I ignored her.

Pál had told me I could not hold his vision of the world without him, but he had always underestimated me. I did not think I could follow the weave back in time as he had, but I did not need that. Only this moment. I closed my eyes, sending all the shared force of my twin souls questing for the weave that held the world together.

At first I saw nothing, only faint traces of light against my eyelids, and I began to despair. But then I caught a glimmer that was not remembered light, and I followed it to another thread of light, laid against it in a careful pattern, and then a third. And then the pattern was before me, not as vivid as it had been when Pál held it, but enough.

Vasilisa, standing before me, was an intricate knot of light weaves, her magic circling in and around the bright core that was her soul.

Unmake this. I tugged at one of the threads of her magic, and Vasilisa screamed. The weaves did not break at my touch, as casual spells did. Like the spell around Franz Joseph, they were tightly drawn together, with no give.

Fire rippled up my arm, and at the shock of pain, my eyes sprang open. I dropped the vision weave. Steam hissed in the air where Vasilisa's water cage had stood. Where before she had been amused, now she was enraged. Her wispy hair stood on end.

I had only a heartbeat of time, if that. I scrambled to find the vision weave again, following the first trail of light until I could find a second, then a third. Though my arm still throbbed with pain, Vasilisa had given me an idea. *"Adure,"* I whispered—but I directed the fire inward, to the invisible plane where magic existed.

A conflagration erupted around the tangle of lights, a burning bright enough for a witch.

The ground shivered beneath my feet, and I fell to my knees, dropping the weave before I could see if the fire had been enough.

I braced myself for another onslaught, cradling my burnt arm in my strong one. But instead of flinging another fireball at me, Vasilisa crumpled to the frosted grass and covered her eyes with her fingers. The veins in her hands and at her temple pulsed thick and blue. She didn't look like a being who wanted to destroy the flawed human world I loved. She looked like an old woman, someone I might have become—someone who loved and hated in equal measure.

The bubble around us evaporated. The wolves were already running from the field, their bond with Vasilisa disappearing with her magic. Hunger shifted to human form and ran to my side.

"What did you do to her?"

"I stripped her magic." After a beat, I added, "I think." I didn't know if I'd unmade all her magic or only some of it, if the damage was permanent or only temporary. But Vasilisa was not attacking, so I had clearly done *something*.

She began to laugh weakly. She dropped her hands and looked at me. "*Brava!* I did not think you had it in you. I could almost forgive you for what you've done."

"Do you yield?" Hunger asked.

"I suppose," she said, rather ungraciously. "And what shall you do now?"

"Win the war," I said. "Negotiate a treaty that gives a place to the praetheria and restores Hungary's independence, that gives a better voice to everyone."

"It's a pretty dream," Vasilisa said. "But dreams have a way of disappointing you."

She started to add something else, but a rumbling shook the ground beneath us, and she fell silent. I turned, braced to face some new disaster.

A praetherian army marched toward us, the low light glinting off swords and shields—and other items that might charitably be called weapons. A shovel, a scythe, a washboard. Above the army a handmade flag waved: Hadúr's gold ash tree on a green field. My gaze dropped back to the front ranks of the army, to the woman at their head, her sharp teeth bared in a grin, her goose feet covered by boots.

"Ild—" I started, then stopped myself. The lidérc had given me her name but had not given me leave to use it publicly. I glanced at Vasilisa, to see her reaction to this new evidence of her loss, but she had already crept away in the chaos. I thought briefly of sending someone after her, but without her powers, she was no longer a threat to us.

Besides, even if she had tried to kill me, she had saved me too. She had taught me what I needed to know about myself to embrace my magic—all of it.

Hunger said to the lidérc, "I see you found them."

"Most were gathered near the World Tree, as you said. And the others—well, a few light-lures managed to draw them out, and they did not kill me when they realized what I'd come for." The lidérc's grin widened.

A weight seemed to lift off me. I'd been a fool for far too long, hoarding responsibility to myself like a miser. This fight was not just mine—it had never been just mine.

Each of the praetheria before me was a drop of hope and, together, a veritable ocean of promise. The tide of battle was turning, and we would ride the cresting wave into a new world.

EPILOGUE

Anna

Debrecen, December 31, 1848

A rap sounded at the door of my bedroom. The hair I had been inexpertly trying to pin came tumbling down my neck, and the pins scattered. I surveyed the pins rather mournfully, then sighed and went to the door.

It was Mátyás. "Anna, there's something I must—" He broke off, taking in the rather fine dress of burgundy silk with gold embroidery that I was wearing. "What are you doing?"

"Dressing for the ball," I said, referring to the celebration planned for the end of the war and the new year in the hotel ballroom that night. The fortnight between the war's end and the new year had been filled with treaty negotiations establishing Hungary's independence and granting citizenship to praetheria in whichever nation they claimed. Both

Hungary and Austria were to hold parliamentary elections in the spring, and the Ottoman pasha had promised to hold a similar election among the ruling class. We had not remade the world entirely, not yet, but it was a start.

I took in Mátyás's clothes: a shirt and trousers that might have been through the war. "What have you been doing?"

"Not dressing, obviously."

János *bácsi* had swept into town two days earlier with much-needed funds and had cajoled two suites of rooms for us in a grand hotel downtown. I had not stayed anywhere so fine in months, and still had not quite recovered from the bliss of a well-constructed bed and hot water for bathing.

"Come with me," Mátyás said. A beat later, "Please."

I followed him down the stairs, through the courtyard, and out the heavy doors to the square beyond. The Great Reformed Church gleamed golden across the square in the late-afternoon light.

"Look," he said, and pointed up.

I looked up. Against a pale opal sky, a pair of birds circled overhead, drifting gradually lower, as if they could sense our attention. I knew almost at once that these were the Lady's turul birds. I cocked an eyebrow at Mátyás.

"They've been following me," he said. "Every time I go outside."

"Maybe they've adopted you."

He groaned. "That's what I'm afraid of." He rubbed his mustache—now back to its prewar shapeliness—and said, "Hunger told me the World Tree is my responsibility now that Hadúr and the Lady are gone."

"You don't have to accept that task unless you wish it," I said.

"I know. Except I think I *do* wish it. I've never been particularly connected to a place, except Eszterháza, but there is something about this place—the tree, the plains . . ."

"The bandits and card games," I suggested drily.

He laughed. "Well, yes, that too. And my dragon is calmer when I'm near the tree."

I gave him a hug. "Then I'm happy for you. You'll have to show me around sometime."

"Of course."

I pulled away. He smelled a bit as if he'd been through the war too. "You should change. And wash. And come to the dance."

He did not look quite as enthusiastic as I'd hoped.

"There will be hundreds of beautiful women."

His face broke into a grin. "I suppose I ought to at least wash."

)(

I caught my name as I passed by the front desk on the way back to my room. A man and woman stood talking with the attendant. Behind them, a maid bounced a small child in her arms.

"No, no," the gentleman said in accented German, "we do not need rooms. We have them in another establishment. We are looking for a young lady who might be staying here. Anna Arden?"

"I'm Anna," I said, my heart beating with a new surmise.

The woman whirled with a glad cry and threw her arms around me before I had done more than register that this was, indeed, my sister, Catherine. "Anna! I thought I had lost you, and then we heard that a young woman had convinced the Austrian emperor to step down, and I knew it must be you and insisted we find you." She did not weep on me, as I'd feared she might, but her eyes were suspiciously damp.

"That," her husband, Richard, said, "and Ponsonby sent me to check on the situation here for the embassy." When Catherine poked him, he added, "But of course you were our first priority."

"Oh, and you have not met Christopher yet!" Catherine lifted the little boy from the maid's arms and presented him to me. Somewhat uncertainly—it had been ages since I had held an infant—I took him. He blinked at me, brown eyes beneath a shock of reddish hair. Mama's eyes, I thought. My eyes. He smelled of warm milk and powder, and I nuzzled my cheek against his hair.

"He's beautiful," I said, and Catherine beamed. Then her smile faded as she surveyed my undone hair. "I heard about the ball tonight," she said. "I have clearly arrived just in time." With an imperious gesture, she sent Richard, the baby, and the maid back to their hotel, demanded the hotel send a hairdresser to her at once, and chivvied me up the stairs to my room.

I could not help but laugh. Once, I might have been offended by her imperiousness, but now I saw that it was only Catherine trying to be kind in her own way. I thought of her long-ago debut, when I had sat on her bed and watched her prepare for the ball, my whole body stiff with envy. I'd broken her spell that night, launching the journey that had brought me here. The ball on this occasion might be a trifle unorthodox, but already I preferred it.

)(

A ball can be many things: an invitation, a hunt, a demonstration. But a ball that is also a celebration is by far my favorite. The wide white ballroom with gold accents circling the ceiling was crowded with people: soldiers in military dress, wealthy women in satin finery, farmers in embroidered cotton dolmans and their wives in colorful skirts. Hunger held court with a cluster of praetheria in a far corner. They seemed wary, and I could not entirely blame them. This reborn world was still new—no one entirely knew the social etiquette.

The musicians struck up a waltz, and couples circled onto the floor. Hunger swept by with Emilija, followed by Mátyás and the lidérc. I introduced Bahadır to my sister, and he gallantly led her into the dance. I hoped Gábor would ask me, but before he could reach me, a squat man with a flowing beard and horns protruding from his forehead bowed before me.

Franz Joseph asked me next, starched and formal. "I'm sorry about your cousin."

I followed him through a turn. "Thank you." We'd buried Noémi just before Christmas, holding her service in a golden cathedral that would have charmed her. Across the room, I caught sight of Franz Joseph's mother, glowering at me. I had to look twice to be sure—the archduchess I'd known would never be so undignified. But there was no other word for her expression: she glowered.

"I'm sorry about your country," I said. One of the conditions of the treaty was that the current ruling heads resign: Kossuth had stepped down as president; Franz Joseph had abdicated his throne. No wonder his mother looked as though she could spit nails.

He smiled a little. "All my life, I've been groomed to serve my people. If it is their will that I resign, I cannot set myself against it. I hope they will allow me to serve in other ways, perhaps in the new parliament."

It was several more dances before Gábor could catch me: I passed from one partner to the next, from praetherian to soldier to János *bácsi,* who had to abandon the *csárdás* in the middle and sit down to catch his breath.

When Gábor joined us, he was not alone. His sister Izidóra stood beside him, radiant in a red skirt and blouse, an embroidered scarf tied around her hair. A young man accompanied her, tapping his feet in time to the music.

I rose and greeted Izidóra with a kiss on each cheek. She introduced me to the young man, her new husband. "My mother wanted to come, but she could not leave her grandbabies for so long. So I am sent to tell you that if you mean to marry Gábor"—here her smile widened until it wreathed her whole face—"you shall have to come and visit so that she can teach you. There is much you need to learn about being a good Romani wife."

"I should like that," I said, recognizing the invitation for what it was: a truce between us. I was not the daughter-in-law his mother had hoped for, but I could learn to become part of Gábor's family, as he could learn to become part of mine.

Gábor caught up my hand and pressed a kiss on it, and a bubble of happiness swelled in me.

When I returned home to England in the new year, to see James and my father and mother, and to let my mother fuss over my trousseau, I would not go alone. Mama might be shocked at my choice of a husband, but Papa and James would like him nearly as much as I did. And the only thing Mama would find truly unforgivable would be my marrying without her help—hence the trousseau.

In the summer, under a bower of June roses, we would be married in the gardens at Eszterháza. I hoped my family and Gábor's would both surround us, but whatever they chose, we would be there together. János might even officiate, if his gout did not flare up.

At that moment, Catherine spun by in Hunger's arms. She looked dazed and more than a little alarmed, and I laughed again. I knew Hunger missed Noémi, as did I. But the spark of mischief in his eyes promised that he would be okay.

As would I.

Gábor tugged me into the dance, and then, as the clock inched toward midnight, the host of the ball ushered us all to the doors, where we might view the fireworks he'd managed to procure.

Brilliant flowers of light bloomed in the night sky over Debrecen, their fiery patterns caught between clouds and the dark roofline of the city. *Fireworks*. I hadn't seen such a display for months.

All around us, illusions were taking shape in the air, spiraling upward to join the fireworks. A phoenix erupted from a spout of flame; a griffin took wing from a parapet near us. A great turul bird swooped low over the square and a couple of ladies shrieked. (I was not entirely certain that one was illusion. I should have to ask Mátyás.)

The bells of the Great Reformed Church began to ring out, and members of the orchestra took up their instruments and began playing a triumphant tune in the square. All around me, ballgoers raised a hue and cry, some of them with noisemakers.

I'd never been in Hungary for the new year, and I turned astonished eyes on Gábor.

"The noise is supposed to drive away evil spirits and bring luck in the coming year." His smile was a white slash in the darkness.

It was midnight, the first day of 1849.

Gábor cried, *"Hajrá!"* and plucked me up off the ground, swinging me in the air.

My heart soared, and I laughed. It was impossible not to be hopeful as the new year dawned, impossible not to believe that this year might be better than the last.

Szilveszter night stretched before us, but it was no longer the cold, sharp expanse I'd feared. The darkness that cocooned us held the promise of days to come, and of nights filled with love and laughter and the hope of peace.

Gábor set me down, gently. I slid my arms around his waist and settled into his embrace.

Being with Gábor felt like home.

That home was not a country, though Hungary shared

both our hearts, or a building. It was a place where we knew and were known.

Gábor bent to kiss me, and I saw my face briefly reflected in his eyes. The girl that looked back was more than the things she'd been named: Barren, chimera, spell breaker, monster . . . hero. She was all those things, and none of them.

She was me, entire, gifts and flaws together.

I hoped when Gábor looked at me, he saw his whole self likewise.

I met Gábor's kiss, then took his hand. A few late fireworks burst in the air above us. As the other guests drifted back into the ballroom, we set off across the silent streets of the city, a new world spread wide before us.

The End

AUTHOR'S NOTE

My favorite thing about historical fantasy is the way it marries the mundane with the fantastic, blending real-world events with magic. As such, while I've taken some liberties with the timeline (and the addition of magic), I've also tried to stay true to the spirit of the historical record.

By late summer 1848, Hungary was at war with Croatia; by fall, Austria and Romania had joined in (both Romania and Croatia were Hungarian territories). Within a year, Austria would emerge victorious. The liberties won in March 1848 would be lost, and Hungary would remain part of Austria until the end of the empire, following the First World War (and the death of Emperor Franz Joseph in 1916). In my fictional version, I've compressed the timeline of the war, moving up, among other things, Franz Joseph's coronation (the real coronation did not happen until Emperor Ferdinand abdicated in December of 1848). In this alternate timeline, the inclusion of the praetheria accelerated the Russian involvement and thereby amplified the war earlier.

While my descriptions of the war include Luminate magic, they also include details from the actual Hungarian war for independence, drawn from contemporary accounts. Where possible,

I tried to use the general strategies and troop movements from the war: for example, the battle at Kápolna was a decisive loss for the Hungarian troops, though not so devastating as I've described. And Dembiński and Görgey were in fact at lunch miles away in Eger when the battle started (much of the description of the lunch and Dembiński's subsequent actions were drawn from Görgey's own account of the war and its aftermath). Of course, the addition of magic makes the stakes much higher—which makes the scenes more fun to write.

Like the war itself, the historical characters have also been fictionalized. I've tried to convey their personalities where they are known, but conflicting accounts make this difficult. Kossuth Lajos has been portrayed as a hero and a patriot by some—and a weak, vacillating egoist by others. Görgey might have been (as his memoir suggests) a soldier's soldier who only sought the good of Hungary, even in the face of Kossuth's opposition; or he might have been a traitor, trying to impede the war effort to stay in the good graces of the Hapsburgs. Josip Jellačić, the ban of Croatia on whom Dragović is very loosely based, was a hero for many, particularly the Austrians—and a villain to the Hungarians. Only Haynau, the Hyena of Brescia, seems universally despised. (Lázár István, in his *Hungary: A Brief History,* records that later in life Haynau retired to rural Hungary, where he was rumored to be a vampire by his neighbors). Most likely the truth of these characters lies somewhere between these extremes.

Some aspects have not been fictionalized: the prejudice many Europeans felt toward the Romani was all too real, and unfortunately still continues today. Bihari János was one of the best-known Hungarians of the early nineteenth century for his music, but few of his contemporaries seem to have known he was Romani. Still, Romani music was profoundly influential on Hungarian music (including that of Franz Liszt). Many Romani fought bravely in the Hungarian war for independence, as Gábor does here, despite the discrimination of some who saw their value primarily as musicians.

The Blood Rose Rebellion trilogy has been a pleasure to write, not least because it let me indulge in historical research and call it "writing." Some of my favorite sources for historical details are contemporary memoirs and novels. From Görgey's memoir, I adopted the scathing critique he gives Gábor of General Dembiński. From Jókai Mór's *Hungarian Sketches in Peace and War,* I borrowed the tradition of the empty basket that Noémi hands to Hunger. So many of the ordinary details of life get lost to history books, but they underwrite the fabric of daily life and the stories we tell about them. I'm grateful I could include a few of them.

ADDITIONAL RESOURCES

These are some, but not all, of the resources I relied on in writing this book (and the Blood Rose Rebellion trilogy), for readers who want to know more about the real historical context behind these books.

Achim, Viorel. *The Roma in Romanian History.* Budapest: Central European University Press, 2004.

Boyar, Ebru, and Kate Fleet. *A Social History of Ottoman Istanbul.* Cambridge: Cambridge University Press, 2010.

Curtis, Benjamin. *The Habsburgs: The History of a Dynasty.* New York: Bloomsbury, 2013.

Deák, István. *The Lawful Revolution: Louis Kossuth and the Hungarians, 1848–1849.* London: Phoenix, 2001. Originally published in 1979 by Columbia University Press.

Degh, Linda, ed. *Folktales of Hungary.* Translated by Judit Halász. Chicago: University of Chicago Press, 1965.

E.O.S. *Hungary and Its Revolutions from the Earliest Period to the Nineteenth Century: With a Memoir of Louis Kossuth.* London: Henry G. Bohn, 1854.

Goodman, Ruth. *How to Be a Victorian.* New York: Liveright, 2015.

Görgei, Artúr. *My Life and Acts in Hungary in the Years 1848 and 1849.* London: David Bogue, 1852.

Hancock, Ian. *A Handbook of Vlax Romani*. Bloomington, IN: Slavica, 1995.

Hancock, Ian. *We Are the Romani People*. Hatfield, England: University of Hertfordshire Press, 2002.

Hanioğlu, M. Şükrü. *A Brief History of the Late Ottoman Empire*. Princeton, NJ: Princeton University Press, 2010.

Hartley, M. *The Man Who Saved Austria: The Life and Times of Baron Jellačić*. London: Mills & Boon, 1912.

Jókai, Mór. *Hungarian Sketches in Peace and War*. Edinburgh: Constable, 1854.

Kontler, László. *A History of Hungary: Millennium in Central Europe*. New York: Palgrave Macmillan, 2002.

Lázár, István. *Hungary: A Brief History*. Budapest: Corvina Press, 1997.

Leiningen-Westerburg, Count Charles. *Letters and Journals (1848–1849) of Count Charles Leiningen-Westerburg, General in the Hungarian Army*. London: Duckworth, 1911.

Lukacs, John. *Budapest 1900: A Historical Portrait of a City and Its Culture*. New York: Grove Press, 1994.

Matras, Yaron. *The Romani Gypsies*. Cambridge: Belknap Press, 2015.

Minamizuka, Shingo. *A Social Bandit in Nineteenth-Century Hungary: Rózsa Sándor*. East European Monographs, 2008.

Okey, Robin. *The Habsburg Monarchy*. New York: St. Martin's Press, 2000.

Pardoe, Julia S. H. *The City of the Magyar, or Hungary and Her Institutions in 1839–40*. London: George Virtue, 1840.

Shoberl, Frederic. *Scenes of the Civil War in Hungary, in 1848 and 1849: With the Personal Adventures of an Austrian Officer in the Army of the Ban of Croatia*. Philadelphia: E. H. Butler & Co., 1850.

Stauber, Roni, and Raphael Vago, eds. *The Roma: A Minority in Europe, Historical, Political and Social Perspectives.* Budapest: Central European University Press, 2007.

Wenkstern, Otto von. *History of the War in Hungary in 1848 and 1849.* London: John Parker and Son, 1859.

Winkelhofer, Martina. *The Everyday Life of the Emperor: Francis Joseph and His Imperial Court.* Translated by Jeffrey McCabe. Innsbruck: Haymon Verlag, 2012.

CHARACTER GUIDE

In Hungarian fashion, the surnames are given first, followed by first names, for the Hungarian characters.

★Denotes real historical person, though fictionalized in this story

Ákos (AH-kohsh): a Hungarian bandit
Anna Arden: our intrepid heroine
Charles Arden: Anna's father
James Arden: Anna's younger brother
Mária Arden (MUH-rye-uh): Anna's mother
★József Bem (YOH-zef BEM): Polish general, leading the Hungarian forces in Romania
Bahadır Beyzade (buh-HAH-deer BAY-zah-duh): a Turkish boy, son of a high-ranking military official
Boldogasszony/The Lady (BOHL-dohg-AHS-sohnyuh) (the final component is voiced as a single syllable): The Joyful Woman; the former Hungarian mother-goddess
Borevit (BOHR-eh-veet): a wood demon, subservient to Chernobog
Chernobog (CHER-nuh-bohg): a Slavic deity whose name means "black god," here a god of the underworld
Ginny Davies: Anna's former maid

*Henryk Dembiński (HEN-reek dem-BIN-skee): Polish general, appointed by Kossuth to lead the combined armies of Hungary

Dobos Borbála (DOH-bohsh BOHR-bah-lah): Hungarian journalist working in Vienna

Emilija Dragović (eh-MEE-lee-yah DRAH-goh-vitch): Josip Dragović's daughter; one of the Red Mantles, an elite fighting troop

Josip Dragović (YOH-seep DRAH-goh-vitch): ban (ruler) of Croatia and leader of the Red Mantles

Eszterházy János (ES-ter-haa-zee YAH-nohsh): Anna's great-uncle, her grandmama's cousin. (The family name is often spelled Esterházy today, but both spellings were used in the past. I opted for the *sz* spelling so it's consistent with Eszterháza, their Hungarian estate.)

Eszterházy Mátyás (ES-ter-haa-zee MAT-yahsh): Anna's third cousin; János's great-nephew

Eszterházy Noémi (ES-ter-haa-zee NOH-ay-mee): Mátyás's sister

*Görgey Artúr (GUHR-gee AHR-toor) (hard *g* as in *gas*): Hungarian general, often at odds with Kossuth and Dembiński. (His English memoir lists his name as Görgei, but he was born Görgey and most history books list him as such.)

Catherine Arden Gower: Anna's older sister

Richard Gower: Catherine's husband, a young diplomat attached to the British embassy in Vienna

Hadúr (HAH-dur): the former Hungarian god of war

House of Hapsburg-Lorraine

　*Archduchess Sophie of Austria: Archduke Franz Joseph's mother, an influential woman in the Austrian court

　*Archduke Franz Joseph of Austria: Emperor Ferdinand's nephew and heir to the Austrian Empire

*Emperor Ferdinand of Austria: head of the Hapsburg royal family; emperor of Austria and king of Hungary

Hunger: leader of the praetheria in Vienna, a sárkány (Hungarian shapeshifting dragon)

*Kossuth Lajos (KOH-shoot LAH-yohsh): political reformer and leader of the liberal party in Hungary

Kovács Gábor (KOH-vatch GAH-bor): a young Romani man

Kovács Izidóra (KOH-vatch IZ-ee-doh-ruh): Gábor's sister

*Count Pavel Medem (PAH-vel MEH-dem): Russian ambassador to Vienna

*Perczel Mór (PEHR-tsel MOHR): Hungarian general, leading armies in western Hungary in 1848

*Petőfi Sándor (PEH-toh-fee SHAHN-dor): a poet and revolutionary, considered by many to be Hungary's national poet

*John Ponsonby, 1st Viscount Ponsonby: British ambassador to Vienna, 1846–50

William Skala (SKAA-luh): a Polish-Scottish revolutionary

Svarog (SVAR-ohg): the Slavic sky god, sometimes described as having four heads (sometimes also equated with fire and blacksmithing)

Vasilisa (VAH-see-lee-sah): a young praetherian woman

Marina Winkler (mah-REE-nah VINK-lur): Borbála Dobos's partner

Zhena (ZHEE-nuh): queen of the samodiva (woodland maidens with an affinity for fire)

Zhivka (ZHEEV-kuh): a samodiva

Zrínyi Irína (ZREEN-yee EE-ree-nah): Anna's grandmother, now deceased

Zrínyi Pál (ZREEN-yee PAHL): Anna's uncle; Mária's younger brother

Some of the praetheria in the book are inspired by folklore
(predominantly Eastern European and Slavic), others are invented.
Individual praetheria are listed above, under characters.

domovoi (DOHM-uh-voy): a protective house spirit, small,
masculine, covered in hair with a long beard

Fair One/Szépasszony (SEP-ahs-sohnyuh) (the final
component is voiced as a single syllable): a female demon
with long hair and a white dress, often appearing during
hailstorms and prone to seducing young men

fene (FEH-neh): a Hungarian evil spirit

griffin: a creature with the head and forequarters of an eagle
and the hindquarters of a lion

guta (GUH-tah): a Hungarian demon who beats his victims
to death; often associated with strokes, heart attacks, or
sudden paralysis

leshy (LEH-shee): a Slavic forest spirit, often characterized
by blue skin and green beard, here described with bark-
textured skin (also, tree-man)

lidérc (LEE-dehrts): a succubus-like creature with goose feet,
believed to steal your breath while you sleep

melusine (mel-yoo-SEEN): a freshwater spirit, usually
depicted as a fish from the waist down, similar to a
mermaid.

samodiva (SAHM-oh-dee-vah): woodland maidens with an
affinity for fire, sometimes having the ability to fly. Related
to vila.

sárkány (SHAR-kahnyuh) (the final component is voiced as
a single syllable): a Hungarian shapeshifting dragon

turul (TOO-rool): in Hungarian folklore, a mythic falcon

that helped lead early Hungarians into the Carpathian
Basin. Here they belong to the Lady.

Valhalla (val-HAL-uh): the great hall where the Norse god
Odin gathers the dead he deems worthy of living with him.

Valkyrie (VAL-kuh-ree): one of a group of Odin's maidens
who conduct dead warriors to Valhalla

vila (VEE-lah): in Slavic folklore, fairy-like warriors, often
believed to seduce or entrap unwary men.

Vodanoj (VOH-dah-noy): a male water sprite, often held
responsible for drownings (also *vodník, vodyanoy*)

GLOSSARY

All terms are Hungarian unless otherwise indicated.

adure (AH-doo-rey): a command to light a fire (Latin)
Allah'a şükür (AH-lah-ha SHOO-koor): thank God (Turkish)
bácsi (BAH-chee): loosely "uncle," a term of respect for older men
betyárok (BET-yaar-ohk): bandits
Buda-Pest (BOO-dah-PESHT): what we now think of as one city used to be two separate cities (they officially joined in 1873). Buda, on the west side of the Duna, was the home of many of the wealthy elite; Pest, on the east side, was a younger, more energetic city.
csárda (CHAR-duh): a country inn
csárdás (CHAR-dahsh): a Hungarian round dance
drága (DRAA-gah): dear, precious
drágo (DRAH-goh): dear (Vlax Romani)
Duna (DOO-nah): the Danube River
Eszterháza (ES-ter-haa-zuh): a formerly rich estate belonging to the Eszterházy family
gadže (gah-ZHEH): non-Romani (Vlax Romani)
hajrá (HIE-rah): an exclamation meaning roughly "Onward!"

hála Istennek (HAH-lah IST-ehn-nehk): thank God

Hapsburgs: the imperial family of Austria-Hungary, formally Hapsburg-Lorraine. Today, the spelling "Habsburg" is more frequently used, but "Hapsburg" was a common nineteenth-century spelling.

lidércnyomás (LEE-dehrts-NYOH-mahsh): nightmare; literally, the pressure of a lidérc

me tut kamav (meh tut kah-MAF): I love you (Vlax Romani)

nyuszikám (NYOO-see-kaam): my little rabbit, a term of endearment

pálinka (PAAL-een-kah): brandy

praetertheria (PRAY-ter-ther-ee-ah) or praetheria (PRAY-ther-ee-ah): scientific terminology used as a hold-all for any supernatural creature released from the Binding spell. Praetheria for plural; praetherian for singular and adjective. (Latin)

puszta (POO-stuh): Hungarian plains

sör (SHYOOR): beer

šukarija (shoo-kar-EE-yah): beautiful one (Vlax Romani)

szalonna (SAH-lohn-nah): bacon

táltos (TAHL-tohsh): shapeshifter and shaman

Ungeheuer (OON-geh-hoy-er): monster (German)

ungeschickt (OON-geh-shikt): clumsy (German)

Változz át üres lappá (VAHL-tohz aat OO-resh LAHP-paa): a command to change to a blank sheet of paper (literally: transform to empty page)

Was wollen Sie? (vahs VOHL-ehn zee): What do you want? (German, formal)

Luminate Orders

Animanti: manipulates living bodies. Common spells: healing, animal persuasion, sometimes invisibility. Less common: shapeshifting, necromancy.

Coremancer: manipulates the mind and heart. Common spells: truth spells, spell re-creation, persuasion, emotional manipulation. Less common: dreams and foresight.

Elementalist (formerly Alchemist): manipulates nonliving substances (light, weather, fire, water, earth, etc.). Most popular order. Common spells: weather magic, illusions, hidings, firestorms, water manipulation. Less common: firesmiths.

Lucifera: manipulates forces (gravity, space, time, magnetism). Common spells: telekinesis, portals, flight. Less common: temporal manipulation.

ACKNOWLEDGMENTS

Writing acknowledgments never gets easier—if anything, with each new book I'm more and more aware of the army of people it takes to create a book. One swallow doesn't make a summer; one author alone can't make a book.

Huge thanks are due, as always, to my agent, Josh Adams, for championing my books and talking me off my not-infrequent ledges. I'm deeply indebted to my editor, Michelle Frey, for loving this book and the characters as much as I do, and for pushing me to craft the best book I possibly could. Thanks also to the wonderful team at Knopf: Marisa DiNovis, Artie Bennett, Lisa Leventer, and Allison Judd. Ray Shappell and Agent BOB continue to astound me with their beautiful covers.

I would not have made it this far without my writing group, the sisters of my heart: Erin Shakespear Bishop, Helen Boswell, Tasha Seegmiller, and Elaine Vickers. My beta readers gave me invaluable feedback at critical points in the writing process: Natalka Burian, Taffy Lovell, Destiny Cole, Yamile Saied Méndez, and Rebecca Sachiko Burton.

I am also deeply indebted to readers and friends who helped me with details of Hungarian culture and linguistics, Romani culture, Islam, the Turkish language, and more, including:

Kovács Ildikó, Glonczi Ernő, Dr. Elizabeta Jevtic-Somlai, Dr. Hussein Samha, and Tuğçe Nida Gökırmak. I take full ownership for any mistakes remaining.

Writing can be a solitary endeavor, so I'm especially grateful to all the people who have made this journey less lonely: Cindy Baldwin, Megan Bannen, Karin Holmes Bean, Elly Blake, Dave Butler, Veeda Bybee, Stephanie Garber, McKelle George, Jeff Giles, Mette Harrison, Melanie Jacobson, E. K. Johnston, Emily King, Sara Larsen, Mackenzi Lee, Jolene Perry, Stephanie Huang Porter, Katie Purdie, Caitlin Sangster, Summer Spence, Joy Sterrantino, Erin Summerill, Jenilyn Tolley, Becky Wallace, Kate Watson, Dan Wells, Allisa White, my Pitch Wars Table of Trust, Sisters in Writing, Storymakers, Class of 2k17, and too many more to list here. My gratitude also goes out to the readers and book bloggers and bookstagrammers who have supported my books, especially Krysti at YA & Wine, Sarah at the Clever Reader, Katie at Mundie Moms, Christine Manzari, Corey Taylor Talks, and members of my street team.

My family makes all my books better—even the ones they haven't read—by making my life richer, so that richness spills into the pages I write.

Lastly, to readers—if you're reading this, you've come a long way with me and my characters. Thank you. You're the reason I'm still writing.